Daniel I. Russell

Mother's Boys

BLOOD BOUND BOOKS

ISBN 978-1-940250-04-5

This book is a work of fiction. Names, characters, business organizations, places, events and incidents either are the product of the author's imagination or are used fictitiously. Any resemblance to actual persons, living or dead, events or locales is entirely coincidental.

Artwork by Andrej Bartulovic

Printed in the United States of America

First Edition

Visit us on the web at:
www.bloodboundbooks.net

Also from Blood Bound Books:

To the whistling man at the crossing between McDonalds and the Ormskirk park, one evening back in 2005. Sometimes the smallest of seeds creates a whole novel.

PREFACE

Real monsters lie within the hearts of men.

By candlelight, he turned the pages of his brother's book. Water had swelled the volume, warping the spine and crinkling the paper. The cover, barely visible through a layer of mould, showed a rugged, aged captain pursuing a white whale across the ocean.

He closed the book and gazed up at the low, brick ceiling.

The monsters walk above, he thought, not in the dark, hidden places.

Movement in the shadows drew his attention, yet he sat still, clutching the book.

The city remained oblivious to the secret it harboured deep below the crumbling, neglected streets. He wondered what dramas would be played out on its tarmac stage, under the street lights and the stars.

The shapes in the darkness separated from the murk, and two squat figures darted towards him. Claws and teeth glinted in the flickering light from the candle.

He closed his eyes, thoughts full of men and monsters.

PART 1

1.

Samantha cocked her head, smiled and glanced up at the hair of her new drinking partner. "Has it always been that colour, Johan?" she asked. The lights of the bar shone through his stark white spikes, like frosted glass growing from his scalp. "I mean, do you dye it or anything?"

He swept a hand through his hair and it sprang back up after his fingers passed.

"People always ask me about it," he purred, his voice clear and confident, matching his ice-cold exterior. Heat blushed in Samantha's face. "It's natural, every strand. Well, when I say natural, I mean I haven't changed it myself. Something happened to make it like this..."

Samantha stirred her drink with her finger, mouth hanging open. "Really? What happened? What could do something like that? It must have been *terrifying*."

Her new companion picked up his beer and took a swig. He finished with a satisfied sigh and returned the glass to the table. He looked up with pale, grey eyes.

"It *might* be terrifying."

"What do you mean?" pressed Samantha.

"Well," he said, gazing past her, "I came in here for a quiet beer, and then I saw... I saw the most beautiful girl sitting alone at the bar. I *had* to speak to her, and the mere thought of this goddess refusing my company horrified me to the core! Turned my hair white."

Samantha's intense gaze shattered. She beamed and punched him playfully on the arm.

"Hey!"

"Hey nothing," she said.

Johan smiled and glanced over her shoulder again. "But yes, my hair has always been white. Used to get so much hassle at school…"

Samantha sipped from her wine and turned to follow his gaze. Behind her, three guys raced to chug down pints of beer while banging on the table with their free hands. The coasters trembled and moved around the surface with the heavy vibrations. Two of them, one with shoulder length blonde hair and the other with thick glasses, struggled to keep up with their chubby friend. He swallowed the last gulp and held the glass on top of his head.

"Howzat!" he cried, flecks of beer shooting from between his sausage lips.

The guy with the glasses choked, spraying beer back inside his pint glass. The blonde quit and shook his head, smiling.

"Are *they* bothering you?"

Samantha looked back and found her new acquaintance studying her. "Not really," she said. "They might be a little loud though. The barman doesn't look so happy."

"Probably just worried about them making a mess. Some people have no class. Unlike the two of us."

Samantha raised an eyebrow. "Two of us, eh?"

"We've been drinking together a good hour now," he said, licking his lips. "I think we can qualify as a twosome." He winked and took another sip.

Samantha fought from shuddering in delight. She'd seen Johan come in and thought her prayers had been answered when he walked over. She didn't normally go all girly over meeting men, but those eyes! Combined with the hair, he looked so different, so mysterious. Like a traveller from a far off galaxy who had stopped off on his intergalactic trip for a quick drink.

I'd climb aboard his spaceship anytime, she thought, loving the way his misty gaze lingered on her face.

"Maybe you're right," she said, raising her glass.

"Maybe it would be nice to be a two instead of a one." She tilted the wine to her mouth, keeping her eyes locked on his.

"Glad we're on the same page," he said, slowly reaching for her hand that rested on the bar.

Samantha snatched the drink away from her mouth as something struck her from behind. Red wine sloshed over the rim of the glass and fell onto her lap, staining her miniskirt.

"Damn it!" she cried, turning around.

The blond guy from the table staggered to the side while his friends laughed. He'd obviously bumped into her, a result of too many beers judging by the state of him.

"Sorry, love," he said, holding a hand up in a quick apology.

She jumped from the bar stool, placing the glass on the bar and holding the damp fabric of her skirt away from her legs.

"Jesus Christ! Look at this!"

Johan climbed from his stool, examining the deep purple stain.

"I only bought this yesterday..."

"I'm sorry," said Johan.

"It's not your fault," she replied. "You shouldn't apologise. It's those arseholes over there!"

Johan placed a gentle hand onto her shoulder. "Go and get yourself cleaned up as best you can. I'll get you that apology."

Samantha shook her head. "Don't. Please. It's not worth it."

He smiled, and she almost forgot the drying stain in her new skirt.

"Don't stress over me. I'm not about to take them on, merely...appeal to their better sides. Go on, I'll be waiting for you."

"Really?"

Johan winked. "Count on it."

Samantha scrubbed with a wet paper towel and cursed as it ripped. The stain remained, spreading out from the very centre of the front of the miniskirt. It looked like the menstrual equivalent of Old Faithful and no tampon had managed to stand in its way.

"Great," she said, grimacing at her reflection. "Really going to impress Johan now…"

She wanted another drink with him; his mystery and charm was brightening an otherwise dull evening after work.

Excited as a horny schoolgirl, Samantha left her reflection behind and pushed open the door leading back into the bar.

"Sorry I took so long, I…"

Her words drifted to a stop as she looked around the bar. He'd gone, leaving behind a vacant stool and empty pint glass. The table, which previously hosted the three lager louts, had also been vacated.

She gripped her handbag tightly and approached the barman.

"Erm, excuse me," she said. "I was just sat here and was wondering—"

"It's okay," he interrupted, throwing his cleaning rag into a small sink. "It's taken care of."

Samantha frowned. "What do you mean?"

"Your friend paid, him with the weird white hair."

"Do you know where he went?" she asked, hoping he was in the toilet. A ball of dread started to form like a large pearl in her stomach.

The barman nodded towards the door. "He left."

"He went out?" she asked, feeling the ball within pop from a kick to the midsection.

This can't be happening.

"Afraid so," said the barman, crossing his arms. "Just after those three jokers left. I'm glad to be rid."

He turned his back on her, attending to another task.

I don't believe this, she thought. He just left me?

She sighed.

At least it stops me having another drink. A wine after work is enough with me driving. I would have needed to get a taxi back if I'd carried on.

Slightly happier with avoiding a cab fare, she headed for the door.

Why do they always have to be like this? Surely a lonely waitress in the city should be allowed a little happiness? Even one night would do for now. Why do all men turn out to be... cunts?

She swung her handbag around her shoulder, curses swirling around her head. Her sudden rush of anger cleared the buzz from the wine and conversation.

The night felt fresh, but not too cold. Samantha took a deep breath, enjoying the freedom from the stale atmosphere of the grotty bar. Accepting her fate of another night alone, she exited the doorway and headed for the small car park at the end of the street.

Above her, the buildings loomed like mountains of brick and crumbling cement. She tried not to look at the dark windows as she passed. Made up of mostly derelict buildings, this part of the city had always been sinister to Samantha. It wasn't the *undesirables* who she sometimes saw huddled in abandoned shop doorways or loitering under bridges like trolls, but the place itself. It waited with a dark purpose all its own, a kraken ready to awake. The empty windows were its eyes, the echo of the quiet streets its ears. The thought of all these buildings standing empty with only wildlife and ghosts occupying their silent rooms made Samantha want to run.

Get a grip, she thought. You've walked this way

hundreds of times on your own at night. Nothing's ever happened.

But doesn't that mean I'm overdue?

She quickened her pace.

She'd be glad when the renovations finally began in this area of the city. A well-lit car park would be welcomed for her after work drinks.

Samantha looked up and down the empty street and crossed the road. On the other side, she turned right and nearly walked into the thin figure waiting around the corner. She snatched in a breath and stepped around him, trying not to show she'd been spooked. Looking straight ahead, she carried on.

"Hey," said the stranger. "Leaving already?"

Samantha glanced over her shoulder.

The glare of the streetlights reflected in the lenses of his glasses.

"You were in the bar," he said, his voice high and whiney.

"Yeah," she said, carrying on walking.

"So, where you going?"

Samantha ignored him, biting her lip. Her heart had sped up, and she gasped on the night air. The guy had scared her, even though he appeared too skinny to actually *do* anything. Samantha believed she could take him if he decided to get physical. She wasn't particularly muscular, but could hold her own, especially with a nerd as thin as him.

A gust of wind might blow him away.

She felt a little better, until a more threatening thought sneaked into her head.

What if he has a knife? Or a gun?

She lowered her head and walked faster, gripping onto her bag so hard her palms grew sweaty.

"Suit yourself," he muttered.

She chanced a second look over her shoulder and saw

him lean away from the wall. Instead of coming after her as expected, he turned his back and disappeared around the corner.

Thank Christ, she thought, hurrying along. Oh, Thank Christ.

Trying to put the thoughts of the strange guy aside, Samantha rummaged in her bag for her car keys. She spied the car parked a little further up the street. Looking behind her once more to check and make sure the nerd on the wall hadn't decided to follow her after all, she pulled out her cluster of keys. Gripping them tightly in her closed fist, the keys no longer rattled against each other. The noise might sound like a dinner bell to car thieves.

Samantha reached her small, white Ford. She inserted the key into the car door and swung it wide. Throwing her bag onto the passenger seat, she climbed inside and slammed the door closed. With her elbow, she hammered down the lock by the side window.

Here, she thought, closing her eyes and lying back against the headrest. Finally, I'm here.

Safe in her metal shell, Samantha shoved the key in the ignition and started the car. In the split second before it fired, she imagined the engine releasing a cry of strained coughs. The guy in the glasses comes running...

She pressed her foot down and the engine revved.

She exhaled a sigh of relief.

Samantha fastened her seat belt and clicked on the headlights. The dark street beyond the windscreen lit up, revealing grimy buildings and litter scattered on the pavement.

Why do you do this every Friday? Coming out here in the dead of night...? Either get yourself a guy, honey, or start visiting friendlier places to drink.

She knew she wouldn't. The bars and clubs at the centre of the city had no character, no... *individuality.*

Checking her mirrors and indicating, Samantha pulled

out and cruised down the empty street.

The five and six-story abandoned buildings fell away as she drove out of the derelict district. She passed the park and turned at the roundabout, still not seeing another car on the road. Samantha looked at the glowing green dial on the dashboard. It showed a quarter to midnight.

Never this quiet, but at least I'll get home quicker.

The speedometer climbed to fifty as she made her way down the two-lane carriageway. After turning on the stereo and tuning to a local station, she drummed her palms against the steering wheel in rhythm.

Need to find a new job; there are closer restaurants to work at. Or move out of the sticks and further into the city. I wonder if Natalie wants a flatmate—

She squinted, pulled from her thoughts by a flash of light bouncing off her rear view mirror. Samantha blinked a few times, trying to shift the ball of colour drifting before her eyes. At the side of her car, an engine roared.

Arseholes, she thought.

She peered to the side and gasped.

Johan, his grey eyes on the road, drove alongside. With the window open, his white hair blew back.

Samantha felt her guts squirm.

He looked to her and winked. With another deafening rumble, his car shot forwards.

"No!" she cried, pressing her foot down on the accelerator.

His car, red and slender as a bullet, shot through the darkness ahead. In seconds, his rear lights had become two glowing red eyes in the distance, like a waiting dragon. He sped into the tunnel up ahead.

At least those guys didn't get him. But why would he leave me, catch up and then leave me again?

He must like games...

Her stomach fluttered and she grinned. The car approached sixty, and she eased it around the slight bend and into the tunnel.

With no overhead lights, the tunnel seemed to head deep into the earth rather than under a small river.

Her headlights lit up the motionless red car, parked across both lanes.

"Shit!"

Samantha plunged her foot down on the brake.

Her body dove forwards, but snapped to a sudden stop as the seatbelt locked. With the belt tight across her chest, she struggled to pull in a breath. She stared through the glass, her leg and foot throbbing with the tension of pushing the pedal. The steering wheel jerked in her hands, and the car began to slide. She turned the opposite direction.

Johan's red car vanished from view as Samantha's Ford spun away. Her headlight beams reflected off the approaching black wall of the tunnel.

"Shit!"

The car smashed into the brickwork.

The force threw Samantha back in her seat, and her head shot forwards striking the upper ridge of the steering wheel. She flopped back.

The engine spluttered and died, leaving her collapsed in silence. Samantha's chest burned, and her head seemed to swell. Both headlights were smashed in the collision. She saw only darkness through the windscreen, like the car had been dumped in the ocean and had sunk to the sea bed. She trembled and drew in shaking breaths.

I've been in a crash. I've been in a fucking crash—

A car door slammed.

"Wow!" said a voice. "Look at that, guys."

"I said it would work," another voice said, cool and relaxed. "And you three thought she'd hit us…"

"Think she's alive?"

"After all this, she had better fucking be."

Samantha raised a twitching hand and rubbed her

forehead. It came away bloody.

"H-Help... me..." she said. Her hand collapsed back into her lap.

"All right! She *is* alive!"

The car shook, and grunts drifted in from outside. Squealing in protest, the driver's door peeled open. Samantha looked to her side. The overhead light blinked on, the electrics somehow surviving the crash. Her rescuer leaned in, the light reflecting in his glasses. He smiled.

"Glad to see me now?" he asked.

Samantha's head fell back. The throbbing pain in the front of her skull seemed to swell in an angry storm cloud with lightening flickering inside its darkness.

The slender Samaritan had little trouble easing over her and unclipping the seatbelt. It sucked back into the wall of the car with a rattle. He tried to slide his arm around her back but failed to force his hand behind her limp body. She felt him trying to push her forwards, clumsily poking her in the kidney.

Samantha groaned. "...hurting..."

He looked down at her and pushed his glasses further up his nose.

"Fuck me, Spence, what you doing to the poor girl? Feeling her up?"

His lips pulled back to form a cold sneer. "I'm doing the best I can! She's too heavy."

Paddling in the shallow waters of consciousness, Samantha let the comment go.

"Let me do it," said another voice. Her fumbling rescuer stepped back and out of sight. A second later, the car lurched to the side. "Not much room in here."

The fat guy from the bar leaned in, surveying her with beady green eyes. His breath smelled of beer when he whispered to her.

"Be still, sweetie. This will all be over soon. I'm gonna get you out of here before it blows. You know, like in the movies and stuff."

Smiling, he coarsely grabbed her right wrist, her skin enfolded in his fleshy palm. Groaning with effort, he manoeuvred out of the car, carrying her like a rag doll.

Her torso emerged from the wreckage and met the cold night air. The plump guy pulled her entirely free, and Samantha's feet thumped the ground. After dragging her away from the car, he let go, and Samantha's head struck the ground with a thud. The patch of road tilted like a funhouse floor. Her eyelids flickered.

"Ouch!" said a male voice.

"Yeah, that *had* to hurt!" said another.

"Shut up, guys." The hard voice quickly silenced the others. "A car could come by anytime."

Samantha, lying spread-eagled on the cold tarmac, tried to raise her head. She rested it back and swung her eyes open as footsteps approached.

Johan looked down at her.

"Say sorry, boys."

"What?" came another voice. Samantha presumed it was the guy with the long, blonde hair, the only one of the trio from the bar she hadn't seen yet.

"I said, 'say sorry.' I promised the girl an apology after you idiots knocked wine on her. So, say sorry."

The three grumbled almost apologies like sulky teenagers.

"There. I told you I'd get an apology." He crouched beside her and studied her face.

"H-Help... me..." she said. Her vision blurred around the edges, framing his face.

He reached down and stroked a finger across her forehead, sweeping aside the plastered hair. He pulled his bloodied finger away and held it up to his face.

"You seem fine to me," he said and stood.

"Don't... don't leave me!" she pleaded, struggling to sit up.

He laughed. The way it echoed in the tunnel made Samantha think of monsters living in caverns deep underground.

"I'm not going to *leave* you," he said, his laughter subsiding. "I thought we were a twosome?" He shook his head with a smile, looking amused. "We are gentlemen and wouldn't *dream* of abandoning a damsel in distress."

He faced his comrades.

"Guys, get her in the car."

2

Johan winced as he urinated, holding his penis with his thumb and forefinger. The skin burned. A welcomed pain. An *earned* pain.

He yawned and shook out the last few amber drops. After flushing the toilet, he walked to the sink to wash his hands. Looking into the mirror while he vigorously rubbed the soap, Johan examined the bags under his eyes and the sparse spread of frosty stubble on cheeks and chin. Pure white on his pale face, it was only noticeable close up. He decided not to bother shaving.

He scratched soap into his skin and around his fingernails. He held his hands for inspection and frowned. Rinsing them under the steaming-hot water, he soaped them up a second time.

Yawning again, Johan rinsed his hands and wiped them dry on a towel. They passed inspection. He scanned the bathroom before he left to be sure none of the guys had made a mess. Happy that the loo remained clean, he opened the door and stepped out.

The bathroom led directly into the living room, where the boys had spent the night. Spence and Kev still played on the Playstation, both sitting on the worn-out sofa, their gaze glued to the flickering images on the TV screen. Kev took up most of the space, leaving Spence to lean over the arm.

"Glad to see none of you women had the nerve to steal my seat," said Johan, stepping over Richie and the girl to get to his armchair. He dumped himself in the seat, sighing with comfort. "Whose turn is it next?"

"Winner stays on," said Spence. He sniffed and pushed his glasses back up his nose.

"Not the game," said Johan. He nodded towards Richie, whose blonde hair swayed on his shoulder as he thrust in and out. *"That."*

"Jeez," said Spence. He paused the game and scratched his head. "I was on before Rich and you had a bash before me. Must be you, Kev."

Kev snorted. "Pass. I'm shattered. Besides, I think I'm running on empty." He glared at Spence, who had restarted the game without warning. "Sneaky bastard."

Johan rubbed his chin and glanced over at Richie and the girl. She'd regained consciousness in the early hours of the morning, so they'd had to gag her. She stared up at the ceiling while Richie pounded away. The wet smacking drowned out the noise of the TV. Her face appeared wrinkled, an illusion created by the dried semen splashed on it. Johan considered picking it off later, like he loved picking dried glue off his fingers.

Obviously, he'd have to wash his hands immediately after.

Richie cried out and arched his back. His convulsions quickened, and his body trembled in orgasm. Panting, he slowly leaned down and kissed the girl between her small, pert breasts.

"All done?" Johan asked.

"Oh yes," said Richie, climbing off her.

Johan peeked between her legs and smiled, watching the white trickle emerge from her folds and drip on the floor. She looked red raw. Still feeling the acidic burning of his own sensitive area, he felt sorry for the girl...for a second.

"She love it?" he asked Richie.

"I think so. You enjoy that, love?"

The girl stared upwards, motionless.

"Hey! I asked you a question." He prodded her in the thigh with his big toe without a reaction. "Think she's gone, Johan."

"Shit," he said, shaking his head. "I thought she'd be a fighter."

From his experience, Johan knew only half their women turned out to be fighters. The other half, the girl lying on his carpet like a corpse for instance, kind of...turned off. They just came to terms with it and took their reward. They *all* loved it, whether they kicked and screamed and shouted, or lay rigid, like they were carved out of marble. Either way, they got what they deserved.

Richie pulled on a pair of jeans and disappeared into the kitchen. The girl stayed put, lying still. Johan wondered if she'd severely injured herself in the crash. Her eyes seemed *too* glazed over, like she was on drugs or in a coma. He turned back to the television.

"Richie's done, Kev can't be bothered and I'm feeling a little tender, if you know what I mean," he said, scratching his groin. "Spence?"

"No thanks. I don't like it when they go cold."

The living room had grown steadily untidy throughout the night. Empty beer cans stood stacked against the sofa and armchair. An open pizza box, containing a few nibbled crusts, lay on the floor. The room smelled of sweat, semen and cigarette smoke. Johan considered putting the woman to good use cleaning the flat.

"Then that's it. Fun time over. Hey! Girl!"

She lay gazing at the ceiling.

"Hey!" Johan called again. "Lazy bitch. I'm talking to you."

Her eyelids flickered.

"You can go now," he called over the din of the TV. "Go on. Off you go."

The girl shook and slowly turned her head to look at him. She bit against her gag.

Johan swept a hand through his white spikes and turned back to the TV. "I won't give you a second chance," he muttered.

Kev laughed and elbowed Spence, who shot him an angry side-glance.

The girl rolled over and tried to push herself up off the carpet. Her arms tottered, but had enough strength to lift her up like she was performing a press up. Her legs buckled, and she landed on her knees, sitting up.

Johan found it strange to see her move after all this time.

She tentatively climbed to her feet and stood with her arms wrapped around her body.

"If you're waiting for your clothes," said Johan, "you'll be waiting a very long time, and I might change my mind about letting you go. In fact..." He turned and looked her up and down. "I think I feel an urge coming on..."

The girl bolted down the short hall that led away from the living room. The three guys turned to watch. Her bare feet pounded across the carpet, her hair streaming out behind her.

As she approached the kitchen door with arms out and cries escaping from beneath the cloth gag, Richie stepped into the hall, carrying a steaming mug. Trying not to spill his drink, he stared at it, concentrating.

Johan smiled and sat up.

The girl, too fast and too panicked to stop, ran straight into Richie. She knocked the mug back against him and carried on past. Hot, brown liquid splashed onto his bare chest and belly.

"Yeow!" he cried, wiping the coffee off his skin with his free hand. "Fucking hell!"

Johan, Kev and Spence burst into laughter.

"Bastards!" Richie shouted back at them. "You let that happen on purpose!"

He turned his back on them and surveyed the girl, who had reached the front door and pulled at the locks.

"Clumsy bitch!" Richie shouted and flung the mug at her. It bounced off her head with a *thunk!* More coffee splashed out on the wall, her shoulders and her back. The girl trembled in the corner. Richie vanished back inside the kitchen.

Johan wiped a tear from the corner of his eye. "That was great. Talk about timing!"

Kev sniggered, his stomach and cheeks wobbling. "Rich won't be pleased with you," he said through his laughter.

"Don't care," Johan replied. "He's a big girl anyway. Oi! Goldilocks!"

Richie reappeared, dabbing a tea towel against his chest and clutching a butcher knife. "What?"

"You all right?"

Richie peered down at the red patch of skin deepening over his chest and lean stomach. It looked like the shape of Spain. He looked back up and met Johan's concrete eyes. "Yes," he said quietly. "It's nothing. And this..." he dropped the tea towel and brandished the knife, "will make me feel a lot better."

Johan raised an eyebrow. "A knife? Of all the things in the kitchen, you choose a knife?" He shook his head. "Disappointing."

The girl continued to cower in the corner. Her fingers fumbled with the lock.

Richie swept the knife through the air. "Does the job."

Johan sighed and stood.

"Look, you're going to fuck up my carpet. Again. You know how much these bitches bleed. Get her in the bath." He kicked Kev's foot. "You can help. Spence too. I'll be in the kitchen, looking for something special."

"All right!" said Spence and leapt up.

Johan walked through the lounge, shooting the girl a wink as he passed, and entered the kitchen. Glancing around and searching through drawers and cupboards, his gaze fell upon a shiny object hanging on a hook. He rubbed the stubble on his cheeks, considering the possibilities.

"Perfect," he whispered and grabbed the handle.

Johan walked through the flat and back into the

bathroom, impressed the boys had forced the screaming girl inside without breaking anything. Spence and Kev held her down in the bath by the shoulders. Richie stood over her, still pointing the knife.

"Look what I found..." said Johan and held up the object. Light glinted off its sides, emphasising the holes and razor sharp edges.

"A...cheese grater?" said Richie. He grinned. "A fucking cheese grater! Sweet! It reminds me of that night years ago when S—"

"Shut up," Johan snapped. "I don't want to talk about that. Ever. We have work to do."

He approached the bath, and the boys parted to allow him space. Leaning over the whimpering girl, he whispered.

"You women. Always so obsessed with looks, aren't you? Well, I think we need to make an example, don't you?"

He lowered the grater and pressed the side against her cheek.

She bucked and tried to turn. Kev grabbed a fistful of hair and held her tight.

"Thanks, Kev," said Johan, and dragged the grater down.

The girl shrieked.

Shreds of twisted skin tumbled from the bottom of the utensil, and blood poured across the metal. Johan, wincing from the high-pitched wailing, pumped the grater a few more times. He enjoyed the rough feel as it bit through the girl's face. He pulled it away. It looked like an animal had clawed her cheek off.

"Not so pretty now," Johan said.

The boys laughed, and Spence reached into the bath, grasping her face and delving his fingernails into the exposed flesh.

"Should have turned the other cheek when we came

3

Willing the sun to stay suspended in the sky a few hours longer, Natalie slid down from her seat in the window and entered her small kitchen, depositing her empty mug in the sink. She'd spent an enjoyable day at home, starting with a lazy morning in bed with Simon, which had quickly become a very non-lazy morning when he'd woken up. Their one year anniversary celebration had started *very* early. After he'd gone to work, Nat had watched a little TV, vacuumed, washed last night's dishes and read the first hundred or so pages of her new novel.

She walked back into the living room and sighed.

The book rested on the arm of the sofa, face down with its pages fanned out to keep her place. It looked so inviting, and she felt tempted to read a quick chapter. Through the window, the beginnings of twilight crept up behind the high buildings. She stared at her reflection. Piercings in her ears, nose, eyebrow and lip winked like stars in the dying light.

Wonder what mother would make of all this, she thought, grinning at the dark punk in the glass. Her mother had always shown such disdain for alternative types, labelling them all as filthy hippies, stinking goths or spotty punks. Funny, as she'd usually been the one that reeked of sweat and alcohol.

"Damn it," Nat muttered, heading into her bedroom. She hated the impending doom of six' o'clock. Her shift at Ginelli's started then, and she'd hate every minute until she knocked off at eleven.

The bed sheets were still tangled and unmade after the eventful morning spent between them. She decided to leave it. If she didn't have time to read, she didn't have time to make the bed.

She opened her wardrobe and took down the uniform, a white blouse and black skirt, from a hanger. She swapped this with her *My Chemical Romance* t-shirt and tasselled dungarees, and after a few finishing touches to her heavy makeup in the bathroom mirror, put on her coat and grabbed her bag. After checking that her apartment door was securely locked, Nat walked down her corridor to the elevator.

She rarely saw any of her neighbours in the cramped hallway that ran the length of the building. It wasn't a bad area to live in, but it seemed the other residents knew something she didn't. They stayed behind locked doors.

Only when coming home at night did she wish for some company, or at least a sound from inside the other apartments, just to ease the feeling of emptiness.

A sign on the elevator revealed that it was broken again. Nat groaned and turned towards the stairway door. Grateful she only lived on the fourth floor, she hurried down the steps, her high heels striking the tiles and echoing up the stair well.

God, I wish Simon were here, she thought. These stairs always creep me out. Probably all those horror films where someone is always chased up a stairway like this, round and round and round.

She picked up her pace.

Simon. Mother would surely have approved of Simon.

After Nat's father had passed away, the young girl had witnessed the ongoing parade of *uncles* through the house and cried herself to sleep over the grunting and slapping that came through the thin walls. Her mother would be filled with regret the following morning. Even now, when Nat would dump the empty wine bottles into the restaurant's recycling, she saw her mother sitting at the kitchen table, mid-morning light twinkling off the various finished bottles.

"Never, ever" slurred her mother, jabbing each word with the smouldering cigarette poked between her fingers. "Never get with a man who don't appreciate you, Nat. You get one that treats you like a princess, and you keep a hold of him, you hear?"

Young Natalie would nod and continue cooking breakfast, or cleaning the kitchen, or doing anything to keep from her mother's attention.

"You don't let no harm come to him. Look at your father. Drank and smoked his life away, and what did I do?" She took a long drag, eyes seeing the past. "I let him. You gotta look after a man. They can get in all sorts of trouble without ya," she said through a cloud of smoke.

Halfway down the dark stairwell, Nat heard the empty bottles being swept from the kitchen table and shattering on the floor, echoing across the years.

I did what you said, Nat thought, keen to reach the ground floor. The place was creepy enough without the ghosts of the past following her with each step. I did something you could never do.

I found a good man.

And I kept him.

Fuck you, mother dear.

Her thoughts of Simon carried her down the stairs, and she smiled on reaching the bottom. She pushed through the door into the lobby and, after checking her post box, walked out onto the street.

The first drops of rain blotched the pavement with dark circles around her feet. Nat held a hand up and caught a few in her palm.

With her head down, she turned left and started a brisk walk, hoping her bus hadn't left yet.

Pushing through the glass door to Ginelli's, Nat glanced down at her watch and then around the room, searching for either of her two bosses. The motion of her head sent flecks of water flying from her dreadlocks, garnering glares from nearby diners.

"Sorry…" she murmured, walking past. She nodded a greeting to the two girls working the bar and slipped through the door at the side.

In the kitchen, waiting staff darted past each other carrying steaming plates of food, young apprentices beat eggs and stirred the huge pans of soup on the cookers. Over all this, the head chef, Gordon, usually yelled out instructions. Today was a little different as Andre, one of her bosses, screamed at Gordon.

"What do you mean, we have *none?*" Andre cried.

The head chef stared back at Andre.

"It's on the fucking menu!" Andre continued. "If a customer wants something on the menu, they should fucking have it!"

Nat normally liked to overhear someone else receiving the brunt of Andre's temper, loving how his fake Italian accent fell away as he got angry. This time, she used it as a diversion, managing to hang her soaking wet coat up and dump her bag in a free locker.

"From one joker to another! Where the hell have you been?"

Nat froze.

"Twenty past six! And when does your shift start, Natalie?"

She slowly turned. "Six."

"That's right. Six!" He placed his hands on his hips. His ample gut stuck out. "Hasn't anybody got a goddamn clue around here? First that idiot Samantha fails to show and now…"

"I'm sorry! It's just that the lift was broke and so I missed the bus and I couldn't call because I left my phone at home and …"

"Excuses!" Andre bellowed. "I don't want to hear them! Just get on with it." He huffed. "And again, Natalie. Sort that hair out and get that metal shit out of your face.

Customers don't want to be served by...whatever the hell you're trying to be. You're here to work, not to make a fucking statement."

Behind Andre, Gordon rolled his eyes and returned to work.

Rant over, Andre barged past Natalie and through the swinging door. She heard him complaining to the girls behind the bar.

"Cock," she muttered under her breath.

"Take no notice," called Gordon. He slammed a cleaver into a pile of steaks but turned to look at her. Nat wondered how he'd never lost a digit. "I think him and Roberto had a bit of a tiff. Haven't seen lover boy in here all night. Normally it's him that likes to ride me."

"You don't say," said Nat, raising an eyebrow and smiling.

"What? You've got a perverted mind, my girl." He glanced down and tossed a few strips of meat into a waiting metal bowl.

Nat removed her white, frilly apron from her locker and hung it around her neck, tying the sash around her back. She examined herself in a nearby mirror. It had a layer of condensation around the edges which framed her image in distorted, frosty glass. She looked more like a gothic French maid than a waitress. Straightening the apron, she tottered on her high heels.

Don't know why he makes me wear these things to work. Probably break every health and safety rule going.

She reached into the wide pocket at the front of the apron and took out a small pad of paper and a biro.

"How am I looking, Gordon?"

The chef looked over, again risking his fingers beneath the descending blade.

"Beautiful, but hiding a deep resentment for all the snooty customers."

"Just what I was going for," she said. "Why didn't

Samantha come in?"

Gordon shrugged his shoulders. "Must be ill or something. We don't know. She hasn't called."

With a sigh, Nat turned back to the door leading into the dining area. Straining to keep a fixed smile on her face, she pushed through.

Time's supposed to pass quickly when you're busy, Nat thought, rushing from table to table with plates of sizzling food, returning to the kitchen, bringing out more, taking a new order and replenishing drinks. Every time she glanced up at the clock hanging in the kitchen, the hands seemed to have barely moved.

At twenty-five minutes past eight, she decided to take her break early, risking the wrath of Andre. She walked through the kitchen to the back door. She pushed down the bar and swung it open, enjoying the chill that cut through the humid air. Stepping outside, she noticed Gordon sneaking a cigarette by the bins. She wandered over.

"Andre will do his nut if he catches you smoking again. You know he thinks you can taste it in the food afterwards."

Gordon grunted. "Most of the snobs complain about the food anyway, so what's a little added flavour?" He took a long drag and blew the smoke upwards. The cloud lingered over his head, illuminated by the security light shining down on them. He looked up through it. "Lovely night."

"Yeah," said Nat, leaning back against the wall of the restaurant. She kicked off her shoes. Her tights did nothing to stop the cold seeping into her feet. "When I moved here, I thought I'd never see a beautiful night again."

Gordon took another puff. "How'd you mean?"

"I thought that all these big buildings would, I don't

know, block out the sky. It's weird moving from a small seaside village to the city. I didn't know what to expect."

"You'd be surprised," said Gordon. "We get some real pretty nights here, not many, but some. Usually just after the rain. Come here…"

Nat tip toed across the yard, watchful for any debris. Arriving next to Gordon, she followed his pointing finger with her gaze.

From this angle, she saw the moon, a pale glowing crescent, suspended in between two skyscrapers.

"Wow," she said.

"Get the moon and the stars above the night sky line…beautiful," he said. "You can get it on post cards and pictures in other cities, but not here. I don't know why. I mean, it's the same stars, the same moon, just the city is different." He laughed. "You know, when *I* first came here, my friend warned me never to look up."

"Why?"

"Because he said only tourists look up, to see the high buildings. He said that looking up made you a prime target for mugging." Gordon shook his head. "But look what you'd be missing."

Nat agreed. Even the stench of the bins behind them couldn't spoil the moment.

A dog yapped on the other side of the wall surrounding the yard.

"From one natural beauty to another," said Gordon. "Jenkins! Is that you, boy?"

The dog yapped again.

"I'd better go and open the gate."

"Are you sure about this?" asked Nat. "The mood Andre's in, he'll hit the roof if he comes out here."

"Relax," said Gordon, approaching the gate and unlatching it. "He won't come outside. He's too busy ruling his gastronomic kingdom." He swung the gate open.

A small dog with short black and white hair dashed

around the corner and into the yard. It jumped up against Gordon's leg, tail wagging furiously.

"Jenkins!" said Gordon, beaming. "You little rascal. Come here!" He bent down and roughly stroked the dog with his large hands. The dog promptly flopped onto his back, exposing his belly for the same treatment. Gordon immediately obliged. "Look at you. Where've you been, eh? Where've you been?"

The dog released a high, excited whine.

A figure stepped around the corner and through the open gate, scraggy black hair hiding his down-turned face. His clothes were a mismatch of soiled and torn garments, with the occasional patch holding them together. He scratched his chin through a curly and dirty beard.

"Hey, Max," said Gordon, looking up from the dog.

Max nodded and began to walk towards Nat.

"Hey," she said, growing slightly nervous. "How you doing?"

"Okay," he said quietly. Nat hardly heard him and the beard hid his mouth, making it hard to lip-read. He arrived beside her and swung one of the bin lids open.

Nat tried to hide her grimace and retreated back across the yard to her waiting shoes.

"*Mate*," said Gordon, straightening. Jenkins sprang up, pawing at his leg. "You know you don't have to do that."

"Yeah," said Nat. "I'm sure we can find you something, that is, if his highness isn't around."

"Andre," said Max, nodding. "Never changes."

"Let me go and find you a bite." Gordon strode across the yard and paused at the back door. "Any preference?"

"No sea food," said Max. "Gave me gas last time I ate here." He winked at Nat. "But, beggars can't be choosers, I guess."

With a chuckle, Gordon pulled open the door and stepped inside.

Max pulled the top of the bin closed and leaned back

against it. Jenkins trotted over to Nat and continued his needy whining.

Nat stepped into her shoes and crouched, giving him a gentle tickle behind the ears.

"He likes you," said Max, watching her. "He's normally funny with women. At one point, I thought I had a little gay dog."

Nat laughed and looked down.

"You're not gay are you?" she said in a soppy voice like she was talking to a baby. "Bet you get all the girls, don't you?" She glanced up to see Max still resting against the bins, eyes locked on her. She nervously cleared her throat.

"Thank you for this," he said, taking a few steps towards her. "There's not many people who'd help me out. I appreciate what you and Gordon do, and I know how much trouble you'd get into." He stopped a few feet away from her.

Nat tried not to wrinkle her nose from the smell radiating off the man. Although he appeared quite young, maybe only a few years older than herself, the old-tramp stench had settled in. The grime and body odours seemed to congeal to form a smell like burning wood. There was something else in there too, something damp and salty, like seaweed.

Jenkins yapped impatiently around her ankles.

Max offered his hand, clad in a dirty mitten with the fingers cut out, sausages sticking out of a ball of wool.

"I…I should be going back inside," she said quickly. "My break is over and if Andre catches me…"

Max dropped his hand down to his side and nodded.

"That's okay. We don't want you to get a toasting because of us. Do we, Jenkins?"

The dog looked up at the sound of his name, tail beating.

"We should go, let you get back to work."

The backdoor opened, filled with a mountainous silhouette.

"Max, here. Grab this quick. He's coming."

Nat felt her stomach twist. She didn't have the courage to go through another lecture. She'd have to get inside.

Gordon moved towards them holding four Tupperware containers about the same size as shoeboxes. He held them stacked one on top of each other. Nat noticed that the food within was still hot; condensation had formed on the inside of the plastic.

"Spaghetti Bolognese," said Gordon, handing the containers over to Max. "We make so much of this shit that he won't notice a little missing."

A little? There's enough there to keep him going all week, Nat thought.

Max hooked one arm underneath and kept the highest container steady with his chin. With his free hand, he grabbed Gordon by the arm.

"Thank you, my friend. You don't know how much this means to us."

Gordon clamped a hand on his shoulder. "Forget about it. I made it and besides, it's wasted on those people. At least you appreciate it." Both men released each other, and Gordon stepped back. "Now go before he comes out. I don't want to see Jenkins on the menu."

"Thank you," said Max again, moving towards the gate. "Both of you."

"Anytime," said Nat. "See you, Max. And you, Jenkins."

The dog turned to her, ears pricked. Before it could run over, Max clicked his tongue and the dog obediently trotted along beside. Without looking back, they both passed through the gate and turned around the corner.

"Poor bastard," said Gordon, watching him go with his hands on his hips. "Been living on the streets for years."

Nat walked to the backdoor and pushed it open.

Checking if the coast was clear, she stepped inside and held it open for the following chef.

"Why doesn't he get a job?" she asked. "He doesn't seem like the typical weirdos you get around here."

"You try getting a job in that state." Gordon closed the door behind him. "A bit of polishing up and I think he could *maybe* try for a job; I think there's a handsome young man under there somewhere. But who'd give him that much? Most people act like he's diseased or something."

Nat looked to the floor, remembering her disgust at nearly shaking hands with him.

Gordon crossed to the sink and turned on the taps. He soaped his hands up.

"You can talk," said Nat.

"Very funny. This isn't because I touched him. I have no problem with that. Jenkins, on the other hand, has fleas. I don't think Andre would appreciate a customer finding one on his pizza. I might pass it off as a peppercorn, but better safe than sorry." He rinsed his hands and dried them on a towel hanging on a rack beside the sink. "What about you. Think he's all right?"

"I just feel sorry for him," she said. "It must be awful, having no food, nowhere to live, no job…"

The door to the dining area swung open and Andre floundered in, his face bright red.

"Natalie!" he screeched. "What the hell am I paying you for?"

Out of the corner of her eye, she saw Gordon tip-toe away and start to sprinkle flour on his work surface. "Waiting tables?"

"I like to think so," he whined. It reminded Nat of Jenkins' desperate pitch. "And how many have you waited on in the last twenty minutes?"

"Well I've just come off my break and—"

Andre snapped an open hand in front of her face, looking up to the ceiling. "Enough!"

He spun on his heels and marched out of the kitchen, the door swinging shut behind him.

Nat sighed and looked over her shoulder. "Hey, Gordon!"

He glanced up. "Yeah?"

"Maybe Max has got it right," she said, smirking. "No job means no shit like this."

He smiled, nodded and returned to work as Nat entered the dining area for the second half of her shift.

At eleven o'clock, only a few tables were still occupied. Gordon and the kitchen staff, apart from the dishwashers, had gone home. Nat waited by the bar, chatting to the remaining girl who restocked the fridges. She turned at the sound of the front door opening.

Not more, she thought. Don't these people ever have a night in?

Simon stepped inside, shivering and rubbing his hands. Nat's heart leapt.

"Hey," she said, swivelling her stool around and leaning an elbow against the bar.

"Cold out there," he said, vigorously trying to generate some heat in his hands. Leaving his coat on, he weaved between the tables to her. He slid an arm around her waist and delicately kissed her forehead. Nat seemed to smell the chill of the outside on him. "Just let me get warm."

Nat stroked his arm through his coat.

"You got time," she said. "I was late in. Andre's forcing me to make it up. Liz here might be persuaded to make you a drink if you ask her nice." She winked at her friend behind the bar and turned back to Simon. "Park it."

He didn't have a chance to sit down. Andre burst in from the kitchen. He looked towards them and began waving his hands.

"No, no, no," he said. "We are closed. No more."

"It's okay," said Nat. "This is Simon. He's picking me up. It's our one year anniversary."

"Oh..." Andre leaned back against the bar, thoughtfully placing two fingers on his cheek and studying Simon. "So this is the reason my waitress has her head in the clouds and turning up late, is it?"

Simon's cheeks flushed red, and not because of the cold, Nat guessed.

Andre's tongue flicked out, licking his lips. "I can see why. You are a *lovely* thing..."

Liz, behind the bar, giggled.

"Anyway," said Andre, still shamelessly staring, "you can all go. I'll close up."

Nat and Liz looked at each other.

"Why?" asked Nat. "You told me to make up that twenty minutes and there's still customers." She gestured towards the few remaining tables. Simon nervously shifted from foot to foot, pretending to study the bottles lining the shelves behind the bar.

"That was before *Roberto* called, my dear," said Andre, clapping his hands together and squeezing them. "He's forgiven me, the beautiful, beautiful man!"

Nat didn't know what Andre had done to spark an argument with his partner, nor did she want to know. "Are you sure? What about the customers?"

"I'll deal with them," he replied. "Now shoo! All of you!" He waved his hands impatiently again and passed Liz to get behind the bar. He crouched in front of the wine racks and slid the bottles out one at a time, reading the labels. Liz looked over at Nat, shrugged her shoulders and walked into the kitchen.

"I guess I can go then," said Nat. "Let me get my coat."

"Should I just wait here?" asked Simon.

"Yeah." She leaned into him, bringing her mouth close

to his ear. "That is, if you're not afraid of being left alone with your new admirer."

"I'm sure I can manage," he said, a small, cheeky smile blossoming on his face.

4

"Happy anniversary," said Simon, taking her hand as they walked down the street. "Thought we could go to The Fourth Dimension for a change of scene as it's a special night. It serves great cocktails and it's only a few streets away."

"The Fourth Dimension?" said Nat. "Sounds groovy!"

"I haven't taken you before?" asked Simon. "Come on, you'll love it."

They turned another corner and nearly walked into a man standing on the pavement. Simon tugged on her hand, pulling Nat away from him and guiding her towards the road.

The man, scruffy with heavy stubble and staring eyes, watched them walk past. He scratched the front of his jumper. It had multicoloured vertical stripes and seemed too cheerful and creepy on such a scary looking man. He began to whistle a merry tune.

"Come on," Simon whispered, pulling Nat along. She allowed herself to be led across the road, away from the strange whistler.

They quickened their pace to the end of the short street and just before they turned, Nat glimpsed back.

The man remained standing in the same spot, watching them.

Simon nodded politely to the mountain behind the bar as they entered. The man, with skin the colour of hot chocolate, gave a small wave back, the golden bands around his wrist jangling together.

"You know him?" asked Nat.

"Just in passing," said Simon, directing her to a booth

near the windows. "It's better to be on the good side of Bubba Hempshead when drinking in his bar. Once, a fella had too many and began shouting his mouth off. Bubba warned him but the guy carried on. He started throwing glasses."

They sat down in a booth of dark wood with red curtains separating them from their neighbours.

"What happened?"

Simon glanced over to where Bubba stood and lowered his voice.

"We thought Bubba would have ripped his head off if he hadn't been pulled back. You gotta treat this place with respect. It's his baby."

"Shit," hissed Nat. "And there was me planning to dance on the tables in these heels. Oh well…"

Simon swatted her playfully on the arm. "What're you having?"

"You've been here before," she said. "You choose, but make it exciting."

"I'll see what old Bubba can rustle up," he said, sliding across the aged fabric of the seats that matched the red curtains. Nat watched him approach the bar. The wide hulk of Bubba Hempshead stared at him through dangling dreadlocks.

"Rather you than me," she said under her breath, "but at least he has taste in hairstyles." Twirling a dreadlock of her own, she looked around the small bar. It wasn't quite what she expected. The decoration was haphazard, with posters advertising local bands, old movies and many different brands of beer and spirits. These posters had been piled on top of each other and looked three or four layers thick in some places. Ancient sofas dominated the centre of the room with small tables at each end containing short candles. The bar was chaotic, crammed to bursting with various bottles on numerous shelves. Comparing it to the sterile order and neatness of the bar in Ginelli's, Nat loved its quirkiness. The only disappointment was the lack of a surfer type guy sitting in the corner strumming an acoustic, or a beatnik with a beret and goatee, armed with a poetry book and bongos. Still, it felt nice and cosy.

Simon ordered the drinks. An older woman sitting at the bar leaned over and started chatting.

Please, thought Nat. Put it away, honey.

The woman wore a skirt that ended just above her knees. Even from the back booths Nat saw a network of veins and wrinkles on her exposed legs, like dark blue worms living under her skin. Her tiny top, probably worn to show off her ample bosom, revealed how they sagged, resting above her stomach. The woman's hair, messy and turning white, hung down to her shoulders, looking like a weave of straw and cotton wool. Even through the scents of the bar, Nat was sure she smelled the woman's sharp perfume from the other side of the room.

Bubba turned, clutching two dainty glasses in each coconut-sized fist. He delicately placed them on the worn bar before Simon, who removed a note from his jeans' pocket and paid. The woman patted him on the forearm and said something as he picked up the drinks. Simon laughed politely and said something back before returning to the table.

"Looks like you have *another* admirer," said Nat, faking jealousy. "How long has this been going on?"

Simon looked over at the old woman before sitting down to face Nat.

"That's Agnes," he said. "I'm surprised you haven't seen her before. She's always hanging around this part of the city and, well, *everyone* knows her. Like Bubba…and me! We're all legends in these parts."

Nat wrinkled her nose. "I'm sure. I just don't like the way you look at her."

"What? Like this?" asked Simon, rolling his eyes and opening his mouth in a horrified, silent scream.

"Yeah," said Nat. "She gets all the attention…"

They both lasted a few seconds before bursting into laughter. Simon reached over and took her hand.

"You're so cruel sometimes."

"Says you, pulling the face," said Nat, still laughing.

Bubba glanced over and, shaking his head, returned to his duties about the bar. Agnes looked around and, finding the barman with her glazed eyes, tried to start a conversation.

"So what are these then?" Nat asked, nodding to the drinks. She didn't like the disapproving looks from Bubba and wanted to keep her head attached, so directed the conversation away from the ol' whore at the bar.

Simon's eyes lowered to the glasses.

"This one," he said, pointing to a frothy blue concoction, "is a Tranquility. Made from curaçao, vodka and other stuff that I couldn't read the labels of. It's strong, but meant to chill you out and calm you down. I got it for you."

"I wonder why?" said Nat with a smile. "And what have you got?"

"A Rainbow Ride," he said.

Nat studied the glass containing a black liquid. It looked like flat cola.

"Doesn't look very rainbow-esque to me," she said, picking up her Tranquility.

"Yeah," agreed Simon, turning the glass on the table and examining its other dark sides. "I did wonder when he put it on the bar."

"Maybe it's supposed to be ironic," said Nat, taking a drink from her glass. It tasted fruity with a very slight tang of alcohol. She licked her lips.

"Good?"

"Yeah, thanks."

"I can get you something else if you like."

She squeezed his hand.

"I said it was good! Jeez, maybe you should have had the chill out drink." She smiled.

Simon's face flushed red and he stared into the black depths of his glass.

A warm feeling spread through Nat's chest, and she tilted her head to watch him longer. It was moments like this, when he still tried so hard after all this time together, that made her feel for him. Other guys were only interested with what lay in her pants, and once that little mystery was over, you couldn't see them for dust. Simon was different. It had been months since that first time, and he was *still* here, still trying so damn hard to impress her and make her feel comfortable. Enjoying the way his fringe hung down to hide his blazing face, Nat felt her heart race.

Whoa, she thought. This Tranquillity doesn't waste any time!

Hell, it's our anniversary. I'm allowed to go all mushy.

"I'm glad we managed to get out after all," said Simon, staring thoughtfully into the contents of his glass. "I was worried when you said you had to work. But anyway, it's been one year. One whole year…"

"No fooling you and your calendar," said Nat and sipped her drink. "What's brought this on? You've never seemed the type for speeches."

His grip on her hand tightened, and he began to stroke her skin with his thumb.

"I've just had a lot on my mind of late. The right person can…change a guy, is all. The other day I was remembering all the crazy shit I used to get up to, I mean, some of the stuff…" He shook his head. "You wouldn't believe it. With you, it all feels so long ago. None of it matters anymore."

"Are you trying to tell me you're a psycho?"

Simon blinked in surprise. "Yes. Will you still have me?"

Nat leaned across the table. "Of course," she said and

kissed him on the lips. "But as your psycho manager, I have to insist that you take a Nat twice a day to manage your mood swings."

Simon kissed her back. "Done."

The door opened, allowing a chilly gust of night air to breeze past them. Nat shivered.

A tall man in a long leather jacket stepped inside and peered around the small bar. Nat guessed he was probably around the same age as her, but his stark white hair leant him an older appearance. He smiled, and a second chill chased up Nat's spine. Three other guys entered behind him, laughing and poking each other. The man with the white hair glanced over, and the smile slid from his face. He frowned.

"Simon?" he said and walked towards their table. "Is this where you've been hiding?"

Nat looked back to her boyfriend, who sat bolt upright in his seat. His eyes locked onto the stranger. His hand tightened around hers.

The man arrived at their table. His friends immediately migrated to the bar. Bubba observed them with cold malice.

"Well?" said the stranger. "Aren't you at least going to say hello?"

"Erm…" said Simon, his bottom lip trembling slightly. "Hi, Johan. Been a while, I suppose."

"Too long." His grey gaze drifted across the table.

Nat looked down.

Their uninvited guest grinned.

"And who's this gorgeous thing? No wonder we don't see you around. I'm Johan." He extended a hand, and Nat briefly shook it. "I bet this guy has never mentioned me, right?"

"Right," said Nat.

Johan held her hand a little long for her liking, and she eased it from his grip. Simon fidgeted in his seat.

"You okay, pal?" asked Johan, grabbing him lightly on

the shoulder and giving him a friendly shake. "You look like you've seen a ghost!"

"I'm fine, really…" Simon started, looking at Nat.

Johan lowered his hand and stepped back. He glanced at each of them and pointed to the drinks on the table.

"I get it. Some friend I am barging in on such a romantic evening." He stared at both of them expectantly. Nat gave a polite smile while Simon reached down and gulped from his Rainbow Ride. "Okay, I get the hint. I'll be staying for a few with the boys over by the bar. If you want to come and catch up, feel free." His gaze lingered on Simon for a second before he turned to Nat. "Have a pleasant evening."

"I'm sure we will," she replied.

Johan turned away and walked past the leather sofas to join his friends at the bar. Bubba had poured their drinks and watched them closely.

Nat kicked Simon under the table.

"Ow!" he hissed. "What was that for?"

"That was rude," said Nat, keeping her voice down. "You hardly said a word."

"I have my reasons," he replied, turning to watch them. "Never thought they'd come in here…"

"What?"

"Nothing." He sighed and turned back to Nat, taking a second and larger swig from his drink.

"Well, who is he?" Nat pressed. "He's obviously done something to upset you. You've gone all weird."

"It's nothing!" he snapped.

"Obviously, it is." She took hold of both glasses on the table and swapped them around.

"What are you doing?" he asked.

"You sound like you need some Tranquillity."

"I do. Thanks." He sipped. "Sorry."

"Forget it. It should be me that's sorry. If you don't want to talk about it, I shouldn't have pestered you." She laid her hand on the table again, and Simon quickly grasped it. He gazed back across the bar.

"They're just a group I knew years back," he said. "We had a falling-out."

"It's okay," she said. "Don't worry."

Raucous laughter shattered the previously chilled out atmosphere of the bar. Nat noticed Agnes necking a green drink from a narrow glass. Johan's three friends whooped and cheered.

"At least Agnes seems to be enjoying their company," said Nat. She winked. "Not jealous are you?"

"No," Simon said quietly. "No, I'm not." Nat noticed he'd begun to chew his bottom lip.

"I can't believe she drank that!" cried Johan's fat friend.

"Let's get her another!" shouted the blond with the long hair. Johan himself leaned against the bar, silently observing.

"They're gonna have to be careful," said Nat. "I think Bubba is about to bust a blood vessel."

Bubba stood at the end of the bar, his eyes locked on the group. His nostrils flared as he exhaled.

Agnes rose from her stool, swayed slightly, and raised her glass. "Barkeep!" she slurred. "G'is me 'nother! These lovely yun' men's buyin' me." This made Johan's group burst into more laughter. "Was you laughin' at?"

She staggered forwards into Johan's fat friend. Still laughing, he grabbed her by the waist and held her up. She leaned against him.

"Go on, Kev," said the one in glasses. "Give her one!"

This sent them all into hysterics again, apart from Johan, who merely smiled.

"Is okay," said Agnes, pushing herself away. She lurched towards the door. "I bes' be goin' anyway." She paused and took a deep breath, her eyes closing and opening. "I 'as got fings to do…"

"I can imagine," said the fatty, making a crude gesture with his right hand.

"That be it," said Bubba, stepping forwards and casting his shadow on the boys. "Time for you to get to walkin'."

Nat watched from the booth. Bubba sounded like she'd imagined. He had a booming voice with a Jamaican accent.

"I won't be standin' for dat in 'ere."

Agnes pulled open the door and walked through, banging her hip on the frame. The door slammed shut behind her.

"What's your problem?" asked the muscular guy with long hair. Although pretty built, Nat didn't fancy his chances against the human tank. "We're only having a laugh!"

"Leave it, Richie," advised Johan.

Bubba stepped forwards, cracking his knuckles. "I won't be askin' you boys again."

"You should treat your customers a little better," said Richie, squaring up to the behemoth. "We've come in here to pay your goddamn wages."

"Richie!" Johan snapped. He turned to Bubba. "I apologise for my friend here. He has a problem holding his drink." He slapped a twenty pound note on the bar.

"But..."

"Don't you, Richie?" Johan glared at him, cutting off his protests, before turning back to Bubba. "I'm sorry for the trouble."

"But, Johan," started his fat friend, gesturing to his full drink still waiting on the bar. "Can't we just..."

Johan stared at him. "No. We can't." He zipped up his leather coat and headed towards the door. "There are other ways we can amuse ourselves."

Fat boy picked up his drink and tried to neck the contents. A growl from Bubba, and he quickly placed it back down.

Johan reached the door and held it wide. "Gentlemen?"

45

The remaining three followed in a group.

"Don't know why we came in here in the first place," muttered blondy, walking past Bubba.

Johan glanced over to where Nat and Simon were sitting. "See you around. Don't leave it so long next time, friend."

Simon's body stiffened.

"See you," he replied.

Johan allowed his three comrades to exit the bar. He winked at Nat and stepped out himself. The room returned to quiet, the few drinkers watching the door. With a grin, Bubba shook his head and moved back behind the bar. One by one, the patrons resumed their hushed conversations.

Nat sipped her drink and looked up at Simon.

"Glad that's over with," she said with a nervous laugh. "I thought they were going to be ripped limb from limb."

"Mmm," said Simon, sounding uninterested.

"You okay? I mean, whatever happened between you and them, they've gone, so forget about it. We should go back to before they came in; pretend it never happened."

"Easier said than done." His gaze lingered on the door.

Nat brushed her leg against his under the table, but he shrugged away. A touch hurt and rejected, Nat polished off most of her drink.

"Simon," she said after a moment. "Are you afraid of them?"

He glanced away from the door for a second. "No. Why should I be?"

"Because you're acting like Johan came in here and put a gun to your head. Bubba kicked them out. They won't be back, so relax."

Nat leaned back in her seat and closed her eyes. From the darkness, a bloody hand reached for her.

"Shit!" she cried, rubbing her temples.

"Nat?"

"Nothing. Just...why the hell can't she leave me alone

today?" Nat had a large swallow of her cocktail. "It's like my mother's fucking haunting me. Don't you hate it when you think you've forgotten something and it suddenly leaps out at you?"

It took another deep drink before she could start. "They followed her home from a bar..." she said. "A bunch of guys did a number on her because she'd taken their drinks but hadn't, you know, gone home with them." She rubbed her head. "I opened the door, and she was lying on the step, reaching up... Jesus! Where the hell has that little doozy been hiding all these years?"

Nat flinched as Simon stood up sharply.

"I'll be back in a second," he said, moving around the table and out of the booth.

"What's got into you?" Nat said, worry creeping into her voice. Their night had taken a nose dive. She'd never seen Simon act like this before. "You're just going to *leave* me here?"

"No...erm..." He fumbled in his pocket and fished out a ten pound note, He dropped it on the table. "Give it a minute and call a cab from the bar. I'll meet you back at your place."

"Simon, it's our anniversary and I want to spend it with you! I'm leaving too." Nat picked up her handbag and stood up. She noticed Simon's eyes bulge. He swallowed.

"No. You can't!" He grabbed her by the shoulders. "Please, just get home."

"What's going on, Simon?" she cried, ignoring the curious looks from the others in the bar. "Are you in some kind of trouble with those guys?"

Simon shook his head. "No. Please believe me. I just need to go and speak with Johan for one minute, put something to rest, and then I'm all yours. Just promise me that you'll go home and I'll see you there shortly. I'll grab us some food on the way. That sound good?"

He kept hold of her shoulders, and she sat back down.

He kissed the top of her head. "One minute."

He quickly walked away, threw the door wide, and slipped out into the inky darkness.

Outside The Fourth Dimension, the temperature had plummeted. Simon looked up into the night sky, expecting to see the first snow of the season drifting down from between the stars. Shivering, he dug his hands into his pockets. The cold already gnawed at his fingertips.

Glancing left and right, the street appeared deserted. The only sounds came from back inside the bar: a faint murmur of conversation accompanied by the occasional clink of a glass. He imagined Nat sitting in there, alone.

"Please," he whispered. "Please rush home, Nat."

A scream rang out from his left between the buildings. Sure *they* were the cause of the cry, Simon ran towards the dying sound. He paused at the first intersection, his lungs stinging from the cold air, and peeked around the corner.

Squinting in the glare of the overhead streetlight, he watched the group of three figures cheer and race away. Behind them, Johan was unmistakeable. His white hair seemed to glow from within the shadows.

Sucking in a deep breath, Simon continued to run, his arms chopping through the air.

Up ahead, Johan stopped dead.

He's heard me, Simon realised.

Relieved that he wouldn't have to shout and bring unwanted attention, he sprinted up the street.

Johan slowly turned. He smiled.

"I knew you wouldn't be able to resist," he said. "The lure of the hunt too much, friend?"

Simon arrived, gasping for breath. He bent over with his hands on his knees, gulping down the sharp and numbing air. "Wait. Please…wait."

"We can't," said Johan. "We've started."

Simon grabbed him by the arm. Johan looked down with subtle surprise and disgust, like a leper had touched him during a high-class dinner party.

"You can call them back," Simon wheezed. "All three of those clowns. You know you can!"

"Can," said Johan, the temporary sickened look leaving his face, replaced with his usual grin, "but I won't. This evening has been a complete waste of time, Simon. You can't deny us our fun now." He looked further up the street in the direction the boys had vanished. "You should see her. My God, Simon, you should see her…"

"Bring them back!" Simon shouted, rising up. He grimaced as a stitch flared, stabbing him in the side.

"Keep your voice down," hissed Johan. "You want us to get caught? Really? Think about it."

Simon did. It took all of half a second.

"I couldn't give a fuck," he said. "This has to stop! You can't just… just…"

"Just what? Give a lady what she wants?"

"I can't just let you—"

Johan raised his hand. "Listen. They're coming back now, so stop fretting."

Simon looked past his former friend and indeed, Richie, Kevin and Spence were running back towards them, passing in and out of shadow along the edge of the road. They moved together in a clumsy, uncoordinated run. At first, Simon put this down to alcohol, but as they neared, he realised they carried something.

Not something, he thought, spying the limp form they carried between them. Someone.

"To be honest, I'm surprised this one got as far as she did," said Johan, blasé, like he talked about the weather or a story in the newspaper.

Not about the figure being dumped on the tarmac.

"She nearly *did* get away," commented Spence.

Gasping, he pushed his glasses back up onto the bridge of his nose. "The fat fuck couldn't keep up."

"You are such a funny little twat, Spence," said Kev in reply. He punched his friend squarely on the shoulder.

"Shut up, fellas," ordered Johan, walking up to them. "Spence, stop rubbing your shoulder, you soft prick."

Spence immediately did so and hung his head. Kev winked at him and grinned.

Johan crouched down next to the figure and grabbed her chin. He tilted the face upwards. A thick, dark splash coated her lips and teeth.

"Who did this?" said Johan. "Her nose is bleeding."

Richie stepped forwards. "It was me. It was just…she…she struggled and…"

Johan nodded and looked back down.

"No big deal. She's no oil painting, but she's definitely not an antique." He glanced over his shoulder at Simon. "Come and have a look at this. I swear you're gonna shit yourself laughing!"

Simon stared down the street. It remained empty.

Run! a voice inside his head screamed. Don't get involved! Get back to Nat! Go!

Johan shuffled to the side, still holding onto the woman's chin. Above his pale fingers, her skin appeared bronzed with fake tan, breaking into a gaudy scarlet splashed over thin lips, barely hidden by the blood.

"No," said Simon. "Why? Why the hell did you do this?"

"It's a laugh," said Johan, standing up. The woman's head flopped back to the ground. "I don't see any hot babes around here anyway."

Simon shook his head. "Are you sick? I mean…Agnes?"

Nat drummed her fingers against the table top, her gaze loitering on the door. Most of the other occupants had left The Fourth Dimension, and she expected Bubba to order her to leave any second.

She finished the dregs of her drink and, without the slightest buzz from the alcohol, started on Simon's. Even if he walked through the door that very second, he wouldn't have time to finish it. Bubba had begun to stack chairs on top of the empty tables.

Nat peered back to the door.

She closed her eyes and called to him in her head.

Simon! Come back! Please…

These psychic messages had never worked, but some divine spirit might be cruising on through The Fourth Dimension—after all, it did have a very spiritual vibe—and pass on her message.

Feeling ridiculously optimistic, she opened her eyes and worked on the drink.

First the flashbacks of mother, then Samantha not showing up at work, now this. What a night, she thought. She licked her sour lips; the drink tasted sharper the more she drank.

"Don't look like he comin' back, girl." Bubba, done with his chairs, stood by the bar. He poured a dark brown drink into a short glass from a plain white bottle. "Rum?"

"Erm…no, thank you," she said, quickly finishing Simon's drink and picking up the ten pound note he'd left. She slid around the table, tugged on her coat and glanced into the next booth. Empty.

Aware she'd been left alone with the man-mountain, she picked up her bag and left her coat unbuttoned. She headed for the door and stepped outside.

Damn you, Simon!

Nat looked up and down the deserted street. She hardly ventured into this derelict zone. A siren blared out somewhere far away, and the streetlight, illuminating the entrance of the bar, emitted a low buzz. Nat buttoned up her coat and crossed her arms to keep the heat in.

The biting cold made her very briefly consider going back into the warmth of The Fourth Dimension...with Bubba...

"Come on, Simon," she hissed.

She wanted to call out, bringing her knight in shining armour to her aid. She didn't dare, and Simon could be miles away by now if he'd jumped into a car.

No. He wouldn't do that to me. He's not like all the others.

A noise came from her right.

Underneath the rotting canopies of long abandoned shop fronts, a lone figure walked along the road, running his hands slowly across the smeared glass of the store windows. He whistled a quick blast of some tune Nat had never heard. The last note rose in pitch, like the melody had asked a question.

Nat didn't need to see his face to recognise the tramp with the colourful jumper from earlier. His range and scales of whistling sounded almost like a voice, distinct and personal. She turned back the other way, trying to show the stranger she wasn't intimidated by his presence. She scanned the head of the street.

Looking back over her shoulder, she noticed the whistler had sneaked forwards a couple of steps. The streetlight managed to illuminate his multi-coloured jumper as he neared the edge of the canopy.

His notes sang in Nat's head, her mind subconsciously adding lyrics to songs she didn't know. They brought images of starlets in glittery frocks on music hall stages.

This is too weird, she thought, backing away. If one more freak comes my way so help me God...

She turned from the slowly approaching whistler and clutching her bag by its strap, walked up the street. She hoped her sense of direction would lead her back to Ginelli's, where she could at least get hold of a taxi.

She paused at the corner and stopped cold. Down the street to her left, Simon stood with a group of people in the middle of the road.

She frowned, wondering why Simon was still with the guys from the bar. He stood talking with Johan, whose bone-white hair made his pale face look bald and pointed, like a drop of milk in the dark.

Keeping close to the buildings, Nat walked towards them, keeping hidden in the deep shadows. Simon was a good guy, and she wouldn't let him get drawn into anything.

Johan's probably a dealer, she thought. Maybe that's what this is. He's a dealer and Simon owes him? He said his life was insane before he met me...

She shook the thoughts out. In the year she'd been with Simon, she knew he wouldn't do anything as irresponsible as that. He was straight as an arrow, steady and predictable.

But seeing him talking to Johan up the street, Nat suddenly didn't feel so sure.

"For the last time!" shouted Simon, seeming to put his hands to his head in desperation. "You can't go through with this!"

Hearing his words, Nat sidestepped into the doorway of another empty building. She pressed her back to the cold brick and looked out, sure that she couldn't be seen.

"Simon, Simon, Simon," said Johan, shaking his head. "Where's your sense of fun?"

"Even if for *one second*," said Simon, "for one insane, crazy instance, I agreed with what you guys did, this," he nodded to the side, "is a joke!"

Nat leaned out further from her hiding place and saw the crumpled figure lying on the floor.

What the hell have they done?

"So, it's a joke," said Johan. He stared into Simon's eyes, his face a porcelain mask, devoid of emotion. "Har, har."

Old Agnes lay on her back, spread-eagle. Blood had trickled from her nose and down across her cheek towards her ear, another shade for the pallet of her face. Beneath her oversized fake lashes, her eyes were shut. Either the drink or some blow had knocked her out.

"This is just…wrong," said Simon.

"I don't think—" Johan stopped mid-sentence and pointed in Nat's direction. She fell back against the doorway, holding her breath.

"What's the matter?" asked Kev, looking around. "I don't see nobody."

"Well *I* did," said Johan. "They're over there, hiding in that doorway."

Nat froze.

"There's no one there," said Spence, his whining voice drifting down the street. "You're seeing things."

"I don't think so," said Johan. Nat listened to footsteps growing closer.

She crouched and retreated further into the doorway, curling up in the corner, trying to make her body as small as possible. Her arms, wrapped around her legs, shook to the sounds of approach. She took a quick breath, but then snatched it back in. The doorway reeked of urine.

The footsteps stopped.

"I can *see you*," said Johan, his voice low and commanding.

Nat stayed put.

"Come out," he said. "Or my boys here will *drag you out!*"

Nat swallowed and stood up. Her feet felt like stone.

"There you are," said Johan. "Wasn't too hard, was it?"

Nat remained still, hidden in the shadows.

From further down the street drifted a single whistled note.

She listened to Richie laugh. "It's all right, Johan. It's that fucking retard who lives on the streets. He can't talk or anything!"

Nat released a long breath, which steamed before her face. She collapsed back against the wall.

Better him than me, she thought.

"Get out of here!" Johan shouted, still keeping his tone of control. "We'll *kill* you if we see you round here again."

Nat listened to a burst of whistles followed by the frantic beat of feet on the road. She imagined the weirdo in his colourful jumper running for his life. The group began to laugh, all except Simon.

"You better be right, Rich," said Johan. "If he says anything…"

"Don't worry. He's a fruitcake."

The guys began to talk, and Nat had difficulty making out the words. Blood rushed in her ears, and her heart still hammered from the close call. She strained to listen.

Most of them laughed. Simon began his pleadings anew.

"It's not worth it, Johan. Let her go."

"You know that's not an option," said Johan. "Not now. Get her up."

Nat sidled along the wall to the edge of the doorway and, after closing her eyes briefly with a prayer on her lips, peered around the corner.

Richie and Kev had hauled Agnes onto her feet. She hung between them, a marionette with its strings cut. Her head slumped forwards like she was inspecting something on her chest.

Standing to the side, Simon grabbed Johan by the shoulder.

"How can this be about sex?" demanded Simon. "Look

at her!"

"Sometimes the sex is just a distraction," said Johan, approaching the limp form.

Nat felt her heart step up another gear as he reached forwards and tilted her head up by the hair.

"What matters is the hunt!"

Agnes's head jerked and she snapped a knee upwards. It connected with Johan square in the groin, and he fell to the ground clutching himself.

"Bitch!" he screamed. "Fucking bitch!" He gagged. "Oh *Christ*."

Richie and Kev dropped the woman and rushed to his aid. She staggered for a second before turning and breaking into a run. Spence stood by, uselessly watching.

"Get her!" cried Johan through his chokes. "Get the bitch!" He rolled onto his back, his features pinched in agony.

The three men abandoned him and pursued.

Nat watched Simon drop to one knee next to Johan. "You okay?"

Johan groaned in reply.

Seizing the opportunity, Nat bent down and scooped off her high-heeled shoes. Ignoring the cold, she eased out of the doorway and, keeping in the shadow cast by the tall building, began a silent dash away from the scene. She threw a cautionary glance over her shoulder, though she doubted Johan could run anywhere in his current state.

He'd rolled onto his side. Simon gazed down at him, looking concerned.

Reaching the corner, Nat slipped around the edge of the building and away.

Johan heaved himself up, roaring with pain. He hobbled a few steps, his balls throbbing. His stomach had a lead weight inside. "Bitch," he gasped. "That fucking bitch."

He straightened up and swallowed a gulp of air. He looked up the street where Spence, Richie and Kev had fled in pursuit.

"It wouldn't have happened if you'd have just let her go," said Simon.

Johan glared at him.

Simon continued. "She'll easily get away from those guys. Just hope she's too drunk to remember your faces in the morning." He walked away.

With a wince, Johan began a slow jog up the street away from Simon. The pain gradually subsided with each step, and his speed increased. He looked back once. Simon watched him go.

Sucker, Johan thought with a pang of regret.

Hearing a shout, he veered to the left, heading down a side street. He lengthened his stride, ignoring the slight protest from his swaying testicles. A little more abuse wouldn't do any real harm. He shot down the street, his coat billowing out behind him.

He skidded to a stop at the corner.

The buildings were spread apart like teeth in a broken mouth. The park, a green jewel in the middle of the grey city, lay between. They spent a lot of time in the area. Being surrounded by the derelict areas the park guaranteed privacy. Occasionally, some stray beauty would get lost or try a shortcut and come wandering into their territory. Those times, Johan thought, the gods were smiling down on him. Easy pickings.

On the edge of the park grounds, Spence, Richie and Kev loitered on the grass. Each looked in the same direction, towards a small patch of woodland. They covered their eyes from the glare of the last street light.

Breathing deeply through his nose, Johan approached them.

"Well?" he demanded, his voice showing only the

slightest sign of exertion. "Where is she?"

Richie pointed towards the woods.

Johan looked at the dark island of trees in the sea of dark fields and swallowed.

"You let her get away *in there?*" He shook his head. "I don't believe this! Of all the places..."

"You want us to go after her?" asked Kev. His chubby cheeks had flushed a deep red and his wide chest rose and fell with rattling breaths.

"If you know what's good for you," said Johan. "I don't think you'll like prison food."

He walked through them, roughly barging into Spence. The three tagged on alongside him, heading for the dark expanse of trees on the far side of the park.

In the dark, one aging building looked the same as its neighbours to Nat as she fled down the empty streets. The soles of her feet had grown sore from running without her shoes, the pavement taking a harsh toll.

She turned left, running past a small and vacant car park.

Did we pass that on the way here?

Slowing to a walk, she looked behind her. No one followed. She scanned the road ahead for anything familiar.

She arrived at a crossroads. An old pub stood on one corner, its door and windows boarded up, paint faded and flaking. Its sign, hanging from rusty hinges, swayed in the slightest of breezes. The corroded metal creaked in a slow rhythm.

Nat stopped and turned full circle. Each road leading away from the crossroads appeared the same. She strained to listen for passing traffic in the distance, but silence prevailed. The moon, her only observer, peeked down from between two four-story buildings. It felt like days since

Gordon had pointed out its beauty.

Completely lost in her city, Nat shook her head and chose the road to the right.

She checked over her shoulder again. Neither Johan or any of his boys had followed her, nor had the whistling man.

Don't relax too soon, she told herself. You need to get home first.

She quickened her pace.

Hell, you need to find *civilisation* first.

Ahead, a building with an aged majesty split the road like a rock in a river. It may have been a bank before the city deteriorated. Nat walked down the right branch of the fork.

She stumbled and cried out as pain erupted in her foot. Using the wall for support, she pulled her leg up and studied her sole. A stone, narrow and sharp, had penetrated the skin and stuck out like a splinter. Hissing through gritted teeth, she plucked it out and threw it on the pavement. A tiny bead of blood oozed out of the pinprick hole.

"Damn it!" she said, dropping her shoes on the floor and stepping into them.

Continuing, the steady noise of her heels on the pavement made her feel even more alone, even more vulnerable.

But better than stepping on something again, she thought. God knows what stuff is lying around.

Her thoughts turned back to what had gone on between Simon and Johan.

They had that old woman, that Agnes, on the floor.

Thinking back to events in The Fourth Dimension, she remembered how Johan's friends had deliberately tried to get the woman drunk. They'd done a good job too, judging by the state she left in. It was planned. Whatever they did to her, it was premeditated.

Mother, beaten and left for dead...

She thought about Simon. He'd been with her all night, and he *did* look terrified when Johan had entered. Could he have been involved in all of this?

The street turned to the right, and following the corner around, Nat was surprised to see The Fourth Dimension up ahead.

"Ah fuck!"

She paused to look around and try and regain a sense of direction, unsure how she'd doubled back and come full circle.

She hurried down the street towards the bar. The lights were off inside. She guessed that Bubba had locked up for the night. She imagined him still sitting by the bar drinking rum.

She approached the street where she'd left Simon.

I will never, ever come back here, she promised herself, reaching the corner. This part of the city is creepy enough without all this shit to go with it.

She took another step and moaned. Her foot stung. She lifted it free from the shoe and again inspected its underside. A minute streak of blood was smeared on her sole. Licking her thumb, she wiped it clean, revealing a tiny flap of torn skin. Grimacing, she plucked it off and replaced her foot in the shoe. She looked up as the figure stepped around the corner, reaching for her.

Barely any light penetrated the thick foliage of the small wood. Johan held his hands out to avoid walking into any trees or branches that might strike his face. He moved in small steps, fearing to raise his feet off the ground in case some root should trip him and send him sprawling into the filth of the land. His nose wrinkled from the smell of earth and wood. The streets weren't exactly hygienic, but they were ordered, lending him more comfort than this green and black maze of nature.

They should have had her in the streets, not here in this grubby wasteland, he thought.

Within the shadows to his side, a twig snapped. Probably Kev. The four of them walked in a rough line. He'd seen the police do this on television, searching for missing kids. It seemed a good idea, certainly more appealing than running around aimlessly in the dark.

He tried to see Richie, but the night and the wide trunks of several trees restricted his view. His hopes of finding the woman were falling fast.

Yet he *smelled* her. Lying underneath the stinking odours of nature, he detected bitter perfume. Like a bloodhound, he followed his nose.

Things might be okay even if we *don't* find her. She was pretty out of it, and with the roughing up Richie gave her, she might be too dazed to remember anything at all.

These were dangerous thoughts. Sloppiness meant getting caught, and this was too much fun to give up. Better to find her and be sure she's in no state to tell anybody *anything*.

He passed between the trees a little faster, pushing leafy branches away and kicking through small shrubs. Desperate to wash his hands, he knew he'd have to wait.

"Here!" It sounded like Spence. "I've got her!"

Good lad. Johan broke into a run.

At the centre of the small wood, the trees thinned out revealing a patch of bare earth. Johan bounded out through a bush, finding the other three already gathered.

On the ground, the woman cowered between them.

"It's about time," Johan said, walking up to them. They spread out, allowing him access to the old woman. Shivering, she gazed up with wide eyes.

He stopped in front of her and placed his hands on his hips.

"Please…" she said, her slur gone.

Johan considered that the run and the shock might have sobered her up, but he believed she'd been faking all along. Again, sloppiness. She wiped the trail of blood from under her nose. "What do you want? Just let me go…"

Begging. He hated begging.

Johan quickly stepped forwards and kicked his leg up. His foot caught her on the bottom of the chin. He heard the sickening crack of teeth crunching together. Her head whipped back, followed by her body. She sprawled back on the ground.

The boys sniggered.

Johan followed up with a boot to her side.

She cried out and tried to roll away from him.

Kev prodded her with his own large foot, stopping her retreat. She had time to suck in a breath before Johan's foot slammed into her ribs again.

"Not nice, is it?" Johan asked. He swung his leg back and kicked her again. She coughed, the wind knocked out of her. "Not nice at all."

Johan turned away and walked a few paces. He raised his face to the moon that glimmered through the ceiling of leaves and drew in a long breath through his nose. His heart thundered in his chest, and he felt a steady swelling in his pants. The woman herself wasn't bringing it on; it was the sounds she made.

Behind him, the boys laughed.

"So," said Johan, turning, "who wants to go first?"

The chortles died down, and he caught them exchange nervous glances.

"Rich?"

Richie scratched the back of his head through his thick hair. "No thanks. I'm good."

Johan raised his eyebrows at Spence.

"Me too." Spence looked down at the woman. "Don't think I could even if I tried. Not much to work with."

Johan smiled and shook his head. "I presume you feel the same way, Kev?"

He nodded.

Johan sighed. "Sorry, love. Seems the boys aren't too keen..."

"Please," she pleaded again. "I won't tell a soul, just let me go." She shuffled back on her rear. Kev crouched down and grabbed her hair. He wrapped it tightly around his fist and tugged upwards. She howled and stopped her retreat.

"Everyone we meet says that," said Johan. He scanned the woodland floor. "And you're right. You won't tell anyone." He bent down, spying the side of a rock protruding from the ground. His fingers found its edge and easily pried it from the loose earth. He picked up the stone and held it with both hands, weighing it up.

The woman's eyes grew wider on seeing the rock. She fought against Kev's hold, reaching upwards and trying to pry his fingers open. He held on tight, tilting his head back in case she tried to strike his face.

"Let her go," said Johan. "I believe her. Who would believe a crazy, drunken *whore* anyway?"

Kev frowned. "Let her go? But after we chased her here..."

"I said to let her go," Johan repeated. "Unless you want her after all."

Kev seemed to consider this for a second before untwining his hand from her hair and standing up. He stepped to the side.

The woman frantically climbed to her feet, clutching her side.

She headed for the dark wall of trees.

Johan heaved the rock, smashing it against the back of her head. Agnes's body pitched forwards, falling back to the ground.

Kev, Rich and Spence cheered, disturbing a bird that

fluttered from its perch above and zigzagged through the branches.

Agnes tried to push herself up with trembling arms, but Johan stepped in again, picking up the football-sized rock over his head and bringing it down with both hands.

The rock made a solid *crunch* as it hit her head a second time. She flopped onto the ground, her spread limbs going into a spasm.

Johan casually threw the soiled rock to the ground. It bounced once and fell on its side, the bloodied edge pointing upwards.

"Let's see her run now." He wiped his hands on the back of his jeans and held them up for inspection. Some dirt still smudged his skin. He wiped them again, harder. "Finish her off. I want out of here."

Like a pack of hunting dogs who have waited eagerly for their master's order, they pounced on the unconscious woman. All three punched and kicked. Spence in particular appeared rabid, stomping the woman in the face over and over again. Johan stepped around for a better view. Already the woman's face had swelled. Blood gushed from her mouth and nose.

He walked back over to the abandoned rock and picked it up again.

"This is going to take all night," he said. He toed the fallen leaves and other detritus with his boot. "The sooner we're out of here the better."

Johan approached Agnes, and the three reluctantly parted. He stood over her, a foot planted on each side of her chest. Beneath him, her rib cage rose slowly and drifted back down. Her head hung to the side.

He focused on her temple and rearranged the rock in his hands. The sharp edge pointed downwards.

"If you want a job done properly…" he said quietly. He hoisted the rock over his head. "You have to do it yourself."

With a roar, he swung the rock down.
It sounded like cracking an eggshell.

Simon had followed Nat all the way along the street, begging with every step.

She allowed him to ramble. Ahead, the road became well lit and cars shot through the junction a few hundred yards on.

How the hell did I miss this before?

"Please," said Simon, keeping pace. "Hear me out!"

"Hear you out?" she growled. "*Hear you out?* You just left me there to go and do…to do God knows what!"

"It wasn't like that!"

"Yeah. It certainly felt like that when I was left alone with that giant, Bubba. He could have done anything, Simon. He might have been a rapist for all you care."

He swallowed and kept quiet.

"And then to leave me wandering the streets at this time. Anything could've happened!"

"Look," he said, grabbing her elbow. She jerked free and continued up the street.

"Fuck off and leave me alone. You seem good at it."

"Listen to me!" he screamed. A more forceful attempt of grabbing her, he managed to wrap his fingers around her arm. She again tried to shrug him off, but he held fast. "Nat, just stop and listen!"

She huffed but stopped her advance up the street and gazed at the dark windows above. On a worn ledge, a bird observed them for a moment before fluttering away through the night.

"Look at me, Nat."

"I don't think I can," she said firmly. "No one has ever done something like this to me."

"I had a good reason."

"Yeah, running off with your little friends. I've had boyfriends choose their mates over me before, but I've never been abandoned in a random bar!"

He shook his head. "It's not like that. I hoped you knew me better."

"I thought I did," Nat replied coldly.

Simon looked back down the street.

"Can't we discuss this when we get back?"

Nat laughed, the sound emerged nervous and weak.

"You expect me to have you come back home with me? You're insane." She turned and started to walk away. Simon ran up to travel alongside her.

"Please, Nat," he said, his words soft, tentative from between his lips. "We need to talk. At least, I need to talk, get all this off my chest."

Nat's throat twitched. She swallowed the sensation down, remembering Agnes lying on the ground between the gathered men.

What the hell was going on?

"Please," he said again, reaching for her hand.

Nat snatched it away and kept walking. Pulling her coat tighter around her body, she dreaded the journey back home. It was hard enough to get a taxi at this hour, and she didn't know a convenient place to pick one up. She pressed her teeth together to stop them from chattering.

"You're freezing," said Simon. He slipped his arm around her shoulders and pulled her in close. His heat radiated through his thin coat, and Nat let him press against her while they walked down the street.

Just until I get a taxi. He isn't back in my good books, whether he can keep me warm or not.

They carried on in silence until they reached the junction, caught in the glare of passing cars.

"Come on," said Simon, gently tugging her to the side. "This way."

She fought against him, standing her ground. "No. I

can find my own way back."

"Yes," he said, "but it's freezing out here. Do you want to get a taxi or not? I know a place."

Nat peered up and down the street, studying the cars speeding past. None of them looked like taxis, and even if one *should* go past, it probably wouldn't pick up a person out here. Tired of roaming the moonlit and deserted streets, Nat grunted and followed Simon.

The bird fell between the branches like a plummeting stone and opened its wings a few feet from the ground. A burst of flapping, and its small body drifted over dried leaves, stones and earth. It landed neatly on its twig-like legs. The tiny head bobbed to and fro, black eyes scanning the woodland floor. Content in safety, the little brown bird hopped along, its tail held high.

Through the trees and out of the solid darkness, echoed a hoot, followed by a whistle.

The bird replied, its own quizzical tweet ringing out to greet the mysterious caller. It hopped forwards for a few feet and, happy with its spot, pecked at the ground, ignoring the mangled face of the old woman lying beside it.

The whistle came again, closer this time.

The bird raised its head and surveyed the trees. It tweeted again and resumed its hunt for worms in the loamy soil. Moving forwards, making faint pattering noises across the ground, the bird paused and tilted its head at the old woman.

Her eyes remained open, staring forwards. She didn't move as the bird hopped closer still. It gave her nose a cautionary peck.

The bird shot upwards into the air with a flurry of wings and feathers as a shape loomed out of the bushes and staggered into the clearing. Circling a tree before landing on a long branch several feet above the ground, the bird peeked down into the clearing.

The figure, its head down, slowly walked up to the body and stopped.

The bird responded to the whistle that escaped from the visitor. Hooking its right wing up beside its head, it began to prune.

The man fell to his knees, running his hands across the

white face of the old woman. He explored the ragged skin across her forehead, his fingers slipping into the crater at the top of her skull. He stroked a thumb across the woman's lips and caressed her cheeks, now painted with deep bruises as well as blush. He raised his head and sucked in a deep breath of freezing night air.

The blast from between his pursed lips caused the bird to panic and burst from the branch. Like a feathered missile it shot through the trees, avoiding each with sharp twists and turns. Whistles reverberated around the small woods, rising and falling in sorrow and seeming to swell in the air. The tiny bird emerged from the trees and flew across the park, swooping higher and higher.

It headed into the city.

The taxi ride over hadn't taken as long as Nat expected, and she stepped onto the pavement outside her apartment block. It bothered her how close the maze of derelict buildings stood to her home. She expected to wander those streets again in her dreams.

Simon leaned into the open window of the car and paid the driver. Nat looked through the glass doors into the lit foyer of her building. She considered running inside and telling the night watchman that Simon was bothering her. That way, she had a chance to retire to her apartment alone. But the voice, the one that *normally* talked her into trouble, sounded its protests in her mind. If she left things as they stood, she'd never know about Simon, Johan and the woman.

"Well?" he asked. "Am I allowed up or am I hopping back inside this cab?"

Nat sighed. "You'd better come in."

Simon waved to the taxi driver. The car pulled away from the curb.

Let's see what he has to say for himself, she thought, entering the building.

Seeing the sign on the lift doors and remembering it was broken, Nat headed for the stairway. She pushed the door open and stepped through, her heels echoing in the narrow hallway. The light fixtures along the walls, made to look like antique wrought iron containing candles, flickered. Shadows made by the banister danced across the cream walls. She took Simon's offered hand.

"Let's go," he said, taking the lead.

They emerged from the stairway onto her floor. Walking to her apartment at the end of the corridor, Nat heard distant voices from televisions behind closed doors. Her neighbours, whoever they were, must still be awake or had fallen asleep in front of their sets. She opened her bag and fished out her keys. They jingled against each other as she separated them out and slid the correct key into the lock.

The door opened into her dark living room. Pinpricks of light glittered in the void beyond the window, a constellation of distant streetlights. Nat groped along the wall for the light switch and, finding its cool plastic beneath her fingers, switched it on. Blinking in the sudden brightness, she stepped inside to allow Simon to follow. He closed the door softly behind them.

Nat tossed her keys into her open bag and dropped it to the floor. She hung up her coat and wandered further into the apartment. Reaching the sofa, she kicked off her high-heeled shoes and sighed.

"That's better. Feels like I've walked across this whole damn city." She inspected the small wound on her foot. The skin didn't sting anymore but still felt tender to her touch.

"How did you do that?"

"Wandering the streets looking for you. It was only a stone."

"I'm sorry," said Simon, lowering his head.

"Enough with the apologising," said Nat, flopping back on the sofa and resting her feet on the coffee table. "You're making me feel like I overreacted."

Simon shook his head. "No, this is my mess." He raked a hand through his hair. Nat noticed his vacant expression had returned, like when Johan had entered the bar. "You still want to talk?"

Nat yawned but nodded.

"If you want to," she said.

"It's late."

"I know, but I can tell you need to. Something happened tonight, didn't it? With Johan?"

Simon hung his head.

Nat yawned again and tried to hide it behind her hand.

"You're tired," said Simon. "It can wait till morning. It's been a long night. Maybe I should sleep on it anyway, it's...it's a lot to deal with."

Nat nodded and groggily pulled herself up from the sofa. The late hour had finally caught up with her.

"I'm sorry," she said. "The night has tired me out. Come on..." She walked up to him and took his hand. "Let's go to bed."

He raised an eyebrow, but his lips stayed straight. "Am I still welcome?"

"You're better at snuggling than my hot water bottle," she said. "But no funny ideas, okay? I don't think I have the energy."

She expected some retort, but Simon silently followed her out of the living room and into the bedroom, turning the light off on the way.

Nat stood with Gordon, looking up into the sky.

"It's beautiful," the chef told her. "A secret just for you."

"What do you mean?" she asked, turning away from the black canvas of night to the sound of his voice. Gordon had vanished, leaving her standing alone on the street. She turned around. The street was empty.

He was here. I heard him.

She gazed back upwards. Gordon, here or not, had been right. It *was* beautiful. The pure emptiness of the night loomed above her; a dark skyscape of desolation. The city tried to interfere with its lights and noise, but for this instant, the sky remained pure and untainted.

Nat watched in awe as the first stars emerged, appearing almost shyly with their gradual twinkling. They formed in a dusty cluster above her.

I'll have to share this with Simon. Get him to drive us out of the city and into the country. We could just sit and watch for hours and hours...

Raucous laughter rang out, and Nat gasped, staring upwards, mouth hanging open.

Four smiling faces gazed down at her from the heavens, blotting out most of the sky. Their skin appeared white. Dead.

"What have we here, boys?" boomed Johan's voice.

Nat fled, holding her hands above her head like a girl caught in a sudden downpour.

"Leave me alone!" she screamed, running from the hovering faces and down the empty street.

Her actions spurred more laughter from the spectres, which seemed to effortlessly keep pace with her.

Left and right and left again, the streets whipped by as she fled in blind panic. Her breaths gasped from her aching chest. Sweat poured down her face in a warm trickle.

"Wait!"

Nat skidded to a stop at the sound of the voice. With her heart pumping and her lungs threatening to burst, she slowly turned around.

"Noooo!" she screamed, seeing Simon. At his feet—

She opened her eyes.

"Ssssh!" said Simon, placing his arm around her neck and giving her a tender squeeze. "You're awake now."

Her thin curtains did little to block out the early morning rays of sun. The yellow of the fabric gave the room a golden hue, creating a sense of midsummer rather than the chilly tail of autumn. Simon's warm, bare chest pressed against her. She gazed around the room taking in quick, sharp breaths.

"That must have been one hell of a nightmare," said Simon. "I've made you a cup of tea. I was bringing it in when I saw you writhing and screaming. I thought you were having some kind of fit."

"No," she said. "Just a dream, I guess."

"Want to tell me about it?" He removed his arm from her and picked up the steaming mug from the bedside table. He gently passed it to her.

"Well," she said, taking hold of the handle, "I can't really remember."

The final image of the nightmare blazed in her mind: Simon standing in the street with the battered body of Agnes at his feet.

I can't tell him about that. Then he'd know I was there.

"It might have done you a favour," he said. "I was going to come and wake you anyway. It's getting quite late. You don't want to spend all day in bed."

"Yeah," Nat agreed. She raised the mug to take a sip, but feeling the heat on her lips, lowered it back down. "I'll make breakfast."

"I'll come with you," said Simon, climbing off the bed. "I've done a lot of thinking while you were asleep. I think I'm ready to tell you what's been bothering me…and what happened last night."

"Okay. Just give me a few minutes to freshen up and we can talk in the kitchen. How does bacon, sausages and eggs sound?"

Simon smiled. "Sounds great."

Ten minutes later, in a long Nirvana t-shirt and her dreadlocks hanging loose, Nat placed a frying pan on the hob and poured in a little oil. The feast of pork was already under the grill and sizzling nicely. She walked to the fridge and removed a box of six large eggs. She noticed how the bottom of her foot felt fine, the wound already healed. She knocked the fridge door closed with her hip and returned to the cooker.

Simon appeared in the doorway, holding his drink.

"Smells good."

"Mmm. Doesn't it just? Nothing beats a hangover like

a good cooked breakfast. My mum taught me that." She sighed. "I did the cooking, she'd have the hangover."

"It's a shame we didn't get to the hangover stage."

"Yeah. It would have been nice to stay out longer, make a proper night of it. At least I can enjoy the day without lazing around the house with a banging headache."

She broke an egg on the edge of the frying pan and tipped the contents inside.

"So how do we start this?" she asked. "I'm not good at these heart to heart conversations. Maybe I've been single for too long."

"Well, what do you want to know? A question is a good starting point."

"First off, tell me who this Johan is. The others seem to do as he tells them and you look...wary at the least."

Simon nodded.

"Johan is...was...an old friend. We met towards the end of school. We were two loners that kind of drifted together, preferring each other's company to none at all."

Nat snorted. "I find that hard to believe. I bet you were fighting the girls off." She added more eggs.

"Things were different then. I was fat for one thing. Johan was always the athletic one, but I ate and ate and never exercised. I've only been able to ditch the candy fat these last few years. The strict diet cleared my complexion too. I feel like a normal person *now*, but back then, I was a freak. I guess hindsight is a powerful thing. If only I used it sooner." He tried to smile, but it fell flat. "Johan didn't have the same problems as me. Okay, his hair brought some unwanted attention from the resident arseholes, but he didn't have the same self-esteem issues as me. In fact, he was the opposite."

"What? Cocky?" said Nat. "He came across that way last night."

"I wish it was that simple. He was just...arrogant, especially towards girls. I think his attitude landed him in loserville with me. He had the brains and body to make something of himself, but it was like he *chose* to be alienated."

"Why did you hang around with him?"

"Like I said, we just found each other. Strange, but we got along great."

Nat crouched down and peered under the grill. The meat was browning nicely. The salty aroma made her mouth water. She straightened up. "Go on. What about the other guys?"

"They came later. Nothing special about them, just three more that seemed to slip into our group. I always saw them as tag-a-longs."

"That's not very nice," said Nat.

"You've seen them," replied Simon. "I don't think they have a brain between the three."

"So what happened? Did you fall out with them?"

"In a way." Simon walked over to the window. Placing his still full mug on the worktop, he gazed out and across the city. "It started as a game at first, one drunken night in our late teens. You see, none of us ever had much luck with women. We'd exchange stories of refusals and knockbacks. In hindsight, I suppose it wasn't very healthy."

"No, probably not."

"But that was what we did. We'd go out as a group and get so drunk we'd not care anymore. We'd try to pick up women, but it was more for a laugh, you know? We never expected any of them to say yes, and none of them ever did. But Johan, he…he…"

Nat frowned. Nothing Simon had said explained why he feared his former friend so much, or what had transpired the night before. These just sounded like old, bitter memories.

"Go on," she urged. "What did he do?"

"It was a night just like all the others, but he seemed different, more *intense* than unusual. We went to a bar and immediately started to pick our way through the women in there. It was all a game until one of them...one of them said yes to Johan and took him outside. Alone."

Nat switched off the cooker and hob. Simon remained staring out of the window, lost in the past.

"We cheered him on, you know." He laughed and shook his head. "We cheered them out of the bar! We were stupid."

He reached down and sipped his tea.

"He did something to that girl, didn't he?" said Nat, approaching him and resting her hand on his shoulder.

Simon swallowed. "I went outside a few minutes later to do something, maybe take the mick, or just see what was going on. I was so drunk, it could have been for anything. I heard someone around the back. I walked round and she..." He shook his head and closed his eyes. "She was on the floor with Johan standing over her."

Nat bit her lip, thinking of Agnes lying in the street the night before.

"Blood ran from her mouth. He'd hit her. When I got closer, Johan smiled at me and told me she'd deserved it, that all of them deserved it."

"What did you do?"

"I won't lie to you," said Simon after a few seconds. "I've held this in for so long, there's no point lying now. I did nothing."

"Nothing?"

"Johan led me away, laughing and joking. The girl was unconscious in the alley. He said she'd never remember when she woke up."

Nat gazed outside at the windows of the other buildings. The sun lit up the glass, making each one glow golden, like a giant candle stood inside.

"Johan has a way of making you feel that everything is okay," Simon continued. "I knew it was wrong, but I, I guess I was a coward."

"What happened to the girl?"

Simon shrugged his shoulders. "I don't know. I guess he was right. She couldn't have remembered. Maybe thought she'd fallen over drunk and knocked herself out or something."

Nat stroked him on the back and returned to the cooker. She opened a cupboard to the side and removed two plates.

"What he did wasn't your fault," she said. "I can see that he's quite intimidating. Just look at how the others jump at his beck and call. He tells them to run and they run—"

"When did he tell them to run?"

Nat looked up. Simon faced her.

"Well, when he told them to get out of the bar. When Bubba stepped in."

Simon closed his eyes. "Yes, of course."

Nat scooped the eggs out of the pan with the spatula and dropped them on the plates. "So what does this have to do with last night? I mean, I presume you stopped hanging around with him after that."

"I did," said Simon, nodding. "I've been polite to him in passing since, but last night, I just thought…"

Nat swallowed. "That he was going to do something like that again?"

"Or worse."

Crouching down, Nat pulled out the grill pan and flicked the sausages and bacon onto the plates. All of a sudden, she didn't feel hungry anymore. "Was he?"

"What?"

"Was he doing something? Is that why you were gone for ages?"

Simon stepped forwards. "Nat, I'm sorry again, I—"

"Stop," she said, holding up a hand. "Forget about ditching me. Was he doing anything?"

Simon stopped and hung his head. "No. No, he

wasn't."

Nat caught the bus across the city and took a deep breath of fresh air as she disembarked. The bus had been packed with no seats remaining. Standing up and grasping a handrail, Nat had spent most of the journey trying to breathe through the corner of her mouth. The guy standing beside her had stunk.

She walked past Ginelli's quickly, her head down. She preferred not to encounter Andre on her day off, and Gordon only started in the evening. Arriving at the street corner, Nat looked left and right, trying to remember which direction they had walked last night.

I can't believe he lied to me. The recollection made her face feel hot. I have to find that bar!

Nat had stayed quiet all morning until Simon left the apartment. Although he seemed genuinely sorry for what had gone on in the past, that didn't excuse him from lying to her. She didn't blame him for what happened to the girl, or Agnes, for that matter. Hadn't he been the one begging Johan to stop last night?

Finally alone, she'd sat in her window overlooking the city streets, a mug of steaming coffee in her hands. Something was bothering her, and while she was far from the villain last night, guilt snagged in her gut like a tiny fish hook that refused to budge.

The lack of action.

Her mother had gone through the same thing. The threats, the intimidation and the violence that had played out on the street; the scene had been what Nat imagined all those years ago. What had been done? Nothing. Her mother never made a complaint to police. Nat herself had left the matter in the hands of her older and supposedly wiser parent. What she wanted was for the best, right?

Wrong. She could see that now.

I did nothing to protect her back then, and nothing to protect poor Agnes last night. I knew something like this was going to happen as soon as she left the bar, and I allowed Simon to handle it.

Simon. Hadn't her mother told her to watch out for the right guy? To keep him close and protect him?

About halfway down the street, she spied a small church, now used as a carpet shop. She remembered seeing it the night before. Confident she was on the right track, she headed down the street.

Finding Agnes would relieve some of the guilt. Correct past wrongs. If she could get the woman to the police and encourage a statement alongside her own witnessed account, Johan and his boys would be put away. Help Agnes, help Simon.

And help myself. Hear that, mother?

Nat passed the carpet shop. The front of the building beside was built up with scaffolding covered in bright orange nets. Nat walked into the tunnel it formed, her eyes flickering across the posters that covered the boarded up doors and windows. She stepped out and narrowed her eyes in the bright sunlight.

Something warm rubbed against her leg.

Nat stepped back in surprise and looked down, shielding her eyes.

"Jenkins?" she asked. "That you, boy?"

The small dog yapped and wagged his tail furiously. He gazed up with big brown eyes.

"Come here," she said, crouching down. The dog allowed himself to be petted. He stood firm, licking Nat's wrist.

"Leave the poor girl alone," said a voice from a nearby doorway. "She don't want to spend her time doting on a mutt like you!"

Nat saw Max sitting in the shadows, an upturned cap

between his feet.

"Hey, Max. How you doing?"

"So so," he replied. He picked up the cap and shook it. A few coins jingled inside. "Looks like people are saving for Christmas. I'll have to cancel that trip to Monaco."

Nat smiled and stood up. Jenkins protested with a whine. She walked over to Max and leaned against the doorway.

"I doubt you'll do much business here. I only saw you because of Jenkins. You should get a better spec, like near the shops."

"Too much competition. Besides, our local constabulary patrols around there. And to think, they call it begging. Have I asked you for anything?"

Nat shook her head.

"Exactly. The cap is there should you wish to make a donation. I ain't exactly asking for it." He stood up with a groan. Nat thought he looked years beyond his age. "I should learn a bloody instrument. Can't move for buskers 'round here. You should see the money they bring in."

He scratched his cheek through his beard. Nat noticed his red, swollen eyes through the long and untidy fringe.

"Max? Are you all right? You seem a bit more...down than usual."

"I'm fine," he said, gazing into the distance. "Fine."

Jenkins barked.

"Here," said Nat, opening her bag. She fumbled inside for her purse.

"No, I couldn't," said Max, turning to face her. "I told you, I'm no beggar."

"I know. You didn't ask for it," replied Nat, pulling her hand out of the bag holding Simon's ten-pound note. "I'm just making a donation."

Max's eyes darted between the white and brown crumpled note in her hand and her face.

"Take it!"

"I...shouldn't. You do so much for us already."

"Okay." She leaned forwards and dropped it into his cap. "Whoops! I dropped it. So clumsy."

Max smiled and shook his head.

"And make sure you swing by the restaurant tonight," said Nat, walking away before he had the chance to return the money. "It's Mexican night. Gordon will probably have something spicy tucked away for you."

She turned back to wave, and Jenkins erupted in a chorus of high barks. Max sat watching her go.

Feeling a little better, Nat carried on down the street.

Even in the daytime, The Fourth Dimension bar proved hard to find. Completely lost on two occasions, only the directions from passing strangers got Nat back on track.

The last guy, the one in the black hat and Hawaiian shirt, had told her to go left at the next junction. She turned the corner. The Fourth Dimension lay halfway down, nestled in among its decrepit neighbours.

Nat had walked straight in the night before, messing around with Simon, and she hadn't really taken the place in. Even on leaving, she'd been more interested in searching for Simon than with the actual building. The frontage, a strange mix of stone and wood, looked ages old. Paint flaked at the corners, and mould clung onto the corner of the wall. The windows were frosted glass that glowed softly from within. Outside by the door stood an old and weathered chalkboard with the day's specials scrawled down it in looping handwriting.

After a deep breath, Nat crossed the road and pushed open the door. The smells that swept out, sweet wood, sharp alcohol and burning spices, brought back another dump of memories from the night before. She mentally pushed them aside and scanned the bar. The tables and booths were empty. An ancient radio on the bar played an old time swing tune. Beside it, wiping in time with the music, a tall, thin black woman scrubbed the bar with a sodden rag. Her own dreadlocks, so thick they looked like twisted branches, were tied back to keep them out of her face as she worked. She paused to wipe her forehead with the back of her hand and looked up, spotting Nat standing in the corner.

"You must be 'ere for the food, girl," she said, resuming her cleaning. "'Cos it be far too early to be drinkin'."

"I'm not after a drink," said Nat. "I was here last night. I'm looking for someone."

The woman studied her and threw the rag down. It landed on the bar with a splat.

"Come on, girl. Don't stand in the doorway like a pretty coat rack. Let Monique tell you a lil' something 'bout the ways of the world...or at least, this hole in the ground we be a findin' ourselves in."

Nat walked up to her and stood by the bar. Monique gestured her to sit, which she promptly did, on one of the bar stools.

Monique put her hands on her hips. The colourful and flower-filled dress tightened across her body. Nat saw the muscle lying just beneath the fabric.

She's built like an Amazon warrior.

Monique turned around and began to pour fruit juice from a pitcher into two glasses removed from the shelves. "A man who leave don't deserve you. And to come here again to find him is foolish, girl." She turned and placed one of the drinks in front of Nat. "Free of alcohol and free of charge."

Nat thanked her and sipped at the drink. It tasted like mango and apple.

"I'm not here to look for a man," said Nat.

"Yeah?" said Monique.

"There was a woman in here last night. I think her name is Agnes. Some guys were giving her trouble, and I just wanted to make sure she was okay."

Monique chuckled.

"We all know Agnes," she said. "Been comin' here for years." She stood up and straightened her back with a small grunt. "Prostitute, you know, but we don' hold dat against her. She's a nice sort. I feel sorry for the woman."

"This was the only place I'd seen her. Thought I'd come down and see if someone knew anything. I take it she hasn't been in today?"

"You be my first customer," said Monique. "Too early for even Agnes. She never have too much money and normally we give her a few handouts, mainly food. I think she fallen on hard times, and fallen hard." She swigged her fruit juice. "You seem a nice girl, but I wouldn't worry. Agnes be tough as leather. She know these streets better then I know me own husband. But that ain't hard; you seen how much there is of him."

Back outside, Nat pulled her coat closed. The day, although bright, had a razor's edge to its chill. She walked away before the temptation of comforting heat and sweet fruit juice pulled her back inside.

Hoping she'd find her way around better in the daylight, Nat turned the corner and started down the street. No Johan and his boys here this time. She paused in the same doorway as the night before.

They'd hurt her, certainly, she remembered. But then Agnes kicked him and ran. She ran quicker than I ever could. And she ran further up...

Gripping her coat near the throat to tighten the fabric about her neck, Nat followed the path the fleeing woman had taken. She passed broken-out windows, the glass like jagged teeth in square mouths. Rot and decay rampant in frames, and stonework that had crumbled after years of neglect. Some of the smaller buildings had lost the fight completely, lying in ruined piles of rubble between their neighbours. Bricks stuck out from walls like jigsaw pieces. The whole scene reminded Nat of the films she'd watched in history class. The war years, when you didn't know if your house would still be standing at the end of each day.

She passed the place where Agnes had been sprawled and carried on. The street rose up a slight slope and curved to the right.

Nat wandered along a little more. Still, no one else entered the street. The bustle of traffic sounded distant, almost background to the whine of the breeze. She pulled her coat tighter again and turned in time to catch a figure slip into a nearby doorway.

Nat stopped. She swallowed and peered around the edge. The doors had been ripped off at some point. The entrance led into darkness.

A single whistle drifted out of the doorway, joining the breeze.

It's him. The whistler from last night. He's been following me....

She remembered how the boys had chased the strange man away, and her fear of getting caught herself.

"Hello?" she said, edging forwards.

Again, she heard the low whistle. It sounded sad, a minor key.

Nat reached the doorway and stopped at the threshold.

The bright light of day barely penetrated the interior. The floor appeared tiled. It was hard to make out through all the dust and debris scattered around. A pillar stood a few feet inside, but Nat couldn't see beyond that. The darkness hung like a black curtain.

"Can you come out?" she called. "I need to talk to you about last night."

No whistle this time, just the sound of movement at the rear. It sounded like he'd kicked a brick. She heard it skitter across the floor.

"Please. I know you're in here."

Opening her bag, Nat removed her phone and pressed a key. The screen instantly lit up with a weak glow.

Better than nothing, she thought, taking a few steps into the building. The smells of mould and rot enveloped her. She inhaled through her mouth.

I'll be safe if I stay near the door, near the light.

"Hello?"

Another step.

She wished the guy would move or whistle again, just to give her a direction to aim for. Giving up on the phone, she replaced it in her bag.

From the right, footsteps moved away.

"No! Please don't go. I have to talk to you."

Her eyes had begun to adjust. She manoeuvred around a pile of broken furniture and stepped over a cluster of shattered brick.

"Please. Just give me a few minutes!"

She arrived at the wall and pressed her hand against it. The rough plaster felt cold and wet beneath her skin. Shivers cascaded down her back.

She stopped, her foot inches over a gaping hole in the ground. She gasped and pulled back, realising how close she'd been to stepping into empty space. Cursing herself for not paying enough attention, Nat crouched down.

Her hands found the freezing metal of a ladder attached to the side of the hole and, holding her breath, she listened to the faint trickle of water from below.

She straightened up.

"Are you still here?" she asked the darkness. She waited for a few seconds.

Nothing.

There is *no way* I'm going down in the sewers. It must be like a maze down there.

Two hands clamped down on her arms. Startled, Nat cried out and tried to jump back, but the huge, cold hands gripped her tighter.

She screamed.

The hands jerked upwards, suspending her several inches from the floor.

Nat kicked out, but her legs merely wheeled through the air. The hands were like stone; thrashing did nothing to loosen their hold.

Her screams burned her throat and echoed around the derelict room. The hands shook her, like a bad mother losing patience with a bawling child. She whimpered.

Through the darkness, Nat saw the hint of two large eyes glistening in front of her.

"Get sack."

The voice boomed out with a blast of foul breath.

Someone quickly approached from behind.

"Girl has fight," growled the deep and husky voice.

"N-N-No," said Nat, forcing her words out through a tight throat and quivering lips. "P-Please…"

The footsteps stopped behind her. A second later, Nat felt something rough placed over her hair. She frantically shook her head, but the sack was efficiently tugged down over her head and upper body. The hands slid from her, grabbed the sack and pulled. She fell back through the air. Sure she'd hit her head on the floor, Nat screamed again. Her attacker pulled the bottom of the sack sharply upwards, trapping her within. Hanging upside down, Nat fought and moaned.

"Come. We go now," said the voice.

A whistle sounded in agreement.

8

The Playstation had been temporarily turned off for lunchtime. The boys sat in the living room of Johan's flat tucking into their various meals. Johan, still watching his body, picked at a chicken salad. Richie and Spence had been to McDonalds for a Big Mac meal each. Kev, who'd originally planned on McDonalds, too, had caved on the journey and called in at Abra-Kebabra. While the others were queuing at the worldwide franchise, Kev ate a bag of chips in a dingy back street takeaway, waiting for his food to cook. He'd returned to the flat with donner and chicken kebabs, garlic bread and a second portion of chips.

With the games turned off, they watched a porn DVD Richie had picked up.

"Kev," said Johan, shaking his head. "You fat fuck."

"What?" he replied through a mouthful of spicy chicken and chips.

"That shit is going to stink out the entire flat. Give the place a douse of air freshener when you're done, yeah?"

"Will do," said Kev, his gaze returning to the film.

Johan noticed the flecks of food that had sprayed from Kev's mouth as he talked. Already he planned to vacuum after lunch.

On screen, an actor, who could have been Richie's twin, lay back on a bed and lifted his legs into the air, keeping them up with his hands behind his knees. A slim, pretty blonde girl immediately climbed onto the bed and applied her tongue to his exposed crevice. She licked in a circular motion.

"Ewww!" the group cried in unison.

"I'm trying to fucking eat here," said Spence, licking along his own exposed crevice of burger.

"Huh huh," chuckled Kev, still watching the screen. "Look at him! The gay—"

"Kev, how can he be gay?" asked Johan. "It's a *girl* that's doing that."

Kev looked at him, then back at the action. "Yeah, but it's a gay thing though, innit?"

Johan pronged a piece of lettuce on his fork and held it up.

"But still, *that's a girl*," he said, pointing at the screen with his food. "Just because she's doing something to his arsehole, it doesn't make him gay. I mean, putting on makeup and wearing frilly dresses is considered a girl thing, but *you're* not a girl." He smiled and ate the lettuce.

Richie sniggered.

"Apparently," said Spence with a handful of limp fries, "men have a spot up inside them which makes them cum instantly. Milking the prostate or something. Probably why he's getting her to do that."

"Firstly, he's not *making* her do that, the director is," said Johan. "And secondly, that internal spot is complete bollocks. If it was true, then why don't we blow our load every time we take a shit? Huh?"

"Ah..." said Spence.

"Good point," agreed Richie.

A knock at the door pulled them from their philosophical debate.

"It's open!" cried Johan, smiling. Only one other person knew of his place, located at the heart of the crumbling derelict district.

Simon entered and closed the door behind. He walked into the living room, looking ashen.

"Well look who it is!" cried Johan, placing his chicken salad on the carpet next to his armchair. "It's our old friend Simon. What brings you to our neck of the woods?"

The others muttered quick greetings and, uninterested, turned back to the screen. Simon glanced over their heads at the television.

"Nice," he groaned. The girl had sucked on two of her

fingers and plunged them inside the man, up to the knuckles.

"Hang on," said Johan, reaching for the remote. "I'll just turn this crap down."

He pressed a button and a green symbol appeared in the corner of the screen. The man wailed in silence.

"Things haven't changed much around here," said Simon.

"You know us," replied Johan, placing the remote carefully on the arm of the chair. "You two, make some room for our visitor."

Kev and Spence, sitting on the sofa, groaned at the request.

"I'd rather stand if it's all the same," said Simon.

"Good," grunted Spence. "There's not much room as it is with this fat bastard."

Kev punched his arm.

"I'm not planning on staying long," said Simon.

"I didn't think you would be." Johan bent down and picked up his meal. "We can talk in the kitchen."

Johan stood and walked around the back of the sofa. Simon followed him inside the kitchen. The moment they entered, the flat filled with grunts, sighs and a rapid slapping from the television.

"Pigs," said Johan, scraping his barely touched salad into a pristine white bin. He carried the plate and fork to the empty sink and began to clean it. "You want to know what happened last night, don't you?"

Simon nodded. "Like I said, this has got to stop."

"Oh," said Johan, rinsing the plate under a steaming trickle of water. "I see. Yes, then. We've stopped. No more. You've shown us the error of our ways." He placed the plate in the drying rack. "Fuck off, Simon!"

"I knew you'd be like this."

"Be like what? Refusing to do as you say? You're damn right there, old mate. We're having fun, that's all.

You know that. You know that most of them have it coming too."

Simon shook his head and closed the door.

"Look, sooner or later, you're going to get caught. Last night you let one get away!"

Johan laughed. "She didn't get away, trust me." He washed his hands and leaned back against the sink, drying them with a tea towel. "I've been keeping track of things. You have to be careful, and that's exactly what I am."

A particularly loud groan of pleasure penetrated through the wall, followed by a cheer.

"Those three will do whatever you tell them," said Simon. "Please, stop this. Enough is enough."

Johan tapped his chin, surveying Simon. "This is *her*, isn't it?"

"Her? I don't know what you mean."

"I think you do. It's the girl, the snail trail you've settled down with. This is her doing."

Simon threw his head back and laughed. "Unbelievable! I should have known you'd blame this on a woman."

"I never thought I'd hear you say that," said Johan. "It's her. She's made you go soft. I wondered why we hadn't seen you around. You've been holed up with her, playing the happy couple."

"This is ridiculous."

"No, no. I get it now." Johan paced the kitchen. "Who would've thought that *you* of all people would finally settle down?" He shook his head and turned back to Simon, the grin gone from his face. "What have you told her?"

"Told her? About what?"

"About this!"

Simon swallowed. "Nothing. Why would I tell her? You think she'd want to stay with me if she knew?"

Johan increased his pacing.

"You had better be telling the truth," he muttered.

"Because if you're not, we could be in a shit load of trouble here."

"Yes!" cried Simon. "I know. Which is why I haven't told her. Believe me!"

Johan stopped and surveyed Simon. "I suppose you're right." He approached the sink and picked up the tea towel. He removed the plate from the drainer and dried it. With a sigh, Johan opened a cupboard and placed it inside. "There. All done for now."

"So where does this leave things?"

Johan laughed. "I don't think it leaves them anywhere. The only difference between now and yesterday is *you* getting nervous. It'll take more than that for us to stop." He walked over to Simon and placed a firm hand on his shoulder. "You know that what we do is right. Someone has to teach them the error in their ways. Women have to *pay*."

"They've paid enough, Johan."

Johan hung his head and dropped his hand.

"I'll make a bargain with you. I've not been thinking about stopping, but maybe cutting down, eh? Things *are* getting a little too risky. Last night was a wake up call."

"I'm glad you're finally seeing sense," said Simon, relief in his voice.

"Listen to what I'm saying," said Johan. "I *won't* stop. Neither will the guys. But we *will* go easy for a while. Come on; let's go watch the rest of the film."

Simon shook his head. "I really should be going."

Johan laughed.

"She really has got you on a short leash. I wouldn't put up with that kind of behaviour."

"Drop it."

Johan laughed again and opened the kitchen door. The sounds of frantic sex grew louder.

"Listen to that," said Johan. "And you want us to stop?"

9

Drip...drip...drip...

Nat slowly looked up, fighting the weight of her eyelids. The back of her skull throbbed. With a shaking hand, she reached behind her head and ran her fingers through her hair. She reached her scalp. It felt slick. An examination of her fingers showed blood, thick and red.

She groaned and tried to sit up, but her beaten body refused to cooperate. She fell back on the cold ground like a drunk. The dripping continued from all around her, like she'd awoken beneath a gentle waterfall.

"H-Help..." she said, again trying to sit. She lasted a little longer before her weak arms gave in. She gulped down a foul tasting breath. "Someone! Help me!"

She rolled onto her back and stared at the low ceiling.

A soft glow rippled across the brick, which curved over her in a wide arch. She realised she was in some kind of tunnel, and the dancing glow was a reflection off water nearby.

She remembered there were two of them. Her kidnappers hadn't talked on the way down here, at least not until she'd banged her head.

Nat moved her legs. The fabric of her jeans had soaked through. She smelled like she'd bathed in shit.

I'm in the sewers, she thought. Those bastards have brought me into the sewers!

She ignored the stench and dragged in another deep breath. Forcing herself, she sat up.

Her head seemed to lurch to the side despite staying still. She fought the sensation and closed her eyes tight. The nausea passed.

She pushed against the floor and rose into a wobbling stand. She swayed on her feet. With her arms wrapped tight around her shivering body, Nat glanced around at her surroundings.

She did indeed stand in a tunnel, the roof suspended just above her head. The rear ended in a wall, long ago dominated by mould. Green streaks covered the brick like a map of a strange new world. A pile of rags and torn clothing were heaped in one corner, the only thing other than Nat in the cell. Thick wooden bars sealed the tunnel from the main chamber.

She screamed and ran at the door to the cell. It too had been crafted from random pieces of wood. Its haphazard design gave it the appearance of some natural surrealist sculpture or something from a fun house.

Nat grabbed one of the criss-crossed planks of wood and furiously tugged and pushed. Her cries and panicked moans echoed around the small room, joined by the rattling of the padlock on the door. She forced a hand through one of the gaps and grabbed the lock. Her pulls did nothing. She gave up, releasing the slippery metal.

Tears threatened. Nat gritted her teeth and held them back. If she started to cry, that would be the end. She knew they'd be back…

Her shoes were missing, but apart from that she appeared untouched. Her bag had gone.

"Damn it," Nat hissed, frantically thinking. She had no hairpin to pick at the lock, or anything strong enough to attack the bars. Her attention turned to the floor, darting around the filthy and moist ground for anything that might help. Towards the rear of her cell, she noticed some of the more rotten bricks poking from the wall.

She scurried over and tried to pry one of them out. It refused to budge at first, but loosened as Nat's fingers dug into the sides and pried it outwards. It fell to the floor with a dull *thunk*.

She quickly scooped it up and staggered to the door of the cell. She felt along its rough edges and ignored the splinters pricking her fingers. She found a hinge: a small chunk of wet metal that flaked under her touch. She pulled her hand away and rubbed the flakes of rust between her fingertips.

It will break, she thought. It *has to* break.

She gripped the brick with both hands and raised it over her head. Her intention to bring it smashing down on the hinge stopped at the sound of deep laughter from the other side of the room.

Nat froze.

A pocket of darkness rose in the corner of the chamber. She peered through the bars and tried to make out the vague shape. Footsteps sloshed through water and towards her. From the poor light from a tunnel, Nat saw a pair of legs step into view. The pants covering them appeared no more than a mass of rags. Patches of denim, sacking, fabric and even animal pelts adorned the two thick legs. Nat gasped at the sheer size of them. Each looked to be as thick as her waist and long enough to reach her chest.

Her visitor took another step forwards. The feet, shoed in some kind of black plastic bound with tight rope, sent waves cascading away in the low level of water.

Nat, keeping hold of the brick, backed away. Her head thumped against the rear of the wall.

"Awake. Girl awake," a voice growled. She recognised the simple speech from earlier.

The speaker stepped up against the cage, grabbing one of the bars with great hands. It peered inside.

Nat screamed.

The thing's head nearly reached the higher ceiling of the chamber. It bent over to study her, hunchbacked. Beady, black eyes surveyed Nat, occasionally blinking out drops of water that fell onto its face. Underneath its messy jacket, a t-shirt was stretched to capacity across its chest.

Oh fuck, her mind screamed.

The creature's skin, even in this light, appeared to be a slightly mottled green, like the mould that had infected the walls. Perhaps it had wormed into this creature too.

The stench of the sewers penetrated the back of her throat. Her screaming became a series of choking barks.

The creature smirked.

"I think she no like smell," it said. Nat stared at its mouth, watching it form the words. The thick lips curled over broken and jagged teeth.

She threw the brick. It sailed through the air and passed between the bars to strike the creature in the shoulder. It bounced off and fell to the ground.

The giant laughed again. "Herman! She threw brick!"

A high and mocking laugh joined the creature's low, guttural chuckles.

"Quickly, before the others come back. Get some! Get some now!"

The creature released the bars and patted its makeshift trousers. It frowned. "Not find it."

"Then use your bare hands!"

It felt around its hips, then up to its chest. "Mmm," it grunted, and slid a hand inside the jacket. It removed a tarnished butcher knife, which appeared tiny between its sausage-like fingers. "Okay. Me find it."

"Then use it," said the second voice. It sounded high and nasally, with a tone of arrogance, like a snotty college professor. "Use it, you fool!"

"Me no fool!" shouted the beast over its shoulder.

Nat watched, her back pressed into the cool wall. She scanned the floor for another brick.

The creature turned back towards her with a grin. It pointed the knife at her. "You be good, girly," it said.

Nat glanced around her small cell, from wall to wall and up at the ceiling in vain. The only way out was through the door.

The creature fumbled with the lock.

"Too small," it grumbled. "Hands big. Need bigger lock."

Nat swallowed and closed her eyes for a moment. She tried to focus and still her trembling limbs.

The creature grinned as the lock clicked. "There," it said.

Nat crept forwards a couple of feet. She closed her mouth to stop her breath pumping in and out. Her heart, now a frantic pendulum, seemed to thump against her ribcage.

"Stop wasting time," ordered the sharp voice from the corner. "The others will be here any second. We can get the good bits!"

The hulking figure grabbed the door and swung it open.

"If you think easy, you come do it," it said, looking over its shoulder again.

Nat ran at the open door and dove at the last second. She hit the floor on her stomach. Pain exploded beneath her. Her body hit the gathered water on the floor of the chamber and she slid along the floor through the beast's open legs.

"Huh?" she heard it mutter.

Before her captor could turn, she jumped to her feet and fled towards the open tunnel. Her stomach and chest throbbed. With wet hair clinging to her face and poking her eyes, she didn't dare look back.

"Get her!" wailed the voice from the darkness. "You can't let her escape!"

With a roar, Nat entered the tunnel and ran down the narrow passage.

The tunnels and junctions passed by. Nat ran through each, not caring which direction she travelled. Left and right and right and left again.

She slipped on a walkway covered in green, fibrous

slime and leaned against the wall to stop from falling. She looked back the way she'd come, but nothing had followed. Besides the rats, which darted around the tunnels in the dozens, she remained alone.

Taking a deep breath, which burned her throat, Nat pressed on. She aimed for the archway at the end.

Rats fled from her path. Her feet, with only thin tights covering them, slapped along the walkway. They had grown numb from the floor and ice cold water. She whimpered and held back the hysterical sobs.

She paused at the end and peered through the archway leading into the next chamber. She listened to her ragged panting, the steady *drip-drip* from the sewer ceiling and the playful splashing and squeaks of the rats.

A dim light glowed from a dirty hub at the centre of the ceiling revealing several wet pillars around the circular chamber. Her breath steaming, Nat descended a few steps into the standing water and gasped from its temperature. A grey scum of foam floated on top. Clear patches of water looked black. Nat shivered. The water reached her knees.

She cried out but quickly pressed her hands tightly over her mouth.

The next step left her standing waist deep in the dark water. She again closed her eyes, trying to find the will to go on.

She waded out into the chamber with her arms held over the surface. The water flowed stronger in here.

At the opposite side, another tunnel led away. Nat aimed for it. She breathed in through her mouth and grimaced. The air tasted sour.

Something scurried above her.

She stared up at the ceiling, her vision barely penetrating the darkness. That darkness seemed to have gathered between the pillars like a storm cloud. Nothing moved.

Rats… Just rats.

Nat strode on, her legs slowly sweeping through the water. Stones and rocks scraped her feet. She nearly slipped on something slimy and continued.

The noise sounded again with Nat halfway across the chamber. She pressed on, the exit tunnel about ten metres away.

Something brushed against her side.

She squealed and jerked away, nearly losing her balance on the treacherous ground.

A rat, its fur black as the water, paddled away. Its thick pink tail steered it like a rudder.

"Fuck," Nat hissed. She stayed still and watched the rat swim away around the back of the closest pillar. She knew worse things lived in the tunnels, but the rat seemed bold.

A high-pitched screech from behind the pillar made her jolt.

She gasped, listening to the sounds of pain accompanied by a wet ripping.

Gaze focussed on the tunnel, Nat thrashed her way through the water. The foam broke. It covered her blouse and arms in a clinging film. Nat ignored the filth and concentrated on reaching the other side.

She staggered twice before reaching the black mouth of the tunnel. She walked into the entrance with her hands held out.

They snagged on something cold and thin.

"No," she pleaded. "No, no, no…"

A metal wire was spread across the tunnel. It formed a lattice, with the gaps big enough to poke her hand through. The darkness of the tunnel had concealed it. Nat grabbed two of the strands and tried to pull them apart. They bent slightly in her grip but held tight.

"No!" she cried again, pushing at the wire.

Something sharp streaked down her back. Nat howled and darted around.

Nothing stood behind her. The foam on the water

remained, riding the ripples her body caused.

Nat panted heavier, bent an arm back and felt the area between her shoulder blades. Wincing at the flair of tenderness, Nat held her hand up to the weak light. If she was bleeding, the scum on her hand masked it well.

Desperate to get out of the water more than ever, Nat tried her best to run back to the entrance. The water held her back, like swimming in syrup.

Her back throbbed in a vertical line running from the base of her neck.

She tripped and despite flailing her arms, Nat fell forwards. Her head slipped under the water, and she shot back up, coughing and spluttering. She wiped her eyes and looked up.

A shadow flitted between two patches of darkness.

"Oh god," said Nat. She staggered backwards.

Something swished through the air to her right. The fabric of her blouse snagged at her shoulder and her skin split. She screamed and clamped a hand down on the new wound.

The surface of the water remained still and the gushing water drowned out any other sound.

Shaken, Nat slid forwards and spread her arms through the water. She swam with her mouth tightly closed. Her head dunked underneath the foam again.

In front, something landed in the water with a heavy splash.

Nat threw her body back and tried to regain her footing on the slippery bottom. Her upper body burst from the water.

A few feet away, a figure blocked the entrance to the tunnel. It stood with the water's surface touching its chin. It looked like a floating head. Thick hair formed two points at either side of its head, lending it a triangular shape.

Nat retreated backwards from the monstrosity.

What *the fuck* is it?

The nose appeared flat with two slits for nostrils. Long front teeth hung over the bottom lip. Its eyes darted around inside their sockets. It twitched.

With her mouth hanging open, Nat backed further away and turned.

A similar creature hung from the pillar closest to her.

Nat's scream echoed around the chamber.

It appeared identical to the other and wore rags the same as the behemoth from her cell. It smiled and held up its hand. Underneath the glow of the central hub, its claws seemed to glow. Thick, ivory nails protruded from each finger. It clutched the mutilated remains of a rat. Still smiling at Nat, it raised the bloody mess to its face and tore a strip of meat free with its pointed front teeth.

Nat stepped back and yelped as pain leapt across the side of her neck. She instinctively covered the injury and looked back.

The first creature had approached her in silence. It pulled a hand away, one of the claws bloody.

Nat looked between the two, rooted to the spot. Any sudden movement could bring on a flurry of sweeping claws and teeth.

She exhaled and prepared to strike the first one to move.

The creature hanging from the pillar tore another mouthful of rat.

"Good. She found."

Their heads tuned at the sound of the deep voice. Nat took a speedy step away, floundering in the murk.

In the tunnel leading into the chamber, a silhouette blocked what light shone through.

"Bring to me," said the giant.

10

Johan eyed the balls on the pool table.

"I know what you're thinking," he said to the boys, "this shot is impossible. But as a hush fell over the crowd…"

He launched the cue forwards and after the clinks of several collisions, a red ball dropped into the corner pocket.

"And the crowd goes wild!" He straightened up and grinned at the others.

"Complete fluke," said Richie. He held his own cue yet hadn't taken a shot in the last five minutes. Johan had been potting balls from all angles. "Let's see you get the next one."

Johan smirked. He glanced over to Kev and Spence, who played on a fruit machine. He laughed at the intense looks on their faces, the flashing bulbs dancing in Spence's glasses. Kev stuck his tongue out from the corner of his mouth in concentration.

Morons.

Johan walked around the table, studying the placement of the red and yellow balls. Spotting a moderately easy red near the centre pocket, he leaned over and lined up his cue.

The door to the pub swung open and crashed into the wall. Simon rushed in, his fists clenched at his sides.

Johan pulled the cue back and stood up. He picked up the chalk and rubbed the cue tip while watching him.

Simon, seeing Johan and Richie by the pool table, strode across the pub. Other drinkers moved out of his way. He didn't seem to notice them. His eyes remained locked on Johan, his rapid breathing flaring his nostrils. Johan placed the cue on the green felt of the pool table, careful not to knock any of the balls.

"Simon, twice in one day," he said. "For what do we owe—"

With a growl, Simon launched himself at Johan, grabbing the front of his shirt and pushing him back.

"You son of a bitch!" Simon shouted. "You fucker!"

Johan tripped over a low stool and toppled, Simon keeping hold. They both fell to the floor. Johan cried out on striking the carpet. Simon continued to scream and shake him.

"What have you done? Tell me! What have you done?"

Johan heard the cries of alarm from the boys and, seconds later, felt Simon being lifted up. He scuttled back, all the time watching Simon thrash in Richie and Spence's grip.

"Calm down," said Richie into Simon's ear. "No need to make a scene."

Johan climbed to his feet and looked over at Kev. Money dropped from the fruit machine into his fat and upturned palm.

"Well I wasn't going to leave it!" he said.

"I'll kill you!" Simon cried. "I'll kill *all of you!*"

"Get him in the toilets," said Johan.

Richie and Spence nodded and dragged Simon away with some difficulty. Kev stashed his winnings in his pocket and added his weight to the task.

With a small sigh of relief, Johan followed. He stopped and noticed most of the bar had been watching.

"Sorry, everyone," he said. He held his hands up in apology. "Our friend there has had a little too much tonight. Got quite a temper."

The other customers returned to their drinks. Satisfied they'd have a little privacy for the next few minutes, Johan joined the others in the men's room.

The strip beam along the centre of the ceiling flickered and buzzed. The tainted air smelled of urine and old bleach. Johan walked across the wet, black tiles to the other side of the room. Kev and Richie had pinned Simon against the wall.

"What the hell's wrong with you?" asked Richie, his voice shaking. "Huh? *What the hell?*"

"Let go of me!" cried Simon. He tried furiously to break free of their hold.

Spence turned to Johan. "We can't get any sense out of him. It's like he's gone rabid or something."

Johan shooed him to the side.

"Simon," he said calmly, "my old friend. If I have done something to offend you, then by all means, I apologise—"

"Offend me?" screamed Simon. "Offend me? You arrogant son of a bitch!"

Kev grunted and shoved Simon back against the wall.

"These two are going to let go of you now," Johan continued. "And if you come *anywhere* near me, they'll break your arms. Understand?

Simon roared and surged forwards. Kev and Richie pushed him back.

"I see. Take the fight out of him."

Kev nodded. Bringing his arm back, he punched Simon in the stomach.

Simon exhaled sharply and sagged. Another few blows finished the job.

"That's better," said Johan.

Richie and Kev held the limp figure up.

"Maybe now we can talk..." He tilted his head and studied Simon. "Or gasp. Whatever works."

Simon sucked in a long breath and slumped back against the wall, clutching his belly.

Richie and Kev looked to each other and nodded. They stepped back.

Johan placed a hand on Simon's shoulder and leaned closer.

"What's the matter? I thought we were fine after our little chat this morning."

"What...have you...done with...her...?" Simon

winced and held his stomach tighter.

"Her?" said Johan. He frowned. "Who? We've been here all night. I told you I'd tone it down, remember?"

"Don't...lie to me," said Simon. He stood straight and groaned.

Johan grabbed one of Simon's arms and lifting it up, he draped it around his shoulders.

"Come on," he said and started to help Simon towards the door. "We can talk about this over a drink. That is if we are allowed to stay after your *little outburst.*"

"We'll check it out," said Spence. He walked out, followed by Kev and Richie. The door slammed shut.

"I won't go anywhere with you," Simon wheezed. He broke away and staggered a few steps.

"What is it I'm supposed to have done?" Johan asked. "You come in here, fists blazing, shouting the odds. At least give me a goddamn clue."

"Natalie!" Simon cried. The word boomed out in the small room like a gunshot. "What have you done to her?"

Johan laughed. "You think that we've done something to *her*? Come on, mate! You think I'd do that to you?"

"The way you spoke about her this morning," explained Simon. "The way you blamed everything on her. I could tell you wanted her out the way. "

"Don't flatter yourself."

"I know you, Johan. I know how you *think*. Not only was she spoiling things in your eyes, but she's a girl. I know what you'd do to her anyway!"

Johan shook his head. "I can assure you, I have nothing to do with this. The boys have been with me all day and besides, they're too chicken shit to do anything without me. What makes you think that something has happened to her?"

Simon leaned against a sink and rubbed his stomach.

"She's gone. I can't find her anywhere."

"What about her phone? Have you tried calling her?"

"That was the first thing I did," he said. He slammed a fist down on the sink. "Where is she?"

Johan approached him. "Don't worry. There'll be some explanation. One that *doesn't* involve us."

Simon turned to him. Johan noticed the way his eyes glistened.

"Swear," said Simon. "Swear that you never touched her. Swear that you have no idea where she is."

"I swear."

Simon gazed back to the depths of the empty sink.

"If I knew," he muttered. "If I knew what had happened to her and knew she was dead…" He turned and met John's eyes. "I could…"

"Relax and move on? Come on," said Johan. "You can't stand in here and read the porcelain all night. We'll get you a drink. Maybe we can come up with something if we all put our heads together."

"It's…it's just so unlike her. I know she's a little feisty, but she wouldn't just disappear like this. Not without telling someone."

"Standing around in the gents' isn't going to solve anything," said Johan. "Go on out. One of the boys will get you a drink. It'll settle your nerves. Try and calm down and we can sort this out together."

Simon nodded.

Johan smiled. "What are friends for, eh?"

Simon approached the door, his head down and shoulders hunched.

"Simon, mate?"

He looked back over his shoulder at Johan.

"It'll be nothing. You'll see."

Simon seemed to try a smile, but failed horribly. It looked to Johan that he would either faint, throw up, or both. "Thanks."

The door swung closed behind him.

Johan approached the sink and turned on the cold

water tap. He stared at his reflection in the overlooking mirror.

"Nasty," he said. "Nasty business." He splashed some water onto his face and observed his dripping face. He ran a hand down his face to sweep away the clinging droplets.

Whoever it is, they've done us a favour taking away that bitch of his, Johan thought.

He thought back to the anger Simon had showed on entering the pub and grinned.

His face still wet, Johan turned off the tap and walked to the door.

11

Nat hit the ground and flopped onto her back, gasping.

The giant slammed the door of the cell closed. It clattered within its wooden frame. The padlock clicked shut.

"You not get out again," he said.

In her absence, candles had been placed around the chamber. Their glow pressed back the darkness to the corners.

Around the edges of the chamber, the ground appeared to rise on a slope, creating a slight ledge out of the water around the room. All manner of furniture lay arranged around the border, above the water mark. An armchair, mould covering its fabric, had been dumped in the corner. Cupboards and chests of drawers stood warped by time and constant moisture, the candles scattered across each surface. Only the far corner exceeded the reach of the flickering light.

Nat moaned and climbed to her feet. She staggered over to the bars of the cell after the giant had moved away.

With Nat still soaking wet, the cold bit into her skin all over her body. She shivered and leaned against the bars, her legs trembling. She forced her teeth together to stop them from chattering.

"Yes," the creature said, falling back into the armchair. It made a squelching noise underneath him. "Cold." He looked upwards. "Go get wood."

Nat followed his gaze and saw a network of thick pipes running across the high ceiling. At the sound of his voice, two pale faces appeared around the rusted metal. They looked at each other, sharp noses twitching.

"Now!" boomed the giant.

The two ratty creatures from the water-filled room leapt down, their feet hit the shallow water causing small ripples across the surface.

Their arms looked too long, the claws adding inches to each. The small monsters darted across the chamber and slipped into the tunnel in seconds.

"Twins get wood. They want to watch."

Nat opened her mouth to speak, but no words escaped her lips. Fear clogged her throat, the sights of the chamber stamping out her thoughts.

"Yes! Yes!" came the high voice from the dark corner. Its whiney speaker still eluded Nat's vision. "We're alone with her again, brother! Do you still have your knife?"

The giant grinned and removed the weapon from his clothing.

"Good," said the voice, followed by a slurping noise. Nat retreated to the rear of her cell. "Then go, Jacob. We're hungry!"

The creature stashed the knife away.

"I think. Maybe leave girl for now. Maybe food come—"

"She snooped and she saw us!" snapped the voice. "Why can't you get it through that huge, thick skull?" It sighed. "She's *dead*, Jacob. Dead. And there won't be any more food, beside the girl that is—"

Nat cried out.

The creature in the armchair growled.

"Don't get in a mood with me," said the voice from the corner. "We need to eat. Edgar is growing weak!"

"Is fine for you. Is us who do work."

"Well, if I could get around better, I would too!"

A squeak rang out in the chamber from the dark corner.

Nat watched on, breathing in quick gasps.

Something black and bulky emerged into the light cast by the candles. It squeaked again, the cry of metal on metal. It moved forwards another few feet.

Nat realised it was a pram, the rusted wheels

screaming beneath the body as they turned. It moved forwards again, propelled by an unseen force, further into the light. A hunched shape sat within.

"We all need feel sorry for Herman," said the creature from the armchair. "All time, Herman complain."

"You would too," said the figure sat in the pram. "If you were stuck in this thing!" It stretched around. "Let's see this girl."

Nat snapped her eyes shut the moment it turned to her. The image had burned in her head.

The thing in the pram appeared skinned. Its surface looked red and slimy, criss-crossed with exposed muscle and sinew. Its mouth was nothing more than a puckered hole at the centre of its face. Two pure black eyes lay embedded above. She shuddered as it spoke.

"Not a pretty picture, eh?" It laughed. "I bet I look better than *you* will this time tomorrow."

Nat screamed.

"More, Herman!" said Jacob. He clapped his hands together and bounced around in the armchair. "Taste better when afraid!"

Nat forced her eyes open.

Herman, with arms like long strips of raw beef, reached down to the wide wheel of the pram. With another squeal, he pulled them around another half turn. The pram crept closer to the bars of the cell. He peered inside.

"Not much meat on this one," he said, his lipless mouth somehow forming the words. "Hope we can get it off her before the others return."

Nat shrank away, moving to the far back of the cell and pressing against the brick wall.

"Seems nervous," said Herman.

"Not nervous when she escape," snorted Jacob.

"Yes," Herman said and rubbed his chin. He brought his fleshy hand away and a thread of slime hung off. "Spirited. Very spirited."

"Leave me alone!" Nat screamed.

Herman chuckled. "Look, Edgar," he cooed and looked down. "Come look at your supper."

The creature fumbled around the confines of the pram and lifted up a dripping bundle. It started to writhe. The object in his hands unravelled in a cascade of pale tentacles, which wrapped around Herman's skinless arms. He lifted it higher.

At first, Nat thought the thing was a squid or octopus of some kind. As the many thin tentacles squirmed and separated, a face peeked out from within. Its mouth opened and released a small laugh of delight.

Nat thrust a hand over her mouth to keep from throwing up.

The grey-blue form clutched at the air with tiny, delicate hands.

"Mon Mon!" it cried.

"That's right," said Herman, in a sing song voice. "It's Herman! Look at what your brother Jacob brought you."

It's a baby, thought Nat. God help me, it's a baby.

She watched Herman cradle the infant to his chest. He pushed aside the tangle of tentacles that sprouted from its body.

"Such a cute thing," he said. "You have your momma's eyes, don't you? Don't you, little one?" He gently popped a finger into its mouth. "There you go, baby Edgar. There you—aargh!" He whipped his hand out and shook it in the air. "He bit me!"

Jacob roared with laughter behind the pram. "Har har! Maybe baby tired of Herman, too!"

"Shut up!" Herman snapped. "Get in there and start cutting. The baby is obviously hungry."

"No point," said Jacob. He spread out in the armchair and placed his hands behind his head. "Need fire to cook. Need wood for fire."

Herman turned quickly in the pram. It threatened to

topple.

"Where have those twins got to?" he roared. "The baby is hungry. So am I. And it's too bloody cold!"

Nat, rolling onto her side, pressed her hands over her ears to block the constant shouting and bickering from these freaks.

"I can't wait!" cried Herman. He bounced up and down in the pram. It bounced and lurched backwards and forwards on its wheels. "I'm so hungry. Go in there *now*, Jacob."

The motion set the infant crying. Its wailing echoed in the chamber and seemed to fill Nat's head. She pressed harder.

"Herman!" yelled Jacob. "Shut baby up!"

"If you got in there and took the meat, it would be quiet. The girl is making noise now…"

Nat squeezed her eyes shut, wailing.

"What *the hell* is going on?" asked a new voice.

The noise in the chamber instantly stopped. Even the baby ceased its din.

Nat slowly opened her eyes. She sensed someone at the entrance to the chamber, standing within the shadows. The voice, which sounded deep and civil, came again.

"I leave you alone for a couple of hours, and this is what I come back to?"

That voice, thought Nat. I know that voice!

A bark echoed in the chamber.

Nat crawled across the floor to the wooden bars, her eyes fixed on the small shape sniffing at the ground there.

"J-Jenkins?"

The dog looked up and yapped again, its tail beating.

Nat looked over to the tunnel.

Max stepped into the candlelight, a white plastic bag in his hand. The twins and the whistling guy from the street lingered behind him.

"I'll ask you *again*, Herman," he said. "What *the hell* is going on?"

12

"Erm…" said Herman. "Nothing! Nothing is going on! We weren't doing anything!"

"Herman want food," said Jacob. He remained watching from the soaked armchair. "He want food for baby Edgar."

Max scowled. "Can't you wait?"

Behind him, the whistling man shook his head. The twins scuttled up the wall and leapt onto one of the pipes and out of sight.

Max walked up to the pram, the bag swinging in his hand.

"It's good that you *did* wait," he said and held up the bag. "I have Mexican. Piping hot."

Herman stayed quiet, but a thick black tongue slid from his mouth and wiggled in the air.

"That is," continued Max, "*if* I let you have any."

The tongue whipped back into Herman's head. "That's not fair! I'm the oldest. Who are you to decide?"

Max passed the bag to the whistling man, who removed the paper bound packages from within and spread them out on a chest of drawers. The smell of spicy beef and peppers fought against the stench of sewage.

"Me not want hot food," said Jacob. "Want meat!"

"There's meat in that," said Max. He reached into the pram and picked up the infant. He gently rocked and cooed it.

Jenkins barked again.

"Stupid dog," said Jacob.

"Less of that," ordered Max. He approached the whistler and picked up a scrap of fajita. He tossed it high in the air.

Jenkins jumped up, caught it and devoured the morsel in a second.

"M-M-Max?" said Nat. She pulled on the wooden bars and climbed to her feet. "Max!"

He turned, his mouth full. It dropped open on seeing her and a shred of food fell out. Jenkins immediately trotted over and licked it up.

"Nat?" His eyes widened. "Nat? From Ginelli's?"

"Get me out!" She thrashed against the bars.

Max handed the baby back to Herman and hurried over. He grabbed the padlock. "The key! Where's the key?"

Jacob laughed.

"Stop fooling around, Jacob. Give me the key. What's she doing in there?"

"She look for us, so that be our food. You bring food tonight. What tomorrow? Or other day?"

The whistling man turned and smiled before poking fajita into his mouth.

"Don't you know who this is?" asked Max. He stepped away from the cell, his odd shoes splashing in the shallow water. "This is Nat!"

"Nat," gasped Herman. "Our... girl?"

"Yes," said Max and gazed at her through the bars of the cage. "*Our* girl."

Nat screamed and shook the bars again. "Get me out of here!"

"Indeed," said Herman. "Get her out of there. Get her out right now!"

The whistler left the spread of Mexican food and walked up to Jacob. He held out his hand.

Jacob looked at him and then to Max. With a grunt of complaint, he dug a hand into his jacket and pulled out a small, golden key. He slammed it into the whistler's hand.

"Still think no good idea," he said.

The whistler ran over to Max and eagerly gave him the key. After a few seconds of fumbling with the lock, he clicked it open. Max swung the door wide and stepped inside.

Nat dashed back into the corner.

"Wait," said Max. He held his hands out and stared at her. "Don't panic."

Nat wiped the tears from her eyes. She looked behind Max at the creatures on the other side of the bars. Her gaze found the Mexican food just as a clawed hand swept down from above, grabbed what it could, and disappeared back in the darkness.

Bet it tastes better than rat, she thought, and nearly burst out laughing. Her adrenaline made her feel giddy with terror.

"Steady," said Max, taking a step closer. "No need to panic. You're among friends now."

Friends? her mind shrieked. How can these freaks be friends?

She ducked left and as Max moved, Nat dashed to the right.

She thought she'd passed him until his arm whipped around her waist. He pulled her close. Nat roared and kicked against him.

"Don't let her go," said Herman. Nat looked over and noticed that he sat solemnly, no longer bouncing around with excitement. The candlelight reflected in his black eyes. His body glistened. "We can't allow her to leave."

The whistling man joined him at the side of the pram, his face creased with concern. He released a small, lingering note from between his lips.

Only Jacob, who thumped the arms of the armchair with balled fists, seemed to be enjoying it.

"Don't fight me," Max whispered. "Please. This is the only way."

Her attention on the tunnel leading out of the chamber, Nat continued to kick out and thrash her arms. The movement caused her fresh cuts to burn. She gritted her teeth against the pain.

"Nat! Calm down! You think I'd hurt you after all you have done for me? For us?"

She stamped down on his foot.

With a cry, Max let go of her and moved back. "Nat?"

She stared at the pile of Mexican food on the chest of drawers. She knew where it had come from. Gordon had sneaked it out, just like he'd promised. She remembered the nights where either Gordon or herself had risked their jobs feeding Max and Jenkins. She recalled wondering why they always needed so much. Now she had her answer.

"Please don't run," said Max. "We won't hurt you, but my brother is right. You can't leave."

She looked at Max. "Brother?"

He nodded and scratched his chin through his thick beard. "Yes, my brother. We're all brothers here."

Herman hung his head and studied the floor. He resembled a half-melted candle, shiny and red. In his arms, the baby muttered its own private language.

She met eyes with the whistling man, who blushed and turned away, only to sneak another quick peek at her a second later. Jacob stayed in the chair.

Nat looked up. She failed to see the twins, but their shadows darted between the pipes.

Brothers?

"Nat!"

The floor suddenly tilted and rushed up to meet her. She fell in a crumpled heap in the shallow water. Max's face hovered over her.

"Nat? Are you okay?"

She managed to shake her head. His face warped, like the air over a fire. For a second, Nat believed he was about to transform into some hideous monster; shrugging off his normal appearance to show he belonged with the others. The candlelight dimmed, and Nat found herself in total darkness.

~

"Come on, that's it. She's coming round, Whistler. Don't do anything to scare her."

Nat lifted her head off the floor. It felt like it weighed a ton, and she flopped back down.

"Just relax, Nat. You've had a funny turn. Just lay there and take a minute."

The voice sounded familiar. She tried to replay the events through her head. She knew she'd been looking for the old woman. She'd bumped into Max.

Max! That's who the voice belongs to! I must have passed out on the street.

She tried to sit up again, but her body protested.

"Please, Nat. Just stay still."

She heard a dripping noise in the background.

What the hell is that? Is it raining?

She listened to a short and low series of whistles.

"I know, but there's little we can do."

Whistles? The whistling man? Where am...?

Panic overcame her sluggish head. Opening her eyes, she sat bolt upright.

Max and Whistler jumped back.

"Steady there!" said Max, again holding his arms up in surrender. "We aren't going to hurt you."

She was still inside their chamber, lying in the mouldy armchair. Besides Max, Whistler and Jenkins, who lay in a basket to the side, it appeared the others had gone.

"Wh- where are they?" she screamed.

Max hushed her. "You're safe. Nothing bad can happen to you down here. Not after all you've done for us."

Whistler nodded and grinned. He fingered a strand of multicoloured wool, which had worked loose from his jumper.

"Safe? How can I be safe? I want to go home..."

Max sighed and bowed his head. "You can't. Not yet,

anyway."

His words sent her heart racing.

"Why not?" she asked. "If nothing bad can happen to me, why won't you let me go?"

"Because you'd tell others about us, child," said a voice from the corner. Herman leaned forwards, his gelatinous face emerging from the darkness. "And others would come."

Nat gasped and tried to jump out of the chair. Max and Whistler held her firmly.

"Please, just try and relax," soothed Max. "I know this isn't easy. Hear us out."

With her eyes locked on Herman, Nat forced her erratic breathing to slow. She leaned back in the chair.

"What's going on? I can't even..." She covered her face with her hands. "I just don't understand."

"Max, tend to her injuries," said Herman. "They should be minor; the twins were only playing." He sighed. "I apologise on their behalf, child."

"Come on," said Max. He gently pulled down the collar of her blouse and examined the shallow cut running down her shoulder. "It doesn't look too bad."

From underneath the chair, he pulled out a first aid kit. Nat glanced to meet his eyes.

"I know what you're thinking." He smiled. "People throw away all kinds of good stuff."

He removed a small vial of clear liquid and sprayed her shoulder. Nat winced.

"Sorry. I thought it might sting a little." He looked over his shoulder. "Herman, why don't you enlighten our guest. It will take her mind off what I'm doing."

Herman pushed the pram forwards a few feet, revealing more of his body.

"Very well," he said and appeared to settle down further in the pram. "What do you want to know?"

Nat looked at Max.

"Go on," he said. "Herman can be surprisingly civil at times." He unwound a strip of bandage.

"He…he didn't sound civil earlier," she whispered.

"I was hungry!" said Herman. "And just because I don't have any ears doesn't mean I'm deaf either." He reached down and picked something out of the pram. His lipless mouth sucked at it for a moment. "This is nice. What is it, Max? A fajita?"

"Yes," said Max, concentrating on patching up her shoulder.

"So much better than people. *Nil desperandum…*" The fajita disappeared into his mouth, followed by a wet smacking sound. "So, girl," he said after he swallowed. "What do you want to know first? We've already covered why we can't allow you to leave yet."

She gave Max another glance. He nodded.

"Okay," she said. "Who are you?"

"I think you know that. I'm Herman, that is Whistler and you already know Max. Jacob and the twins are around here somewhere. We didn't want them to get too excited when you awoke, so they're searching for more wood. Oh…" He lifted up the baby, who had returned to a mass of coiled tentacles. "This little fella is Edgar, the youngest, obviously."

"What *are* you?" Nat asked, now able to study Herman's fleshy form with a little less stark terror.

"Why, we're people," he said. "I won't take it as an insult. It's understandable to wonder."

"You can't be," she said. "You…you just can't be…"

"Some of us are not the most attractive of beings," Herman replied. "Out of the family, only Max, Whistler and Alcazar are *normal* enough to go outside. The rest of us stay down here."

"Alcazar?"

Max glanced up. "He's the second eldest. He doesn't live down here."

"Yes," said Herman. "He's the bird man. He needs to spread his wings a little!" He chuckled.

Nat sat in silence for a few moments, digesting the information.

"I don't understand. How can a family of..." She chose her words carefully. "How can a family live this way? How did you get here?"

"Our...mother..." said Herman. His head dropped. "I suppose it's all down to our mother."

Nat noticed Max had stopped tending to her shoulder. He leaned back, his eyes closed.

Whistler emitted a low and sad tone.

"Does she live down here too?"

Herman shook his head.

"Then where is she?"

"Dead," whispered Max. "Murdered."

"Murdered?" said Nat. "Why would anyone...how *could* anyone...?"

"She walked above. Many people knew her," said Herman. He remained looking at the floor.

"When did this happen?"

"Last night," replied Max. He wiped his eyes.

"You...you seem to be bearing up," she said, unsure what else to say.

"We have others to think about," said Herman, his voice hushed. "We are *survivors*. If we allow our grief to better us, the child will suffer." He stroked the slimy bundle in his arms. "I envy the little one. He's too young to know of the pain we feel."

"We need to plan for the future," said Max. He stood and walked to the cell. "We can't go on like this."

"We need time to come to terms with the loss," said Herman. "There will be time for planning later."

Max roared and kicked the bars.

"No, brother! We need to plan *now*. I cannot feed all of you on my own. We need money, the money that mother brought in. Begging doesn't get us enough!'"

"In time..." said Herman.

"Did your mother work?" asked Nat. She aimed to calm the two down. The noise might bring Jacob or the twins back, and she wasn't ready to deal with *that* yet.

"She...did," said Herman. Thick tears flowed from his obsidian eyes to join his glistening skin. "She lost her dignity to keep us alive."

"Her dignity?"

"She was a prostitute," said Max. He attempted a smile. "I guess it explains why there's so many of us, right?"

"I was the first," said Herman. "When I was born, she hid me down here. She wasn't ashamed or afraid, but mother knew I couldn't live a normal life. Look at me. I know what you think when you see me."

"I...I..."

He held up a gnarled hand.

"Don't try and lie. Mother loved me, which is why she hid me in this maze of pipes and tunnels. She would leave me to go and earn money on the surface. Her family had disowned her when she fell pregnant. We only had each other."

Nat swallowed. "What happened then?"

"Her line of work isn't without its risks. Months later, she fell pregnant again."

Nat thought back. "Alcazar?"

Herman nodded. "When he was born, he wasn't right in...different ways. Not as deformed as me, but still not right. She now had two young children to deal with. Things carried on with her working the streets to buy us food, medicine, things to keep us warm."

Max, his anger dissipated, walked back to Nat, his feet splashing in the low water. He picked up a strip of gauze and pressed it against her shoulder.

"That was it for a while," Max said. "For years, in fact.

But one by one, out we came. The older ones watched the younger children while mother was out. When I grew old enough, I too was expected to work the streets, but begging is all I know how to do." He sighed. "The money was desperately needed. See, our mother began to bring in less and less…"

"Max," Herman snapped. "Dark waters! Be careful what you say."

"She's heard and seen enough," said Max. "She has to know it all."

He took a moment to wrap her shoulder in a tight bandage. Whistler leaned over to help hold the gauze in place. He gave Nat a grin. Nervous, she returned with a small smile.

"Time wasn't kind to mother," continued Max. "Maybe it was her own deformity, but she had a hunger. The older she got, the more it consumed her."

"My God," said Nat. "You mean she… she…?"

"Yes," replied Max. "She liked to drink."

Nat almost blew out with relief. The image of an elderly vampire lurking in the sewers to spawn freaks was replaced with that of an old lush, propping up a bar.

Hang on…

Herman nodded in agreement.

"Isn't something we spoke of," he said. "Being stuck down here makes you crazy with boredom. I read to keep the demons at bay, child. Old battered volumes tossed aside by the uneducated. They always find a way down here to me. From my studies, I believe she had a disease, a problem."

"She grew angry when we tried to talk to her about it," added Max.

Nat nodded and tried to take in all the information. Herman's appearance still made her insides squirm, which didn't help.

"Mother would allow her customers to buy this devil's

drink for her," said Herman. "Although we worried for her, it had little effect on the family. It was when she began to spend her earnings that things became bleak."

"We think it was part of what happened last night," said Max. He applied surgical tape across the bandage to hold it in place. "She must have been drunk again. Mother would never allow herself to be taken by surprise. She was paranoid about us, you see."

He put down the roll of tape and again wiped his shimmering eyes.

With a low note, which trembled at the end, Whistler reached over and patted him on the shoulder.

"What *did* happen last night?" asked Nat.

"We don't know for sure," said Herman. "Whistler found her in the woods. Someone had..." He swallowed. "Someone had beaten her and hit her head with a rock."

Nat snatched in a breath. Her mind instantly found the image of Johan and the others standing over the old woman in the street. She quickly dismissed it. Sure, Simon had told her they were a nasty bunch, but she doubted they would actually *kill* someone. Besides, Whistler had been there. Surely if this was the same woman, he would have done more about it?

"We buried her up there," said Max. "Jacob and myself. We didn't think it was right to lay her to rest in the sewers. She'd spent her life suffering down here in the darkness."

"Like I said, you're coping well," said Nat. "Maybe it hasn't really sunk in yet."

"It's sunk in all right," answered Herman. "We have always expected death, just not our mother. People *do* come down here every so often. We're wise to avoid them and keep our presence secret. Their reaction would be like your own: terror and confusion. If our existence became known..."

"Maybe my reaction would have been better if you

weren't about to eat me," she said.

Herman dipped his head.

Max stepped back to admire the bandage.

"You've done a good job," said Nat, looking down to inspect the dressing. Whistler nodded.

"Turn around. I need to look at your back."

Nat turned, glad to avert her eyes from Herman's glistening form.

"Jacob and the twins are handling this the worst," said Max. He carefully pulled up her top. Nat felt his cold hands on her back. "They are just so angry. I think that's why they played with you. Those three have always been the most savage of the family. We might get our deformities from our mother, but I believe that the men that spawned us also had a major effect on what we've become."

"Easy for you to say," said Herman. "You're blessed."

Nat expected the words to be laced with jealousy, even malice. Herman's voice sounded sad and hopeless.

"But I still find myself down here with the family," said Max. "It's not easy being an outsider up there, you know. At least you don't have to experience that." He sighed. "Anyway, I'm worried about Jacob and the twins. They've become angrier, more vicious. I think the monster in them is taking a firmer hold, feeding on their grief. I want to find out who killed our mother and make them pay. My God, I'll make them pay. But I'm worried that the need in those three is greater, and that will lead to sloppiness. Mistakes might be made…"

"Agreed," said Herman. "Baby Edgar needs to be the priority, not vengeance."

Nat winced as Max touched the shallow cut on her back.

"Whoops. Sorry."

"It's fine, really," she replied.

He proceeded to spray antiseptic on the wound.

"So you have no definite idea about what happened

last night?" Nat asked.

"Apart from where it happened and what was used," said Max, "no, we haven't. We decided to wait until our brothers had calmed down before we started our own way of investigation. The city is like a jungle; there are eyes and ears everywhere. We hope to speak to Alcazar soon. He has ways…"

Herman snorted. "Nonsense! He can no more talk to the birds than I can converse with the rats that scuttle around in this hell hole!"

Whistler chuckled.

Nat felt her top being carefully eased down.

"That one's not so bad," he said. "It would be a waste of time to dress it."

"Thank you." Nat turned around and sat back in the damp armchair.

"Okay," said Max. He walked over to Herman and leaned on the pram. "I know you think Alcazar is a little…nutty."

"Nutty? I think he's crazy!"

"But he might know something. Whether it's from one of his feathered friends or not, Herman. We have nothing at the moment."

Max looked down into Herman's pram. Nat thought he was looking at the baby, but he reached in and pulled out a small square of paper.

"So this is where it got to," he said quietly. "I've been looking for this."

Herman bowed his head again. "Yes, brother. I…I have been looking at it." He used a skinless hand to wipe his eyes.

Max ran his grubby fingers through his beard and tugged on the thick black hair. Nat watched him study the paper for a moment.

"Max? You okay?"

He slowly nodded and lifted his gaze to meet hers.

"Here. Just to show you she wasn't a monster like some of us."

He approached and offered her the small square.

Gently taking it from him, Nat squinted in the poor light. The photograph, despite its colour, looked old. She ran a hand across it to try and smooth out the wrinkles that ran across its surface. It showed a woman, possibly in her twenties. Judging by the hairstyle and décor of the room she stood in, Nat guessed the photograph had been taken in the early seventies. She held the photograph closer to her face. Time and water had done their damage, and the details were hard to make out. She studied the face.

Christ…

Even with the long hair a natural brown, and the skin pure and white, Nat recognised the woman in the photograph. Years later, the face would be covered in makeup and the hair bleached and cut.

She swallowed, praying her face hadn't given anything away. She looked up, all the time expecting Max to see something was wrong. He still looked down at the photograph. She turned to her right and saw Whistler moving away. He looked back over his shoulder.

Nat stared at him.

With a nervous yelp, he turned away and hurried across the chamber. With a final glance back, he disappeared into the tunnel.

"Strange boy," said Herman, and wheeled the pram back into the shadows.

13

Johan glared at the man. He'd never wanted to hurt anyone as much in his life. He balled his hands into fists within his pockets and tried to keep his voice calm and steady.

"All I want to know, sir," he forced out, "is whether or not you have heard from her today."

The man, who towered above Johan with his arms crossed above his prominent gut, sneered. "I cannot see what business that is of *yours*, darling," he said. "Are you family?"

"Yes. I'm her brother."

The man's eyes narrowed and glanced up to observe Johan's stark white hair.

"Mmm," he said. "Obviously. I can see the resemblance. You could almost be twins."

Johan grabbed him by the shoulder and pulled him in. The man seemed to swell with anger.

"Get your hands off me, you young ruffian!"

Johan did. People in the restaurant had turned to watch, their knives and forks suspended over their plates. His confidence began to diminish. Some of the male diners were big, and he felt sure one or more would come to the big fruit's aid.

Be civil, he thought. That's the way here. Time for violence later.

He smiled and looked at the man the way he looked at his women. With his hands behind his back, he tilted his head.

"I'm sorry," he said quietly. "You understand I don't want to cause a fuss."

He leaned in, close enough to smell the man. He reeked of garlic and sweat.

"All I want to know is if Nat has called you tonight. We're friends of hers, and we are very concerned about her, as I'm sure you are too."

The man looked at him with doubt.

Johan looked around, pleased to see the diners had lost interest. With the potential of a good argument gone, they'd returned to their meals.

"She was due to work today. She never showed up."

"And she hasn't called to say why?"

The man shook his head. "My second waitress this week."

"Thank you," said Johan. "Please, excuse me."

Without waiting for a reply, he walked up to the bar. Sitting on one of the stools, Richie idly chatted with the barmaid, a girl who looked about eighteen in a black and white uniform.

"All done?" Richie asked as Johan stopped beside him.

Johan nodded. "Nothing. I didn't think the fat queer would know anything. Come on, let's get out of here. I bet the others are freezing."

Richie looked to the other end of the bar, where the barmaid was refilling a chiller, and back to Johan.

"Can't we stay a little longer? Just one quick drink, I think we have a contender for the night's entertainment."

"If you could drag your brain out of your prick for a moment," Johan hissed, "Simon's bitch has to be *somewhere*."

"Yeah? So?"

"So, my horny friend, we have a trail to follow. We find out where the stupid girl went and who she's with! And when we do…" He rubbed his hands together.

The barmaid cast Richie a lingering look.

"Don't bother, love," Johan called. "He has crabs."

The barmaid blushed and quickly returned to the job at hand.

"Hey!"

"I don't want you distracted by any pussy you come across," said Johan. "Not tonight. We have a job to do." He tapped a fingernail on the bar, deep in thought. "The Fourth Dimension," he said after a moment.

"What?"

"Simon was there with his girl last night, and she might have taken a liking to it, I think we could convince him to go there."

Richie raked a hand through his hair and grinned. "I don't think he's that stupid. If she didn't come here, then I doubt—"

"He's in no state to make decisions," said Johan. "When we get outside, back me up on whatever I say. Right?"

Richie nodded and looked back to the barmaid.

Johan looked over too. She ignored the pair of them.

"Better luck next time," said Johan with a smile. "Come on."

He waited for Richie to slide from the barstool and walk alongside him.

The owner, who'd been talking with some customers, tried to rush over. Johan weaved between the tables and headed for the door.

"Come back later," the man called across the room, "she might have called!"

"Yeah," said Johan, not stopping. "I'll do that. I'll call in later."

He reached the door and pulled it open.

"Fat fuck," he said, watching the owner return to schmoozing with the diners.

"What? I didn't do nothing!" Kev, leaning against the wall beside the restaurant, looked confused. Spence and Simon stood with him, their breath steaming in the cold air.

"I meant another fat fuck," said Johan.

"Well?" asked Simon. He stepped forwards. "Has she called? Does he know where she is?"

"No, I'm afraid not. She hasn't disappeared from the face of the earth, though. She has to be somewhere." He glanced up and down the street. "We'll try down here. Someone has to have seen her."

Johan started to walk, and the rest of the group fell in behind him.

That's it, he thought, follow me, boys.

"Johan?" Simon caught up with him and kept pace.

"Yeah?"

"Do you think something *has* happened to her?"

Simon's eyes appeared glazed, and he stared at the ground. He kept his hands in his pockets and shoulders hunched. Shakes ran through his arms. Johan knew it wasn't because of the cold. The guy was worried sick.

"I still hope there's an explanation," said Johan. "But to be honest, the longer it gets..."

"Do..." Simon swallowed. "Do you think someone's taken her?"

No, I think someone's *doing* her.

"She could have gone out with her friends or anything," said Johan. He smiled. "You haven't had an argument, have you? I don't think the boys will appreciate being dragged around the town over a tiff."

Simon's eyes narrowed.

"Simon?" Johan pressed.

He shook his head. "We need to find her. She... she knows...things."

Johan growled. "I see. Exactly what things, good buddy?"

"Nothing much, but she knows we used to hang out," said Simon. "If she finds the woman and the old bitch talks, you'll all be for it. I'll be linked to it all, and if other things come out—"

"Simon, Simon, Simon," said Johan. "You know us. You really think the woman will be found? If so, that she'll be able to give names and faces? You really have forgotten who your friends are—sorry—your *old* friends."

"We all have things that need to stay buried," said

Simon.

Johan gave a small nod, never removing his hard stare. "Indeed. But if we *do* find this *señorita* of yours, the two of you are going to have a long chat."

"Yes," said Simon. "I guess we are."

They stopped at the end of the street and Johan looked both ways before crossing. Simon walked alongside in silence while the boys idly chatted behind.

"Where are we going?"

"The Fourth Dimension," Johan said.

"Why?"

"You were there last night," said Johan quietly. "I think it would be a good idea to try everywhere. You never know."

People bustled around tables and hung around the bar. Johan waited in the doorway for his group to gather behind him. Expecting trouble from big Bubba Hempshead after last night, he needed the boys at his back.

"I don't think she's here," said Simon.

"Someone might have seen her," Johan replied. "No harm in asking while we're here."

He faced his three friends. Kev's normal jolliness had gone, and Richie hung his head, his hair hanging over his face. Spence looked around, his pupils darting around behind his lenses.

Don't fret, boys. I'm sure things will liven up soon.

Head held high, Johan walked over to the bar.

A tall, dark skinned woman poured drinks.

Johan pushed his way through the customers. The boys followed close behind.

"What can I get you, gentlemen?" the woman asked. With her thick accent, Johan guessed she was Bubba's wife or sister.

"Just information," said Johan. He raised his voice over the bustle of the bar. "We're looking for someone."

"Lot of people come and gone tonight, boy. I been busy, but I help you if I can."

Simon barged in, and Johan was forced aside, bumping into the man standing next to him. "Has a girl been in here today? I came here with her last night."

The woman raised an eyebrow. "I weren' workin' last night, chick. You gonna have to do better than dat, if you catch my drift."

"She's around this tall." He held up his hand. "She has long, dark dreadlocks, normally tied back. Pale complexion. Piercings. Erm..."

The woman rolled her eyes.

"So she *has* been here?" said Simon. He grabbed Johan's arm.

"She been here."

Johan shrugged Simon's hand away. "I don't suppose she told you where she was heading?"

The woman looked him up and down.

Bitch, he thought as she surveyed him. Might have to come back and visit you one day.

"Girl seem upset. Maybe your boy here be the reason. Now why would I go and send you her way, huh?"

"Please?" Johan flashed his well-practised smile. Hell, it had worked on the queer at the restaurant.

She didn't look impressed.

"I don' know where she went," said the woman after a moment. "She was 'ere dis afternoon. But even if I did know, I wouldn' tell you. I know trouble when I sees it."

Johan smiled again. "Thank you, my dear. You have been a *wealth* of information."

The woman smirked and walked away to serve more drinks.

"Finally," said Johan. He turned around and leaned back against the bar. "At least we have something."

"Do we?" asked Simon. "We still don't know where she is."

"But we know she was here. Gives us somewhere to focus on."

But you weren't in here with another guy, Nat my dear. What *are* you doing?

He gave Simon a reassuring smile. "We're getting closer, my friend."

"Hey! You two!"

Johan turned back.

Bubba Hempshead had stepped out of the back and stood behind the bar.

"I kick you jokers out last ni'. You tink you can just come a walkin' in 'ere the next day?"

"Come on," said Johan. "Best we don't draw any more attention to ourselves."

"Dat it," called Bubba. "You keep on goin'. Out me place like good boys."

Johan growled under his breath. He gestured towards the door. Richie, Spence and Kev got the message and headed out of the bar. Simon walked alongside him.

"Say *beer can*," said Kev. "Sounds like Jamaican bacon..."

Bubba remained standing behind the bar with an arm around the woman and a white bottle in his hand.

I'll remember this, thought Johan. I'll remember *her*.

"We're wasting time here," said Simon, leaning against the grime-streaked wall of an abandoned building. "I'm still for calling the police."

"The fuck you will," said Johan. He looked up and down the empty street. "If she was wandering around here, someone else might have seen her. Have a little faith. We'll search all night if we have to."

They hadn't seen another person for the last half an hour, not since leaving The Fourth Dimension. Johan believed they didn't have a hope in Hell's chance of finding the ever-elusive Nat. The streets were a concrete maze. Even he, a veteran of the city at night, had lost his way on a few occasions. The run down area looked the same on every street. Johan wondered how a district a mere twenty minute walk from the bustling city centre could be allowed to rot and decay like this.

He turned at the sound of hurried footsteps. Spence emerged from around the corner. The streetlights reflected in his lenses; his eyes golden circles.

"Anything?"

"Nothing," said Spence and pushed the spectacles further up his nose. "Not a thing. Have the others found anything or anyone yet?"

"They're not back." Johan rubbed his hands together and blew on them. "Let's go find them."

"Look at this place," said Simon. "If she was around here and alone, any weirdo could have grabbed her."

"And if some weirdo *has* grabbed her, we'll deal with him. Me and the boys got you covered. Ain't that right, Spence?"

He nodded with a sheepish smile.

"That'a boy. Meanwhile, you can deal with *her*. Have you entertained the idea she might be with another man? Would explain an awful lot."

"Nat? Never."

Johan laughed. "Come on, matey! Have you forgotten all that life taught us? She's a woman! Women can't be trusted. She's probably choking on some dude's cock as we speak!"

"You're enjoying this aren't you?" said Simon.

"Me?" Johan said and raised an eyebrow. "I'm just helping out a friend. What would you do, Simon? Eh? What would you do if we found her after all this, shacked up with another man? Think about it...see it, mate...right there..."

Johan noticed his friend's fists tighten, and that look, that wonderful look he'd missed all this time, flash across his face.

"I'd..."

"Yeah?"

Simon let out a great long breath. "Nothing. She wouldn't do that. She's different."

"If she knows enough about us, brother, it doesn't matter how different she is. Come on, let's find those other jokers."

They walked for a few seconds in silence, each with their hands deep inside their pockets and breath steaming before their faces.

"I think they went down here," said Spence at the next turn.

Johan gazed in the direction Spence pointed. The street appeared the same as all the others. He frowned.

We might not find this bitch after all, he thought.

"Then let's not hang around admiring all this beautiful scenery. It's freezing." Johan strode on.

Along the street, one of the streetlights flickered. It caused their shadows to blink in and out of existence under its beacon. Johan stopped and placed a hand above his eyes.

"I can't see shit. You sure they came down here?"

Spence nodded. "Positive."

"Well I don't see them."

Further down the street, under the rotten canopy of a shop front, a bulky figure stepped out onto the pavement. It raised an arm.

"That's Kev. Come on."

They ran down the street to meet him. Kev waited outside the derelict building with a huge grin. "You guys are not going to believe this," he said.

"What?" demanded Simon. "Is it Nat? Is she in there?"

"Maybe."

They all peered into the dark doorway.

Richie walked out, also sporting a wide smile. "Look what we have here…"

He held up a black handbag, the head of Jack from *A Nightmare Before Christmas* on the side. He dangled it on his finger with a strap.

"That's hers!" said Simon and stepped forwards to take it.

"We know," said Kev, sounding smug.

Johan narrowed his eyes. "How?"

"Because everything was still inside it," said Richie. He lifted his other hand to reveal a purse in the same design as the bag. He flicked open the clasp with his thumb to show a bus pass in the clear plastic window. "Natalie Freese? Right, Simon?"

He tore the bag from Richie and sank to his knees.

"Simon. You need to calm down. Take a minute."

Simon dug into the bag and pulled out various items of makeup and pieces of paper, which fluttered around on the pavement in the slight wind. Her telephone showed twenty-one missed calls.

"Rich, the purse. Toss it here."

Richie gave the purse a small under arm throw. Johan caught it comfortably and held it wide.

"All the cards and money are still here. Know what that means?"

"She hasn't been mugged," said Spence. "That means she's okay?"

"I don't know," said Johan. The rest of the purse held nothing out of the ordinary. He examined the photograph on the bus pass.

Even nicer in the flesh, he thought. At least you *were* even nicer. You might not have a face left anymore…

Simon dropped the bag to the floor and roared. He clasped his hands over his face.

"You two," Johan snapped. "Get him on his feet."

Kev and Richie both nodded and immediately grabbed Simon under each arm.

"We're going in," said Johan. "All of us. Pull yourself together, Simon."

Simon stared back at him with glistening eyes. "Someone *does* have her. In there. In the dark. Don't they, Johan?"

"If they do, they won't have her much longer. Fellas, show me where you found the bag."

They released Simon, who stayed standing, and turned to the shop doorway.

"There's no light in there," said Spence. "How are we gonna see?"

"No problem," said Kev over his shoulder. "There's light where we're going."

"Enough gabbing, ladies," said Johan and pushed past them. His heart began to hammer the moment he stepped into the darkness. "Time to play hide and seek."

14

Jacob picked up a wooden table and flung it across the room. It exploded against a wall. The few rats gathered beneath squeaked and dashed for cover. Jacob tilted his head back and roared.

Nat clamped her hands over her ears. The sound seemed to swell her head.

"Jacob!" cried Max. He stood in front of the giant, his hands held up. "Calm!"

With another bellow, Jacob pushed his brother square in the chest. Max shot backwards and fell. He skidded in the shallow water.

"Why show her picture!"

Nat saw the trails of tears flowing down Jacob's mottled skin. She remained in the damp armchair, not daring to attract the creature's wrath.

Jenkins jumped around Max with small yelps of concern.

Jacob strode over.

"They walk above," he cried and pointed a finger down at Max. "Murderers! They walk above and you not care!" He roared again. "You not care of hurting. You care only of girl." He spat the words out, his deformed lips curling around each syllable.

"Jacob," said Herman as he wheeled his pram out of the shadows. "This kind of behaviour is helping nobody. Calm down and talk about this rationally."

Jacob frowned. Nat guessed he was processing the words. He slammed a fist against the wall.

"Me want them dead."

"As do we all, brother. But we can't go to the streets and kill everyone, can we? We have to be careful. We have to find out who did this and deal with them in secret."

Why don't you ask your brother Whistler who did it?

Nat thought. He was there.

Jacob returned to jabbing a finger at Max, who still lay on the floor.

"You show her picture. You do nothing though!"

"We *will* do something," Max said, and climbed to his feet. "But Herman is right. We have to think very carefully about how we go about this. Would you like us to make a mistake and bring people down here? You know what would happen."

Jacob's breath hissed from flared nostrils, but he stayed quiet.

Max stood and took a tentative step towards Jacob. He placed a hand on his chest and gazed up at him.

"We will do something. I promise you. I would strangle the life from the person responsible; who am I to deny my brothers their revenge?"

Jacob sobbed and laid a massive hand on Max's shoulder, completely enveloping it.

"My brother."

Max nodded. "My brother."

Jenkins barked and wagged his tail.

"We can't go on like this much longer, Herman," said Max and turned from Jacob. "Tempers are frayed. Blood is needed."

Nat shivered. It sounded strange to hear the normally timid Max talk of murder and vengeance.

Jacob collapsed with a crash. He sat on the floor and leaned back against the bars of the cell. He placed his head in his hands.

"Then what do you suggest?" said Herman. "We can't do anything until we know the identity of the killer. How do we do that?"

Max closed his eyes. "Alcazar."

"Alcazar?" Herman's beady black eyes widened. "How the hell can that loon help?"

"He spends more time than me up top. He might have

seen something."

Herman laughed. "You mean one of his little birds might have seen something. You don't honestly believe all that, do you?"

"You never know," said Max. He approached the armchair. "Look at Nat. Before Jacob and Whistler brought her down here, you think she would have believed that we existed? But we do. Alcazar might be a little…strange, but he's still part of this family. If he says the birds can talk to him, I say we take a chance. What other option do we have? Door to door enquiries?"

Herman shifted uncomfortably in the pram.

I could tell them, thought Nat. I'm sure Johan and his gang must have done it.

She looked over at the crying hulk near the cell and the deformed creature within the pram. Her cuts throbbed to remind her of the claws of the twins.

But what if I'm wrong? I didn't actually see them do it. What if I'm wrong and they turn on me? Would Max allow that?

"Well if you're going to go, then go now," said Herman. "You know what an *ordeal* it is to get to him."

"But at least its night," said Max. He turned to Jacob. "You come too. I think it will do you good."

Jacob looked across from the side of the chamber.

"Me touched with kindness," he said.

"Stay then. Stay and mope around here all night, but I'm going to talk to Alcazar."

"What of girl?"

Nat swallowed. The thought of being left alone with Herman and Jacob made her skin crawl.

Max scratched his cheek. "I suppose you'd better come too, Nat. Just to be safe."

She quickly nodded.

"Then I come," said Jacob. "You soft. You let girl go. People come."

"Considering the job you've done to keep them in the cage," said Herman, his bloody face contorting into a sneer, "I think we have nothing to lose."

"Might get hungry on way," said Jacob and flashed Nat a wink.

Oh God. Maybe I *should* stay here.

"What about the twins? And Whistler? Shouldn't we find them first?"

"No, Herman," said Max. "They could be anywhere. Especially the twins. They know these tunnels better than any of us. I don't want to waste any time tracking them down. You can fill them in when they eventually get back."

Herman nodded. "So just the three of you." Jenkins barked. "And the mutt. Don't linger though. The baby will need feeding come morning, and I'll need some help. I know once Alcazar starts talking, it's hard to stop his crazy rambling. You might be there all night."

"Then I'll bring him back with us," said Max. "I know he doesn't like coming down here, but won't he be better off with his family? Under these circumstances?"

Herman seemed to consider this for a second and nodded.

"I suppose."

You can tell this is a real family, thought Nat. None of them get along.

Jacob hooked a hand around a bar of the cage. He heaved himself up.

"We go now?"

"Yes," said Max. "Nat, you feel up to this?"

She leaned forwards in the armchair.

"I...I don't know. It's all happening so fast."

"You do understand that we can't let you go yet. It's for your own safety as well as ours."

15

Johan crouched and touched the top of the ladder. It poked out of the hole by his feet. He lifted his hand away and felt the moisture between his fingertips.

"You know where this leads, don't you? I can hear water down there." He stood up and leaned over to look directly down the shaft. Somewhere at the bottom a weak light danced across the brick. "Think it's safe to go down?"

"I don't care," said Simon. "If she's down there, that's where I'm going."

He tried to step forwards but staggered back. Kev had grabbed his shirt.

Johan gave the big man a nod of approval. "Let's not be too hasty."

He listened. The flow of water sounded slow and steady.

"Depends how deep it is. But if it's not flowing too fast, we should be fine. And the bag was here?"

"Right next to the hole," said Richie.

Simon tried to dive forwards again. Kev held on.

"Let go of me. Nat! Nat!"

Johan whirled round. "Shut him up. Now!"

Richie dived at Simon and clamped his hand over his mouth. Simon's shouts became muffled moans.

"Keep him quiet," Johan snapped and returned his attention back to the open manhole. "We can't give ourselves away. Not yet."

The sound of a struggle snatched his attention.

Simon jerked from side to side, freeing his mouth from Richie's hand. Kev still held on tight.

"What do you mean?" said Simon. "What are you planning?"

"Cool off, will you? If someone has taken Nat and is keeping her down there, we have to sneak up and get the jump on them. You *do* want to make them pay, don't you?"

Simon glowered at him, his gaze burning. "Damn right I do."

"Then shut your mouth. Kev, let him go."

Kev obliged straight away and stepped backwards. Simon stayed put.

"Good." Johan turned his back on the boys and peered back down the hole. "Can you smell that? Smells like all the shit in the city is flowing at the bottom of this ladder."

Kev, Richie and Spence chuckled. Johan turned and flashed them a toothy grin.

"This isn't funny," said Simon and darted forwards. He shot past Richie and arrived at the manhole.

The smile lingered on Johan's face, and he locked eyes with Simon.

"Problem, mate?" he asked, raising an eyebrow.

"Move," said Simon.

Johan's grin widened and he sidestepped away from the shaft. He made a dramatic bow, like an overly gracious butler. "After you, sir."

Simon grabbed the ladder and turned, his feet descending into the shaft. Johan noticed his hands trembled. He climbed down. The clang of his feet striking the metal rungs echoed and seemed to fill the dark room.

"You just going to let him go?" asked Spence.

"He'll wait," said Johan, purposely loud. He knew Simon would be listening. "If it wasn't for us, he'd still be running around the city like a headless chicken. We brought him here." He smiled again. "*We* found them."

"Them?" said Spence. "Don't you mean *her*?"

Johan gave him a wink. "I know what I mean."

With that, Johan descended. He took a tight hold of the slick rungs.

It's took us most of the night. Last thing I want to do is fall and break my neck at this stage in the game.

The sound of flowing water grew louder, and the

stench intensified beneath the floor. Johan's feet slapped into several inches of water at the bottom. He groaned as icy sewage swept over his shoes and instantly soaked through.

He fought the urge to retch, picturing the filth and germs against his skin.

The dull light came from a hub on the wall, close to the ceiling. It looked like shit was smeared across the plastic cover. Johan imagined the light might be stronger if the thing was clean, but it could stay that way. Nausea bubbled up his throat, but he swallowed it down, trying not to think of the muck surrounding him. He wandered from the ladder; one of the others was on their way down.

"Simon?"

The poor light revealed the small area around the ladder, with mouldy brick, frothy and slowly drifting water and bits of crap that floated on the surface. Johan looked around the darkness.

"Simon? You better not have gone."

"I'm here." The water splashed. Simon stepped into the light, arms wrapped around his body. His breath steamed more than ever. "I'm cold."

Johan nodded. He was right. Being out of the wind hadn't improved things. It felt like they stood in a freezer.

"Why would they bring her down here?"

"There'll be a few of them, probably," said Johan. "Who knows their thinking? There's plenty of places above where they could hide out. Maybe they don't have a fancy place like mine. Or your place, Simon. I miss your apartment."

Another splash from behind. Richie walked away from the ladder, his long legs kicking up the foul water. "Fuck. Look at this! These jeans are ruined already."

"Try and get a man's pair this time," said Johan. He didn't smile. His heart had stepped up a gear once more, the foul stench made his breath come in shallow, frantic gasps. He swallowed again and gazed down the tunnel. Even in the low light, he saw how the tunnel ended in a circular hole. Darkness lay beyond. A glance along the other branch revealed the same.

"Whoa!" cried Kev, jumping from the last few rungs of the ladder. He caused an almighty splash, forming an expanding wave.

"Damn it, fuckhead!" said Richie. The water had soaked his jeans up to the knees.

"Like you said, they were ruined anyway," said Johan. "Quit bitching."

"This reminds me of that film, *Alligator*," said Kev. "You ever seen that?"

"No, Kev. I haven't," said Johan, uninterested,

"It's about this pet alligator that the kid's dad flushes down the shitter. It grows to be twelve foot long or something, and everyone that goes down the sewers gets munched!"

"Thank you," said Johan. "That's very reassuring considering *where we are*."

Kev grinned, his piggy face widening. "I know. That's what reminded me."

Spence stepped off the ladder. He clasped his nose between his fingers. "We're really doing this?" he said, his voice sounding muted and nasally.

"You get used to it," said Johan. He looked left and right a final time. "Simon? Which way do you think?"

Without waiting for another invitation, Simon dashed away. He headed to the left branch of the tunnel, leaving the small circle of light. Johan squinted, watching the vague, moving silhouette against the greater dark.

"Come on," he told the others. "No more joking. I'm expecting trouble." He started down the tunnel after Simon. "Lots of trouble."

16

Max rubbed Edgar's cheek and the baby cooed within his arms.

Nat kept her distance. She knew the baby meant her no harm, after all, it was *only* a baby. It wasn't his fault the way he'd been born. Her opinion of Herman had begun to change, away from the horror at the monster she initially saw, to a kind of pity. The man was disabled and trapped in the sewers; he didn't live this way out of choice.

Nat closed her eyes and took a deep breath. Amazed at how quickly she had come to terms with all this, she tried to picture Alcazar, the final brother. Various hideous forms popped into her head: things mangled and twisted, covered in thick black hair or scales or even feathers. He was called the bird man after all.

But Max isn't deformed, she thought. He might be like Max.

She opened her eyes and looked across the chamber.

Max placed the baby back inside the confines of the pram. He rested a hand on Herman's shoulder.

Nat expected the older brother to scream in agony. The skin appeared raw and sensitive. Herman merely looked up.

"You going to be okay?" asked Max.

Herman huffed. "Sometimes I think you forget who the oldest one is. How many times have you all left me here to baby-sit while you go on your adventures to the surface? Of course I'll be okay. Nothing's happened so far, has it?"

"Maybe it's just this atmosphere," said Max. He removed his hand and wiped it on his pants. Nat noticed the slight yellow smear it left, like a small urine stain. "I don't like this. Things have changed."

"For better, now we move," said Jacob. The giant figure stepped out of the tunnel and into the chamber. He needed to duck so his bald head wouldn't scrape the ceiling. "*They* change things. Not us."

"Still doesn't mean I have to like it," said Max. "Any sign of Whistler?"

Jacob shook his head.

"I'll tell him you've gone when he arrives," said Herman. "Of course, he'll be disappointed not to see his brother..."

"Like I said, hopefully we'll bring Alcazar back with us."

"Damn," said Herman. "I thought you'd forgotten about that part."

"Edgar has been fed," said Max, ignoring him, "so he should be quiet for the rest of the night. He will require something in the morning and there's plenty left over. We should be back by then anyway."

Herman nodded and stayed quiet.

"Are you ready, Nat?" Max asked. "It's quite a journey. Are you sure you feel up to it?"

The baby, its tentacles dangling over the sides of the pram, gurgled and laughed.

"Nat?"

"Yes," she said and stood up. "I'm coming."

"I'll try to get us back before sun up."

17

Kev leaned back against the wall and looked back and forth along the tunnel.

"We're lost," he panted. "It fucking stinks and we're lost."

"Calm down, tubs," said Johan. He squinted, trying to see to the end of the passageway. "It's a tunnel. It goes two ways, so we have a fifty-fifty chance of going the right way." He grinned.

"That logic is so fucked up, I don't know where to start," said Spence. He sucked in a long breath through his nose and coughed. "I think I'm going to be sick if we stay down here much longer."

"No one's going to be sick," said Johan, struggling with his own lunch, thinking of the dirt…the germs…. "We'll stay down here another half an hour, tops. And to put fatty's worries to rest, I've got our route memorised, so we can get back out. Happy?"

Kev nodded, staring at the floor.

Johan took a few steps away from the group. "We've come this far. None of you want to turn back now, do you? Simon?"

He'd crouched on the floor, catching his breath. The frantic pace of his run through the maze of tunnels had taken its toll. He looked up, twin trails ran from his eyes and down his cheeks.

"Simon? Do you want to go back?"

He shook his head.

"I didn't think so," said Johan. He looked from face to face. Spence appeared weary, his eyes dulled behind his lenses. He constantly rubbed his hands from nerves or the numbing cold. Kev, having the most trouble in their hike through the sewers, stayed leaning back against the wall. His wide chest rose and fell. It emitted a low wheezing sound with every exhalation. Richie, in contrast to the rest of group, still seemed keen and full of energy.

Good, thought Johan, at least someone's ready. We're close now. I can almost smell the bastards.

But if she has been taken by another gang…

"We need weapons," he said. "Weapons. Now."

"Weapons?"

He turned to Richie.

"You think they are going to just give up peacefully and hand Simon's girl over? I think they're going to be fucked off with being discovered, and that means things will turn nasty. We might be able to get the jump on them, but I don't like to gamble. I like a certainty." He glanced around the floor. "Find something, anything. There has to be something down here."

Apart from Simon, who remained crouched and swaying slightly, everyone searched the tunnel. Spence returned with a couple of bricks, which he held tightly in each hand. Both contained a sharp edge. He hit them together and neither crumbled. Kev found a plank riddled with mould. The end had decomposed into a sharp point. He held the wood like a sword.

"Simon? You not going to arm yourself? God knows what we're going to find in there," said Johan.

"I know what we'll find," Simon replied. He stared at the wall, the weak light giving his face a sickly white pallor. "We'll find her dead, mangled, raped…"

Johan marched over and shoved him.

Simon toppled over and lay sprawled in the filth on the floor. He looked up at Johan in silence.

"We don't need any of this," he said. "Where has your fire gone, soft fuck? Jesus." He turned to the rest of the group. "And you lot. Does no one care? Am I the only one that gives a shit what happens to this girl?"

"Shut up," said Simon.

"Make me," said Johan. "Seems like you're all mouth

until it comes down to the crunch. Look at you, lying in the shit, feeling sorry for yourself. Nat's probably better off down here."

"Shut up!" Simon jumped to his feet and crossed the tunnel in a second. He grabbed Johan by the jacket and pushed him.

Johan hit the wall, his head flying back. It struck the wall, not quite hard enough to hurt.

"There we go," said Johan. "I knew you still had it in you."

"Son of a bitch!" Simon brought his arm back, the fist poised before Johan's face.

Richie stepped forwards.

"Wait," said Johan. He met Simon's blazing eyes. "Why waste your energy?" He swallowed. "Who would you rather hurt? Me? Or them?"

Simon licked his lips before they peeled back from his gritted teeth.

"Think about it, mate," said Johan, his voice low and soothing. "Make *them* suffer."

Simon released him and spun around. He barged his way through the gathered group and headed down the tunnel.

Johan stepped away from the wall and straightened his jacket. "After you, boys."

Richie flashed him a smile and swept the hair out of his eyes. Kev groaned and faced the head of the tunnel. As one, they marched forwards and paused at the next junction. Another tunnel, appearing almost identical to the one they had just been in, ran from left to right.

"Look at this," said Spence. "How the hell are we going to find our way out of here? It's like a goddamn labyrinth."

"Johan," said Richie, and bent down against the wall. He picked something up from the floor, which clattered with a clang. It echoed in the tunnel. "Here. Catch."

Johan raised his hands in time to catch a slick length of metal. He shivered from touching its grimy surface.

"God knows what they're from," said Richie. He too held a long bar. "Looks like they were part of a ladder or something."

Johan's bar was just short of three feet long with a comforting weight. He gave it a few testing swipes through the air. The momentum pleased him. He released the bar with one hand and examined his skin. Thick, brown rust was smeared across his palm. He wiped his hand on the back of his jeans.

"Let's keep moving," he suggested. "The longer we stay down here, the more likely I am to forget how to get out again."

The boys nodded.

Simon stood further on down the tunnel, staring into the darkness.

"Simon?" asked Richie. "What's up, man?"

Ignoring them, Simon stepped away and vanished into the shadows gathered at the end of the tunnel.

"Move it," said Johan. He kept his voice low. "We can't let him go running around here on his own. If he gives us away…" He led them up the tunnel and held an arm out in front of him as he entered the darkness, afraid of colliding with Simon. The metal bar hung at his side.

"Christ," he heard Kev moan. "I can't see a thing."

"There's light up ahead," said Johan. "Just keep moving forwards."

"Natalie!"

They stopped at the cry from ahead. It seemed to spiral down the tunnel.

"Was that Simon?" Spence whispered.

"Natalie!"

Without waiting for the others, Johan burst into a run, his shoes splashing through the shallow water, which carpeted the tunnel.

Idiot! Johan thought. What the hell does he think he's doing?

Frantic footfalls echoed behind him. The boys were keeping pace.

This is it. We found them.

He tightened his grip on the bar, eager to find some deserving target.

They reached the segment of tunnel where the dim light shone through. The wall opened into a circular area, and the glow highlighted the rough edges of the hole. Simon had already stepped within and stood just inside the room. Johan carefully raised a leg and stepped through the wide hole. His foot splashed in the water on the other side. He joined Simon's side and looked around.

"What the hell?"

Shabby furniture lined the walls with an assortment of rotting drawers and tables piled high with junk. Several chairs, wooden or plastic and all worse for wear, lay scattered around the chamber. Even an old, rusted pram stood in the corner, its hood pulled up. What drew his eye was the entire right side of the room. A portion had been sealed off with roughly cut, thin strips of wood. He stared at the door at the centre of this random network. A dulled lock hung from its frame.

"Jesus Christ," Johan said and ventured deeper into the room. Peering through the gaps, he saw a pile of rags in one corner. A rat sat in the middle of this makeshift bed and cleaned itself, paws sweeping its furry head. "It looks like some kind of cell. A goddamn cell!"

"Natalie!"

Johan winced at Simon's cry and sharply turned towards him.

"Shut up!" he hissed. "Look around. She's not here so quit the shouting. You want them to come running?"

"But—"

"But nothing. She's not here. She probably was at

some point, but she's not now. We have to take a look around and see what we can find, and we have to do that quickly and quietly."

Johan grabbed the hand of a floundering Kev and helped his bulk through the wall and into the chamber. Spence and Richie quickly followed.

"This is incredible," said Richie. "Someone could have been living down here for years!"

"What are we dealing with here?" asked Spence. "Tramps? You think there's a gang of bums living down here?"

Johan walked over to one of the drawers and opened it. A quick rummage inside revealed some torn and dirty clothing and empty cans. "Looks like it. No normal person could live in this...this squalor."

"Kicking a few tramps will be easy," said Spence, smiling for the first time since they'd entered the sewers. "They're probably too drunk to put up much of a fight anyway. And I'm glad we picked up the weapons, means we don't have to touch them, know what I mean?"

"Amen to that," said Kev. He jabbed the sharp plank around in the air.

"Will you guys shut up?" said Johan. "This isn't a joke. We have a problem. They're *not here*. If they suddenly show up and we're still poking around, we could get taken by surprise."

"Then let them come," said Simon. He stared at the cell. Johan noticed two burning patches of red had developed on Simon's pale cheeks. "I'll kill every one of them with my bare hands if I have to."

Johan looked to the other side of the room. The furniture, although mostly pushed against the wall, was piled up in places. This, combined with the weak light from over the entrance, created pits of deep shadow. He had the queer sensation of being watched, like eyes waited in the darkness, surveying him in silence.

That's crap, he thought. If anyone lurked in here, they'd have sounded the alarm by now.

"What was that?" asked Spence sharply.

"What was what?"

"I heard something. A squeak."

"Probably a rat," said Richie. "There's enough of the little bastards down here."

Spence shook his head. "No, it wasn't like that. It was…metallic."

From within the shadows on the far side, the noise came again. This time they all fell silent.

"That," said Spence. "I heard that."

The ground trembled, and Johan wobbled. He spread his feet a little wider apart for balance. It felt like a heavy truck was approaching.

"What the hell's happening?" said Kev.

"Nat!"

Johan's anger rose up in a flash. He shot towards Simon and gave him a firm two-handed push in the centre of his chest. Simon staggered backwards and after colliding with a warped table, fell to the floor and landed on his back.

"If you don't shut up, we'll leave you down here. Then you can shout all you want!" Johan choked out, attempting to be quiet and jabbing a finger.

Beneath his feet, the ground continued to shake.

"Johan?" asked Spence.

"What?" he spat, still staring down. Simon looked back with equal intensity.

"The water. It's rising."

Johan blinked, snapping him out of his sudden rage. "Rising? What're you talking about?"

He noticed the few inches of water around Simon had started to climb his body. His hands were all but submerged and a wave swallowed them within the murk and slid up his arms and his body. Simon remained on the floor with his eyes locked on Johan's. His fast breaths flared his nostrils, emitting small puffs of steam in the chilly room. For a second, it gave Johan the image of an angry cartoon bull.

"Shit, you're right." Johan swallowed and extended his hand. "Come on, man."

After a moment's hesitation, Simon grabbed him and allowed himself to be pulled onto his feet. The foul water dripped from his jacket and jeans.

"We gotta get out of here," said Kev. His voice had risen, high and panicked. "We could drown in here if we don't get out quick enough." He shook his head and looked around at the dark and swirling waters. The rate had increased, and already the water had reached their knees. A few of the lighter pieces of furniture caught in the currents and floated in short, lazy dances. "I knew we shouldn't have come down here. My mum always warned me when I was a kid—"

"Fuck you, and fuck your mum," said Johan. "Use your head. The water can't rise much higher. Look at the hole we came in through. It can't rise above that, it's too wide. We aren't going to drown."

"But why?" said Richie. "Why is it rising now? It's like someone knows we're here."

Again, Johan looked to the shadows, feeling scrutinised.

The water climbed further up and reached halfway along their thighs. Johan braced himself for the awful moment the icy water would slip over his groin. He squeezed his lips together and held his breath.

"Christ," said Spence. "It's stopping."

Kev frowned. "Stopping?"

"The floor's not shaking anymore."

Johan realised Spence was right. The floor felt solid again and sure enough, the water had ceased its climb. He blew out his trapped breath.

The metal squeak, like nails down a blackboard,

echoed from the shadows once more.

"That noise again," said Spence. "What the hell is it?"

A jet of water sprayed up at the centre of the room.

The boys all cried out and backed away towards the wall.

18

"Go a little further down the tunnel," said Max. "It's quite safe."

Nat turned towards the black mouth of the tunnel that led away from her. The dusky, warbled light from the chamber ended a few feet beyond. She heard scratching, probably Jenkins, and something else, a deep pulsing. She placed her hand against the wall to the tunnel and felt a faint throb travel through her fingers.

"What's down there?"

"Machines," replied Jacob and smiled. "Fun machines."

She looked to Max.

"You'll see," he said. "It isn't just pipes and water down here, you know."

Nat rose to standing and walked a short distance down the tunnel, leaving the light behind. With each small step the noise intensified. Again, she touched the wall and the steady vibrations had grown stronger. She even felt it through the soles of her wet feet.

It sounds like drums, she thought, drums in the dark.

A noise like a wet slap made her turn back. Max had climbed into the tunnel and stood at the entrance, his outline silhouetted against the dull glow. He shook himself and water dripped from his patched clothes and thick beard.

"F-F-Freezing!" he said, and rubbed his arms. "The machines will dry us off in no time."

"What do these machines do?"

He shrugged his shoulders and walked towards her. "They do something, I suppose. Ventilation or water pressure or something like that. All I know is we need to get through them to get to Alcazar."

"Wouldn't it have been easier to go through the streets?"

Roaring, Jacob pulled himself up into the tunnel. The wooden planks crashed down behind him. His body filled up the narrow space and blocked out most of the light. "Easier, yes," he said and looked up. "More violent."

"Yes," said Max. "We couldn't just walk down the street with Jacob here. Even in the early hours, someone would notice him, and that would be…very bad."

"For them!" said Jacob and smashed his fists together.

"Let's keep moving. We're nearly through the pipes now. Things will get easier once we get into the buildings above."

Nat wrapped her arms around her body. "Good. It's like a freezer down here."

"Jenkins?" Max called down the tunnel. A sharp bark replied from the darkness. "Follow that dog," he said and started forwards. The dank and mouldy tunnels of the sewers gave way to more orderly, yet no less filthy, surroundings. The ground was dry and tiled, and the air, more breathable than the fetid gases they'd endured, contained the tang of oil. Bright bulbs swayed in time with the throb of the machines ahead. They hung on thick cables along the centre of the ceiling.

Nat placed her hand on the cold, painted wall. The pulsing was still there, stronger than ever. She was able to hear the machines now, a steady thump with splashing sounds, like a washing machine filling before a cycle. She had no idea what the machines were or what purpose they served, but one thing had become apparent since entering the long corridors. The area was maintained better than the run of tunnels and pipes, and there was evidence of recent activity. In the room they ducked into—with Jacob staying quiet and silent, hunched a few feet away and taking little interest in her—a work bench stood in the corner under a heavy set lamp. Its neck was curled over to focus the lamp's beam on the work at hand. A few tools lay scattered on the surface of the bench, as well as a coffee cup with a small, brown puddle inside. Nat had lifted the mug and saw that the dreg of coffee, although stone cold, appeared clear of mould. It had been placed there recently, certainly within the last day or two. Charts and maps covered the walls showing the layout of the sewers. It looked like a map of the London Underground with lines of different colours shooting off in every direction.

Nat crouched against the wall at the far end of the room, away from the doorway Max had gone through minutes before. Jenkins, who looked bored with the proceedings, lay on the floor beside her, his head resting on his paws.

Come on, she thought, get us moving, Max. If these machines of yours can dry us, I don't think I can wait much longer.

As if to answer her, another wave of chills danced across her skin. The sodden denim of her jeans had rubbed against her inner thighs as she'd walked and the skin burned in protest.

Do I want him to hurry up? she suddenly thought. Shouldn't I pray that he's discovered and people come and rescue me? Maybe coffee cup guy can come in, overpower Jacob and whisk me away to the surface.

She slumped back and sat down.

What the hell you want, girl? You may be cold and miserable, but admit it, you be lovin' dis!

Nat smiled. The voice in her head had adopted the brash tones of Monique, the ebony empress from The Fourth Dimension.

"You smile," said Jacob. "Why?"

Nat glanced and noticed him staring at her. She licked her lips.

"Just because of all this." She shivered and another wave of goose bumps stood to attention across her skin. "It's like all the excitement that was missing in my life has been crammed into one day. All it took was to go wandering in the bad part of the city and get kidnapped."

"You nearly dinner. You lucky."

"Yeah," said Nat, the smile faltering on her face. "It was lucky that Max showed up when he did. Were you really going to...you know..."

Now Jacob smiled in a twisted sneer. "Better than rat."

In front of her, Jenkins stretched, his neck arching, before he returned to lounging on the floor.

Nat almost cried out in relief as Max ducked through the doorway and stopped in the middle of the room. Jenkins immediately jumped up and trotted over to him.

"Coast is clear. Not even one of the workers around. Lucky, huh?"

Jacob mumbled and climbed to his feet. Again, his head hung just below the ceiling.

"Is it safe to go through?" asked Nat, also standing up. "Those machines, whatever they are, sound loud."

"And they are, but you'll get used to them. At least it's warm and dry out there. Come on."

He stood aside to let Jacob move past him and squeeze through the doorway.

"Heel," he said to Jenkins and clicked his tongue. The dog wagged its stubby tail and looked up eagerly. "You too, Nat. If we want to be back before sun up, its best we keep moving."

She started forwards. "Why are you concerned about dawn? We're underground."

"We'll be going up top soon, and with my brother, its best to keep in the shadows. Plus, there's more chance of workers being down here in the day. At least we can slip back through here easily if we're quick. After you."

Nat took one last look at the lone coffee cup on the workbench and stepped through the doorway into a plain corridor. A thin pipe, running across the ceiling, leaked at its centre and a puddle had gathered underneath. Jacob was nowhere to be seen, but Nat noticed massive wet footprints leading down the corridor.

"Just keep going," said Max. He stood right behind her but raised his voice over the throb of the machines. "Almost there."

The bulbs also swayed in here, and the floor appeared to tilt from side to side. To Nat, it looked like a corridor from some kind of ship. At the end, an open doorway led to the right, and as Nat turned into it, she clamped her hands over her ears.

The area widened out into a room the size of a school gymnasium. Heavyset machines, which reached up to the ceiling, were arranged in several rows to form an ordered grid of pounding, hissing metal. Some closer to her appeared as solid metal blocks, speckled with rust. Green and red lights blinked from panels on the side. Only the rhythmic vibrations from within gave any indication they were in use. Other machines, located closer to the centre, had moving parts that could be seen. Pistons pumped in and out, long, thick metal pipes reached into the ceiling and pulled out in a constant cycle, driven by enormous pivots. The air contained a stronger scent of dark oil. The floor rumbled.

Something brushed against Nat's leg. She leapt back and looked down, afraid another rat had fancied its chances and taken a chunk out of her leg.

Jenkins dashed between her legs towards the other end of the room, his stick-thin legs kicking out a frantic pace. It appeared he didn't like the noise either.

She turned to Max, who was trying to say something to her, his lips animated in the depths of his beard. Nat shook her head. Max seemed to think for a second and waved his hands in front of his face.

I don't understand, Nat mouthed, not bothering to force the words out. The din of the machines would destroy them the moment they left her throat.

Max pinched his ragged coat with both hands and

shook it like a man who has just stepped in from a rain storm.

Like a man trying to dry off, thought Nat.

For the first time she noticed how warm it was in the room of machines. A slight, hot breeze brushed against her face. It barely had the strength of a hair dryer but the chill had evaporated from her skin.

She looked back to Max and nodded. He smiled and nodded too. He held his hand out in the direction Jenkins had scurried off in. Nat understood and began to walk.

She wondered what Mr. Coffee Mug actually did down here.

19

In the lair, the water had returned to a calm and foamy surface after the sudden splash at the centre. The boys stood in a semicircle, covering half of the room. On the other side, lighter items of furniture floated and bobbed against each other.

"What was that?" asked Richie.

Johan ignored him. He scanned the dark water, trying to see what had caused such a high splash.

If I can just see where it's coming from, we can do something about it. I don't want us to get caught in it again.

Kev wailed.

"What?" asked Spence and took a step towards him. He held his arms out to the side for balance and stumbled. "Kev, what's wrong?"

Kev's eyes frantically moved left and right in his sockets, scanning the water. His skin had flushed, and his rapid breathing sounded like a dog panting. "Something..."

"What?"

"There's something in the water! I...I felt it against my leg!"

Spence looked down and threw his bricks into the water.

"Chill out, fellas," said Richie.

Johan glanced at Simon. He was still staring at the cell, like he hadn't noticed the large splash or panic. Kev looked on the edge of a heart attack.

"It was probably just a bit of wood or something," Johan said, hoping to calm the boys. "Look at how everything's floating around."

He peered around Kev's legs. Nothing floated near him. The water looked clear.

"Something's going on," said Kev who took a wobbling step back. "I'm getting *the fuck* out of here."

"The hell you are. You're staying put like the rest of us," said Johan.

Things had settled and the water lay undisturbed.

"This was probably just a time controlled system or something. These are the sewers. What the fuck do we know about what goes on down here?"

"That's why they've gone." They looked to Simon. "These bastards knew the room was going to flood, so they left," he said, eyes still fixed on the cell. "We have to go after them."

"Amen to that," said Johan. "I didn't come all this way to get covered in shit and be denied now."

Simon frowned.

"We have to find Nat," Johan quickly added. "Before anything else happens."

About to head for the hole in the wall, Johan stopped and pointed at the water. A rat, most likely the one from the cell bed, paddled across the room.

"There's what touched your leg," he said to Kev. "Just a rat. Maybe it was attracted by the smell."

Something darted up to the surface of the water and snatched the rodent underneath. The surface bobbed for a second.

Johan blinked.

"Did I just see that?" asked Spence. "Seriously, guys. *Did I just fucking see that?*"

All four stood rigid and stared at the water.

"Everybody get out," said Johan. "Nice and slow. No sudden movements."

He lifted a foot from the floor and shuffled backwards. Kev and Spence lay between him and the exit. Simon stood on the other side, and Richie remained on the opposite side of the room.

"Spence, you're closest. Go through the hole. Gently."

The chamber seemed to have switched from cold to hot. Johan's armpits prickled underneath his t-shirt and the first trickles of sweat slid down his sides. He swallowed, and his mouth instantly filled with saliva a second later, glands pulsating at the back of his mouth.

Jesus Christ, his mind screamed. Oh Jesus Christ, where have we come?

A small piece of wood, floating in the middle of the room like a canoe, suddenly flipped over and sank.

The movement ignited the panic, which had seeped from each of the boys and built up in the chamber like an electrical charge. They each dove for the hole.

"Wait!"

Johan, kicking his way through the water and about to push Kev aside, glanced over his shoulder. He expected to find Simon wrestling with some beast that had emerged from the water. Instead, he perched precariously on a rotting armchair, which had stayed rooted to the floor.

"Get out of the water!" he screamed. "You can't all get out in time. I can see it! It's in the water!"

Before his words had finished their echo, Richie screamed and fell forwards. He struck the water in a loud splash and vanished beneath the murky surface.

Johan watched in horrified awe.

Richie was dragged along just under the surface.

For some stupid reason, Johan thought of the alligator that Kev had mentioned.

"Richie!" Spence seemed to think about diving in after his friend but then quickly reconsidered. He thrashed backwards in the water and pressed against the wall.

Kev had reached the hole but floundered, unable to pull his leg high enough to get through.

Johan scanned the water for Richie, but the scum-lathered surface had closed up again.

"Richie!"

He leaned down for a closer look, ready to jump back should anything touch his leg.

A hand shot from beneath the water, inches from

Johan's face.

He staggered back, the metal bar raised over his head, poised to strike.

Richie's face emerged, his hair plastered over his eyes. He coughed and sent a spray of water from between his lips. "Help me!" he cried, his eyes squeezed shut, his hand waving.

Johan grabbed him and pulled.

Richie rose from the water, his body dripping. He'd lost the metal bar and most of his right sleeve. His jacket had been torn from the elbow down and hung in tatters. While he lay against the wall sucking in deep breaths of the putrid air, Johan lifted his arm.

A patch of blood had soaked Richie's shirt a few inches below the wrist and, mixing with the water, formed a river flowing down his arm. It dripped off his elbow.

"Oh Christ," Johan whispered. "*What the hell is in here?*"

Richie grabbed his shoulder and gritted his teeth. "Fuck, it hurts, Johan, it hurts... My arm! It got my arm!"

"It's not deep," Johan replied, eyes still transfixed on the bite. "Just a flesh wound." He turned away and headed back for the hole. He stabbed the water around him with the bar.

"But my arm! Christ, it hurts... I dropped the bar..."

Kev still hadn't managed to get through the hole and stood leaning against it with tears running down his face. Spence beat furiously on his back, head turning between the hole and the water behind. "Move! For fuck's sake, move!"

"Shit," yelled Simon from the armchair. "Guys, look out! It's coming!"

Johan looked over his shoulder and flopped back, away from the struggling pair.

A thin tentacle, narrow as a pencil, curled out of the water like an Indian rope trick.

Johan kicked out in a half swim. His scrabbling hands found the edge of a chest of drawers, and he clambered on top. He lifted his feet from the water and held them against his chest, curled up in a ball and shivering.

The blue-tinged tentacle weaved around itself in a weird ballet.

Johan watched in amazement. The creamy grey foam had closed in again and hid the rest of the creature from view. The long, twisting feeler paused for a second just above the surface.

"Guys!" Simon yelled again. He waved his arms. "Move!"

Spence continued to try and shift Kev out of the way. He lacked the strength to move such a weight and merely shoved and punched. Kev remained blocking the hole, blubbering like a six foot baby.

The tentacle whipped forwards.

Kev again attempted escape and lifted his knee high, managing to find the edge of the hole.

The tentacle wrapped itself around his ankle and snapped taught.

Kev looked down and began to scream.

"Someone help him!" Johan, breathless, heart trying to burst from his chest, glanced to the side at the voice. Simon, perched on the armchair, carried on shouting. "Help him!"

The tentacle pulled. No sudden jerk, more a steady pressure, like a chain being wound inch by inch. Kev's panic grew as his leg was quickly pulled behind. The big man hopped in the water, and the tentacle seized the opportunity. It tugged Kev closer.

Spence backed away.

"Hit it!" Simon cried. "With the plank!"

The rotten and pointed bit of wood remained in Kev's hand. Its edge looked sharp enough to cut through the tentacle in one swipe.

"Cut it!" Simon yelled.

Crying, Kev dropped the wood and seized the ledge of the hole with both hands.

"No!" cried Simon.

"Help me! Help meeee!"

Spence, ignoring the pleas, used the bars of the makeshift cell as a ladder and ascended from the water.

"We have to do something," said Richie, breathless and still standing in the water.

For a second, the line of the tentacle grew slack and hung in an arc, dangling in the water. Then its owner pulled again. It snapped tight.

Kev wailed, one of his hands lost its grip and slid free of the ledge. He clung on to the edge with the fingertips of his right hand. He screamed, his face swollen and purple.

"Help meee!"

"We can't just leave him!" cried Richie. Still nursing his bitten arm, he started forwards through the water. Simon jumped from the armchair. Both of them waded towards Kev, who'd been pulled almost horizontal by the tentacle.

"Damn it!" Johan, gripping the metal bar so hard his knuckles burned, lowered himself from the chest of drawers. His own scream nearly escaped his throat the moment his feet slipped into the dark water. He joined the line formed by Richie and Simon and thrashed at the water with his bar.

Kev hit the water, which closed over the top of him. The tentacle vanished beneath the surface.

The boys stopped in their tracks.

"Don't move," said Simon. "It could be anywhere."

"But we have to do something!" said Richie again.

Johan continued to strike and jab at the water in the vain hope he'd hit the thing. He operated purely on adrenaline, the thoughts of Nat and the people who'd taken her gone. Survival was all that mattered.

"Where is he?" shouted Simon. "Can anyone see him?"

"I can't see anything!" called Spence. He'd climbed to the ceiling and showed no signs of budging.

Simon strode into the centre of the room, the exact spot where the tentacle had emerged. He kicked, sending a splash of water in the air.

"Nothing."

20

An archway led away from the machines and into another plain room, its only feature a dulled metal hatch on the far wall. The hatch contained a long handle, the middle connected to the centre of the door by a thick cylinder. Nat thought of the doors on submarines or bank vaults. Jacob stood before it, arms crossed on his expanse of chest. Jenkins waited patiently beside.

"Are we going through there?" she asked Max.

He nodded.

Jacob grabbed the handle at each end and pushed. His biceps bulged. The fabric of his jacket, ending just below his shoulders, grew taught and looked ready to tear.

He tilted his head up and emitted a roar. The handle moved clockwise a few inches but nothing more. Jacob released it and rubbed his hands together. He stared at the bar for a few seconds and tried again, crouching lower and arching his back. The handle turned, reluctantly at first, but then, as it loosened and spun around ninety degrees, Jacob tugged the hatch open.

Darkness lay behind it.

Max leaned in and brought his mouth close to her ear.

"You go first," he said. "There's a ladder on the right as you go through. Be careful. There's quite a drop."

Great, Nat thought. First the ice cold water, now the risk of falling to my death.

"I said it wouldn't be easy," said Max. "Hold on tight and you'll be fine."

Nat walked forwards and quickly crossed the small room. She stopped in front of the open hatch and leaned in. Her head poked over the edge.

The light from the room illuminated a wall some ten feet away, on the other side of the vertical shaft. Looking down, the bottom was concealed in shadow, like the shaft reached to the very centre of the earth itself.

She twisted her head around to peer up the shaft but it appeared the same. The vertical tunnel ascended into darkness.

"I can't see anything," she called back.

Something touched the middle of her back. For a moment, she feared a push and falling head first into the pit.

She felt Max's body lean against her.

"Give me your hand," he shouted. "I'll guide you to the ladder."

Nat stared down into the abyss below. "I... I can't do this—"

"Sure you can. Trust me."

He gingerly took her left hand, and with his arm around her back, they leaned further in together. Nat squeezed her eyes shut. Her feet were on tip toes and she imagined Max suddenly moving his arm away and her body overbalancing.

Their arms, joined by the linked hands, entered the darkness to the side inch by inch. Just as Nat thought her arm wouldn't reach any further, her fingers brushed something attached to the wall.

"Can you feel it?"

"Yes," she said, her eyes still shut tight.

She expected the ladder to be cold and slippery. Everything down here seemed to be covered in rust or mould or slime. But the ladder felt warm and dry, probably kept that way by the warm draught rising up from below. The breeze drifted across the bare skin of her arm.

"Now you have it, keep hold," said Max. His hand lingered for a moment on hers before sliding away. "This is the scary part."

Nat nodded. Max moved away, giving her the space to twist her body and push away from the floor with her feet. She sat on the edge of the hatch, her hand still tightly gripping the ladder. Taking a deep breath, she slowly eased her legs over the side. Her feet dangled over the void.

"So slow," said Jacob, his voice booming over the machines.

"*Shut up*, Jacob!" Max said.

Nat ignored them and shifted her weight over to the left. After moving as far as the hatch would allow, she explored the dark with her foot, eventually finding a rung of the ladder. Steadying herself and refreshing her grip, she swallowed.

'Eere we go, girl, said the voice of Monique. Let's show 'em what we made of!

Nat dove forwards, into the dark.

"He has to still be in here," said Richie, scanning the water.

"What is this thing?" asked Simon. "A fucking octopus?"

"I don't know," Richie said. "I couldn't see a thing under there."

In the corner Kev burst from the water.

The boys jumped back.

He waved his arms furiously, trapped amid thin, blue tendrils. They convulsed and tightened, trying to bind Kev's arms to his body. A concentrated mass of tentacles covered his face in a living mask. His cries leaked out, muffled and choked.

Spence wailed and clung onto the wooden bars like the mast of a sinking ship.

"It's on his face!" cried Simon.

Johan, the closest to Kev, raised the metal bar in two hands. He focused on the thing attached to Kev's face.

"What are you doing?" said Simon.

Johan ignored him and waded forwards another few steps.

The pulsating tangle of tentacles parted.

Are those? No, they can't be. Johan blinked. Hands? Little tiny hands?

Johan's arms shook, and he tightened his grip on the bar. Saliva trickled from the corner of his mouth. He crept closer, raising the bar higher.

"You'll hit him!" Simon said. "Don't swing that thing or you'll hit him..."

Fuck it, Johan thought. It'll kill us if we don't kill it first.

Kev lurched in the water. The tentacles whipped around his body, and he plunged back into the water.

"Don't let him go under again!" said Richie.

Johan paused, the bar still held high. He heard Simon and Richie splashing through the water towards them.

Kev bobbed, not quite floating on his back. The thing shifted a little and revealed more of his face. His right eye almost bulging from its socket. Blood gushed from his forehead and dribbled down into his eye. He blinked, his sclera staining from white to a dark pink.

Johan stared at the small hand that gripped Kev's cheek.

With a cry of his own, Johan let the bar fall and dangle in his left hand. Without thinking, he plunged his free hand forwards and down, straight into the blue mass on Kev's face and wrenched it free.

"Johan!" Simon said. "What're you doing?"

The thing writhed and shuddered.

Johan held it at arm's length and squeezed his fingers tight into the coil of tentacles. It felt like a handful of worms, all squirming against his skin. The creature wailed, crying its protests at being restrained.

"Kill it!" screamed Richie from behind. "For God's sake, kill it!"

Kev attempted to climb to his feet, still moaning. The skin of his forehead had been ripped open. He clamped his hands against the wound and fell back in the water.

"Help him up," said Johan, his heart pumping.

Richie nodded and rushed to his friend's aid. Simon also lent a hand.

The thing in Johan's grasp thrashed, the shorter tentacles whipping against his hand and wrist. The longer appendages hung down, their tips dangling in the water. They spasmed and curled.

Johan swallowed and slowly turned the creature around.

From within the tangled, blue mess, a baby's face peeked out.

"Christ!" he yelled, almost letting go.

The baby, features screwed up from shrieking, stared at him with tiny eyes like dark sapphires. Emitting a small coo, the baby smiled and displayed rows and rows of sharp incisors.

Johan shook his head, mouth hanging open.

The chamber filled with hacking laughter, which swept around the room from all directions. Johan kept his gaze locked on the baby, his fingers clutching the back of its skull.

Richie helped Kev from the water.

"Where the hell is that coming from?" said Simon.

Spence, still clinging high up on the wooden bars, looked down. "What *is* that *thing?*"

Kev and Richie backed away in the water. They neared the hole.

Expecting another tentacled beast, perhaps the baby's giant, angry mother, Johan chanced a look over his shoulder.

From within the pram parked in the corner, a gelatinous red blob sat up and laughed. The pram rocked back and forth, creating small waves in the dank water. It gripped the edge of the pram with a skinless hand and threw its head back. The puckered mouth opened wide, and it resumed its laughter with a new found vigour.

"Nat…" said Simon, sounding deflated. "Oh Christ… Nat… where are you…"

Johan's legs trembled.

Richie and Kev dove for the hole. Above them, Spence remained on the bars of the cell, his eyes squeezed shut and his mouth a thin line.

A long tentacle brushed Johan's leg and instantly whipped around it. The coil tightened around his thigh.

Johan screamed and lifted the baby higher, trying to pull the tentacle away. It seemed to stretch, its hold intensifying.

In the corner, the creature in the pram continued to laugh.

The metal bar in his other hand, Johan whipped it across and struck the tentacle. It unwound from his leg, grabbed the bar and hurled it across the chamber. The metal struck the wall with a clang and fell, disappearing beneath the water.

The baby giggled.

"Richie!" Johan said. His friend had flopped back against the wall, eyes transfixed on the bloody vision in the corner. Glancing up showed Spence still had his eyes closed. "Kev?"

The hole once again proved too difficult for Kev's large frame, and his chubby leg, hindered further in soaking jeans, couldn't quite get high enough.

The squirming in Johan's hand writhed with increased frenzy.

"Har, har!" the thing in the corner bellowed. "You didn't realise, did you? You didn't realise!"

"What is that thing?" screamed Spence.

"You dare come down here? *Down here?*" the skinless creature cried.

The baby in Johan's hand opened its tiny mouth and flashed its razor teeth again. The blue face screwed up and it started to bawl. The tentacles struggled against his hold.

"Here," he said to Simon and held out the baby. "Take this."

His old friend appeared appalled at the thought, but obediently took the squirming body, yanking it hard to free the tentacles that curled around Johan's wrist.

"Now kill it."

"What?" Simon stared at the tiny figure in his grasp.

"Kill it."

Simon studied it with disgust.

Johan grinned. His friend was finally starting to emerge. "Do it, Simon. Kill it. It can't be allowed to live. Look at it! Kill it, Simon!"

"Yeah," said Richie.

"Kill it," said Spencer.

Simon swallowed, leaned back and thrust the baby against the wall. The thud of impact echoed in the chamber.

The laughter stopped. The slimy creature gripped onto the edge of its pram, the toothless pit of a mouth hanging down. Its beady eyes seemed to widen.

"No," it croaked. "No! What are you doing?"

The baby's shrieks climbed higher and stabbed in Johan's ears.

Simon smashed the baby at the wall a second time.

Its skull, the size of a small apple, cracked between his fingers. Creamy blood seeped through. Thrashing and jerking tentacles suddenly hid the sight.

"Leave him alone! He's only a baby!"

Richie and Kev stood motionless.

The baby's cries had dissolved into wet gurgles and chokes.

Simon drove it against the wall a final time. The tentacles hung loose and dipped into the water. The body fell limp and silent.

"No!" the thing in the corner shouted. "Edgar! No!"

Simon flung the body across the room. It looked like a

large, slimy pompom and struck the wall with a splat. The baby bounced off and splashed into the water. A few of the tentacles floated on the surface.

"You bastards!" wailed the creature, its words distorted by sobbing. "Murderers!"

Simon wiped the blood from his fingers on the seat of his jeans.

The tentacles drifted on the surface of the water for a few more moments before they slowly sank under.

"Nooo!"

Johan leaned against the wall, swallowing the rotten air deeply. He inhaled, retched and spat out a glob of phlegm. An inspection of his hand showed dark brown stains. Rather than keep the creature's diseased touch on his skin, Johan dipped his hand into the rank water, choosing its natural germs instead.

"J-Johan?" asked a tentative Richie. "What the hell do we do? *What the hell?*"

Another glob of sputum flew from Johan's mouth, and he closed his eyes to steady his head. Richie's voice had grown distant, echoing down a tunnel. Rough hands grabbed Johan's shoulders and shook him.

"Don't lose it," said Simon, his hands dripping with blood. "We aren't finished."

Swallowing, Johan nodded and looked back at the thing in the corner. It quivered within the pram, its hands, still holding the edge, trembled, and strings of yellowed gloop hung from its fingers. The curses had stopped and it peered around in fearful silence.

It knows, thought Johan. It knows it's all alone now. It can't hurt us.

The realisation sobered him a little and the chamber came into focus.

"I'm... fine," he said quietly. Simon squeezed his shoulder. Johan nodded, and his friend relinquished the grip. "Good work, Simon. Nice to have you back." He took another steadying breath. "Spence, you get down here you weak piece of shit."

From behind the spectacles, which had somehow managed to stay on his face throughout the whole encounter, Spence's eyes darted around in his wide sockets. He moved his head back and forth, scanning the water. He lingered for seconds to stare at the pram bound monster.

"Spence, get down. I won't ask you again. The baby's dead."

"But…"

"I said it's dead."

The boy began his descent.

Using his foot to sift through the contents strewn around the concealed floor, Johan searched for the metal bar. His heart soared at the sudden hard contact, and he bent over to retrieve it. With his face inches above the water, and his hand outstretched in the dark pool, he imagined more tentacles about to drag him under. He forced the images away as his fingers brushed cold metal. Fishing the bar out, he flinched at the sight of a limp coil of tentacle dangling from the end. Johan flicked off the detached appendage and swung the bar in a wide arc through the air. Water flicked off its shiny surface.

"Simon's right," he said, staring at the bar. "We aren't finished yet."

He pointed the tip of the bar at the creature, which brought on fresh tremors through its exposed hide. Johan felt no sympathy. "Boys?"

Following his lead, the rest of the group immediately sought out new weapons. Kev managed to retrieve the plank of wood he'd carried into the chamber and held it out like a shield. Richie and Spence resorted to a couple of wooden chairs, both ridden with green mould. Johan expected they'd fall apart after one good hit but better than nothing.

This should suffice, he thought, hefting the bar

upwards. He ventured towards the creature.

"No!" the thing wailed again.

The word stopped Johan's advance for a second. He closed his eyes, refusing to look at it, wishing it to be quiet. The creature, like its fucking baby, was a *travesty*.

To live down here in such... such squalor...

Even if they escaped the maze of tunnels, Johan knew this couldn't rest. The thought of this thing alive would consume his thoughts until it drove him crazy.

The last few years of his life had been a mission—a crusade—to eradicate the living filth he saw every day. The women, the corrupting, disease spreading women, were just a warm up to this, he realised. We've had our fun, but now the time has come for more serious matters.

Wiping his cleaned hand on his jeans again, he shot Simon a side-glance.

And it's all due to you, my friend. Look what your bitch led us to.

He swallowed.

"This is for you, Simon," he whispered.

His friend stayed quiet, his attention fixed on the creature, which glanced back and forth between the approaching faces.

"No," it whined. "You can't. Please. You can't!"

Johan coughed down his rising bile.

"Th-This is our home. Outsiders!" it screamed.

"I think it's calling for help!" said Spence. "What if others come?"

Johan lifted the bar over his head. "Then we have to silence it, don't we?"

He hammered it down and struck a glancing blow on the creature's head. It cried out and clamped its hands on the wound.

Johan closed his eyes again, the shrill noise from the thing pulsing through his head.

"Hit it again," said Richie. "Please. Make it stop!"

Opening his eyes, Johan noticed Spence had turned away, watching the entrance. Simon hung away a little, hands still on his hips.

"Please," Richie said again. He held his bleeding arm and seemed close to throwing up.

Johan lifted the bar again and pointed it at the creature's face like a sword. Its ebony eyes swelled with tears. It lowered its hands, producing strings of slime that dangled from its head.

"You can't be allowed to live," said Johan. Saliva slipped from the corner of his mouth and he absently wiped it away with the back of his hand.

The creature rested its hands in its lap and stared at him. "You'll... be... sorry."

The words stepped Johan's heart up a notch. "Not as sorry as you."

He thrust forwards, his arms straining to force the bar hard. The creature lifted its head at the last moment, and the sharp point effortlessly slid into the boneless flesh of its throat.

The boys cried out. One of them retched.

Johan remained staring at his victim, enjoying the sight of the dark, viscous fluids jetting from around the dull metal before slowing to a heavy trickle. The creature kept its eyes on him, arms by its side.

Johan pulled the bar out, and slid it free like a knife from butter. The wound, now a second puckering mouth, pulsated for a moment. It mouthed some kind of words, and blood cascaded from within the flesh. Finally, the creature coughed, and a fine spray shot out.

"...be... sorry..." it croaked and shook its head. With that momentum it flopped to one side and lay still within the pram.

21

Nat clung onto the narrow ladder on the wall of the shaft. Her short jump had been successful, and her arm had swung her onto the ladder. She prayed her feet had dried enough to prevent slipping. With her arms curled around a metal rung, she wriggled her toes. Her socks squelched around her feet. She blew out a long breath through pursed lips.

I hope the soles are drier, she thought. She looked down into the endless dark. I can't believe I'm suspended on a ladder God knows how many feet up…

"You okay?"

Max leaned out of the hatch. She guessed the walls of the shaft were thick, as the noise of the machines had been reduced and she heard Max clearly. His words seemed to resonate upwards and all around her.

"I'm fine," she said breathlessly. "I'm not used to all this."

"You will be."

She forced a smile to show Max everything was okay. She doubted he could see her in the dark, but thought it best.

Max appears normal, but he could have unseen abilities, like night vision or something, she thought.

"You want to make a start so the rest of us can get on?"

"Which way am I going?"

"Up, of course."

The shaft revealed no clue to what lay up ahead. Nat began her ascent, her feet making dull clangs on the ladder. After climbing a few feet, the ladder vibrated slightly. Nat glanced down and saw Max below her. She couldn't see his face, only the messy heap of dark hair at the top of his head. She turned back to the ladder and climbed quicker, afraid that Max would reach her and grab her foot by mistake, sending her falling backwards, clutching at the empty air. She gritted her teeth, filled with extra determination for the climb.

The ladder shook violently for a second, and Nat imagined the screws working loose and the whole thing falling away from the wall. She clasped the current rung tighter.

"You okay down there?" she heard Max ask.

"Good," said Jacob. "Go."

It took another deep breath and a second to calm her spiking nerves before Nat carried on up. She climbed the rungs slower, raising a step with one foot joining the other before attempting the next. The stop-start motion seemed safer.

She wondered how Jacob could manage the ladder. After all, his hands alone were almost too large for the rungs. She expected him to use one hand at a time, like vertical monkey bars... and his feet? She had no idea.

Her foot slipped off the rung.

Nat cried out and her body fell. She snapped to a stop, her breath snatched from her lungs. Her arms locked straight, her shoulders strained. The rung above cut into her tight fingers.

"Nat!" Max cried. "Are you all right?"

Nat heard her pulse in her ears and she gasped in deep breaths. With another small cry, she felt around with her feet and found another rung. She carefully stood on it and, sure her footing was secure, slowly eased the pressure from her arms and changed her hold. Her fingers and shoulders seemed to sigh in relief.

"Nat?"

"I'm okay," she sighed. "I'm okay."

"What happened?"

"I slipped."

"Hope she fall next time," said the deep voice from

below. "Want to know how far down. We listen to splat."

"Shut up, Jacob," said Max. "You think you can go on, Nat?"

"The sooner I'm off this *damn ladder* the better," she replied, regaining a little composure. "How high is this thing?"

"About another fifty feet and we should be out. There's another hatch. Alcazar keeps it open in case we drop by."

"Right," said Nat, more to herself than to Max. She took another deep breath and swallowed.

She knew she'd be safe on the surface. She was protected from most of the brothers out of the sewers. Max would understand if she escaped. As long as she kept their little secret, Max would understand.

She paused and hooked an arm around the ladder while she mopped her brow.

I could even make sure that they get food every day, now that I know the truth. Then no one would have to get hurt.

Her thoughts turned to the killers of their mother.

No, she corrected herself. Someone *will* get hurt once the brothers find out who's to blame.

She climbed another few feet.

The image of Johan, with his stark white hair and dazzling blue eyes, jumped into her head. She remembered him standing over Agnes in the moment before she kicked.

I just know it was Johan. If I told the brothers, would that stop innocent people from getting hurt?

She thought about this for a while and decided that she couldn't. She wasn't judge and jury. Just because Johan and his boys were *there* didn't mean they were killers. She couldn't pass judgement without evidence. Jacob and his brothers were planning on killing their mother's murderer, not just scaring them or giving them a beating. How could she condemn a man to death based purely on damning circumstance?

Nat looked up and spied the hatch a few feet above. Light glowed in the open cavity. Allowing her mind to wander, far from causing her to fall, had taken her from the gruelling and dangerous task of climbing the ladder. Relieved, she scrambled up the final few rungs and heaved herself onto the edge of the hatch.

Through the thick darkness beneath, Max still climbed at a steady pace perhaps twenty feet below. Beneath him, she heard Jacob. He puffed and panted and emitted the occasional small curse.

Nat slid around on her bottom and bent her legs at the knees to squeeze through the hatch. She planted her feet back onto the solid ground on the other side and stood up, glad to be off the ladder and already dreading the return trip.

If there is one, she thought and peered around.

She stood in an abandoned warehouse, and she guessed they were still in the derelict part of the city. Dawn had arrived during their journey through the sewers, and the first rays of golden morning light filtered in through smashed windows and an open door. Nat saw the street outside.

I could just walk out of here. All that time worrying how to escape and I can just walk out!

Yet her feet refused to move, her legs almost locked in place.

Should I? She licked her lips. *There will be no one out there, not in this part of town, and this time I'd be alone. Jacob might risk coming out after me and if he catches up...*

"Nat!"

She nearly cried out, wondering if, for a second, her thoughts had been spoken out loud, her ideas of betrayal heard.

Max's hand poked out of the shadows, fingers splayed

wide. "Give me a pull!"

Nat's gaze lingered on the open door a second longer before she grabbed Max's hand. She gripped his slippery skin and pulled. He toppled out of the hatch and fell to the floor, his patchwork coat tangled up around his body.

"Thanks," he said, panting. "Damn ladder always takes it out of me."

"No problem," she said and offered her hand. He accepted it, and Nat tugged him to his feet.

She jumped back and covered her mouth, eyes fixed on Max's chest, which pulsated and convulsed beneath his coat.

Oh Jesus, her mind screamed. This is it. He isn't normal, he's just like one of them.

She stared, her mouth hanging open with a scream loaded and ready to rip through the air.

What is it? A third arm? A second head?

Max reached below his chin and popped the top button of his coat. He looked up and smiled, unfastening the next button along. The coat opened further and revealed his tatty woollen sweater underneath. Below his hand, the fabric continued to bulge.

Jenkins' head popped out and the dog peered around the cavernous room, his tongue lolling from the side of his mouth.

"Come on," said Max and bent over. Jenkins leapt from within the coat and landed on his feet. He trotted around in a small circle, sniffing the air.

Max looked up at Nat. "You okay? You look like you've seen a ghost."

"Just my imagination running wild," she said.

A roar echoed out of the open hatch, and Jacob's wide hand slammed down on the edge. He hoisted his body up and barely squeezed through the small space.

"Hate dumb ladder," he said. He raised his hands over his head and stretched, the muscles on his shoulders and arms bulging.

Jenkins barked.

Nat spied Max frowning at the open doorway.

"It's dawn," he said. "I wanted to be back by light."

"They fine," said Jacob and walked past. "Herman can mind baby okay."

"It's not them I'm worried about," said Max. He swallowed. "The light brings people, even in this desolate place. Let's go find Alcazar and get back home, quick."

Jacob had strode to the other side of the room, having passed under several thick chains and rusted pulleys. He grabbed a horizontal wooden beam and pulled himself up, hanging off it. To Nat, he looked like a clothed, shaven gorilla.

"Max worry too much."

"Max is right to worry," Max replied. "Let's stop mucking about and get a move on."

Squinting in the morning rays, he walked across the warehouse, his feet kicking up small clouds of dust with each step. Jenkins obediently trotted along beside. He created a trail of tiny paw prints running parallel to those of his master.

With a last hungry look at the open and inviting doorway, Nat followed. Though she still hated Jacob, she had to agree with him—the ladder had been gruelling. Her shoulders and biceps had stiffened, and a line of pain still throbbed across her palms from the near fall. The cuts from the twins also flashed with white-hot needles.

Jacob fell to the floor, his feet smashing into the ground. A boom echoed around the empty warehouse. Birds took to the air somewhere above them.

Max shot him an agitated glance.

With Jacob bringing up the rear, the group walked across the floor of the warehouse. At the other side, two ramps on either side led up to a raised platform and a dark archway stood beyond. From the set up, Nat guessed that when the warehouse was operational, trucks had backed up against the raised area for loading. Max headed up the nearest ramp and, without looking back, disappeared into the entrance. Nat and Jacob followed.

The corridor appeared to be in the same state as the warehouse, filthy and empty. Halfway along, Max stopped and turned left. Reaching his side, Nat saw a stairway leading upwards.

"Easier than the ladder," said Max, and started towards them. The first few steps groaned under his feet in a ghostly sigh. Jenkins bounded up each step, his tail beating away.

Something poked Nat in the back, directly over her slash. She winced and snatched a breath through gritted teeth. She rubbed her stinging skin.

Jacob, his thick finger outstretched, pointed towards the stairs.

"Okay, okay," said Nat, moving forwards. "Jesus!"

Max had already reached the first platform between floors and waited for them.

Like a sulky teenager sent to her room, Nat ascended the stairs, her feet slamming down solidly on each step. She didn't care about staying quiet anymore. She'd start showing them some respect when they—or more accurately, Jacob—started showing her some.

They climbed flight after flight. Nat's breath whistled, and her legs burned. She remembered the last flight of stairs she'd climbed, those of her apartment block, and it had been a lot more fun. A fleeting image of a smiling Simon flashed through her head, but it vanished at Max's voice.

"This is the floor."

A smell assaulted Nat's senses, a dank and acidic stench.

"Sure?" asked Jacob. "They all look same."

"Yeah," said Max, "but this one stinks."

He's right. What the hell is that? thought Nat.

"Alcazar will be here," said Max. He held out a gloved a hand. "It can get quite slippery."

Unsure, Nat took his hand. He led her away from the stairs and into a murky corridor. The smell intensified. It transcended Nat's sinuses to attack the taste buds at the back of her throat. She fought back the gags and held a hand over her face.

"I can't believe you can stomach this," she said, her voice muffled.

"When you come enough times..." said Max. "Anyway, it's just until the end."

The corridor turned to the left and Nat suddenly found herself standing in the intense rays of the sun. The light revealed a white splattering that covered the walls and floor. The corridor opened out into a vast room, a large hole in the far wall allowing the golden morning glow to flood in. Wooden beams crisscrossed just below the high ceiling, all coated in the creamy white mess, dripping down in places like melting wax. Despite the fresh air drifting in through the hole, the air still smelled foul and mouldy. Piles had accumulated to form dry and twisted pyramids on the floor, like fetid stalagmites.

"What the..."

"It's shit," said Max. "Bird shit."

Jacob joined their side, fingers pinching his nose. "Even Herman don't stink this bad."

Around their feet, Jenkins sneezed and whipped his head from side to side.

"You don't like it either, do you, pal." Max bent down and scooped him up off the floor with his free hand, still keeping hold of Nat. He straightened up, Jenkins pressed against his chest. "Let's find my brother; he'll be in here somewhere."

Walking further, Nat's foot slid a few inches in the deep bird droppings. She clutched onto Max's hand tightly to stop from falling.

"Whoa! You okay there?"

"Yeah," she said, regaining her footing and ignoring Jacob's sniggers.

Beyond the hole, the city spread out before them, shining gold by the rising sun on the horizon. Nat heard the distant hum of the early morning traffic, broken by the occasional car horn.

"It's... beautiful," she gasped, gazing at the sun.

Jacob snorted. "Take or leave."

One of the piles of bird crap near the edge of the hole had begun to rise.

Nat cried out and took an unsteady step backwards. Max held her tight.

The white-splattered column rose to around seven feet tall and arms swept out to the side. Nat realised the mound was a large coat, completely covered in bird shit. Two hands, fingers curled into claws, held the coat out like a cape. The figure turned slightly, the early morning light creating an eclipse from the hooked nose. Two deep, dark eyes calmly surveyed them.

"Alcazar," said Max. "Finally."

The man smiled.

"Down!" shouted Jacob, already diving to the floor.

A question on her lips, Nat was pulled to the floor. She hit her knees and slid in the muck.

"What...?"

The air above her burst into life in a deafening cacophony of screeches and beating.

Holding her breath, Nat crouched into a tight ball and covered her head.

The dazzling rays of the sun darkened in a premature dusk. Behind the outstretched arms of Alcazar, the bright air grew speckled and buzzed with life.

"Down!" cried Jacob again. He had already spread out on the floor, lying on his front. He folded his arms over the back of his head.

"What? What's happening?" Nat looked to Max.

"Better if you take cover," he said and crouched. "Protect your head. They can be a little… excited."

Alcazar continued to grin at them; the fading sunlight glinting in his wide eyes. An animated black cloud steadily neared the building, the individual members of the flock now visible. Through the hole drifted the furious sound of beating wings.

The first of the birds entered the building and swept around Alcazar. Feathered pawns, they flew around the cavernous room, sharp calls echoing back and forth. Nat watched their meandering paths through the air. One of them, a small black bird with a vibrant yellow beak, stretched its wings and landed elegantly on a horizontal beam of wood. It turned and cocked its head in her direction.

"Watch out," called Max. "Here come the rest!"

The air burst into life with a *whoosh!* from outside.

Nat ducked back down and covered her head.

Wind beat against her, and feathers drifted down like giant snowflakes. A glance up revealed a flurry of wings, a flash of claw, a glint of beak. The room seemed to vibrate with the din of calls and shrieks. The birds raced around the derelict space in a cyclone of white, grey and black.

"Can't you calm them down?" shouted Max, his voice barely audible over the cacophony.

Alcazar stood silhouetted against the clear sky. The birds parted around him, a Red Sea of feathers. Nat wondered how they could fly so fast without colliding. She cried out and ducked down as one of them soared towards her. Its passing blew back her hair. She squealed.

"Alcazar!" roared Max.

"Oh, very well," said a high voice.

Above, the chaotic mass of birds circled, slowing.

Nat watched on, amazed at the sudden order within the flock.

The majority landed on the various ledges and beams that criss-crossed the walls and ceiling. Some chose the floor, where they pecked and bobbed among the filth. In seconds, only feathers, swaying and dancing on the air currents, remained in the air.

"Jesus," Nat whispered and peered around again.

His smile larger than ever, Alcazar lowered his arms and pulled his trailing coat around his thin frame.

With the air clear, Nat had the chance to study him in more detail. He'd been spared the disfigurements of Herman, Jacob and baby Edgar. He resembled the twins in some aspects. Whereas they shared similarities with the rats, this man had the distinct look of a bird. He appeared stretched; his arms and legs were grossly extended and it gave him the appearance of a vulture. His nose in particular, the way it hooked down, consumed his face, added to his avian appearance. His head sported several clumps of bushy white hair. Nat couldn't tell if it just wasn't more of the bird shit, which dotted his coat.

Hundreds of black eyes watched her climb to her feet.

"Look at this," said Max and pulled his coat from around his back. "I'm covered here, Alcazar. How the hell can you live like this?"

"I might ask the same of you, sewer rat," his older brother replied. Alcazar's large nose caused a slight whistle to creep into his voice. He walked towards them, wading through the mess.

The surrounding flock bobbed their heads with interest.

"It's cleaner down there," said Max, his arms out for balance. Alcazar caught his arm and pulled him close before he fell.

Jacob, rather than try and climb to his feet, merely sat back on the floor. He eyed the birds suspiciously.

"It's nice to see you, little brother," said Alcazar and grabbed Max by the shoulders. He gave him a firm squeeze.

"Likewise. I just wish it was under better circumstances."

Alcazar's narrow face drooped. "Yes. I was expecting your visit." He faced the rising sun. "All the friends I have in this city, all the eyes I can see through, and I allowed this to happen."

"It wasn't your fault," said Max. "None of us could have foreseen this."

"Foresight is one thing I don't claim," said Alcazar. "This...evil must have begun at some point: an argument, a chase...something! If only we were warned..."

Aware that her face burned, Nat looked away.

Jacob groaned, drawing the attention of his brothers.

"Birds," he said and shook his head.

With a firm push on the floor, he managed to stand. A grey pigeon on a nearby ledge pecked at him and flapped its wings. Jacob scowled and swept it away. The bird plummeted from the ledge and quickly spiralled upwards. It forced a new space among its kin and stared down.

"Birds," Jacob said again.

"I am surprised to see you here, Jacob," said Alcazar. "I thought you stayed underground?"

"Want answers. We know little."

Alcazar nodded. "And answers you will have, of what I can offer, at least. Who is this?"

Nat's heart seemed to stall like a bucking engine before it ascended back to a solid thumping. Pinpricks crawled across her brow.

"This is Nat," said Max. "A friend."

Jenkins barked.

A small smile fixed on her face, Nat turned her head back towards the brothers. Alcazar stared at her, head cocked like the inquisitive birds.

"A friend, eh? Not often we have company from outside the family." Some of the birds squawked in response. "Can we trust her?"

Max frowned. "Would we bring her here if we couldn't?"

Running a long finger down his nose, Alcazar gave it a small tap. "I suppose. Come."

He walked across the room, between Nat and Jacob, his feet finding the unmarred patches of floor. His long coat billowed out behind him. Nat imagined giant wings hidden underneath, a dirty angel, tramp of the skies.

"Where?" asked Jacob. "Is light now."

"He's right," said Max. "We've left Herman alone with the baby. The twins wandered off chasing rats, and Whistler's been acting weird."

"And?"

Max sighed. "I don't want to leave them alone for too long."

"Dear baby brother," said Alcazar. "I think our eldest can look after a baby for a few hours, don't you? Come into my room. You must be thirsty after such a long journey."

Max seemed to consider this for a few seconds. "Yes, I suppose they'll be fine for a little while longer. But we promised."

"We all make promises and most of them are broken. How is the old boy?"

They could be talking about some senile uncle or distant cousin, Nat thought, not the brother without skin that lives in a sewer.

"And you," said Alcazar, locking her into his intense gaze once again. "Surely you will join us?"

She quickly nodded.

Alcazar smiled. "Very good. Let us get comfortable, for we have much to discuss."

22

Alcazar's private quarters had only received the lightest of abuse from the birds. Nat chose an armchair with only thin white streaks of bird crap on the head rest. She made a mental note to lean forwards. Max shared a sofa with Jacob, who took up most of the room. Jenkins explored the area under a small table and sniffed at the carpet. Beyond them, in an area which served as his kitchen, Alcazar fussed around with cups and a metal kettle. Using a box of matches from his coat, he lit a small burner and placed the kettle on top.

Nat had developed a respect for the tall brother in the long coat. His room, a little way down the corridor from the stairs, was better kept than the lair in the sewers. The furniture, although still torn and beaten, appeared cleaned. Shelves of wood had been knocked up on the walls; their various angles and sizes gave the room a slapdash effect. Tins, pots and utensils were strewn about on them. A strange odour hung heavy in the air. Nat smelled burnt wood and spices. It completely blocked out the stench of the birds.

"You know," said Alcazar, peering back from the makeshift kitchen, "I should be flattered, but I find it quite amusing."

"You find *what* amusing?" said Max. He placed his hand on the armrest of the sofa and immediately recoiled in disgust. He wiped the spongy white gunk from his fingers.

"How many years have all of you doubted my skills? Called me crazy, called me names. Now, here you are, wanting answers."

"Mother dead!" Jacob cried. "Not here for fun."

Nat shrank back in the armchair. The wound on her back burned anew.

"He's right," said Max. "We came to see if you knew

something, anything, about who killed mother. We are underground for most of the day. Only I can venture out, and most of that time is spent begging. Out of all of us, *you* had the best chance of seeing or hearing something."

"You're right. I *have* heard a few things from my feathered friends."

Jacob rolled his eyes which brought a sharp glance from Max.

The water in the kettle bubbled, and Alcazar removed four chipped cups from a shelf. From a tin, he decanted a dark powder into each one. To Nat, it looked like ground charcoal. He added hot water and stirred each drink with a spoon.

"I apologise for the quality," he said and carried them over to the table. "I am a man of simple means, after all."

Nat took a cup and muttered a small thank you.

His hands enveloping his cup, Jacob drank the brew in two quick gulps, despite the heat. He lowered it from his lips with a sigh of satisfaction.

"Feel good to be a little more civilised, Jacob?" said Alcazar.

"Is only drink," he replied. "Maybe I grow more civil and live here…" He paused. "After pound skulls."

Max cleared his throat, cup held in his lap. "Before we get ahead of ourselves, I think it's time to talk about what happened. We're totally in the dark here, Alcazar. We don't know anything apart from what actually happened to her. It was definitely murder. I don't think she caved her own head in with a rock."

Alcazar flinched at the words and turned his back on the group.

Nat sampled her drink with apprehension. The strong, hot brew tasted of dark wood mixed with tea. She took a second sip. It refreshed her mouth, and, her thirst awakened, she tried not to gulp it all down.

Alcazar hunched over his workbench, nodded to

himself, and joined them. He settled down into another armchair, this one heavily soiled.

Max sipped his drink. "It's good."

"Thank you."

"Start from the beginning."

After a deep breath, Alcazar said, "It was probably the day after it…it happened. I was here, and one of my friends spoke of a woman being chased through the streets. I hear anything of interest in the city, and there's been quite a few women in peril over the last few years. More and more in fact. Only this one… this one was different, because… because…"

"This time it was our *mother*," Max finished for him. "If you knew that someone was hunting women out there, why didn't you do something?"

Alcazar laughed. It sounded like a series of sharp squawks.

"Listen to yourself. First, I'm no superhero. I don't watch over the city, ready to swing into action at the first sign of trouble." He gulped his drink. "I can't do a thing. The same way that *you*, any of you, can't do a thing. We have to live in the shadows. Call it fate, call it bad luck. This is how we're forced to live and, for the family, it has to be *maintained*. And another thing…" He stared at Jacob. "You in particular. What kind of hypocrite would I be, eh? Saving lone women in the city like some kind of… some kind of vigilante, knowing what you do!"

Jacob glared back. "Is different."

"Different?" said Alcazar and leaned back in his chair. "You're far from innocent, brother. You and the others!"

"Is for food. Is for survival."

Alcazar snorted. "Is it? Is it *really?* So you have *no choice* in the matter?" He stared back to Max. "I can't believe you let them do it. It appals me to be related to murderers."

Nat closed her eyes, suddenly wishing she was

anywhere but here.

"I can't watch them all the time," Max cried back. "Mother and I did everything we could to feed the family. Everything! There have been... incidents in the past, things done to keep our secret that I'm not proud of. I might not have done the killing, but I know the blood is on my hands." He took a shaky breath. "We can't argue. We don't have time, Alcazar. Please. Tell us what you know!"

"If you insist," he replied. He raised the cup to his lips and surveyed them all over the rim.

Beneath the table, Jenkins whined and lay down.

"There was a group," said Alcazar. "Four. Maybe five."

"How you know?" asked Jacob.

"I just do. I don't exactly speak to the birds, but I can see through their eyes, feel what they feel, and I don't have the patience to put up with your cynicism, Jacob."

"Go on," said Max.

"It happened in the woods by the park. They chased her and... and kind of closed in at the clearing. That's when they..."

"Yes," said Max, his face lowered. "We know how they did it. We found her, remember?"

Jacob slammed his fist onto the arm of the sofa. "We come here! Learn nothing!"

Jenkins looked up from beneath the table. He yawned and replaced his head between his paws.

"That's not everything," said Alcazar. "I know one more thing that will help us. I presume you're out for revenge, little brother?"

Jacob roared in reply.

"Then hear this. The one we seek has hair white as snow."

The cup fell from her hand as Nat jerked. The black drink splashed onto the floor.

"Nat?" asked Max. "Are you okay?"

"Y-Yes," she said. "This is just a little much for me, that's all."

It *was* Johan.

"Would you like another drink?" offered Alcazar. His stony gaze had warmed up some. "There's plenty left."

"No," she said. "But thank you. I'm just clumsy, I guess."

Her mind raced, and she barely registered the words slipping from between her lips. The images of that night flitted before her eyes—Simon arguing with Johan and his boys, the old woman between them, Whistler being chased.

Whistler! He was there! Why hasn't he said anything?

She picked up the cup and placed it on the table.

"We need to head back," said Max. "Herman will be in a foul mood. We need to plan a way to find this white-haired bastard, all of us."

Alcazar nodded. "I will come with you."

They all looked up at a tiny bird that flew in through the open door and swooped in circles around the room. It emitted a few chirps and bounced off the walls like a moth against a hot light bulb.

Alcazar outstretched a hand. "Here, little one."

Obediently, the birds changed direction and, with a stretch of its wings, gently settled on Alcazar's palm.

He brought the bird closer to his face until his sharp nose almost touched it. He emitted strange clicks and whistles in his mouth and throat.

The bird bobbed its head and chirped.

"What's it doing?" whispered Max.

"Sssssh," said Alcazar and lifted his other hand for silence.

The strange conversation carried on for another twenty seconds or so before the bird took off. It fluttered out of the room and away.

"We need to go," said Alcazar, who stood and dashed for the door. "Come on! Now!"

Nat stayed sitting with Jacob and Max. They swapped confused glances.

"What's going on?" said Max. "What's happening?"

"A group of boys have been seen leaving the sewers," Alcazar sighed. "One of them has stark white hair."

23

The light burned his retinas, but Johan forced his eyes to stay open. He breathed in his first breath of clean air. It smelled of grass even though they were a long way from the nearest green area. The long hours spent underground in the dark, wading through the fetid and rank waters, had altered his opinion of the city streets, which he'd always thought of as saturated with filth. They now seemed wholesome and inviting. He fought the urge to fall to his knees and kiss the ground.

His friends looked equally exhausted. Kev and Richie stayed close by each other, Johan presumed for protection. They'd not left each other's side throughout the arduous journey to the surface, both jumping at the slightest noise. Their wounds had clotted to a rusty brown.

Spence looked dazed, like he had just climbed out of bed. Behind his glasses, his eyes were vacant and staring. Johan wondered what carousel of thoughts danced around his head after their little adventure.

Away from them, Simon sat down on the pavement, his feet in the desolate road.

Johan stared up at the sun and closed his eyes, relishing the warmth on his face.

"We have to go," said Spence. "We still aren't safe here."

"Yes," Johan replied. "We are."

"No, no, no. We have to go. We have to move!"

Johan opened his eyes and looked at his friend, who had moved away from the dark doorway and eyed it wearily.

"What if they follow us?"

"They won't follow us, Spence. Think about those *things*. You seriously think they would come out in the day?"

"It might kill them," Kev suggested. "Like vampires. Maybe that's why they live in the sewers."

Johan shook his head. "No. They live in the sewers because that's where they belong, living in the shit." He peered back the way they'd come. "And they can't be allowed to carry on living down there."

He faced his comrades once more.

"This is *not* a surrender," he said. "This is a regroup."

"And what good will it do? We should have stayed and waited for them to bring her back!" Simon snapped.

Johan knew she was nothing more than a floating corpse now. Bitten, clawed, ripped to pieces. Only the rats will love her now, Simon, old friend.

Johan smiled, his head filled with an all consuming, cleansing fire.

"We can't go in there blind again, Simon. They nearly had us down there, but not again." He stared back at the entrance again. "God knows how many of them there are, how many we have to get through until we find your girlfriend. We need weapons, and not just a few bricks or bit of metal. We're going back in, boys, and this time we're going in armed."

The car was still parked around the corner from the pub. To Johan, it seemed ages since they'd played pool and Simon had barged in, all fists and accusations. They climbed inside, and Johan drove them back to his flat.

"You think it could be infected?" Richie asked. He sat on the sofa nursing his right arm. "They live in the sewers for fuck's sake. We were waist deep in that shit! Anything could have gotten in."

Simon disappeared into the kitchen.

"Kev," said Johan. "Help me take his shirt off."

Underneath his own injury, a crescent-shaped cut on

his forehead, Kev's eyes widened.

"Come on, Kev! We need to see what's been done."

Richie's shirt had been ripped by the baby, but it still concealed most of the damage. Johan popped open the cuff.

"You guys need anything?" asked Spence, peering over Kev's shoulder.

"Some wet tea-towels," said Johan. "And a first aid box. There should be one in the kitchen."

"Already got them," said Simon, back in the living room. He clutched a dripping bundle in his hands and a green box under his arm.

"Good," said Johan. "Now, let's see what we have."

He rolled up Richie's sleeve.

"Jesus!"

Close to his wrist, a small chunk of flesh had been removed. The edge was neatly serrated where the teeth had cut through the skin. Johan stared into the hole, roughly the size of a fifty-pence piece. The wound had dried, the inside a dark red, bordering on black. It looked like he'd been stabbed with a white hot skewer that had cauterised as it entered. Grime streaked the skin around it.

"Is… is it bad?" asked Richie.

Johan picked up a wet tea-towel. "It looks worse than it is."

He cleaned the wound, ignoring Richie's complaints, and sprayed it with antiseptic from the first aid box. Kev and Spence held a pad in place while he wrapped the arm in a bandage to hold it in place.

"There," said Johan and sat back. "Not perfect, but it will do." He climbed to his feet.

"Where are you going?" Richie asked.

"To the bathroom." He nodded to Spence. "There's a bottle of brandy in the kitchen cupboard. I know it's early, but I think we could all do with a drop."

Spence nodded and headed for the kitchen.

The morning sunshine had not yet penetrated the

frosted glass of the bathroom window. Johan switched on the light and dashed inside, straight to the sink. Using a strip of toilet paper, he covered the hot tap and turned it. Wiping the light switch and then depositing the paper in the toilet, he returned to the sink and plunged his hands under the already steaming water and rubbed them hard.

Dirt and filth, oh fuck me, all that dirt and filth...

From a bottle between the taps, he squirted creamy white soap into his hands and continued to scrub them. Back under the hot jet, Johan cried out, the water burning his hands. He sucked in a breath and scoured his hands, nearly scratching in the suds.

He whimpered and stepped back. He removed his leather jacket and flung it in the corner. It fell in a crumpled heap, the streaks of dirt clear on the glossy black sleeves.

He cried out at the sight and plunged his hands back under the tap.

Steam filled the small bathroom. Johan looked in the mirror above the sink, his image misty and distorted. After another squirt of liquid soap, he washed his hands again.

He kicked off his boots, and these joined the pile in the corner. His socks, sodden with stinking water, were hooked off. He threw them with a yell, like the sewer water was a concentrated acid that would eat away at his fingers.

He washed his hands after touching them.

Jeans down, they flew across the room, followed by his wet boxer shorts. Naked, he splashed the scalding water onto his body and face and rubbed. Long red streaks formed on the skin across his chest and stomach.

A knock on the door made him jump.

"Johan?"

Simon.

"Johan? Are you okay in there?"

The door opened an inch.

Johan leapt over and slammed it shut, pressing his body against the wood. He turned the lock next to the handle.

"I'm... I'm fine! Just cleaning up, you know?"

"We thought we heard you scream," Simon called through the door.

"Yeah," Johan replied, his voice low and steady. "The water was hot, took me by surprise."

"You need anything?"

"No," said Johan and swallowed. He stared at the bundle of soiled clothes in the corner. "I'm good."

He listened to Simon move away from the door, probably to tend back to Richie. Sobbing, he slid down the door. On the cold linoleum, Johan curled up and wrapped his arms around his knees.

Look what they have done to me. All that filth.

The memory of the baby clutched in his hand— touching his bare skin—reared up and he shivered.

He sprung to his feet, eyes feverishly darting around in his sockets. Bottles around the sink fell over and spun into the basin as he swept up several and headed for the shower.

In the living room, Richie had propped his newly bandaged arm up with a pile of cushions.

It hasn't leaked, thought Johan, watching them from his bedroom, a towel around his waist. That's good. I don't think it will give us any more problems.

Spence and Kev sat with Richie on the sofa. Simon gazed out of the window from the armchair, sipping dark amber liquid from a bottle.

"Glad to see you have time to shower," he called, his tone flat. "They could be doing *anything* to her right now."

"Walking around covered in sewer juice won't help," Johan replied. "We're going out soon and we don't want to draw undue attention to ourselves. I suggest you all take the time to freshen up. I should have clothes to fit you all, even you, Kev."

"Why?" Spence called. "Where are we going?"

Johan pulled a fresh pair of boxer shorts from a drawer. He dropped the towel, stepped into them and pulled them up. They slid up along his legs, the skin raw and scratched. He held his breath until they were in place and comfortable.

"I told you, we won't be caught out again. We're going to see a friend of mine on the other side of the city. He'll help us out." He repeated the painful process with a pair of black jeans. "Which is why you lot can't go around stinking like the sewers."

A figure stepped into the doorway, and Johan spun away to hide his scalded chest.

Fighting the urge to return to the bathroom for another shower, Johan approached the wardrobe and unhooked a t-shirt.

"You think this is the best way forwards?" said Simon from the doorway. "Go in alone? Again? Don't you think we should tell someone about this, seeing as we know what's down there?"

Johan pulled the red top over his head and down to his waist. Happy his scrubbed body was completely covered, he faced Simon.

"You think the police would believe us? A group like *us,* telling tales of monsters and kidnap and killer babies that live underwater? They'd laugh us out of the station. Besides, the authorities are soft. They protect the weak..." He walked to the mirror and studied his face. "They'd probably label us murderers for what we did down there."

Simon shook his head. "I don't care. This is too risky, too dangerous for us to deal with."

"We handled them fine, didn't we? And this time, we're going in prepared. Don't you want revenge?"

Frowning, Simon said, "Revenge for them taking Nat?"

Revenge for killing her.

Johan closed his mouth before the words could spill out.

Need to keep him onside. He has to believe she's still alive.

"Yes. We'll make them pay. For taking her and what that fucking baby did to Rich and Kev." He returned to the drawers. "I'll pick you something out. Go and get a wash."

Simon took a mouthful from the bottle, swallowed and winced from the burn. "You know," he said, a little slurred, "women, eh? Fucking women." He shook his head. "More trouble than they're worth, but then we always knew that, didn't we, right mate?"

Johan paused in his pursuit of extra clothing. "Nice to have you back to our way of thinking."

Simon huffed and took another drink. "What a night. Mutant freaks and my woman in the middle of it. At least she wasn't screwing around."

24

Nat's feet, despite the clumps of bird mess that clung tenaciously to the soles, stayed on the rungs of the ladder and refused to slip. Through her hands, the ladder gently vibrated, throbbing with the pulse of the machines. The vertical shaft echoed with the erratic sound of feet on metal. Below, Max stepped off the ladder and through the hatch, quickly followed by Alcazar. Nat hurried. The eager sound of Jacob rang out from above.

The smell of excrement and mould assaulted her once again. Every breath created images of a thick brown sludge coating the inside of her lungs, lining her passages, infecting her taste buds that shrivelled away at the back of her throat. She gagged and, with the space below her unoccupied, spat a glob of phlegm into the darkness.

From her vantage, and with light streaming in from the open hatch about ten feet below, Nat glimpsed something at the bottom of the shaft. She slowed her decline and stared downwards.

Again, a sliver of light illuminated a ripple of movement far below.

It doesn't just go on forever, deeper and deeper. There's water at the bottom.

She expected the knowledge to reassure her. A fall at this height would not leave her plummeting down to the centre of the earth, nor would it splatter her across a grating or concrete floor. Nat shivered, thinking of hitting the water and rising to the surface, only to find that the ladder started several feet above.

I'd tread water in the dark until my energy ran out. My body would glide under the water and rot for years at the bottom of this shaft.

She returned her concentration to the ladder and quickened her pace.

Maybe it would be better to find an unforgiving concrete floor. Crunch! All over.

Nat eased her left foot from the ladder and with a controlled swing of her body, stepped onto the edge of the hatch. Max, standing on the other side, helped her through.

"How far behind is Jacob?" he asked. The skin of his face had paled and, with the glare of the yellow halogens, it appeared jaundiced, the colour of bad teeth.

"He's right behind me," she said, and looked back at the hatch.

The machines pounded beyond. The air seemed to throb.

The dark rectangle of the hatch instantly filled as Jacob dropped down. He pounced forwards and landed on the floor.

"Move!" he said.

Nat backed away a few steps.

His chest rose and fell heavily. Fists, the size of bowling balls, squeezed tight at his sides.

"Move..." he growled again and ran on ahead.

Nat followed the others into the next room.

The slow beat of the machines filled her head the moment her feet crossed the threshold. The pistons continued to rise out of the large tanks and ease back inside. Red lights glowed in the shadows like the eyes of demons.

Nat, almost at a run, followed the flapping coat of Alcazar across the room. She moved around another machine covered in black and yellow warning stickers. A metal safety rail surrounded it.

Beyond this machine, two other routes ran away from the main path. In front, Max and Alcazar ran straight on.

Nat pushed her legs harder to catch up to them.

A man, dressed in a blue boiler suit and hard hat, emerged from the left walkway. He looked up from a clipboard.

"What the…?" He glanced at Max and Alcazar on one side, then at Nat on the other. "You… you people shouldn't be down here!"

Nat stopped and stared at the man, her heart racing.

"What are you doing?" he continued. From the grey hair that peeked out from under his hard hat and the weathered lines of his face, Nat guessed he was at least in his fifties. He looked between her and the others again, eyes wide.

Max and Alcazar had stopped their retreat and faced the man. Alcazar held up his hands, like the man had a gun aimed at him.

"We don't want any trouble," said Nat, feeling that *someone* had to say *something*. "We're just…passing through."

"This is private property," replied the man. He shook his head. "It's dangerous, too. You shouldn't be down here!"

The two brothers on the other side of the room appeared locked in fear. They stared at the worker with their mouths hanging open. Jenkins barked twice.

Nat chanced a step forwards and held out a hand. "Please," she said. "Just let us through."

An immense shadow separated from the darkness behind the man and loomed up behind him.

Jacob roared and slammed his hands on either side of the worker's head. The hardhat flipped backwards and fell. The clipboard dropped from his hand.

"Jacob!" Nat screamed. "No!"

Jacob's arms tensed and ripped the man's head around.

Nat covered her mouth.

It looked like the man had dressed backwards. Only his feet, which pointed in the wrong direction, revealed the grim reality. The body dropped to its knees.

Gritting his irregular teeth, Jacob once again grabbed the man's head and pulled. The neck showed resistance for a moment, but then gave way with a wet creak. The head tore free, and Jacob lifted the trophy high. Inches of vertebrae dangled underneath, the anchor for twisted blue and purple strands. It all hung from the head like red seaweed.

The body fell forwards and flopped on the floor before Jacob's feet. Blood gushed from the ragged cavity in a scarlet ejaculation.

"Oh… shit," groaned Nat. Her legs buckled and she leaned against the safety rail.

Jacob threw the head across the room. It spiralled through the air in a cartwheel of dripping blood. It struck a machine and bounced off, resting face down.

Crouching, Nat clamped a hand over her mouth and took in a deep breath through her nose. Bile burned the back of her throat.

Max crossed over to her and hooked a hand under her arm. He gently pulled her upwards.

"We have to go," he said. "There might be others nearby." He glanced at Jacob. "Get rid of the body."

"He just… I can't believe…" Nat wailed. "He just…"

"Greater good," said Jacob. He bent down and grabbed the body by the ankle.

"He's right," said Max, his tones hushed and smooth. "We can't let anyone know we're here. Others will come looking." He snaked an arm around her back and guided her forwards.

With the body dragging along the floor at his side, Jacob strode towards the head on the far side of the room. The corpse slid past Nat.

"Oh God—" She turned and vomited. It slapped the concrete walkway and spread, like a pale orange Rorschach test. To Nat, it looked like a severed head. She'd be seeing that head for a long, long time.

"Come on," said Max. "Let's keep moving. Put it out of your head."

Head?

Nat groaned and staggered along.

"He... he..."

"I know," said Max. "Let's keep going."

She allowed herself to be ushered along through the loud, pulsing machines, to the doorway on the far side. Alcazar moved on. He entered the corridor and peered around the corner. After a nod, he motioned them forwards.

Jenkins, snug inside Max's coat, stuck his head out, panting.

Nat recognised the corridor from their journey here. The light bulbs still swayed with the beat of the machines.

Alcazar ran ahead. With just enough room in the narrow corridor, Nat and Max followed, side by side. They paused at the next junction. Voices drifted from the next section.

"Wait here," said Alcazar. "Watch her."

"No!" Nat whined as he slipped away around the corner. Her trembling increased. "Max! You can't let this happen. There must be another way through..."

He bowed his head. "There isn't. I wish there was." He placed a gloved hand on top of her head and massaged his fingers through her hair. "I *know* it's wrong, but this is what it takes to survive, Nat. We've lived down her for decades. I know enough about the world above to see what would happen if our presence was known. They'd be placed in freak shows, or worse, labs where scientists will cut them up to see what went wrong..."

He lowered his hand to her shoulder.

"I think of my family," he whispered. "Protecting my family is the only thing that justifies these... these atrocities."

Ahead, the voices abruptly stopped.

"No!" Nat cried again.

Max gripped her harder. "Shhh. Don't think about it. Picture Edgar and Herman, the twins too. We have to do this so they can live."

At what cost? Nat thought bitterly through her tears. How many people have to die to keep the family a secret? What makes their lives worth more?

Alcazar appeared around the corner.

"Lucky," he said. "It was only a radio. After this room we're back in the true sewers. Max, you'll have to lead the way. I get lost down there."

"Okay." Max started forwards.

"What about Jacob?" said Alcazar.

"He'll be right behind us. He knows the way better than me. Come on."

Nat wiped the tears from her cheeks and trailed behind Max.

Clothes soaking wet again after wading through the deep water, Nat stepped into the tunnel leading to the lair. Alcazar stood in front. The walk through the filthy water had actually cleaned his coat, the dark brown fabric now clear of white smears.

Max grabbed her hand and pulled her to a stop.

"Alcazar!" he hissed. "Stop!"

Alcazar turned and frowned.

"Look!"

The entrance to the chamber lay at the end of the tunnel: a wide circular hole in the mouldy brick. Water sloshed over its lips and formed a small waterfall. This created a fast stream which flowed towards them.

"What does that mean?" asked Alcazar.

"Something must have happened," said Max. "It was something we built but never used. There's a lever that… that fills the chamber with water. This is the overflow."

"Why would you want to flood it?" asked Nat.

Max turned to her, his face ashen. "In case of

intruders." He stared down the tunnel. "It's supposed to make them panic and leave before they find anything… anyone…"

Alcazar nodded to Nat and proceeded down the tunnel.

"Herman," Max cried. "Herman! Are you all right?"

Only the gentle sound of lapping water answered his call.

They splashed through the shallow stream and reached the lair entrance. Max paused, shouted Herman's name again, and climbed inside the round aperture. He splashed in the knee deep water on the other side. Alcazar quickly followed.

"What's happened?" asked Nat. She kneeled up on the edge of the hole and eased her body through. From within the dark circle, she peered inside.

The lair had been partially flooded, but already the waters had begun to recede. Smaller pieces of furniture floated around. A table top drifted lazily like a raft. A few ragged clothes hung suspended in the murky pool, weeds of cotton and wool.

Nat lowered her feet into the water.

The horizontal bars of the cell dripped, showing how high the water had reached. Inside, the collection of rags and other debris had formed a scummy island.

In the corner, the old pram lay overturned, wheels motionless.

"Herman?"

Max waded over, kicking up waves of froth. The water rocked the pram slightly.

"Herman?"

He reached down and grabbed the edge of the metal frame. With a grunt, he pulled and flipped it back.

Underneath, Herman's eyes, orbs of black glass, stared up at the ceiling. His head was tilted back, and his mouth hung floppy as a limp hose. A thick metal bar stuck out of his throat.

"Herman?" said Max, and touched his face.

His brother's body had lost its gleam and appeared dry. A map of shallow cracks ran across the withered hide around various cuts and bruises.

Nat looked away from the horrific sight to Max, who stared at his older brother. His matted hair hung about his face. His lower lip trembled.

"No!" wailed Alcazar behind him. He waded through the water and stood beside. "They can't... they..." His words trailed off as tears slid down his grimy cheeks.

"Where's Edgar?" said Max, still staring. Only his lips moved, the words quick and quiet.

Jenkins barked.

Nat turned her back on the brothers to search for the dog.

Alcazar cried with an increased urgency and held onto Max, his face pressed into his shoulder. Max remained staring; his grief had paralysed him into a statue of sorrow.

Jenkins stood on a pile of rubbish heaped in the corner. His tail beat the air; the dog looked up and grinned as Nat approached.

"What've you got there?" she asked in a soothing voice. Her words nearly choked at the back of her throat. The grief in the room was a palpable gravity. "What you got?"

Jenkins replied with another yap. The water lapped its filth-encrusted coat, and he sniffed around the floating debris. He dipped his head in the water, grabbed a floating length of blue rope between his teeth and pulled back. Out of the water, Jenkins placed the rope by its front paws and looked up, tail wagging again. The end of the rope remained hidden, suspended in the water.

Unsure why—maybe simple curiosity or to avoid the scene behind her—Nat bent down and touched the rope. She nearly recoiled from its slimy, spongy feel.

Probably just been in the water for too long.

Jenkins watched as Nat turned the rope over. Its underside was lined with pale white circles the size of bottle caps.

She held the rope higher for a closer look and dropped it.

This isn't a rope.

She swallowed. "I... I think you need to come over here."

Her knees trembled, and she wiped her hands on her top.

"Max, I said I—"

"We heard you," snapped Alcazar. Nat flinched. "Can't you give us a moment? Herman is... Herman is..." He squeezed his eyes shut, gripping Max even harder.

"Please," she said. Her own grief soared from the aching pit of her stomach.

Leaving Alcazar to mourn over the body, Max crossed the chamber. His eyes glazed over. A frown creased his brow, and he reached down.

He followed the tentacle, running it through his hands. It led him into the centre of the chamber.

Max peered through the murky depths. He dropped the long, thick strand and closed his eyes.

"Max?" asked Alcazar.

He covered his face with his hands. His shoulders hunched, racked with shakes. Nat heard the muffled sobs.

"Max?" Alcazar wiped his cheeks with the back of his hand.

Silently, Max plunged his hands into the cold water. He pulled out a small, dripping body. The tentacles hung beneath it, limp and motionless, dangling in the water. Max held the baby to his chest and bowed his head.

"No," said Alcazar, his arms weak at his sides. "They... they wouldn't have..."

Max didn't reply and remained still, holding the tiny corpse in a tight embrace.

Sitting down on a pile of rubbish, Nat allowed Jenkins to hop onto her lap. She stroked the dog's back, trying to keep it calm. It seemed to sense the sadness in the chamber and grew restless.

Alcazar hugged his brother, the baby sandwiched between them. Besides the gentle lapping of the water, the lair was silent.

Nat closed her eyes, not wishing to see the grief of the brothers, nor the body in the corner. Jenkins squirmed in her lap.

A loud splashing sounded from the chamber's entrance, followed by a deep growl.

Oh no, thought Nat.

"Man gone," said Jacob, voice echoing in from the tunnel. "Thrown in pit. No one find."

Nat opened her eyes and clutched Jenkins harder.

The entrance darkened, and Jacob clambered through. His body slid through with surprising ease.

"What happen?"

He looked at Nat. She shook her head, eyes welling up with tears.

"Where...?" His head twisted to the right. He gazed into the corner at the battered and bloody body of Herman. His broad chest swelled in a deep breath, and a thick vein in his neck pulsed. He clenched his fists. "Edgar?"

Alcazar, staring at the floor, stepped back.

Hands tangled in tentacles, Max held up the baby. Tears poured down his face and met the pool of snot trickling from his nose. His body swayed, ready to fall at any moment.

Nat tasted the salt of her own tears.

The floor vibrated with Jacob's roar. He hooked a hand around the upturned pram and flung it across the room. The carrier flew through the air between Nat and Max and struck the wall with a loud clatter. One of the wheels jumped off and landed in the water with a high splash. The rest of the pram fell on a pile of junk, its metal frame bent out of shape.

Jacob had already gone to work on a set of mouldy drawers. His fists punched through the rotten wood leaving large, jagged holes. Blood sprayed from his knuckles. With another painful cry, he picked up the chest of drawers and smashed it against the wall.

"J-Jacob," started Alcazar. He stepped forwards, his arms held up. "Please!"

He ducked a flying chair. It exploded in a shower of splinters behind him.

"Jacob!" he said, firmer.

Jacob screamed and clutched his bald head.

Nat shuffled back against the wall.

Alcazar pressed his hands against his brother's pumping chest. "Stop it! Why do you have to do this?" He burst into a new fit of tears. "Destroying your home achieves nothing!"

Jacob howled and raised his arms.

From atop the pile of rubbish, Nat watched, her mouth hanging open.

Before Jacob struck, Alcazar punched him the chest.

"Why?" he screamed, face glistening. He rained blows against Jacob, who stood rigid, staring down.

"Stop!" cried Nat. She clamped her hands over her ears. "I can't take anymore. Just stop it! Both of you!"

Jacob's arms dropped to his sides. "Who care what *you* want," he growled. "Should kill you when had chance, girl."

Max spoke, his voice barely a whisper. "Shut up, Jacob."

They all looked towards him. He clutched the small body to his cheek.

"We'll get our blood. Even if we all have to go to the surface, they'll not see another sunrise." He closed his eyes.

A whistle drifted in from the tunnel outside, and a

figure stepped over the crumbling wall and through the hole.

Jacob growled.

"Stop!" Max cried.

Jacob ignored the plea and pushed Whistler back against the wall.

Whistler, shooting panicked glances around the chamber, released a high-pitched note of pain, striking the wall a second time.

"Where?" Jacob accused.

Alcazar leapt onto Jacob's back, but uselessly slid off and stumbled back in the water. He toppled in with a splash.

"Jacob!" said Max, still holding the body of Edgar. "It wasn't his fault. We weren't here either."

Jacob grabbed Whistler's multicoloured jumper and yanked him upwards.

He slid up the wall, feet kicking in the air. He clutched Jacob's thick wrist and frantically shook his head.

"Your fault," Jacob hissed. He turned slightly and, with a massive heave, flung Whistler across the chamber.

Nat watched the thin body soar past, arms and legs circling like he was swimming through the air. Whistler's head dipped, body following. He crunched against the far wall, his back hitting the brick. Whistler plummeted into the shallow water below.

"Brother!" Alcazar rushed over.

Whistler jerked up and spat out a mouthful of water. He gagged.

From the other side of the room, Jacob jabbed a finger in his direction. "Where?" he demanded again.

Whistler emitted fast and agitated notes.

"This is pointless!" screamed Max. "It doesn't matter *where* he was! This happened, and nothing will change it. Where are the twins, Jacob? Are you going to try and kill them when they arrive? We're all equally to blame for this;

we promised Herman we'd be back by dawn." He gave the body in the corner a prolonged gaze. "And look what happened."

Jacob huffed and turned his back on the group.

Whistler slumped against the wall and rubbed his back, glaring at his brother.

"I find twins," Jacob snarled.

"No," said Max. "Alcazar can find the twins. We need to tell them, but *not you*. There are other things we need to do."

He closed his eyes again and stroked the body of Edgar against his face.

25

The last load of dirt fell from the spade in Jacob's hands.

They all stood in the clearing of the small forest. Two mounds of freshly turned earth lay between them. Beside these, another patch of ground appeared recently disturbed, the first few green colonists taking root. Nat guessed that their mother, old Agnes, lay beneath.

On tree branches, various species of birds watched in silence. Pigeons, starlings, blackbirds, seagulls, sparrows; they stood side by side, taking up every available perch. Smaller birds balanced on Alcazar's shoulders, and a large thrush sat atop his head. One of the smaller species constantly chirped its song into his ear.

Nat thought it might have been amusing under different circumstances.

She glanced at each face that surrounded the fresh graves. Alcazar and Max stood on either side of Jacob, heads bowed, hands clutched together. The twins, finally found, looked a little more human in the daylight. They stayed close to each other, almost touching. Their eyes, small and completely black, squinted in the sun. Their snouts emitted long, wet sniffs. One of them wiped the tip with the back of a long claw.

Whistler had maintained a safe distance from Jacob through the tunnels and up through the grate. He stood the furthest away, barely in the circle.

Nat stared at him in bewilderment.

What can be going through his mind? He could have stopped one death. Where was he when Johan and the rest of them called?

Johan. It always came back to Johan.

Whistler looked up at her and, meeting her eyes, immediately glanced away.

Coward, she thought, returning her attention to the two

graves. Edgar's burial place was no more than a foot long. Her hands tightened on each other.

Jenkins trotted around the undergrowth, sniffing the base of the trees.

"Someone should say a few words," said Max, his voice quivering. "I'm... I'm not up to it."

Jacob thrust the spade deep into the earth and leaned against its handle like a cane. "She not be here," he grumbled.

"What?" said Max.

"Not want her here," Jacob replied and shot Nat a look. She saw the cold hate in his eyes.

"She has every right," said Alcazar and wiped tears from his face. "Max has told me all about you, Nat. You might not be part of this family..." He gave a weak smile. "Something I imagine you're grateful for, but you *are* one of us. If you hadn't helped for so long, who knows? This might have happened sooner." He dropped his gaze from her to the graves between them.

"But she not family!"

"Hush, Jacob," said Alcazar. "This is not the time or the place." He walked forwards and the roosting birds took flight to join their comrades in the trees. Stopping between the freshly turned mounds, he outstretched his arms.

"We are here to celebrate the lives and mourn the deaths of our beloved brothers, Herman and Edgar. They were taken away too soon, through hands that did not realise their sin."

The twins erupted into muffled sniffles and hugged each other.

"We pray that God Almighty will welcome them into his Kingdom. Our brothers have suffered on earth and deserve the reward of eternal paradise. Despite our appearance, we are all God's creatures. Amen."

"Amen," the others repeated.

"Now," said Alcazar, a single tear meandering down

his cheek, "let us pray, remember the good times that we shared."

Jacob snorted and received a sharp glance from Alcazar.

With her head down and eyes closed, Nat took the few minutes of silence and gathered her thoughts. Her mind seemed distorted, like her thoughts had been refracted through a prism and lay scattered in her head. She guessed it was due to the lack of sleep and the journey she'd made since entering the derelict area of the city. She realised this was the first time she had actually stopped since her time in the sewers. Her life, in a single night, had become a rollercoaster. No, she thought, that's not right. It's more like a ghost train—full of creatures and horror and shock.

She opened her eyes and again studied the brothers. She shivered at the twins. The wound down her back had begun to itch terribly.

They're *not* monsters, she thought, just fighters. Alcazar's right. I do feel like one of them now. How can you go through so much and *not* feel like one of them?

She closed her eyes again.

I need to speak to Max. He'll know what to do. It's time to tell him everything I know. Johan, Agnes, the whole damn story. Fuck. Will he get mad that I didn't tell him sooner? No, he'll understand. I couldn't prove anything.

She heard a small cry from her left, a low, sharp whistle.

Nat tensed her fists.

And what about him? Should I tell Max that he was there the night their mother was murdered? That he turned and ran instead of helping her?

"Look after him, Herman," said Alcazar, "you cantankerous old bastard."

He raised his arms and all the birds took flight. They rose high into the sky in a tornado of beating wings. The dark cloud of movement dispersed; the sky between the treetops returned to a gentle blue with thin wisps of drifting cloud.

"We have to return underground," ordered Alcazar. "It's been risky enough. Come on."

Jacob strode on ahead and lifted up the thick metal grate that covered a raised concrete platform. Nat jumped as the twins shot across the clearing, bare feet scampering across the earth. They disappeared into the dark hole in seconds.

Alcazar's little feathered friend had returned to his shoulder, chirping in earnest. The older brother's brow creased in concentration.

"Whistler," he said. "A moment inside, if you'll entertain my questions. A little birdy tells me we need to talk."

Whistler studied the grass between his feet.

"Now, brother," said Alcazar, threat creeping into his voice.

Nat watched Whistler plod towards the birdman like a child caught drawing on the walls. Had Alacazar's network finally called Whistler out?

Did the older brother know Whistler was there when Agnes was chased?

Max called for Jenkins and the dog trotted over, blades of grass poking out from its mouth.

"Stupid dog," he said and scooped Jenkins up. "You know that makes you sick. Why do you still do it, eh?"

"Max?" Nat asked and put a hand on his arm. "Can you hang back for a second? I… I need to talk."

He nodded. "It's overdue, I suppose. Alcazar? Can you get everyone back and keep them there?"

Alcazar waved the request away and ushered Whistler into the hole. From beneath his black fringe, plastered down on his forehead, Max gave Nat another worried glance over his shoulder.

"Go on," said Max and placed Jenkins on the ground. "Off with your uncles."

The dog barked and shook its short fur. Tail wagging, it ran off after Alcazar. He picked up the dog.

"Don't be too long," he said.

Jacob growled and lowered his body in after Alcazar. He dropped the heavy grate into place and was gone.

"Can we get back?" asked Nat.

"There are many ways back," said Max. "Now, what's on your mind?"

They sat down on the grass.

Nat looked around the vacant clearing. Not all the birds had gone. Some lingered in the treetops in warbled song.

"It was nice," she said, enjoying the warmth of the sun on her face and the fresh, earthy aroma of the wood. "I'm sure Herman would have approved."

"Funny how he was a devout Christian," said Max with a small smile. "You wouldn't think it."

"Really?"

"Yeah. Apparently he had read The Bible from cover to cover at a young age. Changed his outlook."

Nat frowned. "Doesn't the Bible say thou shalt not kill?"

Max plucked at a patch of weeds by his sides.

"Herman didn't kill anyone. He always left it up to Jacob or the twins."

"Um," said Nat and looked at the ground.

"I'm sure you didn't keep me behind just to discuss how nice the service was. You look drained, distracted. I know what this is about."

Nat raised her head to meet his eyes. "You do?"

"I expected it. You want to leave, anyone would."

The rays of sun highlighted the few ginger strands in Max's thick beard. They glistened like copper wire. Nat wondered what he looked like underneath all the hair and dirt.

"We've been keeping you prisoner," he continued. "Okay, you're out of the cell, but we still haven't let you go." He placed his hand on her shoulder and gave it a gentle squeeze. "We're only in the park, you can hear the traffic if you listen carefully. Go. I'll tell them I lost you in the trees. Jacob will be pissed, but he's got other things on his mind. He'll forget quickly and—"

Nat swallowed. "It's those other things I want to talk to you about," she said slowly.

"What do you mean?"

Nat climbed to her feet and held out her hand.

"Let's walk for a bit. I promise I won't run off. Like Alcazar said, I'm part of the family now."

After a few seconds, Max took her hand and allowed himself to be pulled up. Nat snaked her arm around his, linking them.

"See. You can grab me if I make a break for freedom."

"You shouldn't be joking about this."

"Who says I'm joking?" said Nat. The sun seemed to have washed away the fear and dread of the night's adventures. She felt a little more like herself. "You haven't done anything to hurt me. As for some of the others…"

"It was a mistake," Max pleaded.

"I know."

They followed a thin, winding path through the dense trees. Nat marvelled at the birds darting between the branches above. She watched a red squirrel, tiny hands clutching an acorn, bound through the undergrowth and scamper up a tree out of sight. She sighed.

"You kind of forget about all this," she said. "Living in this hell hole of traffic and people, shitty bosses and even shittier jobs."

"Your shitty job kept my family alive," Max reminded her.

"Yeah, but you just forget what life's about, you

know? I cringe when I think about the years I wasted as a waitress, waiting for something to happen, waiting for something to change."

"It did."

The trees thinned out, and the first signs of the park came into view. Sounds of friendly shouts and children's laughter joined the birdsong. On the very edge of the wood, still within the shadows of the trees, Nat pulled Max to a stop.

"Should…should we go out there?" she said. "I've been missing all night. I'm sure people will be looking for me, especially…" She almost said Simon, but kept the name from escaping.

"We'll be okay for five minutes," said Max and stepped into the direct sunlight. "There's a fountain just over there." He pointed. "We can sit down and talk."

Nat nodded and allowed Max to take her hand and playfully pull her from between the trees. Her stomach tightened up, twisting like a balloon animal.

I hope he doesn't get mad, she thought again. At least I'm with people now. I can make a run for it if he goes all Jacob on me.

On one side of the playing field, a large group of boys played football, using their bags and coats as goal posts. Nat watched as one goalkeeper, distracted by pulling on his gloves, allowed the ball to slowly roll past him. The other team cheered while his team mates ran over, accusations flying. An old couple walked their dog down one of the tarmac pathways. The rest of the park appeared empty, including the stone fountain at its centre.

They crossed the park and reached the monument. Sitting on the edge, Nat gazed into the moving water. The image of that lone blue tentacle popped into her head. She ushered the thought away and dangled her hand in the fountain.

"Excuse me," said Max. He joined her and plunged

both hands deep into the water.

"What are you doing?"

Max sat up and opened his clenched fists. Coins—mostly dulled one and two pence pieces with the occasional tiny five—covered his palms. He grinned and quickly deposited them in his coat pockets.

Nat laughed, surprised at its sound.

"Every little bit helps," said Max and faced her. "Now, what's bothering you? I'm spoilt for choice."

"It's about your mother…" said Nat, her high spirits plummeting like a suicide jump. "… and your brothers."

Max grunted and faced the sun, squinting. "Yeah. I think we do need to talk about that. I know *I* do. Alcazar aside, the others are too fired up to talk rationally. Especially Jacob. And Whistler, he's seething with anger, but he hides it well."

Nat squeezed her fists.

"This is going to be hard for me to say." She swallowed. "I hope you understand that I had to be *sure*, Max. It would have caused mayhem if I was wrong."

Max's face clouded in a frown. "Go on."

Nat swallowed again, trying to wash down the knot of anxiety in her throat.

"The one with the white hair. The one who killed your mother, and your brothers, too, probably? His name is Johan."

Max blinked, and his eyes seemed to focus on something far away. "How do you know?"

Need to be careful, she thought.

"The night your mother died…was killed…I'd been in The Fourth Dimension with my boyfriend. Johan came in. Turned out they were friends at one point." She looked up into the sky, imagining the bar that night. "Later, Simon—"

"Your boyfriend?"

Nat nodded. "He left the bar to talk to him. He seemed upset. I followed them and found…found your mother, I think. She was on the ground, and they surrounded her."

Max's frown deepened. "Was anyone else there?"

Whistler.

"No," she said.

Standing from the fountain, Max placed his hands on his hips. Nat heard the loose change rattle in his pockets. "Why didn't you help her?"

Nat rose to her feet and faced him, struggling to meet his eyes.

"I was afraid, Max. Four guys and me? Besides, your mother got away, and that was the last I saw of her. I thought she'd be okay, but then all this happened, and…" She shook her head. "I can't keep doing this. Every time I should do something—every time the chance has come along to do the right thing—I keep quiet. Scared. Bury my head in the sand. If I'd said something sooner, maybe—"

"We didn't know they'd come after the family, Nat," said Max. "Don't be so hard on yourself."

"It's my mother all over again. I could have saved her. I could have saved your mother and your brothers."

Max watched the boys playing football for a moment. The old couple had strolled out of the park. "I can't hold you responsible. Perhaps what you're doing now is the right thing. Sticking with us and seeing this through. Don't grieve over your mistakes. Just don't make them again."

Nat thought this over. Whistler certainly didn't seem to be grieving over his mistake, but Alcazar would fix that. The tall man had a way about him, like an ancient headmaster, that could make you feel guilty with a mere glance. How could she change things? With a group of murderous thugs in pursuit, what could she do?

"There is always a right time for action," said Max. "Maybe you just haven't reached it yet." He sighed. "So your *boyfriend* will know how to find this… this Johan?"

Nat shook her head. "He used to know him, but that night he seemed afraid almost."

After a long exhale, Max slumped back against the stone wall of the fountain.

"You're angry," said Nat. "I know I should have said something sooner, but I didn't want one of you to go after them if I was wrong."

"I don't think you're wrong," sighed Max. "At every turn, this white haired guy seems to have made an appearance. At least we know who he is. I'm not angry at you."

A gentle breeze blew a dreadlock over her face. Nat subconsciously brushed it back into place. "So where does that leave us?"

Max looked back to the woods.

"You understand what they've done, and what *will* happen to them?"

Nat bowed her head, but nodded.

"We'll make those bastards suffer."

PART 3

26.

The air inside the car hung heavy with soap and aftershave. All of the boys had taken a shower and changed, keen to shift all traces of the sewer water from their skin. Johan drove, his scrubbed red hands clutching the wheel. Beside him, Simon gazed out of the passenger window in silence. Crammed into the backseat, Kev, Spence and Richie stayed unnaturally quiet.

Without taking his attention from the road, Johan let go of the wheel with his right hand and rubbed it on the seat of his jeans, sure he felt some unnoticed dirt. He indicated right at the approaching traffic lights and turned onto a quieter street.

"Are you *sure* this is going to work?" asked Spence. "It sounds…dodgy."

"Of course it's dodgy," replied Johan. "We're buying weapons. What did you expect?"

He swapped hands on the wheel, now rubbing his right hand on the rough denim.

"And you know this guy?" Spence pressed. "You sure it will be fine?"

"For the last time, yes!" said Johan over his shoulder. "Just shut the fuck up, Spence."

He waited for a response.

Spence turned and looked out of the window, his lips pressed shut.

Johan returned his gaze to the road. After a few more streets he spied their destination on the corner of a quiet intersection. He pulled the car over in front of the entrance.

"Is this it?" asked Simon, his voice low and flat. He sounded tired, uninterested. Johan knew better. He was emotionally drained, but once they returned to the sewers…

His lust will come back, just like the old days.

"Yeah," said Johan. He switched off the engine and opened his door. "Come on, then."

They climbed out of the car.

A sign, covered with adverts for Coca Cola, read "John's Supermarket" in bold white letters. The two large windows on either side of the open door were packed full of goods, restricting any view inside the shop. Items had been placed outside: a newspaper rack, bags of charcoal and wood, and a sweet dispenser. Johan wondered how the old fool didn't get robbed blind seven days a week.

"Seriously," said Richie. "A corner shop?"

"Not quite," said Johan. He squinted against the bright sun. It did little to heat up the day, and the temperature had once again plummeted. Keen to get inside, he walked away from the car towards the entrance. His well-trained pack followed closely behind.

A small bell over the door tinkled as they entered. The store was crammed to capacity with shelves, baskets and other display cases. The room stretched away from them, long and narrow. Halfway along stood the counter, surrounded by row upon row of confectionary. The sound of a mandolin drifted through the shop.

Johan carried on forwards, passing tins and toilet paper and bags of potatoes. It had been a while since he had visited John's. He'd forgotten how haphazard the shop was laid out. It could take a customer an eternity to find what they wanted.

Old John Win sat behind the counter reading a newspaper. Behind him, a large unit contained hundreds of boxes of cigarettes. Perched on top was an aged stereo, the source of the mandolin. The owner looked over his paper, eyes narrowed in suspicion.

"Yes? Help you?"

Johan looked up and down the shop. "Is Alan around?"

The shop keeper sat frozen, glare locked on Johan.

"Why? You his friend? Not seen you before." He placed his paper face up on the counter and stroked his long, narrow beard. "None of you."

"It's been a while since we paid him a visit," said Johan, smiling. He remembered how he had used his nice guy smile on that meathead Bubba at the Fourth Dimension. This old fool was sure to believe it. "We're returning some games we borrowed."

John Win's eyes darted down and up again. "I see no games."

"They're in the car."

"Hmm."

He turned his head and began shouting in rapid Chinese. Johan stood with his fake smile plastered across his face. It began to hurt his cheeks.

Come on, Alan. Get your arse out here before I knock some sense into your old man.

The shop keeper paused and listened. A few seconds later, another voice came from the back of the shop, also in Chinese. John looked back to Johan.

"You go head. In back."

"Thank you, Mr Win. I hope you have a profitable day."

The old man glowered and picked up his paper, hiding his face.

"Prick," said Johan under his breath. He walked away from the counter and headed for the rear, the boys following.

At the very back of the shop stood a meat counter, its glass display containing various piles of pink flesh, sliced sausage and cooked chicken portions. Seeing no other way forwards, Johan walked around it and through the door beyond. This led into a living room, the deep and juicy smell of the meat heavy in the air. Johan suppressed a shiver at the set up. To have all that meat so close to where you live?

Alan Win looked away from a TV as they entered. He stretched and replaced his arms behind his head. Spread out, his feet rested on the other arm of the sofa. He yawned.

"Working hard as usual, Alan?" said Johan. He stepped further inside to allow the others to enter.

"Only fools and horses work," said Alan. "Fools like the one at the counter."

A supposed mathematical prodigy, Alan had been forced into the family business immediately after college. John's plan had been for his only son to take over his own shop and expand the Win Empire. He hadn't anticipated Alan's laziness, or his skills at selling products *other* than groceries and tobacco.

"Alan, why do Chinese people always have boring English names?" asked Johan, dropping himself into an armchair.

"So you Brits can get your primitive tongues around them," said Alan. "Now cut the bullshit, Johan—" He nodded to the boys "—and minions. You want something. Let's do it. I get paid; you fuck off. How that grab you, ladies?"

Simon took a step forwards.

"Simmer," said Johan. "If we take his crap we'll be out of here quicker."

Alan swung his body into a sitting position and leaned forward, a slight smile on his face. He scooped up a packet of cigarettes from a small table and removed one.

"So what we after?" he pulled out a cigarette and poked it into the corner of his mouth. "Cheap fags? Or something stronger?" He winked. "I just got a new delivery of DVDs. Swedish. Your kind of stuff, Johan." The cigarette pointed up with his grin.

"We're going on a little hunting trip," said Johan, "out of town, you know? Thought it would be quicker to get the goods from yourself. Less paperwork."

Alan blew out a plume of smoke. It mingled with the

meaty smell.

"I see. Hunting, you say? What kind of thing would you be hunting?"

"Birds, squirrels, rabbits that kind of thing."

Removing the cigarette from his lips, Alan rolled the filter between his fingers. He watched the smoke drift up from its tip.

"Cut the bullshit," said Johan. "Do you have any guns or not?"

"You *know* me." Alan stood up and walked past them to the door. He stuck his head out and surveyed the shop. "You three. Go out there and keep my old man company."

They looked over at Johan, who nodded.

"How?" asked Kev.

"Browse or something, you fucking dummy. Just don't act suspicious or you'll get kicked out. And don't read any magazines; this isn't a goddamn library!"

Richie, Kev and Spence hastily made their exit.

"They seem like losers" said Alan after they'd gone. "Jesus."

"Just get the guns," said Johan.

Alan walked back over to the sofa and pushed it to the side. Kneeling in the corner, he peeled back the dog-eared carpet to reveal the bare floor boards.

"Old man hasn't got a clue," he said and pulled up a couple of wooden slats. Reaching into darkness, Alan pulled up a large holdall with considerable effort. It clattered on the floor.

"Those three still keeping him occupied?"

Simon looked through the doorway. "He's still reading his paper."

"Good. Johan, get over here."

Johan quickly got up from the armchair and joined Alan. He unzipped the bag.

"I never sell anything I don't know the quality of first," said Alan. He reached inside the bag and pulled out a shiny, black metal handgun. He gripped it by the handle, finger on trigger and pointed it into the air. "This is a Fort 12, used by the Ukraine police, I believe. Double action semi-automatic." The clip slid free with a small click. Alan caught it with his other hand. "Holds twelve rounds, but I've only got the one clip. If you want it, twelve rounds are all you get."

Johan nodded, his gaze on the gun.

"Also, I have this."

He put down the Fort and removed a slightly smaller handgun. Its silver finish was slightly tarnished with a speckling of rust.

"A Korth, German. Only single action. Holds ten nine millimetre rounds. Doesn't look like much, but it can still pack one hell of a punch."

"How *old* is that?" asked Johan.

Holding it up to his face, Alan had a closer look. "Around the mid eighties?"

"Christ," said Simon from near the doorway. "How can we trust something like that? I mean, look at it!"

"As long as it shoots," said Johan. "How much?"

Alan lined up the handguns on the carpet next to him. "Call it a hundred."

"Done," said Johan with a nod. He reached into his pocket and removed a bundle of rolled up notes. Counting out the desired amount, he handed it to Alan.

"How do we know they'll work?" asked Simon.

"They'll work," Johan replied. "Everything I buy from this loser works."

Delving back inside the bag, Alan pulled out a handful of short, black sticks. "You might be interested in a few of these. Flashes, like a flare. Just twist of the end and light. Twenty quid for six. Very good if you get lost in the dark."

Johan picked the guns off the floor and passed them to Simon, who once again checked the shop. The flashes, plain and smooth, felt light in Johan's hand on inspection.

He nodded and tucked three in each pocket.

Alan quickly replaced the bag back under the floorboards. The flashes were swapped for another note from Johan's pocket.

"Don't let him see you," said Alan, returning to the sofa. Johan and Simon stashed a weapon each in their jackets. "Oh, and one other thing…"

Almost through the door, they paused to look back.

"If you think I believe you're going to shoot birds, you must think I'm stupid."

Johan opened his mouth to speak, but Alan held up a hand.

"I don't care what you're doing, but you don't do it near here, and you didn't get the gear from me."

"Of course," said Johan. "You're doing us a favour."

Alan nodded. "Then you've been warned. Now, fuck off and take your pathetic friends with you."

Some people stared. Others merely turned their heads in the other direction and hurried on by. Most veered out of their way or, on some occasions, crossed the street completely. The smell might have been to blame, their appearance most definitely, but Nat knew the sad truth. The people walking down the street were too wrapped up in their own lives and problems to worry about a couple of strays. She felt, more than ever, the stranglehold money held over everyone's lives. Since when did you need nice clothes and a wallet full of money to be treated like a human being? Since high school, Nat had vowed to be who *she* wanted to be. The crazy hair, the piercings, the tattoos, these were all for herself—not to stand out or make a statement. She'd had her fair share of curious bystanders and had been treated like the seed of the devil. Some of her friends had even pushed the boundaries with their faces crisscrossed in chains and their hair cut into high Mohawks, all in the name of being unique. What she experienced now, the sheer coldness of the people on the street, *that* was being unique.

I don't need tentacles or claws to feel like a monster.

They had returned to the lair to discuss a plan with the rest of family, who all seemed to be in agreement. Even Jacob, reluctant to wait any more, had eventually succumbed. The brothers prepared things underground while Nat and Max had other matters to attend to.

They'd surfaced through the building where Nat had been taken by Jacob and Whistler. Without money, Nat and Max walked across the city. From the reactions she received from passersby, Nat was a little relieved they hadn't used public transport after all. To be locked in among them in silence, enduring their stares and their comments...

"You're quiet," said Max.

"Yes," she replied, keeping her eyes forwards. Up ahead, a small boy pulled on his mother's coat and pointed. His mother shot them a look and ushered her son away. "Just thinking, that's all."

"Hard, isn't it?"

"Thinking?" Nat smirked without humour.

"Living like this. Not easy being a true freak and drawing attention all the time."

"Which makes this part of the plan even more important," said Nat. "We're not far now."

Another twenty minutes and they arrived at the entrance to Nat's apartment block. After a quick glance around they ducked inside the door. Nat held Max back and peered around the corner to where the watchman sat in his booth.

Empty.

"Come on," she said. "Looks like we got a clear run. Besides the watchman, I haven't seen anyone else here since I moved in."

"Good. We could do with being in and out as quick as we can."

Nat cocked her head and looked at him.

"Jesus, Max. I think this is going to take longer than you expect! Follow me."

At the end of the foyer, the sign had gone from the elevator doors. Seems it had been repaired in her absence. Nat pressed the call button and waited for the familiar noise of the approaching car. Inside, their own odour became noticeable in the small space.

"This is so overdue," she said. "I mean, you don't think at the time it was sewer water and bird shit we waded through all night."

"You get used to it," said Max and sniffed.

The elevator came to a stop and the doors rumbled open. Nat stepped out into the empty corridor and walked its length to her door.

"Wait," said Max. "How can you get in? You lost your bag and everything in it."

"You're used to the smell, I'm used to being a forgetful klutz." She approached a painting hung on the left hand side of the corridor and slid her hand underneath the frame. Seconds later, she held up a shiny brass key. "So I prepare."

She unlocked the door.

The air in the flat seemed overloaded with perfume, soap and other clean fragrances that bombarded Nat from the first breath. She knew that, after spending the night in a sewer, she needed to adjust back to her own smells. Light flooded in between the open curtains.

On the window sill, a red light blinked on her answering machine.

"Simon," Nat gasped and ran inside. She pressed the play button and immediately a robotic voice declared she had four messages.

"Hey. It's me. Where the hell are you? No one's seen you and you didn't show up for work. What's up? Are you ill? Call me straight away."

Max shut the door and stood beside her. "Is that your boyfriend?"

She nodded.

The next message played.

"Nat, answer the phone! You must be in! Pick up..." A long pause. "Nat, pick up the phone! I'm coming round there."

Max scratched his beard. "He sounds really worried."

"Well, I did go missing all day and night."

She imagined how worried Simon must have been, and the idea that he came rushing over here thinking she was sick filled her with guilt.

Why the hell should I feel guilty? It's not like I was out partying...

"Nat!" said the third message. "Stop *fucking me around* and answer the damn phone!"

Max shot her a glance.

"He has a right to be upset," she said, staring at the phone. "I should call him." She reached for the handset beside the machine.

The fourth message began, freezing her hand in midair.

"God help me, Nat!"

That was all. God help *me*, Nat.

Not *are you okay?* Not *I'm worried.*

God help *me*.

"He sounds pissed," said Max, eyes full of deep concern. "Maybe calling him isn't such a good idea right now."

Her hand lowered. "I think you're right. Besides, you know he doesn't really have anything to do with Johan, don't you?"

Max nodded. "Hungry?"

She smiled.

They rushed into the small kitchen and, like a couple of burglars ransacking a joint, they rummaged through every cupboard and the fridge. Two ham and cheese sandwiches were messily assembled, eaten with chocolate bars, and washed down by milk straight from the bottle.

Mouth still full and chewing, Max picked up a plastic bag he'd found and began to drop biscuits, bread and other food items inside.

"You don't mind, do you?" he asked, spraying out crumbs.

"I'll do that," said Nat and took the bag from him. "Of course I don't mind. But we came here to do something and we're running out of time. Everything you need should be in there."

"And you're sure this is okay?"

"Yes! We've been through this, Max. I'll have everything else sorted by the time you're done."

Almost grudgingly, Max turned and left the kitchen.

After she'd loaded the bag to bulging, Nat left it on the worktop. Full and happier than she'd been all night, she returned to the living room and sat down on the cream sofa.

Forget the stains. It'll clean.

On the coffee table in front of her lay a mirror. She'd used it to get ready the previous morning, before her search for Agnes. Using its stand, Nat tilted the mirror until she saw her own face. She studied the dark flesh below her eyes and the dirty speckles across her cheeks. Her piercings easily slid out, and Nat lined them up on the table after each fiddly job.

From the bathroom the first whoosh of the shower sounded.

"Well? What do you think?"

Nat, lost in her own thoughts, hadn't heard the shower

switch off.

In nothing except a towel, Max stood just outside the bathroom door. His lean body glistened in a slight sheen of sweat from the humid bathroom. With his diet and all the climbing and walking, his chest and arms were packed with small, tight muscles. His long hair, now clean and sleek, had been tied back. He smiled, his mouth clearly visible now that his bushy beard had gone. A tiny nick on his chin was its only trace.

"Whoa," said Nat. "You look so... so different."

Max smiled wider.

"I have a problem, though," he said.

Nat closed her eyes and shook her head for a second. Staring at Max had induced a mild trance. She opened them again and instantly found his firm stomach.

"Y-Yeah?"

"Yeah," he said. "I think I'll need to wear more than a towel. This is all to avoid attention, remember?"

"Of course," said Nat. "Sorry. I must be tired after everything. I'm not quite with it. I'll get you some clothes."

She walked past Max, smelling the soap and fruity shampoo that seemed to radiate from him, and into her bedroom. Searching through her wardrobe, she found some of Simon's clothes lying on the bottom. She balled them up and brought them back into the living room. Max stood, still clutching the towel.

"How did you shave?" Nat asked and handed him the clothes.

"There were scissors and a razor in there. I'm not so feral. I know how to use a razor."

"But...that's a lady's razor. Didn't you notice it was pink?" She sat down on the sofa again.

"Yeah, but they all do the same job."

"I use that to do my legs and..." She glanced down.

Max's gaze lowered down her body and quickly shot back up to her face. "Shit. Sorry."

"You will be," said Nat and turned away. "I *meant* my armpits."

"Oh," said Max, sounding relieved.

"Max. You… you scrub up well."

"Thanks. I'm going to change."

Nat listened to him head back into the bathroom.

Half an hour later, Nat and Max, both clean and dressed, sat side by side on the sofa.

He'd amazed her once again. The tramp had gone. Beside her sat a handsome, twenty-something man in a blue t-shirt and designer jeans. He looked as though he'd stepped out of a trendy bar, not rat infested sewers. Only the lack of a strong aftershave stopped him from being a typical lad-about-town. That, and the beaten boots he still wore.

Nat had dressed more conservatively. She, too, wore jeans, with worn trainers and a thick sweater. She didn't plan on taking a swim in the sewers again, so the sweater seemed a wise choice. If the plan went smoothly, she'd be outside anyway. All the piercings and makeup had gone, and her hair, still dreaded, was tied back neatly. Looking in the mirror she had expected the worst but had been pleasantly surprised.

"Forget about *me*," said Max. "You look great. I didn't know you had a face under all that metal."

Nat looked into the mirror again. "Yeah. I don't know what I thought. Maybe that I'd be too plain underneath it all?" She placed the mirror on the table. "But now we look like typical, law abiding young people. Nothing to see here."

"Think it will work?"

Nat's heart sunk to the pit of her stomach. "It should, if you're right about Johan."

"I think I am," said Max, leaning back. "First mother, then Herman and Edgar…" He swallowed before continuing. "For years, we've avoided being found. In fear that we'd be hunted down, one by one. And that is *exactly* what's happening."

"Simon told me a few things about him. Going to the police will be the last thing he'll do. He has his pack with him. That's all he needs."

Max stroked his chin, like his fingers missed the beard.

"He'll be back to finish the job. Definitely. At least to check the bodies and make sure there are no more of us *freaks*." He spat the word out. "Is it wrong to look forward to this?"

Nat took his hand.

"I suppose it is, but it's the only way to bring an end to it all. Maybe things will turn out differently."

Squeezing her hand, Max looked out of the window.

"I doubt it. Jacob wants, *needs*, his revenge. Look, it's nearly dusk. We'd better make a move."

With a deep breath, Nat stood up. "We're going to hell for this."

"Too late," said Max. "I've been there too long."

27

The building loomed before them, not just an empty derelict shell. Now it was the entrance to the labyrinth. In a long leather jacket, Johan stood in front of the dark doorway. With the memories of the horrors still fresh in his mind, the hard bulge of the gun within his jacket brought a little more confidence. The pack of cleaning wipes in his jeans pocket reassured him further. He feared the dirt and germs as much as the creatures.

Kev removed the other gun from his coat and studied it again.

Simon had become withdrawn and silent. Even now, he stood a little away from the group and stared out into the street. Skin paled and eyes bloodshot, Johan imagined he'd spent a good part of the day in tears over his girlfriend. He couldn't admire this emotional mess; it turned his stomach. The friend he'd known from school had slipped away, his drive and passion drained out by a *girl*. She'd looked like a leech, designed to suck out a man's desire in many ways.

At least she's dead now, thought Johan. He smiled.

"Spence," said Johan.

Spence looked up over the rim of his glasses.

"Keep a look out. Anyone comes near, give me a shout. Keep your weapons out of sight."

Spence nodded and patted his hip. A butcher knife was stashed in his belt. The flashes bought from Alan were hidden in a small bag on his back.

With another glance up and down the desolate street, Johan approached Simon from behind. His friend didn't flinch at the touch of Johan's hand on his shoulder. He continued to stare forwards in silence, focus locked on the dark abyss ahead.

"Simon?"

His friend slowly turned his face towards him. "Are we

going in now?"

"What?"

Simon swallowed and spoke his words even slower, more clear. "I said, are we going in now?"

Johan gazed into his eyes, two shiny white orbs, ringed in red.

He's gone. He's so gone.

"Yes, I think we're ready to get this over with. Are *you* ready?"

"I can rip them apart with my bare hands," Simon said. "Fuck being prepared. I *am* prepared." He swung around and grabbed Johan firmly with both hands. "Do you know, Johan? Do you know she would never, ever hurt me? And that I've left her all alone down there with those things?"

"It isn't your fault," said Johan. "She shouldn't have come down here in the first place."

"All day, we've done nothing. I'm not waiting any longer."

He turned from Johan and crossed the threshold of the building. The solid darkness swallowed him up.

"Wait," Johan called, about to follow.

"Guys!" said Spence. "Someone's coming!"

Johan stopped his advance short of the doorway.

A man, around the same age as himself, walked down the opposite side of the street. Passing between the bright patches the streetlights cast on the pavement, he looked on ahead, paying them no attention.

"Must be cold," Richie said in almost a whisper. "He's got no coat on."

"Like I care," replied Johan. He watched him walk all the way along until he turned the corner, out of sight. "Right. Come on before someone else comes strolling along. We *are* carrying, remember."

With the three following behind, Johan walked through the doorway and into the building. The dank smell of rotting wood instantly filled his nose.

Beside him, Richie clicked on the flashlight he carried. Without a firearm, Richie had brought the flashlight for its weight, intending to use it as a solid club should he need to. The circle of light darted around the space in front of the group.

Eyes blinked in the light.

"Get that out of my face," said Simon. "And who was that guy outside?"

Richie quickly did as ordered and lowered the beam to the ground.

"No one," said Johan. "He didn't even look at us."

"Richie. Point your flashlight around the ceiling," said Simon. "I think I heard something when I came in."

"Okay." Richie aimed the beam upwards, finding the corner of the room. The brick appeared green and crumbled.

"Go along," said Simon. "I'm sure—"

A pigeon fluttered in the path of the beam. It perched on an outcrop of brick high up, near the ceiling.

"Just a bird," said Richie. He directed the flashlight along and revealed more birds, all lined up and watching them. Some occasionally tucked their heads under their wings, nibbling at the feathers. "I'm surprised we didn't hear them sooner."

"Have we forgotten why we're here?" asked Johan. "We all know what we have to do, and yet we stand around? Fucking bird watching?"

"He's right," said Simon, already heading for the ladder. "Let's go."

Johan headed down the narrow shaft first. Gun in hand, he struggled to grip the slippery metal ladder. He opted to only use his left hand and aimed the gun straight down into the darkness with his right.

He remembered Kev talking about a film called *Alligator* last time. Wasn't there a scene where it crawled up a shaft like this and dragged the poor bastard away?

He peered down his side and tightened his shaking grip on the gun. Images of teeth and bulging eyes filled his head.

Fuck this, he thought, and quickly climbed down. I'm the most dangerous thing down here now.

Feet splashing down in the few inches of water, Johan quickly checked both directions of the tunnel.

"Get a move on," he called up the shaft.

A few minutes later, the group stood in the tunnel. Simon stared down to the left.

"How're we going to find our way through?" asked Spence. He held a sleeve over his nose. "We could get lost down here. We were lucky last time."

"Don't worry about that," said Johan. "We'll find a way."

The stench overpowered him for an instant, working its way down his throat and into his lungs. Staggering, Johan placed his hand on the wall and recoiled at the slime under his skin.

"You okay?" asked Richie, shining the flashlight in Johan's face.

"Yes," he snapped. "Get that light out of my eyes!"

The beam dropped and returned to studying the walls and darting back and forth along the tunnel.

Hidden in the shadows, Johan pulled a wipe from his pocket and cleaned his hand.

Kev spoke up. "Which way did we go last time?"

"Left," said Simon. "It was definitely left."

Kev removed the gun from his jacket and held it at his side.

After throwing the used wipe on the floor, Johan walked through the group.

"Richie, I need some light over here."

The flashlight beam meandered across the floor, and Richie joined him. Side by side, they walked about halfway down the tunnel, the flashlight fixed on the darkness beyond.

Apart from the steady *drip-drip* of unseen water and the splashes of their boots, the tunnel remained quiet. Johan noticed the lack of rats. The vermin had swarmed here in abundance only the night before. Why had they gone? Could they have sensed what was coming and made a sharp exit?

They reached the junction. Both men leaned through and, with flashlight and pistol, swept the next tunnel. Happy that nothing waited for them on the other side, they climbed through and waited for the others.

"This looks just like the last one," said Kev. "Are you sure we came this way? I remember the walls being different last night."

"We can't be lost so soon," said Johan. "And we *did* come this way."

A knot of tension tightened in his throat. He too remembered the walls being more rotten and wetter.

This is definitely the right way, he thought. Maybe we're all a bit nervous. It's fucking with our minds.

Simon had already headed down the tunnel.

"Wait," Johan said and ran to catch up. He grabbed Simon by the elbow and pulled him to a stop. "If we all go off like that, we *will* get lost!"

Simon glared at him. "So, you don't hear that?"

Johan frowned. "What?"

"Listen."

The dripping continued, and the boys fidgeted behind them.

"Ssssh!" Johan hissed and waved his hand holding the gun. They instantly fell quiet.

Up ahead, enveloped in the darkness, something splashed around. At first, Johan thought it had a natural source, a leaking pipe or trails of water converging. But no, the splashing sounded different, more random... playful even.

"Richie," Johan whispered. "Up here. Now."

Richie jogged up and held up the flashlight.

The patch of light slowly slid up the floor of the tunnel, reflected off the surface of the water, and created a dancing pattern on the ceiling.

Still the splashing continued.

Richie slowly raised the flashlight higher. The light moved up and away from the water. The beam shone directly into the total darkness beyond.

"Can you see anything?" asked Richie, the flashlight gripped tight in his trembling hand.

"No. Get closer."

The flashlight lowered. "What?" said Richie.

Johan turned his head. "You need to get closer. We can't see anything."

Richie's eyes widened.

"You gotta be fucking kidding me! Are you nuts?"

"No. Go on!"

"There could be one of those things down there!"

Johan cracked a smile. "We sure hope so, right, Simon?"

Simon, attention on the splashing noise, stayed silent.

"There's no way I'm going down there alone," said Richie, shaking his head.

Johan pointed the gun down the tunnel. "Just keep to the side. If anything *does* come out? I'll blow its head off." He shoved Richie. "Now get moving."

Richie staggered the first few steps and stopped. He looked back, and Johan motioned forwards with the gun. Back pressed against the mouldy wall, Richie shuffled along, frequently glancing back.

Johan held the gun with both hands and spread his feet shoulder width apart. He pointed the gun down the tunnel, imagining a figure waiting, hidden in the shadows. His finger squeezed the trigger slightly, but then relaxed.

Come on out, he thought. I can *hear* you…

Richie had only moved a little way down the tunnel. His flashlight beam cut through the darkness, revealing more dirt-streaked walls. Still, the end of the tunnel remained cloaked in shadows.

Splash, splash, splash.

"Get a move on, Richie," said Johan.

Kev and Spence had joined them and watched in silence. Kev had his own gun at the ready, and Johan was glad to see he had it trained down the tunnel.

"Just a few more steps," ordered Johan.

The flashlight beam quivered as it crept along the walls and floor. Richie's hand jerked around, failing to hold it steady.

The splashing stopped.

Richie immediately came to a halt and stared back. "I… I think it's gone."

Johan cocked his head and listened.

"Damn it," he said and lowered the gun. "There's nothing there."

Richie released a long sigh and slumped back against the wall. "Thank Christ."

A growl rumbled down the tunnel.

Johan's back quivered like a feather of ice had tickled the skin. He snapped the gun back up.

"Shit!" cried Richie and fled back to the relative safety of the group.

"Get behind me," said Johan. "All of you."

The splashing resumed, closer.

"Richie, the flashlight! Get the light up!"

Richie fumbled and nearly dropped the flashlight. Wailing, he held it up, the beam sweeping down the tunnel.

From out of the shadows, a small dog stopped in the circle of light. It barked once and, with a playful hop, scampered back into the darkness.

28

The night transformed the warehouse into a place of shadow and twisting dark corridors, like a forgotten funhouse of the dead. A breeze whistled through the enormous room unchallenged. It wheezed through the rafters. They groaned. The rows of roosting birds seemed unperturbed.

Nat sat low against one of the walls, sure some monstrosity or murdering rapist would find their way through the vast building and grab her. She shivered and pulled her coat tighter. The hatch, which opened into the deep shaft to the sewers, stood in front of her.

A hand grabbed her shoulder.

Her heart leapt, and she rolled to the side, her arms and legs frantically beating the floor. Rolling onto her back, she prepared to fight off her attacker.

"Nat?"

She blinked. "Max?"

"What's wrong with you?"

"What's wrong with *me*?" she cried, her heart beat making her gasp. "What's wrong with *you*?"

"Sorry. I thought you heard me come in." Max sat down against the wall.

"Well, I didn't," said Nat and slowly crawled back towards him. "It's too creepy in here. I can't believe you left me alone."

"I can't believe you stayed," Max replied. He slid his arm around the back her neck and pulled her in for a playful squeeze. "I thought you'd be long gone."

"I did think about it. But I can't. You know?"

Max nodded.

Nat leaned in against him and dipped her head. Her face rested on his chest. The sweet smell of her shower gel still hung strong. His skin felt warm through the t-shirt. "Did you find them?" she asked.

He stayed silent for a moment.

"Yes," he said finally. "They were at one of the entrances. It didn't take long to track them down."

"How many?"

"Five."

"Hmm. Sounds like they got back up. One more bastard."

"It's not the extra guy that worries me," said Max. He idly played with one of her dreadlocks. "They know what they are up against now, or at least, can take a good guess."

"And?"

"What if they're armed?"

Nat's stomach dropped on hearing the words. She almost gagged. "What?"

"They acted suspicious when I walked by. More than they should've. One of them has a bag. Who knows what's in it?"

"And you think it could be guns?"

Max nodded. "Or worse."

Nat pushed up away from him and sat up straight. The splashing from the hatch seemed to have grown louder. She guessed that the water level had risen again.

"Then we have to go down there," she said. "We have to go down there and warn them."

"I told Alcazar. We know where these guys are, but they can't find us, not unless we want them to. As long as things stay that way, my brothers have the upper hand. We have abilities that will match any gun. He was having a long talk with Whistler. I think they have something planned."

Nat frowned. "You don't sound too worried. It's like you want this."

"I *do* want this. After all they've done…" His eyes narrowed. "It's Jenkins I'm worried about. I don't think killing a small dog is beneath them."

With her hand on his knee, Nat gave him a squeeze. "He's small and it's dark down there. I'm sure he'll be fine."

Max placed his cold hand over hers.

"Max?"

"I'm sorry," he said and quickly removed it. "I'm just… worried for Jenkins."

"Don't be silly," said Nat. She reached across and took his hand, placing it back in position. Their fingers interlocked.

"Is this okay?" he asked.

Nat smiled. "We're only holding hands. I think I can live with that."

"I'm sorry," Max said again. "Just with your boyfriend and everything…"

"Like I said, we're only holding hands. Nothing wrong with that. I think we need a little comfort right now. See it as the calm before the storm, eh?" She released a long breath. "Those messages he left have me worried. He sounded so angry. I've never heard him like that before."

"How long have you been together?"

"A year…and two days."

Max patted her hand and stood up. "Wow."

"Wow? That's not long."

Stretching his legs, Max said, "It is for me."

"A year?"

"Yeah. Anything really."

Nat also stood, forgetting the dark surroundings for a moment. She rested her hands on her hips. "Anything? Come on, don't tell me you've never been with anyone."

Max scratched the back of his neck and lowered his eyes to the floor. "It's always been kind of hard in my situation." He coughed. "We shouldn't be talking about this. Maybe I'm just nervous. We need to be quiet and wait for the others…" He glanced at the hatch. "Or whoever else should make it through to here."

Nat removed her coat and sat back down. "You're right. Come here."

Max returned to her side and slid down the wall to sit. Nat, using her coat as a blanket, draped it over them. Beneath, their hands found each other.

Nat laid her head on his shoulder and closed her eyes.

29

Turn after turn, junction after junction. Apart from a few small differences—the lighting hub had been smashed and a shopping trolley lay in the corner—this tunnel looked like all the others. If the dog had been sent to confuse them and lead them deeper into the network, the little bastard had done its job.

Furry little shit. When I catch up with it…

"Johan?" asked Simon. "You think the dog belongs to them, don't you?"

Johan nodded and resumed his trek down the tunnel. The water had long since penetrated his boots and the fetid water chilled his feet. He imagined the bacteria swarming into his pores.

Should have put bags on, he thought. Plastic bags over my feet would have stopped this.

He planned to use the wipes on his feet at the earliest opportunity.

"Where do you think it's taking us?"

"To them," Johan replied. "Hopefully."

The rest of the group followed along behind. The beam from Richie's flashlight bobbed along the walls.

A bark echoed from ahead.

"It's close," said Johan.

Instead of another wide pipe, the tunnel ended in a high archway, the bricks black with congealed grime. Light flickered from within and cast long shadows across the walls and water.

The bark came again.

"It's in there," said Johan. He shifted the gun to his other hand and wiped the sweat from his palm.

Keeping to the side, he edged closer to the archway. He held up a hand, signalling the others to stay back.

The boys watched, silent.

Johan arrived at the threshold of the next room.

"Kev," he hissed. "Get up here."

Weapon at the ready, Kev crept up to Johan's side, slowly sweeping his feet through the shallow water. He stopped on the other side of the archway and peered around the edge.

"See anything?" asked Johan.

"No," said Kev. "Not really."

"On three?"

Kev blew out a long breathe that made his fat round cheeks bulge out even more. His skin had blossomed the colour of raspberries, and sweat glistened across his brow. He nodded and raised the gun higher.

"One…" Johan whispered. "Two…"

The dog barked.

"Fuck…three!"

Both of them swung around the sides of the archway and stepped into the room.

The chamber, larger than Johan had thought, appeared to be a kind of central junction. Several matching archways led away from the circular hub. At its centre, the floor opened up in a wide pit.

Johan swept the point of his gun across the room. After a few seconds, he lowered it, realising they were alone. No freaks. No dog.

"Clear," he said.

Looking relieved, Kev walked further into the room, craning his neck to gaze up.

"Jesus! Look how high it goes."

"Watch it!" Johan yelled.

Kev glanced down in time to stop before the pit.

Standing still, Johan allowed his stare to rise and explore the upper reaches of the room. It reached an impressive height and ended in a wide grate. Through the slits in the metal, light seemed to flutter in and decorated the smooth walls with twinkling patterns.

"Those look like street lights," said Johan. "It must go all the way up to the road."

"Then we *are* lost," said Simon on entering the room. "We haven't been in here before." He glanced around. "How the hell are we supposed to find their lair now?"

"That damn dog has led us this far. We'll find them."

Richie and Spence filed through the archway. The group stood around the pit a little way apart from one another.

"My God," said Spence. "Look at this."

With his attention on the missing dog and the street above, Johan hadn't noticed the walls. At first, it looked like random scrawls and shapes had been painted, the work of a child or artistic genius. As Johan took a few steps forwards, he saw the true picture. The walls showed a street at night. High up along the walls, chalk lanterns shone down, illuminating the revellers gathered beneath. Higher still, a pale lemon moon glowed amid a tapestry of stars, all arranged in a purple wash of sky. The filtered light from the grate brought the stars to life.

"Incredible," Johan gasped.

On the painted streets, every inch of wall had been covered in faces and figures locked in eternal happiness. Some danced, others laughed. Some made love while more people watched and clapped and cheered. At first, it reminded Johan of a Lowry, with so many people crammed together. He took another step forwards and rested his hand on the cold plaster.

"How long must it have taken to paint this?" asked Richie, staring up in wonder.

"A real long time," said Johan and moved his hand.

From underneath, a face smiled up. Its eyes shimmered with green and just below its hairline sprouted two curly horns.

Johan frowned and leaned in for a closer look.

He wasn't sure if the figure was male or female. It fit with the rest of the party goers in swirling red robes.

Looks like a demon has snuck in, thought Johan.

He looked away and found another scene to the immediate left. Within a group of women in white gowns, a tiny figure danced a jig. He appeared all of three foot tall, his naked body covered in spines. His arms seemed to end in long, sharp points of bone. The women smiled down on him.

"This is fucked," said Johan, looking around. Countless monsters lay hidden among the normal people in the painting, all laughing and joking together. "This is some kind of sick fantasy."

"Yes," said Simon. "I see them too. One of *them* must have done this." He ran a hand over the paintwork. "You think this is what they want? To fit in?"

The idea turned Johan's stomach, and he backed away from the wall, careful of the pit behind.

"Distractions," he said. "That's what the bloody dog was doing! They could all be making their escape while we stand around gawking."

"He's right," said Simon. He looked crest-fallen, guilty for allowing himself to be misled. "Let's keep going."

"But what about the dog?" asked Spence. He gestured around the chamber. "It could have gone through any of these archways. There are what, eight tunnels from here?"

Johan did a quick count. Spence was right.

"Then I don't know," he said after a moment's thought. "I guess it's down to luck."

A shrill whistle rang out and swept around the circular room like an aural tornado.

"What the hell was that?" asked Richie. "Dogs can't whistle."

"Then it wasn't the dog," said Johan and readied his weapon.

The boys waited around the pit and listened to the rise

and fall of the whistling crescendo. It stopped abruptly.

"Here we go, boys," whispered Johan. "Get ready…"

The whistling started anew, this time with a cheerful tune.

"What?" hissed Simon. "What the? It's a song… I know it but can't quite…"

"'Going Underground,'" Johan growled. "This fucker is playing with us."

Behind Kev, something darted past in a dark archway.

"There!" shouted Johan and raised the gun.

Kev ducked, his arms over his head. "Shit! What are you doing?"

Johan hesitated, his finger poised on the trigger. He blinked and stared into the darkness beyond Kev.

"Put the gun down!" said Simon. "What the fuck are you doing?"

The whistling stopped, and Johan gazed through the empty archway. He slowly lowered the gun.

"Someone was there," he said. "I swear."

"You could have killed me!" said Kev and jabbed his gun in Johan's direction.

"Ah shit!" said Spence. Everybody looked in his direction. He pointed to another of the archways. "There. Something… something was there."

Johan pushed past Richie and walked around the pit. He stopped at the archway and took a cautious glimpse through the other side. The tunnel led away into shadows.

"There!" Richie shouted.

Johan returned to the circular chamber in time to see Spence jump away from an archway, his feet landing on the edge of the pit. His arms wheeled in the air, and for a split second, he fell backwards. Spence bent and stepped forwards, away from the void.

"For fuck's sake," said Johan. "Keep away from the hole and keep an eye out. I wanna nail this bastard."

Backs pressed against the wall, the boys fell quiet and

listened to the dripping water from the tunnels. Kev's breathing rattled from his chest. His face had returned to a deep red.

Johan expected one of the leering, painted faces which he now saw in abundance around them, to lean out of the walls and attack. Like old portraits in ghost stories, their eyes seemed to follow him.

Should *not* have fucked with us, thought Johan. He adjusted the sweaty grip on the gun. Should not have fucked with us *at all*.

Movement. In a tunnel to the right.

Johan stayed still, convinced it was the light playing tricks. If their pursuer wanted to show himself then—

"Listen," said Simon. "I can hear him."

Johan blocked out the gasps of the others. He heard faint footsteps splashing through water.

"Think he's going away?" asked Simon.

Johan glanced at each archway.

"I don't think so. I know why we were led here." He pointed. "I think we're supposed to end up in the pit."

"Shit," said Kev. "I nearly did, too."

"Sssh!" Simon hissed.

The footsteps diminished, sounding further and further away.

"He's definitely going," said Kev. "What do we do now? The dog's gone too."

They all looked at each other across the gaping hole, waiting, Johan presumed, for his decision.

A figure emerged from the shadowed archway next to Kev and grinned.

The sight jolted Johan.

Kev stood oblivious. He held the gun loosely at the side of his thigh, pointed at the floor.

The figure leaned towards him, hand outstretched, reaching for the weapon.

Johan recognised him, the stinking, weird tramp, still

in his stupid striped jumper.

Without hesitation, Johan levelled his weapon.

The tramp made it to Kev's gun, and the touch sparked the big man into action. He whipped his hand away, and the weapon slid free. Striking the floor, it slid towards the edge of the pit, scraping the concrete.

With his face still dominated by the toothy grin, the tramp ducked back into the shadows.

Johan squeezed off a shot. The gun jumped in his hand, recoiling hard. The sound of the blast was a chisel blow to his ears and head.

A brick in the archway exploded in a cloud of grey dust.

Johan cried out and clutched his wrist. "Dammit!"

"What happened?" Richie cried.

"Did you get him?" asked Spence.

Johan pushed past them all. His wrist throbbed. "Move!"

He pounced through the archway. The light revealed the first few metres of the tunnel but darkness cloaked everything beyond that. An odd whistled note drifted back to Johan accompanied by the frantic sound of footsteps. He barely heard it with the ringing in his ears.

"Shit," said Johan. "He's gone."

"Are we going after him?" asked Richie. "You want the flashlight?"

Johan stared into the darkness for a moment, blood rushing in his ears. Hunting down the maggot would be fun but may lead to another wild goose chase.

I think we were getting close. This painting... we must be close to their territory.

He growled from the back of his throat.

This is *all* their territory, crawling around in the filth and rot.

"Johan?" said Simon from around the corner. "What are we doing?"

"We keep going," Johan said and walked back into the chamber. "We'll find him another time. We always do." He carefully manoeuvred around the pit.

"Do you think he's with *them*?"

Spence's words slipped between his thoughts with the sharpness of a scalpel. Johan stopped and turned back to the group.

"You think he could be?" He rubbed his forehead. "All the times we beat on him. He could be one of them?"

"I don't think so," said Kev. "I mean, look at him. He looks *normal*. Those other ones..." He forced the words between his trembling lips. "They were freaks, really messed up. He's not a monster."

"Maybe so," said Johan. "But it's something to chew on. Get the gun."

Kev nodded, his chin and throat wobbling. His piggy eyes darted back and forth in his head, searching the floor. "I can't see it."

"Here." They all looked to Simon, who stood clutching the gun. He held it close to his face, studying it intently. "It nearly went down the hole."

A hush descended on the group. After a moment, Johan spoke up.

"Give it back to Kev."

Simon raised his eyes to glare at him over the firearm. "What?"

"You heard me," said Johan. "Give the gun back to Kev."

Simon slid his fingers around the handle and lifted the gun, the barrel pointed at Johan.

Needles seemed to dot up Johan's back. His balls twitched. He reaffirmed his own grip on his gun.

"We're wasting time," he said, voice without a quiver. "Kev, get the gun and let's go."

Kev hesitantly stepped forwards and held out a hand.

Simon slapped the gun against Kev's chubby,

glistening palm and released the handle. Kev snatched it back.

Johan faced the wall to hide his relief. He closed his eyes and blew out through pursed lips.

I can't let this happen. Not after coming so far, he thought. We need to find these things soon. He can vent his frustration on their mangled hides.

He opened his eyes and found several naked figures decorating the wall directly in front of his face. A woman with several eyes was sandwiched between two men, heads tilted back in bliss. A tongue hung from between her lips and reached down her body, its tip wrapped around the base of a penis.

"We're going," said Johan. His stomach bubbled, and a sour taste flooded his mouth. He coughed to try and shift the acid. "This place is too fucked up."

30

Johan entered the lair, alert for the slightest sound of rushing water. The level barely reached the top of his boots. He prayed it stayed that way. The pram lay in the opposite corner from the night before, now a tangle of twisted metal. The room stank more than ever. What appeared to be mud lay in pancakes around the floor.

"Come on," said Johan and headed in further. "It's empty."

He inspected the cell and the various bits of furniture while the others climbed through the entrance.

Simon, gazing around, joined Johan.

"I can't believe we finally found this place and *they've gone.* Who knows how big this network is." Simon squeezed his fists. "They could be anywhere."

Johan kicked a wooden stool that had fallen on its side. It skidded across the floor and struck the wall.

"Then we carry on looking, all night if we have to." He nodded towards the pipe leading out through the opposite wall.

Abandoning the lair, they stepped up into the pipe and ducked through. Kev struggled with his climb. Storing the gun in his belt, he grabbed the offered hands of Spence and Richie. They pulled him up.

The pipe emerged out into yet another tunnel

"I'm getting sick of this," said Johan.

The tunnel had dried out completely and the boys walked without splashing and slipping. No rats scampered against the walls or sat on the various ledges of brick, washing their whiskers. The absence of any noise, especially the dripping water, added to the claustrophobic grip of the tunnel.

"I'm going to need you, Rich," said Johan, taking the

lead again.

Richie caught up with him, the flashlight already turned on.

The two paused at the exit pipe and listened.

"Anything?" Johan whispered.

Richie shook his head.

"Then get some light down there. Be careful. These fucks seem good at coming out of nowhere."

Richie immediately leaned into the pipe without a word of complaint.

He's getting confident, thought Johan. He's realised what this is. A hunt.

Johan waited behind Richie, ready to grab his jeans and pull him out of the pipe at the first sign of a struggle. After a few seconds, Richie shuffled back out.

"It's big in there," he said. "I can't tell you how big. The flashlight beam will only reach so far."

"Signs of life?"

"No," said Richie and swept a hand through his hair.

About to clamber through and inspect for himself, Johan hesitated.

Can't rush in. Need to play this slow. They might have traps like the fucking *Goonies*.

"Spence?"

Fumbling with his bag, Spence peered over.

"Pass me one of those flashes. I wanna see exactly what's in there before we go strolling in."

Spence smiled, apparently glad to be of some use and eager to use his flashes. Releasing the clasp on the backpack, he pulled out one of the black tubes.

"Here," he said and tossed it to Johan, who caught it one handed.

"Let's see if these were worth the cash," he said and unwrapped the top. Revealing a coil of wire, Johan gave it a sharp tug.

The tip burst into a bright pink flame, spraying out

sparks that drifted to the floor.

"Fire in the hole," said Johan. He threw the flash. It spun through the air and entered the pipe. Johan leaned in and watched it land with a hollow clack.

"Well?" asked Simon. "Anything?"

Johan peered inside.

A thick, circular pillar appeared pink in the cast light. The far wall remained in the shadows.

"It's a vast room," said Johan. "I can't see how big it is. I'm going in. How long do you think those things last?"

"Maybe a few minutes," said Spence. "I suppose we should get moving."

Sure that the gun was safely stored in his coat, Johan grabbed the upper lip of the pipe and hoisted his body from the floor. Swinging his body in feet first, he shuffled through the pipe. For a worrying moment, his legs poked out of the other end, dangling out in the open. He hurried along. His feet landed on the floor with a splat.

A groan escaped from between his lips.

The room smelled worse than all the tunnels combined. His boots slipped in the brown carpet of sludge. He held out his arms to keep from falling.

His reflexes took over, and Johan dove back towards the pipe. He gagged. Holding onto the sides, he dipped his head and took a deep breath.

Fight it! After everything you're going to let this stink beat you?

This isn't just a stink, it's like someone took a dump in my mouth!

"What's in there?" Richie shouted, the shape of his head silhouetted and framed in the pipe. "Anything?"

"Oh yeah, it's a dream," said Johan and coughed a glob of phlegm on the floor. "Get your arses in here."

Standing in the pink light, Johan blocked out the glare with his hand and gazed upwards. The room equalled the height of the painted chamber. The light cast by the flare failed to reveal the ceiling. Barely visible, the far wall lay about thirty feet away. A wide tunnel, different from all the others, led into even deeper darkness. Like giant fingers of stone, the various pillars reached up into the shadows. It reminded Johan of a church, despite all the years since he'd entered one.

The beam wavered from the pipe, and a moment later, a hand emerged holding the flashlight. Johan grabbed Richie's wrist and helped to pull him free.

"My God," said Richie, raising his free hand to his face. "You didn't tell us it stank so bad."

"Suck it up," said Johan and suppressed a choke.

Something fizzed at the centre of the room.

Johan nearly fled for the pipe, expecting a sudden rush of water. The flickering pink light flashed brighter for a second before sputtering out with a low hiss. Johan blinked, the flashlight beam in his face.

"Put that down," he said.

Richie lowered the flashlight. The beam revealed his boots and the layer of shit around them.

"What we going to do?" Richie asked.

"The flash ran out, that's all. Cheap shit," said Johan. "I'll get another. Keep a look out."

He headed for the direction of the pipe. Despite it being so close, Johan held out his hands to feel for it. The tips of his fingers found the rounded edge.

Richie shrieked.

"Rich?" said Johan, his heart thumping. "What happened? Rich?"

The flashlight beam found its way onto his face again.

"Sorry," said Richie, his voice drifting out of the darkness. "It was just one of those pillars. Took me by surprise."

Johan closed his eyes and sucked in a deep breath. "Fuckwit."

He retched, the foul stench invading his body.

Need to clean need to clean need to clean…

"Johan?" Simon called from the other side of the pipe. "What's going on in there?"

"Nothing," Johan replied, composing himself. "Just Richie being a dick. Get another flash from Spence. This one ran out."

Johan waited in the dark. Shuffling sounds came from the pipe.

"Guys?" said Richie. "I think I hear something in here."

The flashlight beam pointed upwards and bobbed from pillar to pillar. Johan watched it over his shoulder.

"Probably just you," he said. "Simon, give me the flash."

Emerging from the pipe, Simon pressed the cylinder into Johan's palm. Without hesitation, Johan unwrapped the tip and yanked the wire. It burst into a glittering flame. Holding it at the bottom, Johan raised the flash over his head.

Simon pulled himself out of the pipe and almost fell head first onto the floor. With a twist of his body at the last moment, his feet hit first with a splat. On the borders of the rosy light, Richie still aimed the flashlight beam upwards, studying each of the pillars.

He glanced over. "I swear I heard something up there," he said.

Ignoring him, Johan called through the pipe. "Kev. You come through next. Spence can give you a hand up."

Muttering from the other side.

"What's the hold up?" Johan said, concerned the stripy jumper freak had returned.

"Spence doesn't want to be left alone," said Kev.

"Well tell Spence he can come through next, but expect me to beat the piss out of him if he does. Understand?"

More whispers echoed through the pipe.

"I'm coming through," said Kev after a few seconds. "Can you grab the bag?"

Johan reached in and removed Spence's bag of flashes. He placed it on a reasonably dry patch of floor underneath a wide plastic pipe. The pipe rose from the floor, bent ninety degrees and ran into the wall. Its surface had congealed with dust and grime over the years. Its joints looked rotten.

Leaving Simon and Richie to investigate the room, Johan began the arduous task of pulling their fat friend through. For one sickening moment, Kev became lodged in the pipe and refused to budge. After some wriggling and frantic pushing and pulling, he popped free. Johan tugged him out by the arms and kept hold to stop him from falling in the muck. Short and thin, Spence slipped through the pipe with ease.

"I think Rich's hearing things," said Simon. "There's nothing. Let's keep moving. We have to go through here." He pointed to the wide tunnel leading away. "There's no other way out."

"Makes the choice easy then," said Johan. He crossed the chamber and approached the tunnel. On closer inspection, the entrance had been covered with a mesh, like chicken wire.

"I think we're getting close," he said and touched the cover. "Who else would do this?"

"Can we get through?" asked Simon, joining him.

"I think so." Johan bent down and hooked his hands underneath the edge. Thankfully, it hung a few inches from the floor. His hands stayed relatively clean, but he couldn't help but think of the bacteria crawling over the metal. With a pull, the wire curled upwards and the gap between the floor widened.

"Help me," he said. "This is pretty tight."

Simon leant a hand and the metal curled easier. They created a sizeable gap.

"You guys," said Johan. "Go under while we hold this thing up."

Richie, giving the upper reaches of the room one, final, cursory glance, clicked off the flashlight and walked over. He ducked underneath and waited on the other side. Kev quickly followed. He removed the gun from his belt.

"Wait," said Johan as Spence stepped forwards. "We forgot the bag."

Spence's eyes darted from the bag back to Johan. "But…"

"We'll still hold this open," said Simon. "But get a move on."

"Yeah," said Johan. "Come on, Spence. Move it!"

Spence grunted and headed for the other side of the room, his head held low. Johan willed him to hurry up. His arms ached from holding up the coiled wire.

The flare fizzed, and its flame sputtered out.

"Guys?" said Spence from the pitch darkness. His voice quivered. "Guys? What's going on?"

"Keep still," Johan called. "Richie?"

"Yeah?"

"Get that flashlight on. Quick."

He listened to the fumbling from within the wire mesh. Closing his eyes made no difference. Johan imagined how Spence must feel, out there on his own.

The light blinked on, and the beam darted around the floor. It found Spence's boots and rose up his body, finally revealing his face. His eyes narrowed. The beam reflected in his lenses as burning circles of light.

"There you are," said Johan. "Rich, find the bag."

The beam lowered and explored the floor. The plastic pipe appeared in the light.

"That's it," said Johan. "The bag's underneath. Spence, go and get it."

A figure dashed through the beam without a sound.

Richie darted the light around.

"I'm coming back!" said Spence, sounding on the verge of panic.

"No," said Johan. "Keep very still. It's that fucking tramp again! I knew he'd follow us. If you can't see him, he can't see you." He released the wire mesh. "Simon, drop it. Let's sort this out here and now. Rich? Find the bum."

Holding out his arms, Johan wandered across the chamber. He aimed for the last spot he saw Spence. The light continued to drift around the room, revealing dank corners, dripping mould and skeins of rust on the walls.

"Spence, go and get the bag. I'm close."

The light beam shot up one of the pillars.

"Rich?" asked Johan and stopped.

"I *told* you I heard something earlier."

"Just find him. He's a retarded tramp in a striped jumper, for fuck's sake!"

Footsteps echoed close by in the darkness.

"I think I'm at the bag," said Spence. "I can feel the wall, but I can't see it."

"Richie," said Johan, "point the flashlight his way."

He looked back as the beam found Spence. "Spence! Look out!"

"What?" Spence paused, his hand inches above the bag.

Behind him, the short figure raised a knife that glinted in the light.

"Spence! Move!" Johan cried.

The figure whipped its arm down.

Spence froze, face caught in the light. His mouth dropped open and a wailing scream echoed around the chamber.

"Spence!"

The figure behind Spence leapt and shot straight up. Somehow, it managed to turn in the darkness and dropped in from the side, feet first and pressed together. It struck Spence hard in the shoulder. He fell into the shadows.

Bang!

The noise boomed in the chamber.

Hissssssssssssssss...

That's impossible, thought Johan. How...?

The flashlight beam whipped around the room for a second and found another of the short creatures clinging to the wall. Suspended upside down, it grinned at Johan, showing off long and pointed front teeth.

Oh shit, there's two of them!

Behind him, Richie shrieked. Darkness swallowed the creature.

Johan struggled to remove the gun from his inside pocket. His friends yelled from the tunnel mouth, and the strange hiss continued from the corner. He looked up while his hand pulled on the gun handle.

In the corner, the circle of light centred on him, Spence lay over the pipe. The old plastic had cracked. The back of Spence's coat was slit down the middle. Blood gushed out and flowed over the black leather.

"Fuck!" Johan screamed. He tugged the gun free and held it out with both hands. "Richie, find the damn things!"

The flashlight beam slid away from the motionless Spence and slid along the shit-caked floor.

Johan stepped back and brought the gun closer to his body. In the total darkness, one of the things could be standing inches away, ready to strike the pistol from his hand. The hissing had grown louder, and Johan smelled something other than the suffocating stench of the room.

"They won't be on the floor! The walls... the walls!" he yelled.

Whimpering, Richie raised the flashlight. The light snaked across the wall. Exploring the darkness to the left revealed one of the creatures lurking on a pillar. It scuttled away with the grace and speed of a spider.

Simon and Kev began to shout.

"Shut up!" said Johan.

They immediately fell quiet. Despite their hushed moans and sobs and the hiss from the broken pipe, Johan strained to hear anything else.

"Spence?" he tried, praying that his friend would reply.

"Mmm?"

"Spence!" Johan cried.

"What's…?" He sounded dazed but alive.

Johan readjusted his sweaty grip on the pistol. "Stay there. I'm coming to get you."

"My back hurts, Johan."

"I bet it does. One of those bastards has a knife. You'll be fine, Spence. Just stay there."

Richie shone the trembling light back on Spence. He'd straightened up some but still leaned over the busted pipe. His glasses lay cockeyed on his face. He coughed.

"That… smell…"

"I know," said Johan, quickly advancing. He kept his head tilted up, expecting one of the things to leap down at any second. "Something's leaking out of that pipe. Smells like gas," he said, keen to keep Spence talking. "I'm nearly there."

Johan began to cough, too. The gassy smell overpowered the low, dank stench of shit and stuck to the back of his throat. The gun held out in one hand, he clamped the other over his mouth.

A cry nearly made him squeeze the trigger.

Back at the tunnel, Richie pointed the flashlight at Simon. Both he and Kev screeched.

Simon grappled with one of their attackers, each gripping one another's shoulders. Despite towering over the creature, Simon's face contorted in effort. He gritted his teeth.

The creature hadn't held a knife after all. Sticking out from its hands, close to Simon's face, long, hooked claws ended in sharp points, one streaked with dark blood. The creature's face had a flat nose and severely slanted eyebrows. The pointed chin and its hair gave the face a triangular look. The protruding teeth reminded Johan of Nosferatu or one of the countless disease-ridden rats that lived down here.

Johan aimed the gun.

"No!" cried Kevin.

Behind Simon, barely visible in the beam of light, the second fiend dropped down and lowered its hand in one smooth motion. It jumped and disappeared. Simon roared and dropped to his knees. The first creature slashed a claw across his face, opening Simon's cheek, before leaping away.

"Simon!" Johan lowered the gun.

"Get Spence," gasped Simon. "Before they come back." He took a deep breath and coughed. "Get him!"

Richie shone the flashlight over to Spence.

Careful not to slip, Johan quickly crossed the chamber. The overpowering reek of gas hung heavy in the corner. Johan felt the gas rushing out as he passed the wide crack in the pipe. The colour had drained out of Spence's face, and Johan wondered whether it was the halogen-yellow of the flashlight or loss of blood. He remained lurched over the pipe, spluttering and hacking.

"Come on," said Johan, grabbing Spence's arm. He slung it around his neck and placed an arm around his back.

"Aargh!" cried Spence, his body jerking.

"Suck it in," said Johan, his arm slipping on the blood-smeared leather jacket. He pulled Spence off the pipe. "Come on! You gotta help me here. We're going to suffocate if we stay in here much longer..." He glanced up into the darkness. "Or worse."

Spence staggered against him and took a few steps away from the pipe. Johan dragged him along. Shadows jumped in and out of the light.

Spence slipped. Johan hoisted him back up.

"Come on, Spence!"

He groaned but continued. "My back... it hurts too much..."

"We're almost there."

"Here!" said Simon. The flashlight found him. Clutching the back of his right leg with one hand, he strained to lift the wire mesh with the other. His cheek was washed with blood. It flowed from the neat line running from ear to nose under his eye.

Johan tugged Spence a little further. His boots slid on the floor.

"I can't hear them!" he said. "Where are they?"

"We don't know," said Simon. "Just keep moving."

In Johan's hold, Spence jerked to a stop.

"Spence? Keep going! Keep moving!"

The flashlight beam moved and illuminated Spence's face inches away. Eyes wide, he blinked once and coughed. A thick jet of blood sprayed out and dripped from his bottom lip.

"Spence?"

"Oh my God!" cried Richie. "Behind him!"

Johan looked over his shoulder.

One of the creatures grinned back at him, hand buried deep in Spence's back. It snapped its arm back, revealing a dripping claw, a red, glistening coil hanging over the hook. Spence wobbled and spat out another stream of crimson.

"No," said Johan. Spence's body fell limp. "No!"

Two hands shot down out of the darkness and clamped down on Spence's shoulders.

From the tunnel, the others screamed anew. Johan stared upwards. The creature's eyes shimmered in the shadows. It clung to a pillar.

"Let go of him," Johan growled and tightened his arm around Spence. He pointed the gun upwards.

Spence rose in the air, the creature effortlessly lifting him up. Its claws penetrated Spence's coat and sank in deep.

Johan wailed and, forgetting about the gun, used both hands to grab onto his friend. Even leaning back, the creature managed to pull both of them up.

Spence jerked free and shot up in the air. His butcher knife, freed from his belt and, without a chance of use, fell to the floor. Johan fell back and landed on his hip. Pain flared down his leg.

"No!" He held out a hand.

In the flashlight's glow, Spence's legs dangled, his feet swinging back and forth.

"Johan! Get over here!" screamed Simon.

Johan clambered to his feet.

Suspended above, Spence's legs began to spasm, like a marionette dancing a jig. A wet ripping sound accompanied the dance and almost drowned out the hiss of gas. Blood poured down in abundance.

Johan froze and stared at the scene a few feet away.

"Johan!" Simon bawled.

Fingers tight around the handle, Johan raised the gun. His hand shook.

"Bastards!" he screamed into the dark. "You fucking freaks!"

Simon continued to scream to Johan, joined by Kev and Richie. The flashlight beam darted around the chamber, flitting between Spence's twitching body and the figure on the wall, slicing chunks out of their friend while his companion held him from the pillar.

Lubricated by blood, Spence's glasses slid down his nose and fell from his face.

Johan grabbed him by the ankle, choking on the fumes.

"Bastards!" he screamed again. The cascade of blood showered down. "Fucking bastards!"

The creature performing the butchery glanced down and smiled. It plunged a hand into the hollowed-out body and pulled out a fist-sized lump of dripping red meat. With a chuckle, it flung the organ down. It struck Johan across the forehead and flopped off his face.

He cried out and rubbed the blood from his eyes. Arms around his waist brought on a further bout of cries. He beat the gun handle against the hands of his attacker.

"Let it go," Simon yelled in his ear and tugged him away by the waist. "He's dead."

"Fuckers!" Johan screamed and levelled the gun.

"No," Simon placed a hand on the pistol and forced it down. "You might set the gas off!"

Simon pushed him past Spence's hanging body and towards the tunnel. Johan flopped against the wire mesh, eyes still blurred by blood and tears.

"Get him in," cried Simon.

Richie and Kev attempted to lift the metal. Achieving a few feet from the floor, they held it steady.

Using a hand against the back of Johan's head, Simon forced him down. Kev grabbed his arms and hauled him through.

"Spence," he pleaded. "We can't leave him!"

"He's dead," said Simon, crawling through. "No way could he still be alive. They've... they've fucking carved him out!"

Something struck the wire mesh and landed on the floor with a splat. The creatures laughed, a high-pitched chatter.

"We need to move," said Simon. "Spence is doing us a favour keeping them occupied."

Johan gagged.

"Carry him," Simon ordered. "Quickly!"

Kev, his face bright red and shiny with sweat, bent down and grabbed Johan. He picked him up over his shoulder.

"Shit," Richie murmured. "Oh shit!"

"What?" shouted Simon.

"Look."

Richie directed the flashlight beam in the corner. One

of the creatures, done with carving up Spence, stood over the discarded bag, in front of the broken pipe.

"The flashes," said Simon and shook his head. "We forgot about the flashes!"

In the dark, something hit the ground and the second creature joined his partner.

Over Kev's shoulder, Johan lifted his head. He imagined Spence's corpse landing on the floor in a tangled mess of broken limbs, face lying in the shit. His head swam, his vision doubled.

"Damn them," Johan said, voice weak.

"Move!" said Simon.

Kev started his dash down the tunnel.

Head still raised, Johan bobbed up and down on Kev's wide shoulder. Richie lingered, flashlight pointed at the monsters in the corner. One of the things reached into the bag and removed one of the black, short cylinders. It seemed to frown and look to the other.

"Run!" said Simon, tearing down the tunnel.

Johan dropped his head, his chin striking Kev in the back. His fat friend didn't seem to notice and carried on running down the tunnel.

"Keep moving," said Simon.

Richie also fled. He shone the flashlight ahead, revealing a bend further on.

Their frantic footsteps echoed off the tunnel walls, the sound of hissing gas more and more distant.

"How... much... further...?" Kev gasped.

"Keep going," replied Simon.

Johan lifted his head again and looked back down the tunnel.

"Spence!"

The end of the tunnel flashed.

"Wha...?"

The ground lurched.

Kev fell, spilling Johan onto his back. Simon toppled

forwards. Busy staring back, Richie tripped over him and rolled onto the floor.

Whoosh!

Gritting his teeth, Johan raised his head from the floor.

The end of the tunnel had erupted into a giant fireball. Blue at the core, yellow flames licked along the walls of the tunnel, heading straight for them.

Johan flopped back and closed his eyes.

Got them, he thought, his mind hazy. We got the bastards...

The hot air rushed across his face.

31

Nat snapped awake, feeling the last of the tremors ebb away beneath her.

"What was that?"

"I don't know," said Max beside her. "It didn't feel like much. We're right above the machine room. Maybe one of them kicked in."

Nat sat up and wiped her face.

"You nodded off," said Max. "Seemed to be having a hell of a dream, but I figured you needed your sleep." He placed an arm around her.

"I miss anything?"

Max chewed on a nail. "Not much," he said, his words slightly muffled. "It's been about two hours. Surely *something* should have happened by now. I mean the twins, Jacob… how can something not have happened? They were all ready for tearing them to pieces."

"It's a big network down there. Maybe we lost them."

"My brothers know the sewers better than anyone. We've had our entire lives to explore. They wouldn't lose them."

The hatchway looked the same as before.

"We could go down," said Nat. She snuggled deeper into Max, enjoying his warmth. "Alcazar is in the machine room, isn't he? It wouldn't take long to head down there and see what he knows."

Max shook his head. "Watch. It started while you were asleep."

Nat waited, unsure of where to look.

Her answer arrived by the flapping of wings. Seconds later a bird shot out of the hatch. It circled the open space of the warehouse before gliding out through the open door. It screeched into the night. The moment it left the building, two smaller birds flew inside. They headed straight for the hatch and disappeared inside.

"My brother seems to be keeping an eye all over," said Max. "I think if we were needed, he'd send a message. We should sit tight."

"And do what? We aren't helping anyone just sitting here."

"We have to be patient," said Max. "Play the waiting game. Hopefully, we can let them have their fun and we won't get involved."

"But I thought you wanted revenge?"

"I do, but my brothers are so much better at this than me. I can get my vengeance through them. Keeping you up here, keeping you safe, that's my priority."

His hand sought hers and their fingers interlocked.

"So, what did you dream about?"

"I can't remember now," said Nat. "Something about giant rats chasing me in a maze. Weird, huh?"

"Did one of them have white hair?" said Max, all trace of humour sapped from his voice.

"No. I don't think so."

"Good. Then it wasn't a prophetic dream then."

"I hope not."

"Come on," said Max. "Let's give our legs a stretch."

They stood, still holding hands. Max pulled her in close to him.

"Just around here," he said. "I still want to be within earshot of the hatch."

They walked slowly, careful not to stand on any of the discarded wood or rope that lay scattered on the floor. Heading up the ramp that led to the raised platform, they both turned and looked out across the empty room. More birds flew into the hatch, passing those on their way out.

"Don't you wish we could have met at a different time?" asked Nat. "A different place?"

"No," said Max. "Despite what's going on beneath our

feet, right now, I'm here, with you. I wouldn't have it any other way. You know why?"

Nat squeezed his hand. "Why?"

"Because right now, I'm here, with you. To change things, well, who knows what would have happened."

He stepped in front of her, stroking her arm with his free hand.

Nat stared back up at him, her heart thumping fast. It filled her with a fiery tingle reaching down to her stomach.

Kiss me.

Forget Simon and his fucked up old friends.

Forget freaky brothers and living in the sewers.

Just kiss me, Max. Kiss me!

He gently reached for her chin and tilted her head upwards.

In allowing him, Nat became a little light headed. Her fingertips tingled.

Kiss me! Her mind continued to beam out physic messages to Max, in the vain hope he would hear them. Kiss me right here, right now.

32

Johan wheeled his head and slowly opened his eyes. He rubbed his cheek.

Simon stood over him, blood seeping from his opened cheek. "Thank God."

"Where... where are we?"

"Still in the sewers. You haven't been out for long."

Johan sat in a wooden chair, his back to a cluttered desk. Maps and charts of various networks and circuits decorated the walls. The floor had been covered with wet footprints, darkening the concrete. The sharp and sour smell of the tunnels had been replaced with the dark and earthy smell of oil.

"This isn't the sewers," he said. "What happened?"

Richie, leaning against the wall in the corner with Kev, glared at him. "You don't remember? About Spence?"

Hanging from the ceiling, glasses sipping from his face, the fire.

"Of course I remember," he said and dipped his head.

"He didn't even want to come," Richie snapped. "Hell, I don't think any of us wanted to after what happened the last time. What are we doing down here?"

"None of you had a gun held to your heads," said Johan. "You knew what you were getting yourselves into."

He raised a hand to his head and, touching a wet patch, brought his fingers down for inspection. A smear of dark brown coated his fingers. Even inches away from his face, Johan smelled the biting stench of shit. He released a high moan and pulled out his wipes. He hastily scrubbed his hands, discarding the soiled wipes on the floor one by one. Once his hands had been washed, the skin red and the nails cleaned, Johan worked on his face. He scoured his skin. More used wipes drifted down to the floor. He pulled more out of the small plastic packet and advanced to his neck.

"Johan?" said Richie. "What the fuck?"

"Just… a… minute," he replied and removed the last two moist wipes. He screwed them up and shoved one up each nostril. Twisting each around, his nose filled with lemon-scented fabric. Done, he threw them both on the floor.

"Feel better now?" said Simon.

Johan breathed in deeply through his nose. "Much."

"Fuck this," said Richie. "We're going."

"Right," Simon agreed. "The sooner we find Nat…"

"Ha!" cried Richie. He shook the flashlight like a club. "Wake up, mate. She's dead, long dead. Those things have sliced and diced her by now. Those two looked well fed to me, right Kev?"

He nodded in reply.

"Bet they carved your piece and served her on a goddamn platter!"

"Shut it! Don't you dare speak about her like that," screamed Simon.

Richie brandished the flashlight. "It's *your* fault we came down here in the first place and your fault that Spence is… is…"

Johan closed his eyes. "Dead."

"We couldn't just leave her!" said Simon.

Richie snorted. "We were helping you. Paying you back for everything you did for us. You think we give a shit about one of *them*? About some *cheap slut*?"

Johan opened his eyes.

Simon darted across the small room and pushed Richie in the chest. He staggered back and struck the wall. The flashlight fell from his hand.

"I'm gonna kill you!" Simon yelled and slammed him back against the wall.

Blond hair flapping about his face, Richie's head struck with a solid thunk.

Let them get this out of their system, thought Johan. Might fire them up enough to finish the job.

Snarling, Simon dove forwards for another attack.

"I wouldn't," said Kev. He held the gun at arm's length, fat finger wrapped around the trigger. He aimed it at Simon's face.

Looking pumped with adrenaline, Simon glanced at Richie.

"I said, I wouldn't." Kev held the gun steady.

Simon backed up, hands to his chest.

"Really. Take it easy."

"You okay, Rich?" said Kev, his eyes still locked on Simon.

Rubbing the back of his head, Richie said, "Yeah. Let's get out of here."

They both backed towards the doorway on the far side of the room.

"Where are you going?" asked Johan, suddenly worried. "We can't split up!"

Kev pointed the gun at him.

"Our friend is dead because of *you*. Both of you. Simon wants to rescue his dead girlfriend, and you, what the hell is going through *your* head?" Kev wiped the gathered sweat from his face. "I mean, what the hell, Johan? We should've called the police or something the moment, the *very* moment, we knew about these things. And what did we do? We bought guns and explosives and came down here like fucking exterminators! We're going, and the first way up we find, we're out of here."

Kev and Richie left the room. Their footsteps echoed away down the adjoining corridor.

"Come on," hissed Johan. "We have to follow them."

"Leave 'em," said Simon. "We don't need the hassle."

"No, but that gun would come in useful."

Johan stepped towards the doorway, but Simon held out a hand and stopped him.

"You don't think she's dead, do you?"

Yes, thought Johan. Dead, carved and eaten.

"She's down here somewhere," said Johan.

Simon sighed. "Paying me back, Richie said. I hope that's not true. What happened in the past, especially the night we met…"

Johan walked to the doorway and turned back.

"This isn't the time. We'll lose them."

The corridor seemed to sway back and forth with the overhead bulbs swinging on their chains. Vibrations throbbed through the walls and floor. Spying Richie and Kev at the end, Johan hurried on. Simon stayed close behind, his walk marred with a severed limp.

"You okay?"

"Yeah," said Simon. "One of those things got me in the leg. Hurts like a bitch, but it doesn't feel too deep. How is it?"

They paused and Johan inspected the back of Simon's leg. The blue denim was soaked in blood. The fabric had been sliced in a clean vertical line just behind the knee.

"It's better than your face," he said after a second. "You'll live."

They pressed on and followed the two boys around a corner. The corridor led into a large room about half the size of a football pitch. The air buzzed with noise and movement. Various machines stood in a grid separated by narrow walkways and safety railings.

At his side, Simon attempted to talk, but Johan pressed a finger against his own lips.

Richie and Kev had reached the centre of the room and stood looking around. Despite the throb of the machines, Johan heard them quite clearly.

"What is this place?" asked Kev.

"Some kind of pumping room, I guess," said Richie. "I don't care. It's civilisation! Like the workroom we were in. If people work down here, there must be a way up."

Johan gestured for Simon to follow. They walked to the left, up against the wall, careful to keep their footsteps light. Their route led them into the corner. From behind a thick branch of pipes that reached into the ceiling, they peered around.

"What do you think?" whispered Simon.

Between the machines, Johan managed to keep Richie and Kev in sight. They stood between two of the larger pieces of equipment.

"We'll follow them. I have a feeling we're close to the end of the line. Richie's right. This isn't the sewer anymore. They wouldn't stay this close to people. If they find a way out, we'll join them and talk them into another sweep through tomorrow night."

"And Nat?"

He slapped Simon on the shoulder. "Don't give up yet. Who knows what else we'll find tonight."

A wide shadow slid between two of the machines close by.

"What was that?" whispered Johan. "You see anything?"

Simon shook his head.

"Keep a look out," said Johan. "I don't think we're alone in here."

At the centre of the room, Richie and Kev stood close together. Johan and Simon still able to see and hear them.

"I can't see a ladder or anything," said Kev.

"There has to be." Richie leaned over the rail of the closest machine and unhooked a clipboard that hung from the side.

"Careful," said Kev and pointed at the yellow and black warning signs. "Looks like this thing has a high voltage."

"After everything we've been through tonight, I don't think a few warning stickers will put me off." He waved the clipboard at him. The few sheets of paper attached fluttered. "See? I'm alive."

He ran a finger down the first column of the first sheet.

"The latest date on here is yesterday. Someone was down here to sign this, so someone had to get back out. We can't go back, because it's blasted to pieces. Can you remember seeing a ladder or stairway yet?"

"No," said Kev.

"No. Which means the way out has to be further on. Let's go."

A shadow swept over the ceiling.

Richie and Kev cried out and stopped.

"What is that?" hissed Simon to Johan.

Johan moved around the pipes for a better view of the far wall.

Standing in an archway, a figure stood holding the folds of a long coat outwards, like a giant pair of stained brown wings. The stronger light from behind threw his shadow upwards. He watched the boys at the centre of the room with narrowed eyes lodged above a long, hooked nose.

Johan ignored the movement behind Kev and Richie. His attention remained locked on the tall, wiry man.

"It's another one of them," said Johan, keeping his voice low as possible. "This one looks normal compared to the others."

"So, you're finally here," the man said, the words cutting through the hum of the machines with authority. "I expected more. Where is the one with the white hair?"

Johan's heart rocketed.

"He... he..." Kev looked to Richie for support. His friend merely stood staring at the man. "We left them behind."

"And why did you do that, young sir?"

"Look," said Richie and showed his hands, "we don't want any trouble. Please."

The man cocked his head. It reminded Johan of a bird.

"Don't want any trouble? You come down here, with guns, and don't want any trouble? You should have thought about that before you killed our mother and our brothers..."

Mother? thought Johan.

"I sent my younger brother to scare you off, to give you a chance to make the right choice. He was there, the night you murdered our mother. I'm sure you remember. He's easily memorable in such a loud jumper, of course. Let's just say after some encouragement, he's finally standing up for himself. He won't rest now until debts have been paid...young sirs."

Johan gritted his teeth. That whistling freak. Of course! They were all brothers. One big fucked up family.

"We're sorry!" Kev pleaded and took a step back. "Please, just let us go. It wasn't our idea. We were made to come!"

The man seemed to consider this for a second.

"Okay."

Richie and Kev glanced at each other.

"You seem like nice enough boys. Perhaps you got caught up in something you couldn't control. Am I right? One big misunderstanding."

They frantically nodded.

"Unlike my brothers," the man continued, "I'm not a violent person. I'm not going to stand in your way..."

Simon glanced away. "Is he really going to let them go?"

"Sssh," whispered Johan.

The man dropped his arms. "But my friends... *they* aren't so understanding."

A sound rose from behind him, a rapid flapping, the beating of wings. Johan expected a swarm of bats to emerge from some unseen cavern.

The air filled with movement. Birds of various size and shape swept around the room and swung between the machines. Kev and Richie raised their arms against the flurry of beaks and feathers.

"My God," said Simon and fell back. "Look at them."

Johan held out a hand and pulled Simon back to his feet.

"Let's move while they're distracted."

At the centre of the room, Kev dropped to his knees and flopped onto his front. With the gun still in his hand, he covered the back of his head. The birds swooped low, striking him in the sides, back and legs. He yelped with each attack, his body curled up tighter and tighter on the floor.

"Get them off me," he cried. "I didn't do anything!"

Behind him, Richie had managed to stay on his feet. He spun on the spot and beat his arms against the marauding birds. They flew into him again and again, ricocheting only to turn in the air and dart in for another strike. His blows rarely found their targets. A few of the birds, larger species like the pigeons, were unlucky enough to be brought down. They flapped around on the floor, injured or startled. One or two had the tenacity to peck at Richie's boots or hop over to Kev and take their beaks to his face. It brought more cries and begging.

Johan and Simon crossed the walkway in silence and hunkered behind the next machine.

A large seagull plunged from the air and hit Richie in the forehead. He reeled and staggered backwards.

"Have fun, my friends," said the man. "Peck out their eyes!"

He pressed his lips together and surveyed the two boys.

Two more birds, fluttering around each other, separated at the last moment and struck Richie in the shoulder and stomach. He howled and tumbled back against a railing.

"Good," said the man while nodding. "Good…"

The circling birds seemed to grow restless and arched

around the room with increased vigour.

"Shouldn't we help them?" asked Simon.

Johan held his hand up. "Wait."

The birds had remained silent up until now. Like a signal had passed between them, they began to squawk and whistle, adding to the chaotic noise of beating wings. They flew faster around the room.

Richie, blood emerging from a cut on his forehead, stared up at the birds and whimpered. A cluster of birds headed towards him. He turned and vaulted the rail.

The man laughed.

Kev, granted a reprieve as the birds seemed to lose their interest in him, raised his head from the floor. "Richie, no!"

The birds dropped from the air in abundance, striking Richie over and over. His arms weakly floundered in front of him and missed all of the feathered assailants. Following another hit to the face, Richie's head snapped back. The slash had opened further. Blood draped over his skin like a thick, liquid curtain. It flowed into his eyes, down his nose and into his mouth.

Johan darted across to the next machine. Simon hobbled along behind.

The bombardment increased. The birds flew into Richie in quick succession like a boxer's combo. Rarely did a second pass without a scratch to his skin or a harsh peck to his body. No longer screaming, he fell back, spent of energy.

The moment his body touched the machine it jerked. A sound like a cracked whip snapped through the air, instantly followed by a shower of white sparks. Richie jolted again, his face screwed in a twisted grimace.

Still the birds attacked. He threw his head back and thrashed his arms.

The machine threw up another cluster of sparks like a Roman candle. They brightened the room for a second before fading out on their descent.

"Richie!" Kev called from the floor.

With one final spasm, the electricity pitched Richie forwards. His stomach hit the railing with enough force to send his body rolling over it. Flipping in the air, he fell to the floor on his back.

Kev wailed.

"What's going on?" Simon hissed.

Johan moved to the side for a better view. From a little way back, he saw the damage the machine had done and closed his eyes.

Richie's face had blackened. The skin looked like charcoal had been smudged across it. His hair was burnt and curled at the tips. Still twitching, his hands had tightened almost into claws. A gurgle escaped Richie's throat and, with a final shudder, he lay still.

"Richie?" said Kev. He stayed low; the threat of the birds still circled the air.

"Shame," said the man. He walked forwards. "Such a shame."

He strode passed Kev, who cowered on the floor in a fetal position.

Shoot him! thought Johan. He's right next to you, shoot him!"

The gun hung uselessly on Kev's finger.

The man's long coat brushed against Kev. He approached the burnt body of Richie and knelt down.

"A pity," he said, flipped the body over and reached for one of the birds unlucky enough to be pinned by Richie. He held the tiny body against his cheek and stroked the back of its head with a fingertip. One by one, he picked the fallen up and held them in his arms, as if he had merely dropped a clutch of apples rather than murderous birds.

"Has he... has he killed Richie?" asked Simon. He'd limped next to Johan and watched with his jaw hanging low.

The circle of birds, emitting a final burst of cries, broke their uniform circular flight path. They all headed for the doorway in which they'd entered. A second later and they had gone. Their calls echoed and grew more distant.

The tall man continued to pick up those that remained.

Johan removed the gun from his jacket.

Damn it, Kev. Shoot him!

Behind the crouched man, Kev, swaying on his feet, slowly rose. He aimed the gun at the man's back.

Continuing in his morbid task, the man seemed to have no idea of the poised weapon behind him.

"Wait here," said Johan. "I'm going to make sure he gets what's coming to him." He raised the gun. "Birds or no birds, this fucker's dead."

Simon stepped back, eyes fixed on something over Johan's shoulder.

"What?"

With a trembling hand, Simon pointed. "Look."

Johan turned.

A huge figure stood in the entrance, his back lit by the swinging bulbs of the corridor beyond. The light gleamed off his bald, mould-coloured head. His wide chest rose and fell deeply.

"Jesus," said Johan and staggered backwards. His back thumped a machine and he quickly hid behind it. "What the hell is that thing?"

"We... we should warn Kev," said Simon, voice shaking.

Johan waited a few seconds, watching the beast in the doorway.

"It doesn't know we're here," he whispered finally. "Let's keep it that way."

"B-But Kev—"

"Kev's dead already. But at least *we* can get away."

And return with more firepower, thought Johan, appalled by the creature. With bombs and flamethrowers and fucking machine guns. Anything to wipe out the rest of these freaks.

The creature stepped forwards, revealing its uneven eyes and protruding, broken teeth.

"Behind you, brother," it said.

The man with the armful of dead birds glanced up.

Behind him, Kev turned, his knees shook and his body wobbled. He blinked away sweat. The gun quivered in his hand.

Staring at the ogre that had entered, Kev sobbed and raised the gun.

The creature growled.

Kev screamed and pulled the trigger.

The sound punched through the air. Johan and Simon flinched. Immediately a metallic *ting!* rang out.

"Missed," said the beast.

The man had gathered all the remaining dead birds and stepped over Richie's charred corpse, retreating to the side.

"Run, Jacob," he cried. "Don't be a fool!"

Kev squeezed off another shot. This time, a spark jumped from the wall next to the creature.

Jacob roared and, ducking his smooth head, stormed down the walkway at Kev.

Seeing the thing charging at him like a gorilla, Kev wailed and squeezed the trigger again and again. The gun jerked around in his hand.

Bang! Bang! Bang!

The first bullet caught Jacob on the outside edge of his shoulder. It ripped straight through in a spray of dark blood. The skin and flesh left in its wake hung in a messy flap. The impact, which would have spun any normal man like a top, didn't faze Jacob. Stone faced in determination another bullet struck him in the stomach. The tattered and dirty shirt seemed to pop over his stretched abdomen in a red splattering. Still, Jacob steamed on, now halfway across the machine room.

"Help him!" said Simon.

Johan stood his ground and watched.

The next two bullets shot wide and hit the machines. The gun clicked. Empty.

Jacob, stepping on Richie's corpse, thrust a large hand out. He grabbed Kev by the throat. In one effortless motion, the ogre scooped Kev off the ground.

The gun dropped from Kev's hand.

"Christ!" cried Simon.

Johan struck him in the upper arm with the handle of his gun. "Shut up," he hissed. "You want it to come after *us*?"

Swept through the machine room, Kev clutched at Jacob's hand, struggling to unwrap the thick fingers from around his throat.

On reaching the wall, Jacob pressed Kev against it. The thud echoed around the room.

Kev kicked, his feet inches from the floor. Held at arm's length, his desperate attacks flailed and missed.

"Waited," said Jacob. "For you…"

He pulled back his free hand and curled it into a fist.

"No," Kev choked, struggling to shake his head within the tight grip. "No, please!"

Jacob's fist struck Kev in the stomach and ripped through his t-shirt, punching into the sagging bulge beneath the fabric.

Kev thrashed against the wall, heels beating against the brick.

Jacob pushed in further. Viscera poured down and slapped the floor between them. With his arm submerged almost up the elbow, Jacob grunted and jerked Kev up like a giant ventriloquist dummy.

Kev coughed out a glob of blood which hit Jacob in the face.

The monster licked his lips.

"Oh no," groaned Simon. "Oh *shit!*"

Smiling, Jacob twisted his hand and pulled it out with a wet sucking sound. Dripping with gore, he held up his fist.

An off-white tube, speckled with blood, hung from his hand and trailed down between Kev's legs. The other end hung from his open stomach, amidst a collection of other entrails, ripped veins and clustered yellow fat. It looked like organic tape had been pulled from a cassette and suspended in a tangled mess.

Jacob squeezed the tube and a clear liquid burst from its split sides.

"That's it," said the man with the birds in the shadows. "He has to learn."

Simon gagged and spat on the floor.

Kev's high-pitched warble faded, like someone slowly turned down his volume dial, until he hung in silence, his body shuddering.

Dropping the section of long intestine, Jacob lowered Kev.

He slid down the wall, his boots, sodden with blood, touching on the floor. Jacob removed his hand from Kev's throat. Something purple and crisscrossed with blue veins dropped out of the young man's stomach and hit the floor with a splat. Somehow, Kev managed to stay on his feet, slumped against the wall.

The man carrying the birds stepped forwards, his sharp nose sliding out of the darkness first. He cocked his head. "I think he's still breathing."

"Move!" whispered Johan.

Together, he and Simon dashed behind the final machine in the row.

Jacob clamped a hand on Kev's left shoulder and, with his other hand, grabbed the upper arm. The ogre's bicep tensed. Kev's arm cracked as it twisted.

More blood dribbled from Kev's mouth.

Working it loose, Jacob twisted Kev's arm further, back and forth. The skin split just below the shoulder, instantly spattering the surrounding wall and Jacob's front. It seemed to be the breakthrough Jacob needed. He pumped the arm up and down. The fingers twitched.

With a scraping noise, the arm popped free of the socket. Jacob held up his trophy, a clear ball of bone protruding from the tattered stump. Blood jettisoned from the haggard flesh left on the body. It painted the wall in a long streak.

"Don't look," said Johan under his breath. "Keep moving, Simon. You don't want to look."

Johan himself wished he hadn't seen. He knew that no matter what happened, that first crack would echo in his mind for decades.

Jacob flung the arm down the walkway. It landed a few feet away from Richie's body.

"More!" cried the birdman.

Jacob released Kev and staggered back. He hunched over, hand pressed to his own wounded stomach.

Kev, his spasms over, slipped down the wall and collapsed in a sitting position. His head drooped forwards.

Sucking in a deep breath, Jacob straightened and stretched his arms. Approaching Kev again, he grabbed the remaining arm, stepped back, and planted a foot against the shoulder. Jacob arched his back and pulled.

Johan and Simon quietly moved along the final row of machines, heading towards the wide doorway. Johan caught glimpses of Jacob between the throbbing mechanisms, straining with Kev's arm grabbed by the wrist.

Crack!

Johan's stomach turned.

At the final machine, they pressed their backs against the vibrating metal. Johan peered around the side.

The second removal hadn't caused the same mess as the first. With his heart stopped, Kev had nothing to spray the blood out with. But blood did drip onto the floor from the hanging arm, which Jacob still held. A few stubborn veins and arteries, snarled strands of blue and red, kept the arm connected to the body. Jacob broke through them with a finger like they were nothing more than a spider web. Wincing, he hefted the arm in the same direction down the walkway. With a final look at the body, Jacob swayed and dropped to his knees.

The floor pulsed with the impact.

"Jacob?" The birdman carefully placed his dead feathered friends on the floor and ran over. He placed a hand on the giant's back.

Jacob clutched both hands to his stomach and doubled over with a low moan.

"Let me see," said the man and moved around to face him. "Jacob! Let me see."

He forced Jacob's hands away. They hung at his sides.

"No," the man cried after a few seconds. "This… this is bad. Jacob, can you stand? We need to get you to Max."

Jacob released a sound like a sigh of relief and flopped to the side. His shoulder struck the floor.

"Jacob!" cried the man fussing over him. "Look at this blood…" He pressed a hand to his brother's stomach and another to his shoulder. "Jacob!"

Johan poked Simon in the arm. In the bad light, his friend looked tired, yet alert. Johan motioned towards the doorway.

"Now?" whispered Simon. "But what about…?" He nodded towards the freaks.

"Trust me," said Johan. "Run!"

Without waiting for a response, Johan dashed for the exit. The moment his boots struck the main walkway, he threw a look over his shoulder.

The man, hunched over the fallen Jacob, glowered at him.

"You," he said. "The white hair. It's you."

The birdman stood.

Jacob cried out, his hands shooting to his stomach again.

The man shot Johan one last venomous glance.

"If you think this is over, you're more stupid than I thought," he said. He returned to tending his comrade, who quieted slightly at his touch. "My brother owes this family after his cowardice, and he will repay us with your blood."

"Don't... leave me," the monster said.

"I won't, Jacob," said the man. "I won't."

33

Johan recoiled at his first touch of the ladder. The metal felt salty under his skin, saturated by the stench that rose from the pit beneath. He imagined the years the ladder had stood in the stagnant water he saw below, the rust, filth and bacteria had probably crawled up it, rung by rung. His groan echoed in the shaft.

"What's wrong?" said Simon, halfway through the hatch and leaning in. "Can't we get up? Please tell me we can get up."

Johan swallowed. "It's fine. Watch your grip."

"You sure this is the right way?"

"It's the *only* way," said Johan. "And it goes straight up. Unless you want to go back to the Vulture and Incredible Hulk?"

"No," said Simon. "I've seen enough."

Fighting his body's reaction and regretting the loss of his wipes more than his friends, Johan climbed the first few steps of the ladder. Simon clambered on beneath him.

"This is fucked up," he said.

"I know," Johan replied.

"You... you don't sound too bothered. About... well..."

Grabbing the next rung, something squished in Johan's palm. He flinched and whipped his hand from the metal, wiping it on the rear of his jeans.

"Sorry, I slipped," he said, hearing Simon stop. He hurried on, holding the sides of the ladder. "We can't take the time to linger and mourn. We need to keep on our toes, stay alert. If we'd have put a foot wrong down there, you know what would've happened?"

"Yeah," said Simon. "We'd have been ripped limb from limb."

They climbed in silence for a few seconds.

"Birds," said Johan and whistled. The conversation helped to occupy his mind, kept it away from the dirt beneath his fingers and the putrid waters below. "Claws, yeah, can deal with that. Giant mutants? Hell, shoot it. But birds? How could he control the birds?"

"Did he?" asked Simon. He sounded a little out of breath. "They could have just got in."

"And attack like that? Have you ever seen birds attack someone like that?"

"No," Simon said quietly. "No, I haven't. But still, it's pretty hard to believe."

"Nothing will surprise me after this. Nothing. But look on the bright side..."

"There's a bright side?"

Johan almost laughed.

"Yeah. My gun's still got plenty left inside. The rest of the bullets were in the fucking bag, but just a few should do it, like with that huge fucker. They mentioned one called Max...."

Simon snorted. "Max. I can't believe these freaks have names. And brothers? Have they been living down here in a big happy family?"

"Until we came along."

Johan looked up and spotted an open hatch further on.

"We're nearly out of here. How you holding up?"

"I just want Nat. I know that... that she's probably dead, but I have this gut feeling..."

"So you think you love her?" Johan asked.

"Think? I know. Would I come down here and go through all this for just anyone? I think you've forgotten, Johan."

"Forgotten what?"

"The old days," he said. "Those wild times we had in this shit-hole of a city."

His words startled Johan. "It's strange hearing you talk

like this," he said and reached out to the side. He had climbed up alongside the hatch. "I thought this girl had *changed* you."

He pulled his body across and stood on the edge of the hatch. Darkness cloaked the water pooled at the bottom, but Johan heard it lapping the sides of the shaft.

"She has," said Simon, ascending to the same height. "She just... I don't know... focuses me in a whole different way."

Johan held out a hand. "Come on, you pussy."

He pulled Simon across and together they stepped through the other side of the hatch.

"She'll be just like the others, Simon. Just you wait. One day you'll be begging me to have some fun with her, and I can't wait for that special moment."

The room was the largest yet, and for a moment Johan feared they'd stepped into another subterranean chamber. Only the streetlights outside, which twinkled in through the vacant windows and open door, revealed they had indeed reached the surface. A breeze ruffled Johan's hair, like a hand of ice across his scalp. He shivered but relished the feeling. Somewhere in the rafters of the high ceiling an unseen bird flapped its wings. The sound clamped Johan's relief away and reminded him the night wasn't over yet. He gazed up and squinted at the ceiling. Although the flickering light from outside made it possible to see, the upper reaches remained hidden.

There could be hundreds of birds up there, he thought, just waiting for the signal.

"The door," Simon whispered. He stayed close to Johan and spoke into his ear. "It's left open. Think it's some kind of trap?"

Johan shook his head. "I doubt it. How could they know we'd end up here? I say we go and come back with more firepower. We can kill them all with the right equipment."

He started towards the door.

"Wait," said Simon and grabbed Johan's shoulder. "We can't leave!"

"And why not? Think we should wait and see if they're coming after us?" He removed the gun and peered up at the ceiling.

"But Nat... We came all this way for her, and now we're going to just leave?"

Yeah, we came all this way for here. Can't he see the bigger picture?

The bird in the shadows again flapped its wings. The sound made the butterflies in Johan's stomach flutter *their* wings. He itched to break for the door.

"Five minutes," he said. "Just in here." He looked around. "This place is huge. It could go up God knows how many floors. We stay in this room and we split up to get it done quicker. Stay within earshot." He rubbed his free hand on the back of his jeans. "I'm exhausted, and my head feels fried."

Simon nodded and, without waiting for further confirmation, walked away to the left.

Johan stopped and listened. Simon had disappeared around the other side of the shaft, which reached up into the darkness like a wide chimney stack. About to call, Johan closed his mouth. If the birds were on guard, a shout might bring them down in a feathered fury. The darkness might be the only thing keeping them at bay.

He headed for a raised platform on the far side of the room. Beyond, a double door stood open like a cave set into the wall.

Johan walked alongside several large wooden boxes and ran a hand along the top of the closest. He instantly regretted it, feeling the layer of dust on top. He wiped his hand on his jeans, wishing for home and a shower.

The boxes reached up to his chest and had been lined up in a perfect row to form a barrier before the platform.

Johan reached the end, each step taken carefully to avoid any noise. The thought of the birds above hung in his mind.

He froze.

Something close by *had* made a noise.

Johan glanced around. Still alone, he took another step.

The noise came again, a very slight smacking sound.

On the tips of his toes, he sneaked around the last of the boxes. Despite his disgust, Johan pressed a hand against its dirty surface. The wood beneath his palm felt perfectly still. He quickly wiped his hand again and continued around.

Movement in the shadows.

The sight nearly made him laugh. He suppressed the urge and smiled with difficulty. He pointed the gun at the closer of the two figures. Oblivious, they squirmed in each other's embrace, lips pressed tightly together, eyes closed.

Bang, he thought.

His smile widened.

Such a special moment.

34

Nat swept a hand up the back of Max's neck, making him shiver against her. She smiled through her kiss and grabbed his head. Forcing him against her, she pressed her lips forcefully against his. His tongue again prodded against them. Nat opened her mouth a little wider and slid her own tongue over her teeth. She met him in the wet cavity between. Filled with an almost static tingle, her chest rose and fell in deep, quick breaths. Her nipples stiffened and poked against the fabric of the t-shirt underneath the coat. Done stroking her back, Max's hand snaked further down and clasped her buttock. Even through the thick denim of her jeans, she felt his fingers press eagerly into her flesh. It caused warmth to spread between her legs.

It was never like this with Simon, she thought. No heat, no... fire.

Again, guilt snagged at her heart like a cat with a ball of wool.

She broke away for a second, intending to catch her breath and compose her thoughts. Instantly, Max pulled her back in and continued kissing.

She allowed him to plant small and delicate kisses at the edge of her mouth.

In her arms, Max snapped rigid.

Nat pulled back.

"What's wrong?" she whispered.

"Nat?" said a familiar voice behind her.

She stared at Max, horrific realisation spreading through her like a rotten cancer. Her stomach seemed to plummet from her body. Blood rushed in her ears.

"S-Simon?" She slowly turned her head.

Standing beside one of the wooden boxes, with his face a canvas of astonishment, Simon gazed down at them.

At his side, the white-haired friend gave a tilted smile.

"I told you," said Johan. "That *is* her, isn't it?"

Simon's expression never changed as he nodded.

"Amazing," Johan said, smirking.

He raised the gun.

Nat broke away from Max, who shuffled back, eyes locked on the two figures.

"This... this isn't what it looks like," she said, her body rigid.

Head drooped, Simon studied the floor, averting his stare from her. "It's exactly what it looks like." Simon squeezed his eyes shut, his expression like he'd bitten into a lemon. His fingers curled into fists. They shook with ferocity. "Exactly..." he spat.

Leaving him trembling, Johan stepped in front. He pointed the gun.

"You," he said to Max. "Get up. Now."

Max stayed seated against the wall, still staring with a burning intensity. His eyes had narrowed to sharp points of hatred.

"I said get up," said Johan, his voice raised. He glanced upwards at the sound of a bird flapping across the warehouse. After a swallow, he spoke again, voice hushed. "I'll kill you where you sit, you fuck. Get up."

Max slowly climbed to his feet without so much as blinking.

"Now walk away from her," Johan continued. "I think her *boyfriend* needs a few words with her." The corner of his mouth curled up in an acidic sneer.

"No," Nat cried. "Max, don't!"

Johan blinked.

"Max? You hear that, Simon? All this time, she's been with one of *them*..."

"I… don't care… who… or what," said Simon. His throat sounded blocked with rage, the muscles of his neck pulsating. He raised a hand and jabbed a finger at her. "How… could you… do this?"

Nat opened her mouth. "Simon—"

His hand whipped across her cheek. Her head swung to the side.

"Bitch!" Simon screamed at her. "After everything I did?"

Max dove forwards, hands outstretched, reaching for Simon's throat.

"Na-ah," said Johan. He thrust the gun upwards and caught Max just below the chin with the barrel. The force of the blow knocked Max's head back. Johan pressed the gun higher. The tip bit into Max's skin. With his free hand, Johan grabbed a fist full of hair and held Max in place. The sly grin never left his face.

"Max!" Nat screamed.

She turned, hearing the hand whip through the air. It smashed into her other cheek. The sound of the blow echoed in the empty building.

"Nat!"

"Hush up, lover boy," hissed Johan. "I think *we* also need a little chat after what your brothers did."

Pain erupted across Nat's scalp as Simon yanked her by the dreadlocks to a stand. He brought his face close to hers. His skin burned deep red. Pressed together so tight, his bared teeth seemed in danger of cracking.

"How could you do this?" he asked. His hand released her hair, but before she could escape, it clamped around her throat. "Little whore. Aren't you? Just like the rest. Say it!"

Nat just choked in his hold.

He pushed her back. Nat's head knocked against the edge of the raised platform.

"Should have known, should have known," Simon continued, his words rambling together. "What the hell is it with women, huh? Why can none of you be fucking trusted?"

"They're filth," said Johan. "I wonder how many times has she done this to you?"

Simon pressed harder.

Nat coughed, feeling her windpipe narrow. Her breath whistled in and out through her nose.

"How many times?" Simon screamed. "How many?"

He pulled her forwards and jerked her back, banging her head on the platform.

"One?"

Forwards.

Back.

Thunk!

"Two?"

Thunk!

"Nat!"

She heard Max's call, but he sounded far away. Sparks danced in front of her eyes like a snowstorm.

"Three? Four? Five?"

Thunk thunk thunk!

With each strike she sagged a little more in Simon's grip.

Out of breath and sweating, he threw her down. She landed on her hands and knees, gasping. She rubbed her throat.

"We've come all this way to find this bitch," said Simon. His voice had regained a little composure and sounded more like himself. It disturbed Nat more than his raving. "I think the journey has made me realise something, Johan."

"And what's that?" asked Johan, grinning. He seemed to love every minute of the ordeal.

"I've learned who my friends are," said Simon. He stared down. "Finally."

"I saw it in your eyes," said Johan. "It was the killing,

cleaning up the scum again."

"No!" Max struggled more and whipped his hands up, aiming for the gun.

Johan pulled it back and struck him across the face with the grip.

Max staggered backwards and tripped over a coil of rope on the floor.

Johan leapt on top of him. Lifting the gun high, he brought it down on Max's face once, twice, three times. Max fell limp, arms flopped to the sides. Johan poked him in the chest with the gun and, satisfied, climbed off.

"Not so pretty now," he said. "Take a look, Nat."

Nat stared at the floor, massaging her bruised throat.

"He told you to look," said Simon and booted her in the side. The blow knocked the wind from her. Simon pounced and, gripping her head with both hands, twisted her head. She tried to resist, but as the pain in her hard neck muscles grew unbearable, she relented.

"Open your eyes," said Simon as he moved a hand to her jaw. With his fingers, he painfully squeezed her cheeks inward.

She opened her eyes.

Max lay sprawled on his back, arms spread at his side, palms up. His eyes were closed, something Nat could barely make out with so much blood. It poured from a large gash above his left eye and travelled along his nose, now a dark purple blob.

"Max... no..."

"Max yes," said Simon. He stepped back and kicked her in the side again.

Clutching her ribs, Nat curled up on the floor.

Johan pointed the gun down and slowly raised it up along Max's body, stopping at his head. He squeezed the trigger just a bit.

"No," said Simon. "Not yet."

Nat nearly cried out in relief.

"Why not?" asked Johan as he lowered the gun. "One less to worry about."

"Think. We can get information from him. We have no idea how many more of those things are down there. If he's in the family, he's bound to know. He'll be in a more helpful mood when he wakes up."

Johan prodded the limp body with his boot. "That is, *if* he wakes up." He replaced the gun in the pocket of his jacket. "But I like your thinking. It's good to have you back, man."

"I was stupid, I realise that now. To think I was against it. That was all due to *her*."

"Against it?" said Johan. "How could you be against it? Things might have been different if *you* hadn't started our little mission. I'm glad you did. I'd have been a mess without the focus."

"It was *you*?" Nat spluttered, still clutching her chest. "You said you'd caught him and tried to save the girl."

Simon chuckled and faked a third kick.

Nat flinched.

"What was I supposed to say, that it was me all along? I feel it may have soured our relationship, Nat. I had to say something. The thing is, and sorry about this, mate, I wanted to keep all that in the past. I thought... I was happy. That night in the Fourth Dimension, seeing Johan and the boys, brought it all back."

Leaving Max behind, Johan walked over and stood on the opposite side of Nat.

"How could you forget? Seriously, the things you used to do." He knelt down next to Nat. "You should have seen him back then. He didn't just have his fun and quietly get rid of them like we did, oh no. He really *butchered* them. Made such a mess. Even I felt a little put off by some of it. I tried to match his... genius with the last few girls, just to show the boys I was as good as him. No one can fuck up whores like the master. He's an artist." Johan straightened up, leaving Nat to sob. "You remember the big red head?"

Simon seemed to focus in the distance, dredging his memories. "What was her name? It's hard to remember them all. Something foreign, wasn't it? Natalya?"

Johan nodded. "You really did a number on her."

"She was disgusting," Simon spat. "Not only a woman—another scheming, evil woman—but a disgrace. She made me sick."

"We still had our fun though, right?"

Simon grunted. "It may have looked like fun, and you might've got your kicks, but I hated it." He sniffed. "Still, had to be done. They need to know their place. I think the fat pig actually enjoyed it. Probably the most attention she'd ever had."

Johan sniggered. "She lost a lot of weight in the week we had her, as I recall."

"Oh yes," said Simon, a grin spreading across his face like a crack splitting glass. "We did remove most of it." He made a sawing motion with his hand.

Nat burst into a run, shoving herself forwards with her feet. She burst past Johan and headed for the open door. Her shoulders whipped back. With her legs running full pelt, she slipped and fell back, hitting the floor hard.

Johan released the back of her coat.

"Nice try," he said.

"How about him?" asked Simon. "Still out?"

Johan glanced down. "Like a light."

Simon licked his lips. "You know, I think Nat needs to learn a little about respect. Bring her over here."

Johan immediately obeyed. Again, he grabbed the hood and used it to yank Nat to her feet like a leash.

"You're letting him order you around?" said Nat, desperate to find a way out of her situation. With no way to overpower them, especially not with Max unconscious and Johan with a gun, she hoped that talking might get her out of this alive. "I thought *you* were the bad boy."

"Compared to this guy?" said Johan and pulled her along. "He taught me and the boys everything we know. It's nice to have him back."

"You're both fucking crazy," she screamed.

Simon watched the ceiling. "Shut her up, Johan."

Johan clamped a hand over Nat's mouth, and he too glanced upwards.

What are they so afraid of up there? Nat wondered.

She tried to scream. If they wanted her to be quiet, she'd make as much noise as possible. Hopefully, the brothers would come running.

Johan's hand felt tight as a second skin. Her scream came out as a low humming sound.

"That'll do," said Simon. "We don't want to disturb the birds. Get her over here."

With one hand on her mouth, Johan used his other arm to grab her around the waist and pull her forwards. Nat tried to beat herself free, battering his chest, stomach and face with short slaps and punches. He appeared to barely feel them and threw her across the floor.

Simon caught her before she fell and hoisted her up.

Taking a deep breath, Nat prepared to unleash an ear-splitting scream.

A knee to her diaphragm reduced her to a gasping, sputtering wreck.

"Naughty," Simon whispered. Two more hard slaps swept her head left to right.

"Are we taking her with us?" said Johan. "I still think we should get back soon and come back tomorrow night with more guns. She could keep us amused until then."

"Just like old times?"

Johan nodded. "Just like old times."

Simon ran his hand up across the red and blotchy skin of her face, mopping up the shed tears with his fingers. He gazed into her eyes, which hung half open.

"I thought you were different," he said. "The one that

could change me."

He pressed her back against the platform.

Nat's head lolled back on her neck.

"But you were far worse than any woman I've had the misfortune to meet," he said and smiled. He grabbed the zipper of her thick coat and began to slide it down.

"Simon," said Johan, nervously looking up at yet another sound from the rafters, "we should get out of here. The birdman could be back at any second."

"Just a minute. She needs to learn, and she learns *now*." He unfastened the zipper and spread the coat wide.

His hand explored the warmth of Nat's skin. His fingers slid over her breasts; his hand felt like a fat spider.

"We don't have time for this..."

"Of course we do," said Simon. "Don't tell me you've lost your sense of adventure! We can double-team her."

Even in the poor light, Nat saw the intensity in which Simon studied her. She shuddered.

"Is she... clean?" asked Johan.

"The cleanest."

"Well..." Johan stepped forwards. "I suppose a few minutes wouldn't hurt. Birdman has a lot to deal with down there, finding a box big enough to bury his brother in." He chuckled, his voice still low. "Who's going first?"

Simon hitched up Nat's jumper and t-shirt underneath the coat. It revealed her bare stomach and the underside of her bra.

"I've had enough of this bitch already," he said. "You might as well have some fun with it." He hitched the fabric higher. "Don't expect much."

The room burst into light from above.

Nat closed her eyes. The hands around her slid away.

"What the hell?" said Simon. "What.... where the hell did he come from?"

Nat forced her eyes open again.

On the far side of the room stood Whistler, Jenkins at

his side. In his hand he clutched a short metal bar that protruded from a panel on the wall. Large light bulbs burned above.

"Whistler?" cried Nat.

"You…" growled Johan as he reached into his jacket pocket.

Birds covered every ledge, every wooden support. They nestled against each other in nooks and crannies within the crumbling wall. Staring down, they bustled restlessly. The sound of rustling feathers echoed.

"Birds," said Simon and released Nat. She slid down the side of the platform and landed on her knees. Her coat hung open, her chest and stomach still revealed. "The birds are back, Johan."

"I know," he said. "Bring the girl. We're getting out of here."

Simon stepped forwards and stretched out a hand. He reached for her throat.

Nat shrank back against the platform.

One of the birds, a small thrush or sparrow, darted through the air like a fluttering brown arrow. It shot between Nat and Simon. He jerked his hand back.

"Did you see that?"

"It was only *one* of them," cried Johan. "You wouldn't have felt it. Grab her. We'll be okay as long as…"

His words tapered off at a sound from behind.

Whistler loitered by the switch, watching in silence. The sound had emerged from the open hatch, still open in the shaft at the centre of the room. It came again, the clang of metal.

"That's him," said Simon. "The birdman! He's coming."

"Forget the games," said Johan and pulled the gun from his jacket. He held it aloft. "Let's do what we came to do and get the fuck out. First, our little lover boy while he's being so well behaved."

He looked down.

During their short spell of staring upwards at the birds and the sudden light, Max had vanished. All that remained was a small splash of blood on the dirty floor.

Johan roared and glanced around the wide room. "Where is he?" He turned on the spot. "Where the fuck did he go?"

"We're not leaving until he's dead," growled Simon. He lurched towards Nat and grabbed her by the hair. She scratched at his hand and screamed.

"Shut it!" he cried and hauled her up. He paused to pick up a short piece of wood that narrowed into a sharp point. "Watch him!"

Whistler had ventured further into the room, his footsteps silent underneath the shouting. He stopped, realising all eyes were on him.

Johan aimed the gun and fired.

35

A small cloud of dust sprang out from the wall a metre to Whistler's left.

"Shit," cried Johan and glanced to the ceiling.

Some of the birds had dropped from their perches, disturbed by the explosion of the gun. They circled overhead and called to each other. This seemed to agitate their audience further, who, in turn, flapped their wings and paced back and forth along the rafters.

Hands still over his head, Whistler ran for the door, garish jumper flapping around him.

"No!" Nat cried, watching her vain hope vanish through the door and into the night.

Coward! she thought.

More birds joined the swirling mass above. The number of cries increased with each clang from the hatch.

"Simon, he's almost here, and when he gets…"

"I know," snapped Simon and jerked Nat's hair.

She cried out and stood on her toes, trying to relieve the tight agony across her head.

Max? her mind screamed. God, Max, where are you?

She scanned the room, searching around every box, within every shadow for any sign of him.

He's… gone.

Realisation hit her harder than any of the blows dealt by Simon. Her heart seemed to tug in her chest. She felt sick.

He's escaped, just like his chicken shit of a brother.

She sniffed.

It's all about the family. As long as the family's safe…

Another noise echoed from the hatch, louder than before.

Alcazar!

Simon jammed the splintered spike under her chin. The point broke the skin. Nat swallowed, and her throat strained against the point for a moment.

"Come on," Simon shouted to Johan. He dragged Nat back and manoeuvred her around the platform. Their feet clopped on the wooden ramp leading up to it. "In here."

Johan stood at the centre of the room, following the circling birds with the gun.

"You can't shoot them all," cried Simon and pulled Nat further along the platform. They reached the entrance to the dark corridor.

If we enter the rest of the building, thought Nat, we could be hidden for days before anyone finds us.

She kicked Simon in the injured leg.

He yowled and thrust the wooden spike even higher.

Nat feared that if she so much as swallowed, the stick might plunge up into her mouth. She remained on her toes and tried to force her head away.

Two gloved hands emerged from the open hatch, followed by a thin face dominated by a sharp nose. Alcazar looked around and soon found Johan. He proceeded to climb out.

"Johan! He's here!"

Averting his eyes from the birds, Johan glanced down and saw the approaching figure.

Alcazar paused, taking a second to study the white-haired boy that stood between him and the platform. "You..."

In the doorway that led to the street, Jenkins whimpered and circled on the spot.

"Run," called Simon as he ducked into the shadows of the corridor. He pulled the struggling Nat along. "Get in here!"

Johan raised the gun and levelled it at Alcazar's chest.

"Fucking freak," he said.

One of the birds, which had been flying in a slow and

graceful circuit, dove down. It struck the outstretched gun and swept back up into the air.

Johan pulled the trigger.

The shot rang out.

Still, Alcazar stood watching him.

"Shit," cried Johan and lined up a second shot. Before he had chance to aim, more birds dropped from the rafters and flew into him, pummelling his body. The second shot missed. He beat the attacking birds off with the gun.

Alcazar watched him like a statue, his face a porcelain mask.

"Johan!" Simon screamed.

Nat continued to pull away, but the movement dug the spike in deeper. The underside of her chin and her throat grew warm and sticky with blood.

Again and again the birds smashed into Johan. He bled from various small nicks and cuts caused by beaks and claws. The crimson stood out stark against his pale skin. He whipped around on the spot, assaulted from all directions.

Despite the onslaught, Johan managed to lift his arm holding the gun and fired. He missed Alcazar by a good distance, his aim towards the exit. The large light switch by the door exploded in a shower of burning bright sparks.

Jenkins barked and fled in the opposite direction.

The warehouse fell into darkness.

"Fuck," muttered Simon and dragged Nat even further back. They stood on the inside of the corridor. "Johan?"

The sound of beating wings and the raucous cries of the birds replied.

"Fuck," he said again. He quickly moved behind Nat and, with one arm around her waist, dragged her deeper down the corridor.

"What are you doing?" she asked, each word pressing her throat against the wood.

"Getting away from all this," he said. "Place seems big enough. They might give up looking for us after a while."

"I'll scream," she said, quivering voice not helping her threat. "I'll scream and scream until Alcazar can—"

"Alcazar?" said Simon, almost with a laugh. "You really have gotten to know these weirdos, haven't you? I take it Alcazar is ol' bird fucker out there. You bang him too? Just like that other bastard?"

"I didn't do anything," she said, hoping that playing dumb might buy her a few more moments. If they stayed close to the main area, Alcazar had a chance to—

"I bet you did," sneered Simon.

It dragged her back from her thoughts.

Simon huffed, the effort of dragging her taking its toll.

"Why?" he asked. He sounded more upset than angry.

"Why, what? Why did I kiss Max?"

He took a moment to answer. "Yes."

"I don't know, okay? I hadn't planned this. I didn't want to be taken down to the sewers and put in a cage! It was all because of you! You and your screwed up friends did this. But I'm glad it happened. Now I know all about you!"

He responded by pushing the wood further up. Nat winced.

"Now I know what you really are." He took a deep breath. "Johan!"

Deep inside the corridor, even the doorway had been swallowed by the darkness. With no sight or sound of Johan, Simon continued back with his reluctant companion.

"In here," he ordered and shoved her into a room to the side.

On the far wall, a window—the glass smeared with dirt and mapped with spidery cracks—let in a meagre amount of light from the street.

Simon threw her down. She landed in a pile of soiled newspaper pages and empty beer cans. They clattered around on the floor. Simon tried to close the door. The wood was green with paint or rot. The bottom edge scraped along the floor, and Simon forced it with his shoulder. Almost closed, it refused to move any further.

"You don't think they'll find you in here?"

"Not if you keep your mouth shut," said Simon. He pointed the wooden spike at her.

Nat rubbed her throat. Blood still seeped from her skin.

"And what do you mean, find *me*? We're in the same boat."

Fearing a laugh might bring more pain, Nat forced it back and calmly asked, "What do you mean?"

"They're crazy! Psychotic! If they find us, we're both dead."

"Oh no," said Nat. "*We're* not. It's *you* they want, you and Johan. You were the ones who killed their mother, the ones that slaughtered their defenseless brothers…"

"Defenseless? After what they did?" He tried to close the door again. "Johan was right. They're freaks and they need to be exterminated." He smiled. "Thank you for leading us to them. Maybe you're not completely useless."

Nat stared up from the floor, mouth hanging open. Her hand fell from her bleeding throat.

Was he right? If she hadn't searched for Agnes, she wouldn't have found the brothers. Simon and his boys would not have searched for her and never come across Herman and baby Edgar.

She dipped her head.

"You didn't realise, did you? If it wasn't for you going missing, we'd probably be in your flat now… happy…"

"We could never be happy," she spat. "How long until you felt the urge again, Simon? The urge to go out and *hunt* with the boys?"

"I… I don't know what you're talking about."

Nat stood, kicking cans out of the way.

"You know exactly what I mean. Being a killer isn't something you can put aside because you think you found the right girl. How long, huh? How long until we had an argument and you decided to put me in my place?"

Simon swallowed. "No, I would never…"

"Looks like it," she said and jabbed a finger at her blood-slicked throat. "You know, like you, I thought that monsters lived down here but turns out I was wrong. *You're* the monster, you and that white-haired fuck out there. I hope he's dead, Simon. I hope Alcazar's birds ripped him to shreds and Jenkins is lapping up the blood."

"That's enough!" said Simon and pounced on her. He lifted the spike high over her head and grabbed her with his other hand.

Nat screamed and grasped his wrist. Her muscles strained trying to keep the spike in the air.

Simon drove it down hard.

"No…" said Nat.

The pointed wood hung inches from her face. Nat gazed up at its tip. Exhaustion built in her arms.

The trembling spike drew closer.

"Bitch," Simon growled. His spittle flecked Nat's face, and she blinked it away.

He pressed the spike further still. Its tip poked her in the forehead.

Nat cried out and twisted her head away.

"You're just like… the rest of them," Simon strained. A manic grin splashed across his face. The light from the window glinted in his dark eyes. "Nothing special. Just another… walking fuck! All you're good for is spreading your legs…" He pressed even harder, and the spike stabbed her again.

Over Simon's shoulder, the door opened a couple of inches.

Nat closed her eyes waiting for the wood to stab through her skin. Her arms burned and felt like weights had been hung from her wrists. She knew to fight him had been a mistake. She should have kept him talking. The brothers would have found her eventually and—

A snarling filled the room as Simon thrashed against her.

Nat let go and fell back into the littered cans on the floor. She kicked out, moving backwards until she thumped against the wall.

Simon raged, hopping on one leg and waving his arms in the air.

Jenkins, teeth embedded in Simon's ankle, growled and snorted. His tiny legs slid on the floor, seeking purchase. Fabric ripped.

Simon bellowed and managed to grab the door and stay upright. The wooden stake fell from his hand. It hit the ground and rolled into the shadows.

"Get off me!"

Simon kicked higher, but the tenacious Jenkins held on. For a second, the dog hung freely from Simon's leg, kicking feet inches from the floor. Jenkins made a strange noise, halfway between a snarl and a high-pitched whine.

"Jenkins!" Nat jumped to her feet.

"Little shit…!" cried Simon as Jenkins, all four feet back on the floor, reaffirmed his grip.

Simon kicked out, but the dog held on.

The green door swung open revealing a rectangle of darkness. The sounds of the birds still resonated down the corridor.

Screaming, Nat ran at Simon, shoulder barging him.

Jenkins let go and trotted back.

Simon tumbled through the doorway on one leg, grabbing the frame before he fell. He stood straight and glared at Nat.

Jenkins growled and barred his teeth again but stayed put.

"I'm going to snap that dog's neck and then choke the shit out of you." Simon wiped the corner of his mouth with the back of his hand, like he'd been drooling.

Nat searched for anything she could use for a weapon.

The room appeared empty as a prison cell.

"Shame the boys aren't here to enjoy this," Simon continued. "Johan showed me the fun in being a team player again..."

Out of the doorway, two hands clamped down on Simon's shoulders.

Max leaned in before Simon had the chance to turn and brought his beaten face down to Simon's neck. Gripping him hard, Max opened his mouth wide and plunged his teeth into the throbbing flesh.

Simon screamed.

With a noise like a choke, Max jerked his head. From between his lips blood dribbled. From Simon's skin, it gushed.

"M-Max?"

Max lifted his head. A clump of dripping flesh poked from between his teeth, thin strands of sinew still joining it to the gaping hole in Simon's neck. Within the ragged gash, blood washed over the pulsing tissue.

Simon's wailing rose to a crescendo.

Max whipped his head to the side and snapped the connecting threads. He spat out the red glob and dove in for a second mouthful. He violently shook his head from side to side, working his teeth in deeper.

Nat raised a hand to her face and held it over her mouth.

Another rip and Max tore his head free, chewing on the meat.

Blood spilled down Simon's neck and covered his shoulder and right arm. He flopped to the side, released from Max's hold, and landed on his back.

Max spat out the chunk of flesh and slowly raised his gaze to Nat. His lips and chin glistened red in the light from the dirty window.

"I'm... sorry."

"You're sorry?" asked Nat.

Simon fell still. "Help... me!" he gasped. Tears meandered down his cheeks. "Please..."

"You shouldn't have seen that," said Max, ignoring him. "But when I saw him touching you, hitting you..."

Nat ran to him. He enveloped her in his arms.

"Please!" Simon wailed. His body trembled and his eyes rolled up to show all white. Blood pumped from his neck anew and his hand slid down to lie palm up on the floor.

Jenkins, tail beating a frantic tattoo in the air, licked at the gathering pool.

Nat hugged Max, breathing in his scent. She felt his fingers in her hair.

"Are you okay? What did he do to you?"

Nat shook her head. "It's fine. He didn't get the chance to do much. Jenkins got here just in time."

Max squeezed her harder. "Hear that, fella?"

Jenkins continued lapping at the blood.

They broke their embrace. Max pulled up his t-shirt and used it to wipe his mouth.

"You're not disgusted? I mean, this isn't normal..."

"I've never wanted normal." Nat looked down at Simon's body. His eyes and mouth were open. "Looks like I never had it."

A figure stepped through the doorway, slamming a hand onto Max's shoulder.

Nat screamed.

The hand pulled Max from his embrace, and a figure stepped between them.

"Jesus!" said Nat. "Alcazar."

He glanced at Simon's body with little interest.

"We still have the other one out there," he said quietly. "The one with the white hair. The one with the gun. Whistler seeks redemption, but I don't think he can do it alone!"

36

Huddled between two of the large boxes, Johan opened his eyes. In the dark it made no difference. Eyes open or eyes closed, he saw nothing. He concentrated, listening hard.

Overhead, the birds had returned to their moderately passive circling. Johan listened to them flap their wings. Those who'd returned to their perches chirped and cooed, like they discussed the recent events and the parts they played.

As long as they stay up there, he thought.

His forehead stung in a patch over his left eye. A particularly vicious bird had gone to work with its claws and had taken a heavy punch to remove it from his face. He patted the skin and winced. His body complained where the feathered missiles had pummelled him. He wondered if they had the speed to crack a rib. It felt that way.

Can a bird carry rabies? I bet they can. I need to clean.

He cautiously stood up, ready to duck back down between the boxes at the first sign of attack.

He squinted and peered around the room.

Johan crept around one of the boxes. Nothing stood between him, the open door, and the street beyond.

Fuck him, thought Johan and ventured forwards. Home first, clean, come back...

He scratched his arms, his neck and his face. The dirt had accumulated, grown inches thick and seeped into his pores. It flowed in his veins and swam higher, higher up into his brain.

"Shut up," he told himself and scratched with increased vigour.

Half way across the warehouse he glanced upwards, expecting a winged bullet to swoop down. Satisfied that the birds hadn't yet noticed him, Johan quickened his pace.

Lots of soap with a thick lather, his mind continued, wash it all up and scrub until you *bleed*.

He reached the doorway. The night outside had grown chillier still; Johan's breath steamed and drifted away. He zipped up his coat, no longer needing quick access to the inside pocket. The gun still poked into his side, now empty of bullets. He had used what ammo he had shooting at the birdman. The rest of the bullets bought from Alan had been in the bag with Spence, blown to pieces.

Johan breathed deep. The clean, crisp air still smelled of the sewers. He hoped a good, hot shower would rectify the problem.

He scanned the warehouse one last time.

No sign of Simon. I bet he's holed up with the girl somewhere, lucky bastard. I hope he makes her *really* suffer.

He turned and stepped through the doorway and onto the street.

A fist smashed into his nose, knocking him back inside.

Hands clamped to his nose, Johan staggered and blinked away the sudden tears from his eyes.

A figure stood on the other side of the doorway, silhouetted against the yellow streetlight.

"We should have done this earlier," Johan said, "and done a proper job too. I wouldn't have this shit to deal with now."

Whistler stepped inside.

Johan struggled to see him in the gloom. He'd removed his striped jumper, revealing a dirty white vest beneath. His arms, surprisingly solid and muscular, rose into a fighter's stance.

Johan laughed. "So now you want to fight? You never have before. Maybe now that I'm alone you fancy your chances? You piece of fucking chicken shit. Get out of my way."

Whistler crossed the short distance in seconds and swung at Johan's face.

Johan leaned back but Whistler moved too quickly. The blow glanced the side of Johan's head, and he retreated further back.

"I don't have time for this," he shouted and ran forwards, head down.

Whistler gave him a hard shove back.

"Fuck you," Johan roared and dove at him. He drove a fist under Whistler's arms and into his stomach. Whistler gasped and doubled over. Johan straightened and followed the blow with a sharp knee, connecting with a hip. He dove in for another attack.

Whistler struck out with a foot and caught Johan on the knee. The blow, although not strong enough to break his patella, inverted the joint enough to bring sickening pain.

Johan screamed and ducked away, clutching his knee. Each step brought jolts of electricity shooting up his leg. He limped a few metres and screamed again.

Another song drifted over from Whistler. He paused between bars to suck in heavy, ragged breaths.

Johan didn't recognise the song, nor did he care. He stepped forwards and snarled at the burst of pain from his knee. "You're nothing. You live in shit!" Standing upright he tried to block out the pain. Screaming, Johan ran forwards, arms outstretched. He grabbed Whistler by the stained and stinking vest.

Whistler grabbed Johan in return and they slammed into the side of the shaft. Johan received the worst of the impact, his head striking the brick.

"Fuck you," he spat again.

Whistler pulled Johan in and headbutted the bridge of his nose.

Johan flopped back and slammed against the bottom edge of the hatch. The tramp had the upper hand and bent Johan back, a palm under his jaw. Johan pushed, but a kick to his damaged knee ended that resistance. Whistler pressed Johan's moaning body further across the edge of the hatch.

"P-Please..." said Johan. "We didn't mean to... do anything. We were scared, it was a mistake."

Whistler, his face inches away, glared at him.

"Please," Johan continued.

Whistler released him and stepped back, eyes still locked on him.

Leaning up and away from the hatch, Johan rubbed his back.

"Th... thank you," he said. "I meant every word I sa—"

A slim figure rushed at him like a speeding train from the shadows, hands slamming into Johan's chest.

The edge of the hatch struck Johan at the base of his spine. The impact swung his body back and into the void.

Nat grabbed his legs.

"No!" Johan screamed. "Please!"

She flipped him backwards.

Johan plummeted through the darkness, screaming all the way down. He caught a glint of light on a moving surface a moment before he plunged into the water, sinking deep. He thrashed, cheeks bulged.

Johan pumped his arms and kicked. Eyes closed, he thrust out a hand and, feeling the lack of resistance, realised he'd broke the surface. He burst from the water, gasping and spluttering.

"Help me!" he cried.

The bottom of the shaft reeked. Sweeping his arms through the water, Johan felt lumps floating on the surface. He cried out with vomit spraying from his mouth, and dipped under the surface. Pushing his body up, he coughed out the putrid water.

"Please," he wailed upwards. The open hatch at the top of the shaft allowed in a square of light. A shadow appeared, someone looking down.

"Help me!" Johan screamed again.

"There's always a right time for action," said Nat at the top of the shaft. The hatch slammed shut, bringing total darkness.

"No!" Johan tread water but his legs were already tired from the fight. His head slipped below a third time, the taste of shit and chemicals invading his mouth, his throat... his lungs.

Johan waved his hands above the surface and choked, inhaling more of the churned sewage.

Vanishing beneath, the foam closed over his body, silent and undisturbed.

EPILOGUE

~

ONE YEAR LATER

Nat chuckled and elbowed Max, sitting next to her in the booth.

Accompanied by two guys, both looking too young to be in the Fourth Dimension, the girl approached the bar. She wore knee high black vinyl boots and a red tartan miniskirt. Fishnet stockings covered the skin in between. Her tight black t-shirt had some band logo splashed across the front. Her hair, platted and tied in two long ponytails, hung from her head like droopy horns. Two circles of thick black makeup covered both eyes.

"And to think," said Nat, "I used to walk around like that."

"Things have changed," said Max and sipped his drink. He winced. "What the hell is this?"

"Something Bubba made up. Told him it was our anniversary and he made something special. Why? Don't you like it?"

"It's too sweet," he said and placed the glass back on the table. He smiled and scratched his head through his short hair. "But thanks anyway."

At the bar, Monique glared at the three newcomers. She leaned on the bar. Bubba, bottle of rum and a glass in his hands, watched with interest.

"You think I be crazy, girl?" said Monique "You be eighteen, I be the Queen o' Sheba."

"Wouldn't surprise me," whispered Max.

The girl attempted to argue back, but Monique's upturned hand cut her short.

"Unless I be seeing some ID, you be leaving." Monique placed her hands on her hips.

"Do as she say, boys," said Bubba and laughed. "Tha does not want to see ma woman get angry."

Defeated, the three walked back out, their faces hung low.

Nat watched them go. "She'll learn," she said. "Probably not the way I did, but when she grows up…"

"Learn what?" Max took another sip and winced.

Bubba glanced over.

Max raised the glass and took a deep swig.

"You don't need to stand out to be different," said Nat and grabbed his hand, "to be happy."

In the lift, they ascended to the fifth floor. Walking along the corridor, TVs played, actors' voices muffled through the doors and walls. In well over a year, Nat still hadn't seen any of her neighbours. Now, more than ever, she appreciated it.

At the end of the hall, she dug through the contents of her handbag and removed the key. Nat unlocked the door and swung it open.

"Agnes?"

In the living room a large, half-naked figure stood over the crib. Agnes lay in his arms.

"What… what are you doing?" cried Nat.

Jacob lifted the baby to his face and brought her head to his mouth.

"Jacob! No!"

Jacob gave the baby a small kiss on the forehead and gently laid her back inside the crib.

"I *told you* not to wake her up after nine," moaned Nat and removed her coat.

"Can't help," said Jacob and turned around. The round scars on his chest and stomach stood out on his mottled skin. "She cute. She like Uncle Jacob." He collapsed on the wide sofa beside Whistler, who quietly watched television.

Nat worried that the cheap sofa would snap in half every time he sat down.

"Not winding her up again, are you?" said Max and quickly closed the door. He approached the crib.

"Me?" said Jacob. He raised his eyebrows and smiled. "No."

"Pain in the arse," said Nat and joined Max. "We're going to get Alcazar to sit next time, even if his birds do shit all over the flat. You two should get jobs."

"No jobs," grunted Jacob. "Watch TV."

Nat sighed and slid her arm around Max's waist.

"I know it's not perfect," he said. "But isn't it better that we're all together?"

She sighed again and gave him a squeeze.

"Better a dysfunctional family than no family at all." She smiled and looked down into the crib.

Their daughter gurgled contently and yawned. All of her three eyes closed.

"A family," said Max and kissed her on the head.

Daniel I. Russell is the author of *Samhane, Come Into Darkness, Tricks, Mischief and Mayhem, The Collector* and the Australian Shadow Award Finalist, *Critique*, currently living out in the country of regional south west Australia. All the sharks, spiders and snakes keep him awake at night, but his four children tend to scare them off.

Made in the USA
Las Vegas, NV
28 January 2021

16745473R00198